WITH ALL MY HEART

The Love Story of

Catherine of Braganza

Margaret Campbell Barnes

WITH ALL MY HEART

MACRAE SMITH COMPANY: Philadelphia

For
MICHAEL
my son
who was killed in battle

"Je maintiendrai"

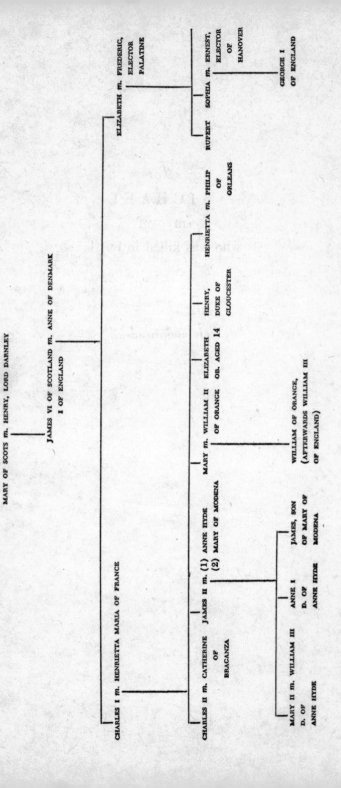

How do I love thee? Let me count the ways.
I love thee to the depth and breadth and height
My soul can reach, when feeling out of sight
For the ends of Being and ideal Grace.
I love thee to the level of everyday's
Most quiet need, by sun and candle-light.
I love thee freely, as men strive for Right;
I love thee purely, as they turn from Praise.
I love thee with the passion put to use
In my old griefs, and with my childhood's faith.
I love thee with a love I seemed to lose
With my lost saints,—I love thee with the breath,
Smiles, tears, of all my life!—and if God choose,
I shall but love thee better after death.

ELIZABETH BARRETT BROWNING
from *Sonnets from the Portuguese*

WITH ALL MY HEART

The Love Story of

Catherine of Braganza

 CHAPTER ONE

hen Catherine of Braganza first came home from the convent where the good nuns had educated her, even the strict court etiquette of Lisbon could not quite subdue her spirit or stifle her warm heart. By the time she was two-and-twenty she was both devout and desirable—and quite incredibly innocent.

Most of her friends, who were daughters of Portuguese grandees, had made good marriages while still in their teens. They came to the palace sometimes to show her their babies. Catherine coveted the babies, but was not even betrothed. She remembered that there had been some talk of it when she was small and her parents, beset by Spain, had been most anxious for her to make an alliance with Great Britain. But Charles the First had not considered her important enough for his heir; and soon afterwards some of his subjects had shocked Europe by cutting off his head, and the young prince had become a penniless exile.

And so Catherine had loitered contentedly enough through the sheltered years, thankful not to have to leave home but shamed sometimes because of her spinsterhood. "It cannot be because I am ugly," she decided, peering into the fabulously carved mirrors imported from her family's eastern possessions. "My nose may be too short and my mouth a thought too wide; but even Mother Superior, who abhors vanity, said at the *Festa* that my hair was lovely." Unlike many princesses, Catherine had sense enough to realize that, even in her most becoming farthingale, she was no breathtaking beauty. What she did not realize was that her big, sherry-brown eyes held all the allure one small woman can possibly need, because naturally she herself could not watch them sparkling with animation or softening to compassion.

And in the end she found that her marriage had waited upon far more momentous matters than the degree of her good looks.

"The English monarchy has been restored," her mother told her impressively, after summoning her to a family conclave.

"And the poor exiled prince has gone home at last!" said Catherine, before she and Donna Elvira, the duenna of her ladies, were well risen from their sweeping curtsies.

"So you have heard, my dear Catalina?"

"Yes, Madame. My ladies can talk of nothing else, can they, Donna Elvira? It seems to them so romantic the way he went back and fought for his crown at some place called Wor-ces-ter, and then had to escape all over again. We made the Abbot Aubigny, who has been in England, tell us about this second landing. All the church bells were ringing, he says, and the people laughing and dancing again!" Catherine's dark eyes were sparkling; for when you have nearly been married to a person, even if he did not want you, it is difficult not to take an interest in what happens to him.

"He is King Charles the Second now," said Don Francisco de Mello, their Chancellor, watching her with unusual intentness.

"And I am sending our good Francisco to London," her elder brother, King Alfonso told her portentously.

Something in the way her younger brother, Don Pedro, was looking at her made Catherine begin to understand why so much interest was being focused upon her. Her gaze came to rest upon her capable mother, who really ruled their small kingdom—who had ruled it since her husband's death and made unbelievable sacrifices to bring it out from the bondage of the Spanish yoke. "Then, after all . . ." Catherine began unsteadily.

"Yes, after all!" confirmed Luiza of Braganza, smiling at her with eyes full of pride, yet moist with the sorrow of approaching parting.

"How fortunate that we did not accept the other proposals," remarked young Don Pedro.

His sister swung round towards him with a stiff swaying of

hooped skirts, betraying her pretty ankles. "Then there *were* other men who wanted to marry me," she exclaimed, filled with a sudden strong delight.

"Scores of them!" he teased. "You can hardly suppose that the grasping Courts of Europe were completely dumb and indifferent when our sailors took Tangier and Bombay."

"Oh! For what they could get, you mean?" she pouted, considerably crestfallen.

"Whatever the motive of these ducal suitors, her Majesty had faith—and waited," explained Don Francisco dryly. "She believed in the destiny of Charles Stuart. Your mother, my dear, is a very astute woman."

The Dowager Queen preened herself like a triumphant little pouter pigeon in her Chancellor's approval. "The British are very like ourselves—a seaboard race with tradition. Like us, they cannot live beneath a drab tyranny for long! So when the mothers of the disappointed dukes said to me nastily, 'Is it not high time your daughter married?' I forbore to tell them what shortsighted fools they were. I waited for the alliance that could consolidate the strength of our country—the alliance your dear father always desired."

They all crossed themselves devoutly and Alfonso asked ponderously, "Does it please you, Catalina?"

"It is—a great honor," she answered, sinking to a stool at her mother's feet because the firmness of her familiar world seemed suddenly to be cut from under her.

They went on discussing the matter at length although she, whose whole life it concerned, was too dazed to listen.

"Six of our ships the cursed Spaniards sunk last month!"

"They'll be sailing up the Tagus with their new three-decker galleons next—and *then* God help us!"

"If we had this new, strong alliance they would never dare—not after the way England bested their vaunted Armada!"

"No. But how are we to make sure of England? What plums does *she* pick out of it?"

"Some of our possessions, perhaps," suggested Don Francisco.

"They have been too busy fighting each other during their disastrous Civil War; but now—being a sea-faring nation—they will want to expand."

"It is true that they want trade. But above everything else Charles Stuart himself must want ready money," said Luiza shrewdly. "His family was ruined during the Commonwealth. Even their plate and pictures were sold. He will have nothing but what his upstart parliament cares to grant him. And as long as he has only that, he will be but a puppet king."

"Money?" repeated Alfonso, caressing his mean little moustachios. "He can scarcely expect much of me after our long struggle with Spain. The sum which *our* parliament voted——"

"By careful economies I have saved the bulk of it, for my daughter's dowry," interrupted Luiza firmly. "Five hundred thousand pounds sterling you can offer Charles Stuart, Francisco."

Successful as their foreign trading had been, the Braganzas had had no idea there was so much in the royal coffers. To them the bargain seemed as good as made. "The only pity is that the man is a Protestant," summed up handsome Don Pedro.

At sound of the hated word Catherine came out of her abstracted trance. "Marry a heretic!" she cried, remembering all she had heard of them in her convent.

"Do not distress youself, dear goddaughter," soothed grayhaired Don Francisco. "None of us will let you go without promise of full religious freedom. You will have your own private chapel and confessor."

"But what about her children?" asked Don Pedro, who loved her dearly.

"It is regrettable, of course. But England is a Protestant country——"

Queen Luiza hastened to lay a comforting arm about her daughter's shoulders. "Charles Stuart's mother, Henrietta Maria, is an ardent Catholic. Also the youngest daughter who has always been with her in France. And now I hear rumors that his brother, the Duke of York, may be converted. It is often like that in these mixed State marriages, Catalina *querida*. You will probably be allowed to keep your daughters and some of your younger sons in the faith."

In her optimistic enthusiasm she spoke as if Catherine were sure to produce the proverbial quiverful, and Alfonso began making tentative plans for a proxy wedding in Lisbon Cathedral.

But the sagacious old Chancellor felt it his duty to point out one unavoidable embarrassment. "In the event of the negotiations going through, I make no doubt the Pope will grant the necessary dispensation," he said. "But I would remind your Majesty that his Holiness has never yet brought himself to offend mighty Spain by acknowledging Portugal as a separate kingdom. Consequently in all documents from the Vatican our dear Catherine will be referred to simply as the Duke of Braganza's sister."

"Oh, not to be thought of!" cried the new young Portuguese King.

"It would debase us utterly in the eyes of England!" protested Don Pedro.

It was, in fact, a contingency which even the practical Queen Dowager had not taken into consideration. Her daughter's prestige was dear, but Portugal came first. She drew a deep breath and rose from her chair. "Then there can *be* no proxy wedding," she decided.

They all stared at her, aghast. Even Alfonso and Pedro, who were no better than they ought to have been, would almost as soon have sent their cherished sister to walk alone among the brothels on the waterfront. And Donna Elvira raised her skinny, shocked hands to heaven—hands in which lay responsibility for the morals of every young girl at Court. "Madame, I beseech you!" she exclaimed. "Send our Princess unwed to some strange man! An unprotected virgin!"

"You and I would be there—protecting her," pointed out Don Francisco, with a gleam of tolerant amusement. "To say nothing of a whole retinue of priests and ladies."

"But even so what could we *do*—in a barbarous island where they behead their kings?"

"Oh, come, come, dear lady," grinned Don Pedro. "Since this

regicide Cromwell died they have at least admitted the error of
their ways by inviting their sovereign back. And from all we hear
he is a fine, cultured man."

"And a notorious profligate!" snapped the outraged duenna.

Knowing there was truth in what she said, the Braganzas remained silent. The idea of delivering Catherine unwed to any
foreign country was utterly unconventional. But, whatever their
individual feelings, there was one emotion which predominated
in all of them—a patriotism capable of triumphing over much
greater things than prudery, the kind of patriotism which absorbs
and directs and unifies a people whose whole existence is one
heroic fight for national freedom. And as a matter of course their
own personal safety and desires had always been subordinated to
it.

It was the Unprotected Virgin herself who accepted the sacrifice. "I am willing to go—just as I am—for Portugal," she said
simply.

To go, leaving these loved ones, would in any case mean desolation, although it had always been her recognized destiny. To go
without married status or consecrated contract was frightening.
Yet somehow, although Charles Stuart was a heretic and someone
had just called him profligate, he seemed to Catherine different,
since she knew at the back of her mind that nothing, nothing
would have induced her to go unwed to any of the unspecified
ducal suitors, trusting to their marriage arrangements when they
met her.

But in spite of her courageous willingness there was so much
delay in settling the negotiations that the poor girl began to
wonder if even now, with the wealth of Tangier and Bombay
and an attractive dowry as bait, the restored King of Scotland
and England considered her important enough. She was not to
know that Vatteville, the Spanish ambassador to that country,
who had never in his life set eyes on her, had whispered through
the anterooms of Whitehall that she was both sterile and de-
formed; or that Charles, who loved children and liked his women
piquant, had in consequence become distrait and dilatory; that

he had sent someone he could trust to look at her and that, finally, when Vatteville, given the lie about her looks, had had the effrontery to threaten war if a Portuguese marriage went through, Charles—in one of his rare rages—had dismissed him from the Court of St. James and sent him back bag and baggage to Spain. There were many ugly things about human nature that Catherine had yet to learn. All she did know was that it seemed a long time before her godfather came back to Lisbon.

But when at last he returned he brought letters to her mother and to herself, and on hers Charles had written in his own fine hand, "To my Lady and Wife, whom God preserve!"

"So you *see*, Madame!" she could not refrain from chanting triumphantly, as she waved the imposing looking document beneath Donna Elvira's sharp, disapproving nose.

"He is dark and ugly as a Spaniard," commented that disgruntled lady, looking at the miniature which Don Francisco had also brought.

There were days full of dressmakers and dowry discussions and the selection of a suitable retinue, followed by a great fervor to sail while the dreaded Bay of Biscay was still relatively calm. But still Charles did not send for his bride. His ships must go and garrison Tangier first, Francisco de Mello explained. But as the autumn days passed and all the gorgeous dresses were packed and the seas grew rougher and rougher, Catherine could have wept with mortification.

And then suddenly everything personal was forgotten in the calamitous tidings that a Spanish army was massing on the border and the great Spanish galleons her brothers were always talking about were harrying the merchantmen from Brazil. The Portuguese merchantmen, hopelessly outclassed, were flying before the wind trying to make Oporto. Defeated in diplomacy, it seemed that by piracy and bloodshed the angry Spaniards would reduce her country to a dependency again and so prevent Catherine's marriage. And then, just when the galleons were on the point of overhauling the merchantmen and grappling the treasure from their holds, fourteen ships of the English fleet hove in sight and, under the very eyes of their new allies, blasted the enemy out of Portuguese waters.

Never had so great a cheer gone up from the waterfront. Never had disembarking foreigners received so warm a welcome. Mariners who spoke no word of each other's language embraced like brothers as they tumbled ashore. Every house in Lisbon was hung with flags; the air was rent with salvos and the delirious ringing of convent bells. By day there were bullfights and feastings, and at night barges of musicians and fireworks made a fantastic carnival of the Tagus.

Tears of a divided pride ran down Catherine's face as she went with her family to welcome the English admiral. No longer would there be need of diplomatic missions and tedious scriveners' treaties. The great, gallant ships had come for her at last, to take her to be England's Queen. No royal marriage had ever been more popular with her people, and though the waves might break like mountains out beyond the bar, she would be proud to go.

But first she must bid good-by to Mother Superior and the good nuns, and visit the shrine of her favorite saint, praying a little forlornly for happiness in her foreign marriage. And the last evening, snatching an hour from formality and fireworks, she talked quietly with her mother.

"I leave so much love here," she sighed. "I beg you, Madame, pray our Blessed Lady that I find some to replace it over there!"

"You are one who needs it as the opening hibiscus needs the sun's warmth," mused Luiza. "But it is not given to many women to find love in a royal marriage as I did. You will have to walk very warily, my child."

Catherine gazed out unseeingly at the conflagration of colored lights that signified rejoicing. "You think—with Donna Elvira— that it will be difficult because King Charles admires other women?" she asked.

"He does more than admire them," Luiza told her bluntly. "But you must try to bear in mind that he had to waste the best years of his vigorous manhood skulking about Europe, cruelly deprived of his natural inheritance and occupations; and that now, suddenly, every ambitious beauty throws herself at his head. It is better that you should understand this, Catalina."

For the first time Luiza was talking to her daughter as woman to woman; but she had left it a little late. And it was a far cry from the mature judgment of a woman who had been sure of her husband's affection to the uncertainty of a convent-bred girl being sent to the most experienced lover in Europe.

There was a long pause during which each of them thought that Catherine understood. "You mean—I must not be jealous?" she faltered.

"I mean that you must shut your eyes."

"Shut my eyes?" repeated Catherine, opening them very wide indeed. There was a suggestion of something hard, half-understood and wholly unfamiliar in the way her mother spoke, which made Catherine feel vaguely uncomfortable. "Did he—for instance—love that woman Don Francisco mentioned?" she asked, trying to speak as casually as if she had not been thinking about it for days.

Luiza shrugged the question aside as if it were of small importance. "He may have done," she said. "But it is neither the clean loves nor the peccadilloes of a man's youth that signify. Nor, for that matter, the occasional brief fires that may consume him later. We wives in high places have to overlook such things. It is the woman who has become a bad habit that matters. They have a saying in France: 'The King is what his mistress makes him.' And there is such a woman in England."

"But surely if he is going to marry *me*—" began Catherine, in all the terrible vulnerability of her innocence.

"I am sure that my future son-in-law will behave with dignity and discretion," Luiza assured her. "When Francisco left London this woman had gone back to her husband's house. But she is handsome as a goddess, they say, and greedy as a gull. Only quite recently Charles has bestowed some ridiculous title upon her— as a reward for past services, let us hope. Something to do with a *casa*, I think. . . . Yes, Castlemaine—that was it."

"Ca-stle-maine." Almost soundlessly Catherine repeated the

strange, foreign name, lisping the *s* a little with her southern
tongue.

"Yes, you will do well to remember it," approved Luiza.

Uncertainties more terrifying than homesickness and the tumultuous waves were tearing at Catherine now. "But even if I
know it, what can I *do?*" she asked.

"Do?" Luiza turned to look out at the proudly dressed ships
which assured the survival of her country. At that moment she
was more queen than mother, and success had given her a fantastic sense of power. "What should a daughter of Braganza do
but ignore her, and see that she is not received at Court?"

CHAPTER TWO

The bride-to-be sat bolt upright against her pillows in the King's house at Portsmouth, horrified at the thought of a strange man coming into her bedroom.

"You say, Madame, that his Majesty wants to come in *here?*" she asked huskily, her eyes still bright from a slight bout of fever.

"He not only wants to, he *insists,*" replied Donna Elvira, with a sniff indicative of her disgust at the coarse customs of the English.

"He has traveled posthaste from London," said Don Francisco.

"Then why could he not have come five days ago, when I first landed?" demanded Catherine, a trifle inconsistently.

The aging statesman might easily have attributed her rare burst of petulance to the feverish cold which she had caught aboard ship, and to the horrible crossing which they had all endured. But Catherine had proved an excellent sailor and he knew her well enough to recognize signs of spirited personal affront. "His Majesty had to prorogue parliament. He sent his brother," he reminded her.

Catherine's thoughts flew back to a morning on the sunlit Solent when James, Duke of York, had boarded the *Royal Charles* between South Hampton and the Wight. Tall and florid in his fair peruke, he had looked much as she had expected any Scot or Englishman to look. She had not been in the least afraid of him. Indeed, because he was shy and awkward, it had been she who had set him at ease; and, obviously, he had liked her. And now, because her nose felt snuffly and she knew she was not looking her best, she almost began to wish that it were the uncritical

James whom she was to marry—except, of course, that he already had a wife.

"We could say that your Grace is too ill," Donna Elvira was suggesting, quelling the squawking of the excited maids-of-honor with a gesture.

In spite of her own agitation Catherine found herself wanting to giggle at the scandalized expressions on their faces. All the clatter and commotion of the King's arrival certainly was very exciting. "But I am not really so ill as all *that,*" she objected.

"And Charles Stuart always sees through excuses," added Don Francisco, speaking feelingly out of his own recent experiences.

"My poor Don Francisco!" Even at so personal a moment Catherine found time to be sorry for him; for had not he, poor man, had to make excuses for a half-paid dowry, explaining away Queen Luiza's optimistic promises on the grounds that much of the vaunted five hundred thousand had perforce been spent on defense during those days of panic when Spain had risen against them. To Luiza's businesslike mind this might seem a triumphal example of persuasive diplomacy, but to Catherine's more honest one it seemed the supreme humiliation. "I suppose—since we have not kept our part of the bargain—he could send me back again?" she whispered, remembering that the fleet was still down in Portsmouth harbor.

Her godfather patted her hand encouragingly. "Take heart, dear child," he whispered back. "Remember the wealth of Tangier and Bombay!"

"Well, if he is coming here at least let me get up," she implored, feeling that dressed and bejeweled she would have more dignity with which to meet her bridegroom. But the physicians grouped about her would not hear of it, and her ladies were already bumping into each other in their efforts to insure that her informal toilette was completely modest. Before they could do much about it the door was flung wide and the King was in her room.

Completely unhurried and composed, he crossed to her bedside and, bowing, kissed her hand. Because it mattered so supremely what he was like, Catherine scarcely dared to look at him. All she knew was that the fingers beneath her own were strong and tapering, and that the voice bidding her welcome was deep and pleasant and indolent. She was aware of a little group of gentlemen standing, plumed hats in hand, at a respectful distance; among them York and the admiral, whose discreet smiles wished her well, and a martial looking cousin called Rupert who was presented to her. And then Charles was enquiring after her comfort on the voyage and Catherine knew that she must answer. Slowly her shy gaze traveled upwards from the rosettes on his shoes. It had a long way to travel, for Charles was even taller than she had supposed, taller and swarthier. His face was grave between the long folds of a dark, curled wig, and his somber eyes were quizzing her. "Your Majesty's admiral was goodness itself," she said; and heard Aubigny, her confessor, repeating the words in English.

"And my brother tells me he has already forestalled me in your friendship, boarding the *Charles* in mid-Solent."

"It would have pained me had he delayed in doing so," answered Catherine, with formal courtesy, bringing herself to smile across the room at James and wondering how two brothers could possible look so unlike.

"And now I find you sick abed, poor soul! Had they told me I would somehow have made shift to come sooner."

There was such genuine concern in his voice that Catherine, in gratitude, found herself making a vast effort to recall some smattering of her hurriedly acquired English. "Already—I become —better," she pronounced cheerfully; and because everybody laughed and seemed inordinately pleased the pink color came back into her cheeks.

For the first time Charles smiled, perceiving that she was not just the prim brown sparrow of a woman he had at first supposed. His full, protruding lips parted over excellent teeth, and amusement crinkled the corners of his almond-shaped eyes.

"Then your medical gentlemen must admit I am no mean member of their profession," he laughed, acknowledging their presence with a gracious inclination of his head. And when Donna

Elvira and other members of Catherine's household had been presented to him, he fell to discussing the wedding plans. "I had
made arrangements for the ceremony to be held here tomorrow,"
he told her, through the interpretation of the hovering Aubigny.

"Then I do not have to go to London to be married?"

"I am sure, Madame, you would sooner travel as my wife, and
that your mother would wish it so."

"And the sacrament? Please, Father Aubigny, ask his Majesty
about—the private ceremony we spoke of."

But Charles seemed to understand without being asked, and to
have no objections. "We can be married privately according to
the Catholic faith at once—here, in your room," he said. "And if
you wish, the public Protestant ceremony can wait until you
are feeling stronger."

"No, I would like that too—tomorrow," declared Catherine,
nodding her head vigorously. "Only you must tell me what to do."

Apparently she was not the little bigot he had been led to
suppose, or else she wished very much to please him. "I will
always show you what to do," he promised gravely. "I know only
too well what it is like to be exiled in a strange country." And
then—because his kindness seemed likely to make the ever near
tears of homesickness overflow—he set himself to tease her back
into laughter again. "I believe you are relieved that we do not go
immediately to London?"

"There are so many people there," she murmured, with an uneasy feeling at her heart that many of them might be less kind to
her than the Stuarts.

"Truth to tell, we are not going there for some weeks. There
are usually some cases of plague during the hot weather and before leaving Westminster I bade parliament have the streets
cleaned up before I brought them home a Queen," he confided. "It
is all very well for us bachelors to splash through puddles of
water to our saddle girths, but Whitehall is like to become an island if they do not see to it soon. An occasion like this is an opportunity—while they are all so prodigiously set up about the Tangier trade—and life has taught me to sieze my opportunities!"

With a new little fluttering of her pulses, Catherine decided that he looked like the kind of man who would make the most of all of them. "Then where do we live in the meantime?" she asked.

"I am carrying you off to a riverside palace in the country which I am sure you will like in summertime. An old Tudor building, mighty inconvenient in some ways. A cardinal built it, but it seems designed for dalliance with its privy gardens and pleached walks. And I shall not be the first of our kings to use it for a honeymoon."

"And what is it called—this honeymoon palace?"

"Hampton Court."

Catherine set them all smiling again by her efforts to pronounce the strange foreign name which was to come to mean so much to her.

"Your Majesty will come to fathom our language in time," the kindly admiral assured her, and James promised comfortable arrangements for the journey. "Don Francisco de Mello will perhaps do me the honor to travel in my coach?" he suggested courteously. "And our cousin, Prince Rupert of Bavaria, will escort the ladies."

"They will travel with drawn blinds," insisted Donna Elvira, with an unnecessarily distrustful glance at that attractive soldier of fortune.

James blinked his sandy lashes. "Why, certainly, Madame—if your ladies so desire," he stammered protestingly. "But England —in Maytime—"

It was Charles's own month, the month of his birthday and his restoration when he had brought back merriment to his people with music in the summer evenings and maypoles on the village greens. Now, two years later, it was to be the month of his marriage—a marriage which did not look like being so prosaic a business as he had anticipated. And at no time in his misspent life had he had much recourse to drawn blinds—though "More's the pity!" some men said. "Everything shall be arranged as you think proper, Madame," he promised, coming suavely to his brother's assistance. "And although I must confess myself more impatient than ever to arrive at Hampton, we will break the journey wherever necessary and find lodgings for the night."

Unfortunately his kindly assurances resulted only in a bobbing together of outlandishly coiffured Portuguese heads and a whispered foreign conversation from which the main outcome appeared to be an urgent desire for "virgin beds."

"But naturally, my dear Aubigny," protested James testily. Whereupon it became necessary for the embarrassed abbot to explain. "My Lord Duke, it is more than that which Portuguese etiquette requires. Donna Elvira would have you understand that many of these maidens committed to her care are the unmarried daughters of exalted families and that in no circumstances could she permit them to sleep in any bed that has previously been lain in by a man."

If James Stuart—fresh from Whitehall where people chose their beds with far less circumspection—stepped back a pace or two in his astonishment, even the admiral, upon whose gouty toe he trod, could scarcely blame him. "There will be beds and coaches and baggage carts for everyone," was all that he could promise.

Catherine's eyes were bright now with excitement, not fever. At no shrine that she had ever visited had a *malaise* been cured so miraculously. "And for my *guarda-infantes* too?" she demanded. "There are seventy-two of them, and we must take them all with us." Charles, who had traveled so light at times that he had had no change of shirt, looked anxiously round the crowded room, amazed that so small a person should need so great an entourage. All these maids, priests and apothecaries, and now some kind of bodyguard, he supposed. "Who are they—these *guarda-infantes?*" he asked cautiously, wondering if now, before his fleet weighed anchor, he could decently ship them back again to Portugal. His people, he knew, were touchy enough about a Catholic marriage, and Rupert's soldiery would certainly resent some oddly dressed foreign escort.

Catherine wrinkled her short nose in perplexity; but when Charles, tired of all this interpreting and remembering that he could speak Spanish, tried out his question haltingly in that language, her gravity broke up into a ripple of relieved laughter. "So you speak my mother's tongue? That is wonderful!" she exclaimed. "But they are not *who* in any language. They are *what*."

Then, seeing that her prospective bridegroom looked more mystified than ever, she bade her dressers open a large closet where stood innumerable coffers of a peculiar round shape, each one containing a carefully packed farthingale. Before the astonished gaze of their hosts her ladies proudly lifted some of these bejeweled dresses, each one more gorgeous than the last—and each with a short wide skirt that stood out from the hips as stiff and round as a cartwheel.

At this display of feminine fashion, formality seemed suddenly to vanish from the scene. With a swift stride or two Charles approached the nearest farthingale and poked with lean, experimental fingers at the wide hooped wires upon which it was stretched. He had watched far more women than he should have being dressed in a variety of garments, varying from a modern shift to the fashionable abandon of the pseudo-classic style so beloved of portrait painters. But never had he seen anything like this. "Why the stiff wire, Madame?" he enquired of his bride's forbidding, hook-nosed duenna.

"As the name implies, your Majesty—to guard the Infanta's virginity," replied Donna Elvira, with folded hands and lowered eyes.

"Oddsfish!" ejaculated Charles. His dark, puzzled eyes traveled over the small figure scarcely molding the covers of the big bed. "But why seventy-two of them?"

"Oh, they are not all mine!" explained the bride-to-be blithely. "There are at least two apiece for my ladies."

Charles sauntered back across the room, catching his brother's eye with mock solemnity. "You heard that, I trust, James!" he remarked. When he turned back to the bed he was still looking stern but Catherine fancied his wide mouth was quivering to a grin. "Does her most Catholic Majesty, your mother, imagine that we English rape our visitors on sight?" he demanded.

But Catherine only looked up at him admiringly. "What is it
—to rape?" she enquired politely.

And Charles, who even in his most inglorious moments had
always contrived to remain master of any situation, sank down
upon her bedside stool, defeated. His Spanish, which he had been
so set up about, appeared suddenly to have deserted him. "What
were the good nuns thinking about?" he asked in his mother
tongue of nobody in particular.

"Their devotions, undoubtedly, Sir," murmured Aubigny with
a smile.

"At least they were capable of instilling faith and hope!" added
James, reviewing the plain foreign damsels with distaste, his
slower mind still working upon the extraordinary measures for
their protection.

But Charles was looking only at Catherine. In the embarrassing
beauty of her innocence she had brought him something which,
in his wildest hagglings over her dowry, he had not bargained
for, something he had not encountered for many a long day. And
he was both humbled and touched. He began to talk to her about
the home she had left, and the one she was coming to, trying to
set her at ease. When Charles Stuart took the trouble to be kind,
he had a way of stealing people's hearts. He began to tell her of
the pleasant river which flowed past his palaces, and the way in
which it ministered to so many of his pastimes.

"We also live beside a river—the Tagus," said Catherine. "My
mother, my brothers and I."

"Was it very grievous saying good-by?" asked Charles, who
knew all about the grief of partings. At his request she had dismissed most of her people, and his gentlemen had tactfully withdrawn to the window whence they were watching the cheering
crowd assembled in the street below. "I, too, have someone I
adore, but seldom see. A sister who lives in France," he said. "And
my young brother Henry died of the pox not long before you
came. We had all been separated because of—what happened to
my father. And Henry and I were just beginning to know each
other——"

"Tell me about both of them," urged Catherine, forgetting how embarrassing it was to have a strange man sitting so casually beside her bed; and when tears trembled on her dark lashes, partly for him and partly for herself, they were brighter than any of the priceless pearls she had meant to wear.

"It was good of your remaining brother to be so pleasant to me," she said, drying her eyes with the handkerchief Charles offered her. "My mother feared he might show me resentment because he is still your heir."

"Only until we have a son of our own," Charles reminded her.

Catherine smoothed the embroidered C.R. on the kerchief and handed it back to him with complete confidence. "I should like one quite soon," she said, much as if she were ordering some new furnishings.

"With all my heart!" agreed Charles. "I cannot think of anything which would make my people—or me—love you more. But now you had better rest. And presently I will send to you the Duchess of Suffolk and the other English ladies who are to attend you, and they will advise you what to wear for the wedding. I think, perhaps, *not* one of the farthingales."

"Not—" began Catherine, with pouting mouth and an ominous darkening of her expressive eyes.

But Charles was quite experienced at forestalling women's tantrums. "I have brought you as a present an English dress. Rose satin with knots of blue ribbon down the front, which I chose especially to become your dark loveliness," he said. "And I can scarce restrain my impatience to see you grace it!"

And after so tantalizing a compliment, neither could Catherine, although she knew that her ladies would not approve. "You see, Donna Elvira, he did not send me back again!" she yawned in drowsy content, after all the company had withdrawn. "I don't think that he even wanted to."

Yet outside her door James of York was still looking vastly perplexed. "What good will come of it, throwing an unshorn lamb like that—to Charles?" he burst forth, falling into step with Ad-

miral Montagu, whom he found pacing the gallery as briskly as if
it were his own quarter-deck.

But Edward Montagu was mightily pleased with the way things
were going. Had he not been responsible for the royal wench's
safe arrival and, sooner than humiliate her, taken the risk of severe reprimand for stuffing his holds with half her dowry in merchandise instead of gold? And was she not already proving a
credit to him, so much so that he had just been created Earl of
Sandwich for his pains? "The Braganzas may have wrought more
subtly than you think, Sir," he made so bold to say. "For such is
the King's goodness of heart that her very innocence may move
him to protect the lamb from the wolves. When his Majesty spoke
just now of cleaning up Whitehall, he may have had in mind more
than the fouled streets. And consider, I pray you, the blessing it
will be to have a virtuous Queen and all things conducted more
seemly, so that we can take our wives to Court again!"

And as there were many decent living men who felt the same
as he, all went forward with high hope.

That same evening the King nearly shocked the poor Portuguese ladies out of their senses by supping merrily in Catherine's
room, spreading the viands before her on the bed and reducing
her to helpless laughter; and on her marriage morning the
Duchess of Suffolk helped her with her new English clothes. No
one was more delighted than Charles to see his taste so thoroughly vindicated. For Catherine and the rose satin dress were
such a success that no sooner had the Bishop of London pronounced them man and wife, and the good citizens ceased deafen-
ing them with cheers, than all the principal guests began begging
one of the little blue bows as a souvenir. "And not a single one
left for me to press in my prayer book for 'ever after,'" mourned
Catherine between smiles and tears, when the Duchess's scissors
had ceased snipping and the last favor had been thrown.

It was a tired little bride who was bedded that night, worn out
with so much strange excitement and still indisposed; and Charles,
who never lay long abed, was astir before she wakened. He had
several urgent letters to dispatch which were of too intimate a

nature for a secretary to attend to, and which he preferred to
write while still undistracted.

In the early summer morning he stood for a while by a window
absently flicking the feathers of his quill across his freshly shaven
cheek, and watching life begin to stir aboard his beloved ships.
For the first time in all that turmoil he had time to think of Barbara, his mistress, lying in her bed at Richmond, and of the child
she was about to bear him—and for the first time he thought of
her and of Palmer, her proud, cuckolded husband, with shamed
reluctance. Because she had become the strongest habit in his
life the temptation to write to her was great, but on this his first
morning as a married man he resisted it.

Instead, with a prodigious sigh, he said his prayers and sat
himself down to address a letter to the Earl of Clarendon, his
Chancellor, so that the waiting courier might be getting on his
way to London. Charles was glad enough to have something good
to tell faithful old Edward Hyde, who had shared his exile and
tried to coerce him into the paths of virtue, and who loved him
like a disappointed father. "It was happy for the honor of the
nation," he wrote, "that I was not put to the consummation of the
marriage the night I arrived for, having slept but two hours on my
journey, I was afraid matters would have gone very sleepily. . . .
She cannot exactly be called a beauty, Ned, but her eyes are excellent and she has much agreeableness. I think she must be as
good a woman as ever was born and you would wonder to see
how well we are acquainted already! . . . Do not expect me at
Hampton Court until Thursday by reason that there are not
enough carts to be had to transport all our *guarda-infantes*, without which there is no stirring."

And then to his beloved sister, so recently and so disastrously
married to the little, strutting Duke of Orleans: "Today I was married, and I think myself happier than you, *ma chère Minette*. But
the fortune that follows our family is fallen upon me, *car Mon-
seigneur le Cardinal m'a fermé la porte au nez! Tout de même*, I
flatter myself I was not so furious as Monsieur your husband. . . ."

And finally, and a little more decorously, he wrote to his new, unknown mother-in-law—thinking for her as he so often thought for others—imagining how hard the day must have been for her and how she must have been hungering for news. "In this spring-time I am enjoying the company of my dearest wife. I cannot sufficiently either look at her or talk to her," he wrote, as the morning larks rose up to meet the new day from the Hampshire hills. "I am the happiest man in all the world."

CHAPTER THREE

"I shall always love this place. I have been so happy here," murmured Catherine, gazing lazily across the lawns of Hampton from the grassy bank on which she lay.

"Happier than at home in Lisbon?"

"Happier than I had hoped to be this side of heaven!" admitted Catherine, incapable of caution or caprice in the prodigality of her new, absorbing love. "I do not wonder that your great ruddy ancestor, whose portrait hangs in the hall, brought all his brides here. Is it really true that he had six of them?"

The hard structure upon which her head rested, which happened to be the King of England's shoulder, began to shake most uncomfortably. "Even Henry Tudor did not have them all at once, sweetheart!"

But to Catherine the subject seemed more meet for anxiety than for laughter. She began plucking at the pink-tipped daisies which starred the grass beyond the stiff grandeur of her skirts. "He beheaded two as soon as he was tired of them," she remarked uneasily.

At so much unexpected knowledge of the seamier side of his country's history Charles Stuart heaved himself up abruptly, tumbling her from his heart in order to shake her gently by the arms. "Who has been putting such grim ideas into your pretty head?" he demanded.

As they sat there unconventionally on the ground, her eyes looked back into his searching dark ones with the translucence of a clear running brook. "Last evening just before the torches were lit I sent two of milady of Suffolk's women to fetch something, and when they did not bring it I found them huddling in a corner, frightened of the ghost of some other Queen Catherine. They do not like lodging here, they said. As well as I could make out from their English talk she runs shrieking and headless and wringing her hands."

"That will be poor, frail little Catherine Howard. She cuckolded him but I am afraid Henry was a brute to his women," admitted Charles, in the very bad Spanish which had become their most usual means of communication.

"But, *carissimo*, whoever she is, it is not a very comfortable thing to have in my gallery!"

"A pack of old wives' tales, my dear. And, anyway, it all happened a long time ago."

"But Donna Elvira said before we came that in a country where they——"

"Before God, I will wring that old she-vulture's neck!" swore Charles.

Catherine's pouting lips widened in appreciative laughter. Out there in the sunshine, with the young lime trees he had planted scenting the summer air, it was impossible to be seriously perturbed about ghosts. And the mellow brick range of private apartments looked too homely ever to have been the scene of such high passions and tragedies. "All the same," she persisted obstinately, "if—whichever Henry it was—could divorce his wives whenever he was tired of them, I suppose you could do the same."

"Do I look as if I were tired of mine?" asked Charles, taking her into his arms and kissing her until she had no thought left for the love-making of his ancestors.

"*Madre de Dios*, it is not decent that a woman should be so beset!" she cried at last, trying to push him away. "People from the windows can see us."

"Alas!" complained Charles, "what is there for them to see, with you in that damned farthingale?"

"Let us move into the shade."

"Where we shall no longer be observed?" he teased.

"No," denied Catherine sedately. "Where the sun will be less hot."

"The coolest place is on the river."

"Oh, lovely!" she cried, clapping her hands. "Except that here ——"

With exquisite delight her husband read the thoughts betraying themselves so ingenuously on her expressive face. "We can still be alone," he said gently.

"Alone—in a State barge?"

"No. In a skiff."

"You mean that you will just take a skiff—and row—like anyone else?" she asked aghast.

"Why not, my dear? The Almighty gave me tolerably good muscles."

It was a way of aquatic progress entirely unknown to an etiquette-ridden princess, but she let him pull her to her feet—then hand in hand, laughing and running, to the water's edge, where a small boat lay moored against a secluded flight of steps. "Always keep a boat at hand as a means of escape," he advised flippantly, as he stepped aboard and lifted a breathless little bride in after him. "Once in my direst need I spent six of the most uncomfortable weeks imaginable trying to find one."

Too thrilled for speech, Catherine watched him divest himself of coat, hat and wig and throw them across a seat, then cast off with expert ease and pull out towards midstream. "When Alfonso goes on the T-Tagus he would not think of r-rowing himself," she said, still nervously gripping the sides of their precarious-looking little craft.

"Probably Alfonso has never been too poor to hire a boatman," observed Charles grimly, staying his long, leisurely strokes to shoo aside an over inquisitive bevy of swans.

"Are not your subjects—shocked?"

"I make no doubt they were at first. But it was through their bungling experiments that I was forced to live by my wits and so come to know the value of occasional solitude and the pleasures

of the common man. A lesson which one cannot unlearn, my
Catalina. And now I should be hard put to it to live without
these things. Even at Whitehall—in spite of all the frenzied
anxiety that goes on in the guardhouse—my brother and I make
shift to slip out by the privy water stairs and swim at Putney or
Barn Elms most summer mornings."

"And the crowds—do they not collect and stare as they do
whenever we leave the palace at home?"

"Most of them are still abed, except the ferry men and the
drovers coming in to market from the country," laughed Charles.
"And if it gives them any amusement to see their King mother-
naked—oddsfish, after the dismal, psalm-singing time they must
have endured these last twelve years, I am content to be their
reinstated raree-show."

Served by the tide, his skiff sped swiftly over the shining water,
and every here and there a fine ducal house or a humble cottage,
half-hidden by hawthorn blossom, lay snug on either bank; and
his companion, forgetting all her fears, trailed her pretty fingers
in the cool water and thought that no other land could ever have
looked so pleasant nor any other woman felt so free. Yet in the
midst of her happiness strong maternal instincts moved her to
yearn over all he must have suffered. "You were only a boy when
civil war separated you from your parents?" she prompted softly,
watching the rhythmic movements of his manhood's lean, athletic
body.

"James and I followed them from one battlefield to another,
while the younger children stayed here. I was only sixteen when
I was put in command of the remnants of our Royalist army in
the west. And afterwards I was happy enough in Jersey. A lanky
adolescent, learning to handle ships."

"And then?"

"For my own safety, my father sent word for me to join my
mother in France. My young cousin Louis and I got on famously
as long as they left us alone with his horses and dogs; but I am
afraid my poor mother, who had been at such pains to train me
in civility, found me very dumb and gauche. Later on, after they

had—when my father was no longer alive, I sailed for Scotland, tempted by the promise of an army with which to wrest back my land from Cromwell. As you love me, Catherine, do not ask me to tell you of the rigors I endured at Holyrood beneath the precepts and preachings of the Elders of the Kirk! And for my pains, when I had marched into England, I suffered defeat at Worcester and brought death to many loyal men. After that," he added, with a deep sigh, "there came the long waste of years at my sister Mary's Court in Holland. It would have been better for my soul, perhaps, had I been killed at Worcester."

Because she loved him, his new young wife was aware of his omissions and already sensed that his family's flight from Whitehall and his father's execution were actually the things of which he never spoke. "Tell me, then, how you escaped after the battle," she begged.

Charles's shrug was a legacy from his sojourn at his French cousin's Court. "I have told it so often," he protested.

"But never to me—who must care the most."

So he tied up beneath an overhanging willow tree, and as he leaned forward and talked his face was all dappled with shade and sunshine filtering through the swaying boughs that dipped green fingers in the Thames. "The most wonderful thing of all was the number of quite ordinary people who risked their lives to help me," he mused.

"I would have given mine," said Catherine, very softly.

But he did not hear her. He was back in the west of England, a young man of twenty, living the most desperately exciting hours of his life. "There was a price on my head, which to some of the men who recognized me would have meant a fortune for life. Yet I swear it never occurred to them to betray me."

"Perhaps they knew that their neighbors would not let them live long to enjoy it," she suggested, swatting quite savagely at a circling gnat.

"That of course is possible."

"You are not very vain, are you, Charles?"

"I have too many things to be ashamed of. More, *ma petite in-*

nocente, than you could ever guess." For a moment his somber eyes seemed to implore forgiveness while he stretched out a hand to touch her knee. Then he took up his tale more lightheartedly, poking fun at the poor figure he must have cut in borrowed rustic clothes and a Puritan's steeple hat. "At first I had not even so much elegance as that," he said. "I had lost a shoe trying to get a man who could not swim across a muddy river. And there is nothing much less heroic than hobbling about in hiding with blistered feet. Yet one of my most beautiful memories is of the kind old woman who cleansed and bound them up for me. Another which I cherish is of a young priest who also stood in daily peril, for celebrating Mass, and whose calm faith in God upheld me. And there were absurd things too, Catherine. Did I tell you those accursed Roundheads came and searched one of the houses that offered me hospitality, and how I found there Colonel Careless who led the charge with me through Worcester streets, and how he and I had to hide a whole day in an oak tree? And how in the end I fell asleep across his knee and he durst not speak because of the soldiers snooping below and so suffered a veritable martyrdom of pins and needles? He and Lord Wilmot and Will Crofts helped me from port to port, that I might get away to France. But often we split up our company, and always for safety I must needs travel as a servant. You should have seen me trying to turn the kitchen spit at Long Marston!"

"*You*—turning the roasting spit!"

Presently Charles stopped laughing and, clasping his hands about his knee, looked up appreciatively into the green canopy above them. "There was a girl called Jane Lane. Colonel Lane's daughter," he went on ruminatively. "I was supposed to be William Jackson, her servant. She rode pillion behind me, having a local official's permission to visit a pregnant relative at Bristol, where it was hoped we might bribe some master mariner to take me across to France. I used to sleep on a truckle bed in the kitchen quarters and sometimes, when I had helped her dismount and led the horses round to the stables, the inn yard would be full of old Noll's soldiers. 'By your leave,' I would say, and push past them—praying to God that none of them had particularly noticed me on the battlefield."

"And this Jane—was she very beautiful?" asked Catherine.

"Beautiful?" Charles's gaze came down to earth again as if to consider the matter. "She was kind and brave, and many a time her quick wits saved me. There was the evening when she sent Will Jackson to bed with an ague because we had seen a doddering old doctor from Whitehall playing on the bowling green who would probably have recognized Charles Stuart. And then the awful moment next morning when I found myself drawing a drink at the buttery hatch next to one of my own guards. He'd fought at Worcester and was bragging to the other servants about it. 'Seen the King?' he answered one of the maid servants he was ogling. 'Why, I've been as close to him as I am to you, Moll, and "the black boy" he's rightly named. Not unlike this fellow standing beside me, but at least three inches taller.' And after he had drawn all eyes upon me like that you may be sure I made what haste I could out of the buttery."

Catherine hung upon his words. Enviously, she contemplated the close companionship he and this girl must have shared in common danger, the excited conversation and crazy high spirits which must have ensued each time that momentary danger passed. "Have you ever seen her since?" she persisted.

"Unfortunately suspicion fell upon my loyal Lanes after my escape and they, too, had to fly to France. When I heard she was coming, although I had scarcely a *sou*, I borrowed Louis's best horses and rode out of Paris to meet her. She is back in England now, of course, and I have written more than once inviting her to Court. At first she made all manner of unreasonable excuses; but now that she is married I am hoping——"

Whatever he was hoping, Catherine heard no more. The long, soundless sigh that passed her lips was a *Deo gratias*. Jane Lane —that was an easy name to remember, even for a foreigner. And, God be praised, the wench was married! "I like you so much better with your own short, uncurled hair, Charles," she hurried to assure him irrelevantly, lest he should suspect her of the jealousy her mother had warned her to eschew. "It makes you look less stern, and so much younger."

"I am thirty-two—and a whole decade more in experience," he said, a little sadly.

"But sitting there in your shirt sleeves you still look like William Jackson. Promise me that while we are honeymooning here at Hampton you will not wear your periwig except in public!"

To the consternation of some peacefully employed waterfowl he rose to his feet, setting the boat rocking violently. Catherine screamed and clutched, but with one lithe movement he had steadied it and was on the seat beside her. "Will it please you to make a bargain, Kate?" he offered. "I will forswear my wig if you will discard your farthingale." But somehow in spite of it she found herself crushed, wire and all, in his arms.

"When you behave so crudely and I am angry with you I shall call you William Jackson and send you to sup below stairs," she threatened.

"And when you love me?" he enquired, his lips persuading hers.

After an idyllic interval during which the nesting moor hens considered it safe to return to their domestic activities, Catherine pulled herself free with an ecstatic sigh. "It seems," she said, "as though I should have to call you Charles all the time."

They returned to the palace in companionable silence, Charles pulling hard against the tide. "I will confess to you, rigidly brought up little royalty as you are," he told her once, between long, satisfying strokes, "that when I first came back I had to check myself from doing things which I could do better than my servants, like saddling a horse, mending an ill-set timepiece, vetting a sick dog. These hands of mine—they are so strong, Kate. . . ."

"So strong and so sensitive," she agreed, guessing joyfully that it was the first time he had ever spoken to anyone of so personal a trial. And while he rowed she fell to pondering upon the first of those marital lessons which, lovingly conned over the years, may bring a woman understanding of her husband's character.

Charles, she saw, could never be like other kings who had lived their lives in palaces. In spite of all his inherited dignity, never could he lose the warm knowledge of humanity he had learned in adversity or return to the cold, separate heights of kingship. Though he might seem to stand there, more easily regal than any Stuart, those wise, patient eyes of his would always be seeing cynically through the illusion.

And so the days of Catherine's happiness sped by, swift and sunlit as the flowing river, until the inevitable day when State duties claimed her husband. Catherine and duty were no strangers. Even her marriage might have been a lifelong personal sacrifice for Portugal had not God and the blessed saints bestowed such new richness of life upon her, for which she fell upon her knees night and morning in passionate gratitude. So when the great royal barge came to take him to a council meeting at Westminster she made no remonstrance, but stood at the water gate to wave him a dignified farewell.

"We shall not have to leave our beloved Hampton yet, shall we?" she had asked wistfully, while he was being dressed in all the splendor of his formal town clothes.

"Not until the summer is spent, sweetheart," he had assured her. "But I must go back and forth, lodging sometimes at Whitehall. For I would remind you, little witch, that while you beguile me here, poor Ned Clarendon, my Chancellor, bears the whole weight of the kingdom in his aging hands."

"You trust him utterly, do you not, Charles?"

"He is far more trustworthy than I!" he had laughed, taking the ring of state which Chaffinch, his groom of the back stairs, brought him, and slipping it on his sun-tanned finger. And Catherine, watching him, had remembered with an unreasonable pang of regret how those same capable hands had looked, unhampered by lace frills, knotting a rope or straining on a pair of oars.

And her regret was not so unreasonable after all, for when he came back, although he was equally kind, she found him different —more withdrawn and distrait. "His holiday is over and cares of State begin to weigh upon him," Catherine told herself, with admirable common sense. "We cannot always be honeymooning, but all our lives we shall be married. And between his public duties I shall be able to give him companionship, refreshing that part of him which belongs to me and not to Britain."

But a bout of restlessness was upon him, which had more to do with the man Charles than with the king. He would go for long walks, outdistancing his handful of attendants, or take the little skiff up the river without asking her to come.

"Are you trying to tire yourself out?" she remonstrated, when he came in after riding in the rain, as wet and muddy as his mount.

To her surprise he had answered her brusquely in English, passing her on the stairs. "Myself—or the devil in me!" she thought he had said.

For two nights he slept in his own apartments, with only his adoring spaniels for company. And one morning, venturing to go and see him there, she had caught sight of him through an open doorway, kneeling at his prayers. Kneeling desperately at his prayers, one might suppose, by the way his dark head was buried in his arms. But though her heart yearned over him as it did whenever she thought of his tragic boyhood, Catherine signed Chaffinch to silence and tiptoed away. That night her husband came to her and she had her reward. Instead of his usual lighthearted love-making it was as if he tried to give her his whole self in a way which he had never done before—as if it were the last time that he would have anything unmarred to give her. It was the night of tender perfection from which a gifted heir should have been born. And yet in the very intensity of his loving she felt the same desperation that she had beheld in his prayers.

"It is to be devoutly hoped, Catherine, that our sons will take after you!" he said, when the world was brightening to a roseate June dawn. "Even my mother had to apologize for me when I was a baby. I was strong and lusty even then, it seems, but black as a Saracen and incredibly ugly."

"I find it a mighty attractive ugliness!" laughed Catherine, sleepily.

"I have never been loved so charitably before," he said, smoothing back the curled luxuriance of her hair.

"But everybody loves you!"

"Because I am the fount of all preferment!"

Of a sudden there was so much bitterness in his voice that Catherine knew how recently he must have been preyed upon. She was silent for a moment or two, casting about in her drowsy mind for some constant thought with which to comfort him. "You were no fount of preferment when Jane Lane rode with you through Cromwell's soldiers and scores of men scorned the price on your head," she reminded him.

He kissed her then, very gently, without passion. "You do well to remind me," he said gratefully. "I will try to think on it when people badger me for high places."

He left her to sleep and went swimming, instead of to his chapel. When he came to bid her farewell he was already cloaked and booted.

"Listen to the cuckoos in the meadows, Charles!" she entreated, sitting up combed, scented and delicious in her bed.

But instead of smiling down at her he stood shifting some important looking papers in his hands. His eyes were no longer warm and shining. They had a guarded look as if he were disillusioned with mankind—disillusioned most of all perhaps with himself. "There are unimaginably tedious arrangements to be made for our taking up residence at Whitehall," he explained. "Lists to be made out for the new appointments in your household. Navy expenses to be passed. Warrants to be signed."

"But today, Charles?" she had persisted, in spite of all her good resolutions. "Is it such a matter of life and death?"

He had laughed, but without allowing himself to dwell upon the sweetness of her eager face. "Nothing so serious as death, my love," he had assured her, bending over the bed to kiss her before hurrying away. "I would say rather to do with life."

And although he did not return for a day or two his Secretary of State, Sir Edward Nicholas, duly waited upon her with an imposing looking document bearing the names of the Queen's household. "For her Majesty's approval," was written upon it in a hand which might have been either the Chancellor's or the Secretary's. But because Charles's familiar signature was set upon it Catherine smiled and laid it on the table beside her and began immediately asking after his health. "I pray there be no cases of plague in London?" she asked anxiously, airing her rapidly improving English.

"Since your coming, Madame, we have been singularly blessed in that respect, and the people take it as a good omen," Sir Edward Nicholas assured her.

Catherine led him on to tell her about life at Whitehall until he reminded her that the council was awaiting his return thither and begged her—a thought nervously—to approve the appointments.

"With all my heart!" agreed Catherine, proud to be able to pronounce so glibly the gracious words so often on her husband's lips. Almost casually, she began to read them through. Handsome Lord Cleveland was already her Comptroller, and Lady Suffolk had proved a good friend. Donna Elvira and her own Portuguese women would still be with her. There were several names which were unknown to her and which all looked alike in their foreign style—but of course Charles would know best.

But heading the list of ladies of the Queen's bedchamber was one name which she had learned to know only too well before ever she set foot in England. Lady Castlemaine. Catherine's heart almost stopped beating. She could hear again her mother's brisk voice saying that evening before she left Lisbon, "Some ridiculous foreign title he has conferred upon her . . . something to do with a *casa* . . . in return for *past* services, let us hope."

Lady Castlemaine. Her husband's mistress. Catherine rose to her feet with a dignity amazing in one so small, and as she stood staring down at the hated name she saw all Charles's strange restlessness in new guise. She knew that when he was away in London he must have seen her and been pressed for the appointment that the woman might remain near him. "How dare he? Oh, how *dare* he?" cried her proud, hurt heart, remembering how shamelessly and passionately she had given her whole being into his keeping.

"Bring me a pair of scissors!" she called.

Sir Edward, who knew his master's humors better than most, made a swift, deterring movement. "Madame, the King himself. . . . I beg you to consider—" he stammered.

"This is a matter which needs no consideration," cried Catherine, in her outraged young righteousness. And taking the scissors from one of her frightened women, she stabbed at the parchment, scratching through the name Castlemaine as though it had been mud.

CHAPTER FOUR

*A*ll through Oliver Cromwell's rebellion Barbara's family have been our most loyal subjects. As children we Stuarts always played with the young Villierses. And it is only meet that I should grant her this preferment," stormed Charles.

"And I am your wife and it is meet that you should not try to humiliate me," cried Catherine.

"No one is trying to humiliate you. But surely that pompous brother of yours taught you that a King must remember services rendered. I tell you Lady Castlemaine's father was killed in my father's defense."

"And I tell you your consideration for her has nothing to do with so respectable a service. It is because she is your mistress. And I will not have the woman in my household!"

They stood facing each other across the great crimson bridal bed, resentfully conscious of how recently they had lain there enamored in each other's arms, and secretly shocked to find themselves hurting each other with bitter words, quarreling like any browbeating City merchant and his shrewish wife.

Charles's face was white beneath his summer tan, and twin red spots of temper flamed on Catherine's cheekbones. His voice was blustering and hers was harsh. In a few brief hours the beauty of their honeymoon happiness had been torn to shreds and their raised voices carried through closed doors so that frightened Flemish waiting women wrung their hands, and grooms of the bedchamber, accustomed to the imperturbable good humor of their master, listened in excited groups. Already, although they could not hear their betters' actual words, they had started the

rumor of royal domestic strife which ran like wildfire through the
galleries and back stairs of the old Tudor palace, to be borne hot-
foot along Surrey lanes and spilled before morning into the
gossip-loving streets of London and the astounded courts of
Whitehall.

As if aware of this Charles, who loathed bad manners, took a
belated grip upon his dignity. "So you know?" he said, more
quietly.

Catherine nodded, her mouth set in outraged self-righteous-
ness. And the very fact that she had every reason to be both outraged and self-righteous made him all the angrier. "Surely you
did not suppose that I waited like a monk until my ministers
saw fit to fix up some political marriage for me?" he demanded
sulkily.

Poor Catherine made a brief, infinitely pathetic gesture with
her little hands. "I—scarcely understood enough—to suppose anything," she murmured, great tears welling in her lovely eyes.

Better than anyone in the world, Charles saw the truth of it.
Her innocence had been his keen delight, and was now become
in some sort his shame. Because it was not in his nature to be deliberately cruel, he went and sat upon her side of the bed and
took her hands in his. "My poor child, I love you the better for
it," he assured her remorsefully. "But now that you have been out
in the world a while surely you realize that I must have had other
women before you came?"

"Have I ever reproached you for that?" she asked, remembering her immature jealousy of Jane Lane and some Dutch princess
he had wanted, and standing unresponsively before him.

"You have been the very soul of tact and sweetness. But why
this obstinate antagonism against one woman now?"

"My mother told me that what was past is none of my business.
And when Donna Elvira called you profligate——"

"The sex-dried old grimalkin!"

"I pointed out that you had had an unfortunate life——"

"You all appear to have discussed me very thoroughly—in spite
of your need of my warships!"

"But I did not think that now, since you are married . . . and, in any case, that type of woman one does not *receive*."

Even Charles's wrath and determination to get his own way had to melt into amusement at her stiff, disdainful dignity, which he guessed to be an exact replica of his mother-in-law's. But what to do when his way of life and his wife's were so incongruously opposed? Could one ever hope to reconcile the strict chastity of a convent-bred girl with the easy morals of the French Court which had influenced his own adolescence? True, he, too, had been carefully brought up in youth, the cherished child of parents whom the breath of scandal had never touched. But his father's murderers had changed all that. At sixteen he had lived with rough soldiers, then been thrown upon a foreign world with nothing but his charm, a strong constitution, and his nimble wits to help him. "When I first saw you I wrote to Ned Hyde, my Chancellor, that I must be the worst man living if I proved not a good husband to you; and I meant it," was all he could think of to say in expiation.

"But you will not keep your good resolution." Suddenly, impulsively, Catherine was plucking with conjugal intimacy at the fine laces of his cravat. "Oh, Charles, how can you expect me to be civil to a woman whom you have had the same pleasures with—said the same things to——"

"Not at all the same, I warrant you! And if you love me as you protest you do, how can you refuse the first distasteful thing I ask you to do? Barbara Castlemaine has promised that if you will take her into your household she will behave herself with every humility and do your bidding in all things."

"So she herself plagued you into making this shameful appointment. That night you left me alone to go to Westminster—on State business."

"There was neglected business enough!" protested Charles, surprised at her acumen.

But, feeling herself to be grossly deceived, Catherine would believe him in nothing. "How *could* you go straight to her when we—had just been so happy?"

He walked away towards the window. So much had gone into the making of his complex character that good and bad now mingled in him beyond either his caring or his comprehension; but looking back to that hard struggle with conscience he remembered how his whole nature had been torn. "She was about to be brought to bed of my child," he said.

Catherine's hands flew to her breast. "Even *that*—before me—" she moaned, almost inaudibly.

He had lived according to his lights, taking it for granted that princes should enjoy traditional privileges, and it was not easy for him to express the contrition which he felt. For a long time there was silence in the pleasant room garnished with exquisite furnishings. And the little bride for whom he had so carefully selected them all sat rigid in a high-backed chair beside a backgammon board where the flung dice still lay as he had left them when he had broken off a game to make love to her. "And as a reward for filching my right—for forestalling what might have been my supreme happiness—your trollop is to be brought here—where you can see her whenever it pleases you," she was saying, fumbling exasperatingly for each word in slow, mispronounced English.

Charles knew that he was behaving like a brute, but the woman who had held him in thrall for so long had nagged him to it. "Barbara is in trouble—" he began.

With a shrill spurt of laughter his wife swept the backgammon dice spinning to the floor. "One would imagine so!" she jeered, having, it appeared, learned more of the English idiom than he had supposed.

"Her husband has left her and disowned the child," he explained, reddening with annoyance.

"One can but commend his sense of decency. Some of us are not of the stuff of which complaisant cuckolds are made. But you Stuarts seem to think you can buy anybody's soul with a title!"

"Hold your peace and do as you are bid!" Charles shouted back in execrable Spanish. "A public rebuff from you would leave Lady Castlemaine the butt of every cheap wit in the country, and she is a proud woman."

"So am I—and with more reason."

"But not over merciful."

"Is no mercy to be spared for me?"

In her desperate fury Catherine had thrown discretion to the winds and Charles, who had expected nothing but gentle acquiescence from her, was amazed. "Have I been ungenerous to you? Can you not come down off your righteous pedestal and put yourself in my position? Or see that some such position as this was inevitable?" he beseeched, in a final effort to coerce her. "And if you will but accept this one demand I swear that I will put no more hard thing upon you, and that if this woman does not behave with deference towards you I will never see her face again. I ask it of you, Catherine. It touches my honor."

"Your honor!"

"Assuredly. I would not leave her and my newborn son unprotected."

His son—whom he would see constantly if this woman were about the palace, and whom he would grow to love and who would not be hers. The words were like a sword in his wife's heart. She stood pondering how this might be avoided, her eyes averted from the ivory crucifix before which she had prayed privily for this very gift. "Since milady Castlemaine is so promiscuous, could not you too disown him?" she suggested.

By the surprised way in which Charles's dark head jerked up, she knew that the idea had never even occurred to him. "That could, I suppose, be your Portuguese idea of honor," he observed contemptuously.

Glimmeringly, grudgingly, she admitted the moral hypothesis that, having sinned, he should stand by it, make what reparation he could. "But if I, too, should have a son—" she began, more temperately.

Immediately he was at her side, his persuasive arms about her. "Please God we shall, and soon, my sweet!" he said. "And then how trivial all this pother will seem. You will forget it and we can live in contentment again."

To live with him in contentment . . . never again in the

complete radiance of trust and dalliance from which she had
been so rudely awakened. But in her bewildered misery the
warmth of his caress was such physical relief that for a brief
moment she almost let herself be persuaded. If she let him coax
her back to love, meeting good humor with good humor, she
would look desirable again—for hers, she knew, was the kind
of beauty that depended upon the glow of happiness. And if
she could but put all this ravaging indignation from her would
not all the advantage be with her, the propitiatory, magnanimous,
forgiving wife? Now that she had learned from Charles to over-
come her prudery, could she not match any mistress in the world
in the ardor of her love for him? And keep him—keep him——

Alas! there was no one in this strange country, save Charles
himself, to whom she could turn for advice. Endlessly she had
listened to a constant stream of prejudices and criticisms from her
own indignant people, though every prentice lad and chambermaid knew that this woman whose famous beauty she so much
feared was a termagant and that the King, already weary of her
greed and tantrums, was a man who preferred peace at any price.
And wise old Clarendon, the Chancellor, could have told her
that Barbara Castlemaine was a bad habit of which marriage had
half broken him, and that now was the moment when an easy,
amiable wife might so point the contrast as to make the break
complete.

But her sense of righteousness held her firm. And her seething
sense of injury made her too bitter to win him back by wiles.
Her upbringing had not taught her how to compromise with
life, whereas her husband's whole life had been a compromise.

"It would be condoning mortal sin," she said obstinately withdrawing herself from his embrace.

"You talk like a prig. It is those miserable, whining priests you
have about you!" complained Charles, exasperated beyond
endurance.

"Why revile them? You promised me religious freedom."

"And, God in heaven, have you not had it? Even to the point of spending hours in your oratory when you should have been serving your husband's pleasure in bed!"

"That is all you think of with a woman," she accused, forgetting how patient he had been with her. "We Portuguese women are not loose like the English. We are brought up to be virtuous——"

"And so ill-favored, most of those you brought, that no man seeks to deny them the privilege. I can promise you that if you persist in making difficulties here and they encourage you, Madame, I will pack the whole cluther of them back to Lisbon!"

"And if you insist upon making this Castlemaine woman a lady of my bedchamber I will go back to Lisbon with them!"

Catherine, now as white-faced as her husband, stood trembling like a threatened thoroughbred in the middle of the room. And her tall husband stared down at her in baffled, impotent rage. Never before had any woman threatened to leave him. Terminating love affairs had hitherto been his prerogative. Long after he tired of them they always cajoled him to return, and whatever their wiles, he had always known how to manage them—good-humoredly, using a little strategy or an absurdly generous recompense or perhaps the help of Chaffinch, his groom of the back stairs, when they became too persistent. And here was this foreigner, whom he had believed to be so meek, defying him on a matter in which she had no legal right at all. By what power, he wondered, could she so enrage and hurt him that he must needs bellow at her like a Thames wherryman, so that the very pages at the doors could hear him? Not, surely, just because she was his wife? If so he had been a fool to let them talk him into marriage—he who for thirty years and more had sauntered through life foot free!

For hurt he undoubtedly was, in heart as well as pride, when she talked so highhandedly of leaving him.

"Better wait and see how your mother will welcome you!" he hit back brutally, and strode out and banged the door.

Poor Catherine sank to the floor, dissolved in tears. Her women came running to her and, not having been trained in any kind of independence, she sent for Don Francisco and Donna Elvira and was so foolish as to pour out her private wrongs before them all.

"To condone his Britannic Majesty's way of life would be to lower the standard of your own," her confessor told her.

"That it should come to this—after ceding Tangier and Bombay!" bemoaned her harassed godfather, smoothing the single strand of hair he wore so strangely across the shining baldness of his pate.

"And the heartless fiend probably gone straight to that Jezebel's bed!" shrilled Donna Elvira. "Did I not tell Queen Luiza how it would be if we came to this immoral country?"

Between them they bolstered up Catherine's indignation and inflamed her self-pity. Not one of them had the tolerance or wit to try to mend matters, instead of ranting about the prestige of Portugal. Only the half-blind and aging Donna Maria Penelva who had been allowed to come because she had had the care of Catherine when she was small, had one word of sense to say. "Far better not to spoil your lovely eyes which the King so much admires, Madame," she advised, sending for warm water and lamb's wool with which to bathe her mistress's red and swollen face, and staying with her long after the others had gone to bed, their tongues ceasing to wag only for want of further invective.

"Do you suppose that he will come here any more?" asked Catherine, when they were alone.

"A man needs a wife to come home to," answered Donna Penelva.

"When he has nothing more exciting to do? I do not want to be needed like that."

"It is, perhaps, the best way in the end."

Long after the candles were extinguished Catherine clung to the old lady's kind, thin hand. Her sobs were small and desolate now because she no longer made pretense that they had anything to do with pride and anger. "Do you believe what Donna Elvira said—that he has gone straight to that awful woman's bed?" she brought herself to ask.

There was no love lost between the two old women, and Donna Penelva sniffed disparagingly. "When Lady Castlemaine has not yet risen from childbirth?" she scoffed. "He is probably much disturbed himself, and if he goes to bed anywhere it will be with those everlasting yapping spaniels of his."

"What, *here* you mean? In Hampton?" Some of her natural animation came back into Catherine's voice.

"I made it my business to ask one of those pert pages. They will tell me things sometimes because I get them to help me across the courtyards and I have the gratitude to talk to them about the way the English ships saved Portugal. They are not bad lads at heart. And they assure me that his Majesty hasn't left the palace, but at midnight was still in shirt and breeches, acting midwife to his favorite bitch."

"Dear Donna Maria!" For the first time the little Queen, tired out, relaxed comfortably against her pillows.

"That is right. Go to sleep, my poppet, and things will look more hopeful in the morning," soothed Donna Maria Penelva. "I am not managing and capable like Donna Elvira, but at least I have been married to a man who was not always faithful to me, and borne his babies and been desolately widowed. And I can tell you that the first grasping, romantic years are by no means the whole of marriage."

hings scarcely seemed more hopeful in the morning. Standing in proud dudgeon at her window, Catherine saw the State barge pull away from the palace water stairs bearing Charles to Westminster. He was ever an early riser. She looked at the French chiming clock he had given her and the hours of the day lay heavy as lead before her. Without his gay teasing and his varied interests the galleries and gardens she had loved so much seemed dead. He had been teaching her to dance and she loved it; already the charm of English music was spoiling her for the crude pipes and harps of the few musicians she had brought with her.

Now that Charles was gone there seemed nothing to do.

She sat down and wrote a long, unhappy letter to her mother and then retired in tears to her oratory. "Oh, Mother of Sorrows, why must this have happened to me when I was so happy?" she cried aloud in bewildered desolation. "Is it to punish me because I am wicked enough to find joy with a heretic and for drinking too greedily of earthly happiness?" And then, persuaded by her confessor, she prayed with simplicity. "Help me, dear God, to turn my husband to the true faith, so that if evildoers take him from me now I may find him hereafter!"

Then, calmed and fortified, she drew her dignity about her and walked with her ladies in the garden chatting and admiring the water lilies as if nothing had happened, though her eyes were always covertly upon the winding reach of the river watching for the return of the King's barge. But she knew that they were whispering together about the night before; and then some busybody amongst them must needs tell her that as soon as Lady Castlemaine could rise from her bed she had taken all the best furnishings from her husband's house and moved to Richmond.

"Where is Richmond?" enquired Catherine.

"A few miles down the Thames, between here and London," they told her.

So no wonder Charles tarried. No doubt, even now, his barge lay moored there. Complaining that she felt chilled in this inhospitable climate, Catherine went indoors. During the long, tedious evening while her priests read aloud from the Saints she persuaded herself that Charles must have arranged for the Castlemaine woman to go there, so that he could lodge there every night, no doubt. No use to sit up and wait for his return, Donna Elvira declared. Since the Queen rightly refused to have his paramour brought under her roof, Hampton would see him no more.

But Charles gave them the lie. He was now a married man and his good resolutions, if frail, had been sincere. Whatever his private differences with his wife, he would not have the world point scorn at her. So when Catherine had at last fallen into an uneasy doze she was awakened by his step and felt him clamber into the great bed beside her. Supposing her to be still asleep, he did not speak. They lay in silence back to back and although Catherine lay fuming for many hours, Charles, who had had an extraordinarily busy day, slept soundly; and although she was furious with him for disturbing her, she dared not speak of it, for at least his coming had put a stop to the busy tongues which she herself, in hasty indiscretion, had set wagging.

During the ensuing wretched week never once did he sleep anywhere else; yet they always rose to wrangle, or, worse still, to sulk in silence. More than once he tried to fondle her back to reconciliation, but always her hurt pride rose like a barrier between them. She wanted no other woman's leavings, she told him. As life became more and more unpleasant at Hampton, he began to spend yet more time away from home. And even though he might have come straight from working with his cousin Rupert in his fine new laboratory, or from an evening at the

theater, Catherine was always firmly persuaded that he had come
from Richmond.

But there came a day when, outwardly at least, they were
forced to smile and speak each other fair, showing a united
front to the world. For the summer months were drawing to a
close and, since the Court would soon be moving to Whitehall,
plans must be discussed for the new Queen's state entry into the
capital and all the various dignitaries and new members of her
household must be presented to her.

Being so sore at heart, poor Catherine was very much on her
dignity for the occasion. Flaunting her foreign patriotism, she had
herself arrayed in one of her bejeweled farthingales so that, sitting
upon the dais of the Great Hall—that most English of all places—
she blazed bizarrely beside the more somber sartorial perfection
of her husband. She would show these arrogant islanders, with
their long established line of kings, that Portugal, for all her
struggles, was not unaccustomed to the etiquette of state occasions. But when her brother-in-law James presented his ill-chosen
wife, Catherine's dignity dissolved into natural kindness.

Because Anne of York was plain and frumpy, and only Chancellor Hyde's daughter, Catherine went out of her way to set
her at ease, inviting her to sit upon a stool at her side. For
the Yorks, she supposed, must have incurred the King's displeasure
too when James married this commoner—hastily, and probably of
necessity.

"Did he not even ask your Majesty's consent?" she asked in
a conjugal aside, forgetting their estrangement.

Charles smiled wryly. "James has a genius for doing the most
tactless thing at the most inopportune moment," he said.

"He might have waited until you—until we—" floundered
Catherine, realizing the importance of the lady's progeny, since
the Duke was still heir presumptive to the throne.

"I scarcely think so, judging by the promptness with which their
daughter Mary made her debut," observed Charles; but to
Catherine's surprise he treated his bourgeois sister-in-law with
every kindness.

With Rupert, the Bavarian cousin, Catherine could never find anything in common; but she was glad to meet again her old friend, Admiral Montagu, Earl of Sandwich, and she was graciousness itself to Chancellor Hyde, remembering how loyal a friend he had been to Charles throughout his exile. Much as she had valued the seclusion of Hampton during the first halcyon weeks of her honeymoon, she was now thankful to see the hall packed with guests because their presence eased the strained relations between her husband and herself.

After the rural life they had been leading, the rambling old Tudor palace seemed alive with a foretaste of the brilliant formality of Whitehall; and Charles appeared to be particularly anxious to make the proceedings a success. With his happy blend of unconventionality and dignity he made a point of presenting the more important of their guests to her himself, helping her to say the right thing by giving her a brief thumbnail sketch of each. But, except for those whom she knew personally, their strange foreign names sounded all alike to Catherine; and, because of a succession of sleepless nights and the difficulties of the language, the seemingly endless line of bowing men and curtsying ladies began to weary her. Their jewels sparkled dazzlingly in the pools of candlelight and many of them were so elegant in the French fashion that, while still smiling automatically, she fell into an inward reverie, regretting that she had not worn one of the charming dresses which Charles had given her. It would have pleased him, and he was being so particularly pleasant to her tonight.

"My friend since boyhood, George Villiers, Duke of Buckingham," he was prompting, as he stood tall and debonair beside her. "And m'lord Albemarle who, as General Monck, of the Parliamentary Army, considered me preferable to Cromwell's sniveling son and invited me back to take again mine own."

"The Dowager Countess of Shrewsbury, who stood firm for my father."

Catherine made a yet more determined effort to concentrate on what he told her and to take in all the ramifications of the British aristocracy, and had the satisfaction of knowing that she was pleasing him by receiving all his subjects so graciously. Somehow she felt that it must be very important, for all present were looking in her direction and she was aware that the little social sounds of discreet conversation and laughter and the coming and going of the servants were no longer breaking the silence of the proceedings. Although the casements of Henry the Eighth's great oriel windows stood open the evening seemed very airless, and either the warmth from the tall wax candles was becoming oppressive or the guests were crowding closer. Even Charles's voice seemed to be trailing off, mumbling the names, and he was no longer making pleasantries or bothering to explain who the various people were. Perhaps even he, the indefatigable, was tiring too. Or wanting his supper, more likely.

"Lady Wymess."

"Sir Charles Berkeley."

Each of them in turn kissed the new Queen's hand.

"Lady Barbara Palmer."

The lovely, auburn-haired creature who curtsied before her rose so gracefully that Catherine smiled at her with real warmth, murmuring her carefully conned words of formal welcome. But at the same moment she felt someone from behind tugging urgently at her elbow. *"That is the infamous Lady Castlemaine!"* hissed Donna Elvira's shocked and penetrating voice.

Too late, Catherine snatched away her extended hand. In spite of herself she turned from English guests to her own people. "But he said—Par-mer—or some such name," she gasped.

"It is her husband's name," explained Don Francisco grimly.

No wonder Charles had mumbled and purposely omitted the notorious title! No wonder his whole Court had been watching so intently! He had tricked her—before them all. And now the brazen beauty was grinning at him triumphantly.

It was true that Charles ignored her intimate glance. He was frowning, and motioning her impatiently to join the other ladies who had been presented. And he looked supremely ill at ease.

But realizing what had happened was like a sudden foul blow upon poor Catherine's heart. As through a mist she saw the next

approaching figure—a large dowager in a plum-colored gown—
dissolving into a series of plum-colored dowagers; as through a
thundering of waves she heard Charles's voice announcing the
lady's name. She felt her face flame and the blood beating in her
ears. With an instinctive effort born of royal discipline, she tried
to extend her hand again, only to find it groping for help. Her godfather was beside her, supporting her. "I must make no scene in
public. Charles will be furious," was the last coherent thought in
her reeling mind. Mercifully the tension of her brainstorm had
snapped; but to her horror she saw great gouts of blood splashing
down onto the silver brocade of her dress. Of all ignominies, her
nose began to bleed violently. "Charles!" she moaned, calling
upon him in the very shame and extremity which he had brought
upon her. Diamonds and candles were all running together into
one shimmering pool of light, and the great square tiles of the
floor were rising up to meet her. Her women began to scream as
Don Francisco caught her.

Catherine did not know until afterwards that it was Charles
Stuart himself who, shamed and furious, waved aside Portuguese
and Englishman alike and carried her through the long galleries
and laid her abruptly on their bed. But when she recovered consciousness, although he had sent his own physician with orders
to care for her, she took the prescribed sleeping draught without
protest knowing full well that her husband would come no more
to disturb her.

And his physician was not the only man Charles sent. A few
days later a very reluctant Lord Chancellor waited upon her, and
it was a very pale, obstinate Queen who received him.

"Do not imagine, milord, that because this shameful trick has
been played upon me I will ever receive that woman into my
household!" she warned, as soon as ever he was come into her
audience chamber.

"And do not suppose, Madame, that I am come to excuse it,"
countered Edward Hyde, Earl of Clarendon, with that downright
honesty which sometimes made him appear more like a plain
country squire than a politician.

Catherine was a little taken aback. She was not to know how unwillingly the poor man had come, or that he had been arguing with Charles on her behalf far into the night. Or that in common with the bulk of the nation he hated the King's grasping mistress, and deplored the influence she exerted over him. Nor could Hyde in loyalty let her know how he, who so seldom took advantage of the old intimate relationship born in cheap lodgings abroad, had told Charles bluntly that making Lady Castlemaine a lady of the bedchamber was putting an indignity upon the Queen which flesh and blood could not bear.

"Then you appreciate my indignation in the matter?" she cried eagerly.

But whatever Hyde's personal opinion, Charles Stuart was the *raison d'être* of his life, whereas this new Portuguese wife was merely a pawn in the political game—useful in increasing the West Indies trade and in curbing the power of Spain. "I appreciate the fact that it lies in your Majesty's power to do much for both your country and my own by means of a successful marriage," he answered dryly.

"But surely, in the circumstances, you do not hold me responsible for its success?"

"Our King is not a difficult man to live with," pointed out Hyde, remembering how often Charles's cheerfulness had been the one bright spot in infinitely more depressing situations.

"As a man, no doubt you find him so," countered Catherine. "But I have good reason to resent an affront to our virtuous affections!"

"Good reason? My dear lady, let me remind you that when the Queen Dowager of France, as a bride, complained to Cardinal Mazarin about her husband's mistresses, there were *five* of them in her procession, all in the same carriage! Not that I uphold such immorality. But I would ask you—when your esteemed brother gets him a queen do you really suppose that she will find your Court at Lisbon full only of 'virtuous affections'?"

Reviewing her brothers' divagations in the light of a more worldly understanding, Catherine was obliged to smile. "But you must admit, milord, that if our marriage be not a success, it is not *I* who have broken our marriage vows," she argued.

But with more perseverance than tact, Hyde insisted that she had broken at least one of them. "Surely no woman should refuse to accept into her household someone recommended by the husband whom she has promised to love, honor and obey?"

The specious argument was the last straw. "Since his Majesty has but sent you to upbraid me—" Catherine's rising voice was choked by angry sobs, and she flounced away from the embarrassed Chancellor to stand with her back towards him by the window. "Love—God help me—I do," she said, as soon as she had regained sufficient control over herself. "Honor—against my conscience—I cannot. And obey—when it comes to conniving at something which is likely to give opportunity for sin—I will not!"

She stood there tearing her kerchief to shreds and staring out at the desolate English rain, and although he could not see her face, Edward Hyde knew that the tears were pouring as desolately down her cheeks. He was miserably torn between the twin conclusions that he was a brute and that women were the very devil. Aware that he had none of his master's subtlety in dealing with them, he yet remembered that he had a headstrong daughter of his own who had also made trouble. Perhaps if he were to approach this unhappy, excitable creature as a father rather than as a solemn minister of the Crown. . . .

"Though it is my duty to point out some sharp things which render me ungracious, I do assure your Majesty that it is for your own good," he said, more gently.

Catherine's response was instant and generous. She came and sat down and turned to him appealingly. "Indeed, milord, you are welcome to show me my faults," she said, "for I begin to see that I am little beholden to an education which has so ill prepared me for this worldly life. So I pray you be seated too and guide me to some chance of future happiness."

Gratefully, because of his gout, the once powerful Earl of Clarendon lowered himself to a chair near hers. "His Majesty has been a bachelor king for two years now," he said, "and even were

he a wheelwright or a farrier for some reason past my understanding women would still throw themselves at his indulgent
head. In these matters he takes for granted the freedom of his
French cousin's Court. It is scarcely to be expected that he——"

"He and I have already spoken of these things, milord," said
Catherine hastily. "And my mother warned me that I could not expect him to—have waited for me."

"I commend your charity and common sense, Madame," said
Hyde, beginning to feel that he was making some headway at last.
"And his Majesty for his part would have me assure you that if
you will put aside these resentments and meet his affection with
good humor as you used, your marriage shall be full of felicity."

"As you used. . . ." From where she sat Catherine could see
the river and the gardens where, for so short a time, Charles
had made such ardent love to her. Instead of answering directly
she rested her chin upon her palm, studying her companion's
florid, round-cheeked countenance as if she would draw from him
some of his many recollections of his master. "You love him very
much, do you not?" she questioned quietly.

Hyde looked up in surprise, seeing in her sudden warm gentleness limitless possibilities for holding the King—holding him to
the ways which were best for him and for the State which both of
them had to steer through all the difficulties of a restored monarchy and the impoverishments and bitternesses which are the
inevitable aftermath of civil war. If only she would not be such
a bigoted little fool! "You, of all people, should know that it is
difficult not to, Madame," he answered.

In spite of his bluntness, Catherine was beginning to like the
man. "Charles says you love him like a disappointed father,"
she teased.

"If I occasionally criticize him adversely, it is only to his face,"
he blustered truthfully.

With the swift veering of her mercurial temperament, her
southern brown eyes were laughing at him. "And always do his
bidding, even against your own conscience, milord? Like coming
here today, for instance?"

The Chancellor of England puffed out his fleshy lips. It was *he* who had come to do the questioning. And now this chit was making him speak of matters he had no thought of touching on. "I have great cause to be grateful to him," he told her ponderously. "There was the unfortunate matter of my daughter, as no doubt you have heard."

Catherine settled herself back in her chair so that her face was in shadow, her own grievances momentarily forgotten. "Tell me about it," she begged.

Since formality seemed to be forgotten, Hyde rested his elbows on either arm of his chair and joined his pudgy finger tips together with characteristic precision. "You must know that my daughter was with child by the Duke of York and he married her secretly. I knew nothing of it, but my enemies bruited it abroad that I had encouraged my daughter's dishonor to advance my own ambition. I do not blame them overmuch. It was what many men would have supposed. It was in my own house that Anne married the King's heir without the King's consent. Many a monarch would have had my head off for less!"

"It was a grievous dilemma. What did you do, milord?"

"What I have always done. I went straight to King Charles himself."

"And he?"

"He was furious, of course. But not with me. It was his brother he was berating. It had lost England a powerful marriage alliance and interfered with the succession. 'Own flesh and blood as she is, I would to God he had taken her as his whore rather than have done this thing!' I cried out. I was beside myself. I went down on my knees to the King. As soon as we came home from exile he had given me my fine house, my title, Hyde Park, everything! 'Your Majesty does not believe what they are saying—Buckingham, Sir Charles Berkeley and the rest of them—that I plotted this thing?' I beseeched him."

"And what did Charles say?" Catherine's beautiful, low-pitched voice came eagerly from the shadows.

"He pulled me to my feet and told me I was almost as big a

fool as his brother. 'Zounds, have I not known you all these years,
Ned?' he said, grasping me by the shoulder. 'Why in the devil's
name should I believe you changed now?' And when later on the
Duke tried to get out of an unpopular situation by pretending
that my foolish wench had enticed him and had had other lovers
before him, it was the King who squashed the scandal. 'What
is done is done, and must be stood by and made the best of,' he
said."

A maxim which, whether right or wrong, it would appear
Charles tried to conform to in his own *affaires du coeur*.

Hyde's thoughts were back with his narrative. His gaze rested
abstractedly upon the long vista of grassy walks which would in
time be shaded by Charles's lime trees. If the good God had
permitted—instead of plaguing him with politics—he too would
have enjoyed planting a garden.

"One does not forget things like that," he said, almost as if
speaking to himself.

A new peacefulness pervaded the room, much as it had begun
to pervade their conversation, so that it was some moments before
he realized that the Queen had risen with a sigh and he must
perforce scramble hastily to his feet. "I pray you thank his
Majesty for his graciousness and assure him of my future obedience and duty. I, too, would willingly go down on my knees to
him—begging forgiveness for my peevishness which I do assure
you was born only of my passionate love for him," she was saying
with quiet dignity. And Hyde, prematurely elated by such success,
perceived that it was none of his carefully prepared arguments
which had moved her.

"I will do as you wish, Madame," he promised; and a subtler
man might have left it at that, trusting the rest to Charles's
superior powers of persuasion. But Hyde was a born mentor, and
so conscientious that he was accustomed to carrying out instructions to the letter. And there was one thing, and only one thing,
which his master wanted carried out at this moment. "But I would
point out, Madame," he added, "that the proof of your promise
lies in your acceptance of Lady Castlemaine."

Catherine had for the moment almost forgotten the woman's name. But although Charles could never ask too much of her, even to life itself, it was always with the exception of this one thing, which the very quality and depth of her love forbade. The brooding softness of her eyes changed to fire. "Let him keep his mistresses out of my sight!" she cried. "If he still insists upon having his own way in this it can only mean that he hates me and would pour contempt upon me before all the world! And sooner than give in I will charter some small vessel or return to Lisbon with my poor people whom he has so heartlessly threatened to turn out!"

Goaded by her sudden change of mood, Hyde pointed out brutally that there were plenty of his political enemies who would be only too glad to see her go. In vain did he try to make her see that the dismissal of her people after a few months was only the normal diplomatic gambit adhered to in the case of most royal marriages, and not any personal revenge planned by her husband.

"Then why did he taunt me the other night because the whole of my dowry had not been paid?" she enquired, with that maddeningly polite, incredulous smile on her lips.

"Probably because he was exasperated beyond all endurance!" thought Hyde, knowing it to be quite unlike the King. Aloud, he asked her if she did not suppose that Charles, too, had been hurt by her extravagant talk of leaving him. "And for your own sake I would advise you to please him of your own accord," he advised, preparing to take his leave, "for do you really suppose it lies in your power to resist if the King insists?"

"I will not despair of his sense of decency's delivering me from the persecution of such a command," she answered, amazing the poor bewildered man by such courage in the face of such an untenable position.

But Catherine knew that she was cornered. By the time the Chancellor had bowed himself out she realized that she could not even leave the house she was in without the King of England's consent. Hampton, which had opened to her the gates of such radiant happiness, had now become a prison. Waves of helpless

homesickness engulfed her. If only she could talk to her own beloved family! "Do everything to preserve the alliance of our two
countries," her brothers had exhorted her. Yet everything in her
upbringing urged her to count self-respect above the temptation
to placate. Although her whole married happiness might turn
upon it, nothing, nothing would induce her to take her husband's
mistress into her household.

So neither of them would give way, and both of them were
supremely miserable. And their quarrel became the main topic
of conversation throughout the land. It never occurred to Catherine that Charles, so long his own master, might be absurdly
sensitive about being nagged into giving up his own way by a
childish-looking little scrap of a wife. Busybodies were not wanting, of course, to tell her that he was supping with Barbara
Castlemaine again; but there was no one wise enough to suggest
to her that while he plunged into a nightly round of gaiety he
might be almost as miserable at heart as his sullen, neglected
queen. She only knew that whenever circumstances forced him
into her presence he would bow formally over her hand and leave
her as soon as the bare claims of politeness permitted, to talk
with godless flippancy to all the most harebrained of his courtiers
or to flirt outrageously with all the prettiest girls in the room.
She knew that he was trying to hurt her. What she found it
difficult to believe, as she surreptitiously watched his suave,
dark face or overheard his witty comments, was how cynically
he was loathing himself. Portuguese Catherine knew him only
as the lighthearted lover, so little as another human being; and
had no idea how one tender appeal, one show of faith in his
better resolutions, could have helped him and brought him back
gratefully to her side before the Castlemaine's possessive wiles
and reproaches had recaptured him.

"If only I could go back to the convent!" she cried bitterly
sometimes to Donna Penelva, deliberately forgetting those honeymoon weeks when Charles's initiation into ecstacy had spoiled her
for any life but marriage.

CHAPTER SIX

*A*nd now, as if things were not bad enough, my mother-in-law is coming!" With a dramatic gesture Catherine laid down Edward Hyde's formal letter apprising her of the fact. Realization that her family life was reduced to a few formal notes exchanged between Hampton and Whitehall, where her husband now spent most of his time, had as much to do with her feeling of flat despair as the arrival of Henrietta Maria.

"The Queen Dowager is returning from France?" chorused her new English ladies, with an unflattering revival of high spirits.

"Almost immediately, I understand," said Catherine, unhappily aware of how deadly her deserted Court must be for them. "His Majesty and the Duke are preparing to meet her."

Since it was to be a family occasion, and she missed her own relations, she would have liked to go too; but the letter said nothing about it and here at Hampton she seemed to be left out of everything. From time to time news floated into her quiet little backwater about the gay swirl of doings in London; but evidently she was not wanted there. And when Charles had his mother she would be wanted less than ever. Probably, too, thought Catherine, it would mean yet another person to criticize her conduct and laugh at her old fashioned ideas of respectability. An influential woman from the licentious Paris Court. . . . "She is sure to think everything her eldest son does is perfect," she prophesied, sticking a vindictive needle into her embroidery.

"Not Charles the First's widow," smiled the Countess of Shrewsbury, who was old enough to remember the contentious days before the Commonwealth. "It was always her husband who was perfect."

"She was inclined to be rather domineering with her children," confirmed the Duchess of Suffolk, settling down to a good gossip. "And I myself think that if she *had* a favorite son it was York."

The Duke was tall and florid and, as everyone knew, a fine courageous fighter, but he had neither Charles's wit nor Charles's charm. "I cannot comprehend how anyone could prefer—" began Catherine; then, remembering her resentment, bit off the words with her thread.

"They do say that it is because he is secretly of his mother's faith," whispered the old Countess, leaning close to the Queen under the pretext of passing her some fresh silks.

"Although her Majesty will want to meet both her sons, surely it will be a very sad visit for the poor lady—seeing again all the places where she was once so happy with the murdered king?" suggested Donna Penelva, out of that gentle capacity she had for putting herself in other people's places.

"But it will not be for the first time," explained the Duchess of Suffolk. "She came on a visit with her daughters, the late Princess Mary of Orange and young Princess Henrietta—Minette, as the King calls her—soon after the Restoration."

"To share in the rejoicings, I suppose?" sighed Catherine enviously.

"The King wanted her to, of course. But she came partly to try to prevent the York marriage. Only the Channel was so rough she arrived too late."

"Domineering *and* interfering," thought Henrietta Maria's daughter-in-law.

"The Dowager Queen always did hate the Hydes," added the gossip-loving Duchess.

"Well, if she goes about breaking up her sons' marriages and thinks that I should be treated as I am—" muttered Catherine.

"Oh, but she was delighted with *your* marriage, Madame," young Lady Ormonde assured her. "Did you not read us the charming letter of welcome she wrote?"

"Making the best of a Portuguese princess instead of a French one," smiled Catherine, who knew something of European diplomacy.

"And there was the gold toilette set she sent," Donna Penelva reminded her.

"Which I certainly like best of all my wedding gifts," allowed Catherine, glancing with pride at the long box fitted with comb and beauty patches and mirror, before which she had so often made herself desirable for Charles.

"Well, let us hope devoutly that she does not stay long!" summed up Donna Elvira, looking down her own domineering nose. "There are enough Stuarts in this country already!"

"It is *their* country," snapped pretty Lettice Ormonde.

"And if you do not like it you can always go back to your own," old Agnes Shrewsbury reminded her tartly.

Whether they sat down to embroider or strolled in the gardens to chat, Catherine's Portuguese and English attendants never failed to finish up by bickering; so in order to preserve the peace she remembered that it would soon be time for vespers and bade them all bestir themselves to change her dress.

But she was still in her crimson petticoat with her dark hair curling about her shoulders when the door was flung wide and the King himself was announced. Although he had come by road and his cavalcade must have clattered into the courtyard, all sound of their arrival had been deadened by the rain beating against the casements and the blustering wind in the tall elms. Catherine stood petrified before her mirror with one of her priceless pearl necklaces dripping from her hand. It was the first time he had been in her private apartments for weeks.

He was an astonishingly different Charles.

All his grim sulkiness was gone, and even his habitual pose of indolence. He was as completely natural as when he was working in his laboratory or doing things with boats. His tall riding boots were splashed with mud, and his almond-shaped eyes sparkled beneath their sleepy-looking lashes. "Why, Kate, that petticoat becomes you!" he cried throwing plumed hat and leather gloves

across her table as informally as though he and she had parted
the best of friends but yesterday, "You've heard the good news?
That my mother leaves Calais tomorrow morning?"

Catherine stared at him in bewilderment—at a more genial, un-
guarded Charles than she had ever seen. "I have been officially
notified of the fact by your Chancellor," she said stiffly.

"Ah, yes, I told Ned to write you as soon as it was known in
council, and I hoped to get here sooner to tell you myself. But I
was delayed seeing Admiral Montagu and that naval secretary
fellow, Pepys, about the escort ships." Although his wife was still
standing, he threw himself unceremoniously into her special chair,
stretching his long legs comfortably before him, still full of his
plans. "I have sent Ormonde to have my mother's old apartments
at Greenwich prepared so that she can land immediately and rest
before coming to London. And I would have you take coach
and wait upon her there."

So, after all, she was not to be left out. This was a family affair
in which a man's mistress, however possessive, could have no part.

"B-but what about yourself?" she stammered, almost too over-
come by conflicting emotions for intelligent speech.

"James and I will be sailing down to the Nore as soon as the
tide serves, then embarking on the *Royal Charles* to meet my
mother in mid-Channel. To surprise her," he answered, as eager
as a schoolboy.

Catherine, in her petticoat, came closer. "And you want me to
go to meet her—alone?" she repeated, feeling very young and
inadequate. She was remembering the painting of Henrietta
Maria which hung above the old fashioned dais in the Great
Hall—a dark, slender, energetic looking woman, of great dignity.
The famous widowed queen whose name had been on everyone's lips a decade ago, and whose faraway misfortunes had
stirred even the girls in Catherine's convent. A capable daughter
of the great Henri Quatre of France.

Charles viewed his wife's evident perturbation with understanding amusement. "She will probably have been very seasick
and you are good at being kind to people," he suggested, knowing

full well that none of his kin was ever troubled by the elements, but seeking to dissolve Catherine's awe. To which end he levered himself up from her chair and crossed to a window to survey the angry, swollen Thames. "Just Mam's ill luck at sea!" he laughed, thereby reducing the stiff regality of Van Dyck's portrait to the easy conception of a teased and human parent.

While his back was turned Catherine had signed to her women to complete her toilette, but her husband would have none of it. "That crimson thing becomes you vastly," he repeated; and disregarding the vesper bell, he waved them all away, bidding her come and talk to him on the fireside settle and so while away an impatient hour while he waited for the tide.

"Does her Majesty, your mother, always have bad weather then?" enquired Catherine, striving to hide her resentment that he should suddenly see fit to treat her so pleasantly and expect the same response.

"It has become a family joke," said Charles. "When I was small my father used to jig me up and down upon his knee. For us it was riding a horse. But Mam always insisted it was the waves rocking her ship when she first came to this benighted country to marry him—a shy little foreign bride like you!"

His devastating brown eyes quizzed her, softening her animosity. It was an unfair advantage, Catherine felt. But she felt too, as often before, that even his most frivolous remarks were made deliberately, prompted by a deep understanding of human nature. Certainly the thought that the imperious Queen had once been as frightened as herself should help her in the coming *rencontre*. Charles stretched his arms casually along the back of the settle so that one of his fine, long hands lay close to her shoulder; but he made no attempt to touch her. And Catherine, wrestling with the flesh, prayed dutifully that she might become less physically aware of him. "And years later when my father and I were being driven from battlefield to battlefield," he went on, "I can remember Mam's going to my sister at the Hague and bringing back stores and arms for him through one of the worst storms in history. 'No English queen has ever yet been drowned at sea,' she told her shrieking women; but she admitted to me afterwards that she quite expected to be the first."

"She must be very brave," said Catherine, comparing the drama of the Stuarts' lives with the tameness of her own and at the same time wondering how recently those fine hands of his had been fondling Barbara Castlemaine.

"As brave as she has been misfortunate—losing husband, home, crown and three children," he answered more thoughtfully. "One of the stories Mary and I enjoyed most was about our mother's reception at some northern English port after that same awful voyage. It appears that Cromwell's guns began pounding the house she was lodging in, and she and her ladies had to go out and lie in a ditch. In the excitement her favorite dog, an ugly old brute called Mitte, had been forgotten. Mam suddenly remembered that she had left him asleep on her bed, so she picked up her skirts and ran all the way back up the street through shattering gunfire to get him."

Catherine began to think that there must be much of his mother in Charles. "I suppose you love her very dearly?" she said, struggling to combat fresh jealousy.

"Of course I love her. But that does not signify that we agree about any mortal thing," he laughed. "She manages and meddles until she drives me mad. And I imagine I have been a disappointment to her ever since the day I was born."

"You? A disappointment?"

"Why, yes. Being such an infernally ugly baby, and then disgracing her by speaking abominable French when she had cajoled all her rich European relatives into giving me refuge. And, of course, not being a Catholic—nor even a good-living Protestant like my father."

Catherine had to laugh at his airy diffidence. "And now you are making her coming an excuse to escape from all your tedious councils and parliaments and get away to sea," she accused.

But Charles was wont to assume a misleading air of indifference where work was concerned. "London is quite amusing now we have gaming again and two good theaters," he told her, with one of his inimitable shrugs. "But I wager neither James nor I is ever so well content as when we have a lively deck beneath our feet."

So it seemed that love-making in Lady Castlemaine's luxurious apartments was by no means the high light of existence for him. "I have been in your country three whole months and never yet seen London," Catherine ventured to remind him.

"It is not overhealthy in summer."

The lines at the side of his mouth looked stern, and Catherine still wondered if it were her health he had been considering or just that he had wanted to enjoy himself without her. But his next words dispelled her doubts.

"Did I not tell you that when my eldest sister, Mary, who was so unimaginably good to me in Holland, came over for my coronation, she caught a pox in London and died," he reminded her. "And a few months before that it was my favorite brother, Henry. He was blue-eyed and fair—as a Scotsman should be—and barely twenty-one. . . . We had planned to do so many things together and never till then had I had a spare groat to spend on him. . . ."

"Oh, my dear!" Touched to her tender heart, Catherine slid a hand through his arm as he sat staring before him, and without looking at her he patted it absently. No wonder he had kept her through the hot summer months at Hampton. "I will come whenever it shall please you," she said meekly. "And in the meantime I will pay my duty to your mother at Greenwich."

"Then I will send coaches for the Portuguese ambassador and all your people," he promised, rising to take leave of her.

All that night and the next the autumnal gales blew, and Catherine scarcely left her oratory where she prayed that her husband's ship would ride out the storm. Thanks either to her fervor or to superb seamanship, her prayers were answered. And when at last beacons were lighted from hill to hill and church bells rang out the good news that the ships were met and sighted off the Nore, she ignored her brother's instructions about converting foreign fashion to the modest farthingale and set out for Greenwich in black velvet elegant enough to please even a Frenchwoman's taste.

The great palace of Greenwich and the ships lying at anchor in the broad slapping river were an impressive sight. And the concourse of people was so great that Catherine hoped Charles would not notice that, in spite of her entreaties, the disgruntled ambassador from Portugal had excused himself from using the proffered coaches on the plea of sudden illness. Whether he noticed or not—and little, she knew, escaped him—he was graciousness itself to her, giving her fingers a secret encouraging nip as he led her up the wide staircase.

It was the first time Catherine had appeared in public since that hateful day when her rival had been presented to her and she had swooned, and it seemed to her that all the people who had witnessed her humiliation were pressing close behind her now, watching to see what would happen next. Standing at the top of the stairs—waiting to look her over, she felt—was her mother-in-law, who would no doubt already have heard a garbled version of her gauche behavior. "And to think that we do not speak a word of each other's language so that I cannot try to explain," thought Catherine, desperately searching for some dutiful phrase in English.

In spite of her lined face and perpetual aura of mourning Henrietta Maria, in her late fifties, still retained traces of past beauty, and she held herself so that people were deceived into thinking her tall. Charles kissed her hand and presented his little bride and Catherine, still in speechless confusion, sank down in a curtsy before her.

But the slender, compelling hands she had kissed were raising her. A kindly finger lifted her chin for inspection and a warm, vivacious French voice was saying, "*Mais, Charles, comme elle est charmante, ta petite brunette!*" Henrietta Maria kissed Catherine as affectionately as her own mother might have done and led her by the hand into the magnificent audience chamber. She made more of the new little daughter-in-law than of either of her stalwart sons. "Come and sit beside me and let us take some refreshment *en famille*," she invited, in clear penetrating tones so that all who had ever slighted Catherine should hear. "For I would not have come to England except for the pleasure of seeing you, to love you as a daughter and to serve you as a Queen."

It was the kindest thing any woman could have done for her, and utterly unexpected. And although Catherine felt, and would always feel, that she was in the presence of the *real* Queen of England, she realized gratefully that the older woman, with her self-composure and wider experience, was deliberately making every courtier present aware of how the King's wife ought to be treated and was, by her own example, shaming all who had neglected her. Catherine, subdued for weeks by lack of appreciation, rose to the occasion. Her manners were demurely charming, her pearls no brighter than her eyes—and Charles was smiling at her approvingly.

During the happy hours they spent at Greenwich he did his best to translate to her the gist of the fraternal allusions and to include her in the brilliant quick-fire of a bilingual family conversation, while Catherine in her turn tried to pass on some of the Stuart kindness to James's poor disapproved-of wife. There was much talk of the eldest sister's orphaned boy's being invited on a visit to England, and of the youngest sister's recent marriage to the Duke of Orleans. Indeed, most of the conversation between Charles and his mother seemed to be about this Minette, as he called her; and although Catherine could not follow the half of it she noticed how their voices softened to affection whenever they spoke of her.

"It is the first time I see you—all together—as a family," she managed to say in English. But the words so painstakingly assembled appeared to be ill-chosen after all, for although the Queen Mother patted her hand encouragingly the happy animation was wiped from her face, leaving it worn and tired. "Those of us who are left," she said sadly. "Last time I came to England we were all here together—except, of course, my beloved husband and our little daughter Elizabeth who died in captivity with those vile Cromwellians."

"And this time," added Charles somberly, "Mam could not bring Minette."

But Catherine had been received into the Stuart family and was surrounded by their easy charm. In high spirits, planning her next visit to her mother-in-law and their state entry into London, she rode back to Hampton. It was wonderful to be driving through the country with Charles again, and for the first time since their quarrel they supped together in public, so that the old palace seemed to come to life and a wave of joyful excitement swept spectators and servants alike. After supper there was dancing and Charles insisted upon teaching her the steps of the popular new *bransle*—so as to be ready for Whitehall, he said.

And later, in her great crimson-curtained bed, Catherine lay wondering if he would come to her. After so happy a day it seemed as if their disagreement had never been. Yet nothing was any different, she supposed. For she was beginning to learn that, in spite of his easy-going manner, Charles could upon occasion be as obstinate as she. He was often supping again with Lady Castlemaine and still intended to make her a lady of the bedchamber. Only last night, for all Catherine knew, he might have slept with her. And if so, how *dared* he come? Yet, covering her hot cheeks in the darkness, Catherine knew that if only he would come back to her she would forgive him anything. "I, who have been so proud for Portugal, have no personal pride left at all," she thought.

Her door opened quietly and he was there.

"Do I disturb you, Catherine?" he asked.

"No one in my life has ever disturbed me more," she answered, folding defensive arms across her heart and almost hating him because he could make it beat so wildly.

"I am not good enough to kiss your little finger, Kate. I will go away if you would rather."

If she refused herself to him he would certainly make no bluster, but go. Charles was always so civilized about these things. But then, thought Catherine, he can afford to be for he does not really care. And she knew—or thought she knew—that if she sent him away he would only go to Barbara Castlemaine or some other trollop. She could not bring herself to answer either way.

"I can, of course, go and sleep in my own stuffy room with the spaniels," he offered. A glimmer from the nightwick flickered on the side of his swarthy face, and she could see that he was grinning as if he had read her thoughts.

She stretched out a hand and caught at one of his. "No, stay!" she implored, with a pitiful catch in her voice. "The nights are so long—alone."

It was utterly humiliating to love a man so desperately; but once he took her in his arms she would no longer see his amusement, nor remember anything but his expert love-making and her own need of him. And perhaps she was wrong about her honeymoon's being all a deception and his not caring at all.

"My poor lonely little *religieuse*," he mocked tenderly, throwing aside his gorgeous dressing robe.

"I am not a—how you say it—a nun!" she protested furiously, and when he bent over her to kiss her lovely hair she reached out warm arms and drew him down to her. In this horrible country where simple goodness was made a mock of she would show him that just because a woman kept her body for one man she was not necessarily inept or cold. And this time she must keep him from promiscuous beauties—compete with them. If only she knew the tricks by which they held their men—those tricks so furtively and fiercely envied by virtuous fools like herself!

The floodgates of her pent-up love were loosened, so that the surge of her southern passion surprised and shook him. It cleansed him temporarily of all desire for the counterfeit and the tawdry, and his loving became a rededication. "May I be the worst man living if after marriage I keep a mistress," he had been wont to say, criticizing his newly wed cousin, Louis of France. And when he had first seen the sweet defenselessness of Catherine, in spite of all his worldly cynicism, he had honestly believed and hoped that marriage would cure the easy, indulgent habits of a lifetime.

"Is it foolish to give and to forgive too readily?" pondered Catherine next morning, walking alone with Donna Penelva in the garden after he was gone to Westminster.

"It may seem prodigal at the time, Madame," said the wizened little Portuguese countess, clinging to her mistress's arm because of her physical blindness, "but if one's love is the kind which lasts a lifetime one can afford to be foolish. For it is to the place where a man is sure of unquestioning giving that he always comes back."

"And in order to attain that far-off felicity you think it right that a wife should be prepared to accept slights—to take second place—to forego all decent pride?"

"I think it is not a question of right or wrong, but of how she loves. For those of us who love a man better than self or pride there is no choice."

Catherine lingered by the lily-covered moat which had bounded her honeymoon, but her thoughts were of the future in Whitehall. "You are a wise old woman, Maria Penelva," she said.

The Countess listened for a moment or two to make sure that the Queen's other ladies were still out of earshot. "How much do you love him, dear child?" she asked.

And suddenly, standing there in the morning sunlight, Catherine knew and accepted the implications of her answer. "With all my heart," she mimicked softly, in her husband's tongue.

CHAPTER SEVEN

*S*o come kiss me, sweet-and-twenty, Youth's a stuff will not endure," sang the pretty chambermaid, puffing up the velvet cushions on the Queen's window seat, and quite unaware that the Queen herself had come into the room behind her.

"What is that pretty song?" asked Catherine of Braganza, startling her out of her wits.

"Oh, Madame! Just something the prentice boys used to whistle—out of some old play, your Majesty." The girl was in a limp, self-effacing obeisance on the floor.

"Well, at sweet-and-twenty you sound uncommonly happy, Druscilla!"

"I crave your Majesty's pardon."

"In this country does one have to ask pardon for being happy?" asked the Queen, with a note of bitterness in her lovely voice.

"Oh, *no*, Madame, no! Not *now!*"

Catherine had been brought up in the belief that queens should not talk to chambermaids. But perhaps one gleaned truer information that way than from sitting with obsequious courtiers. At any rate, Charles talked about race horses to Toby, his valet; and the girl, rising in obedience to an indulgent nod, looked fresh as an English rose. "Was it so very bad, then, when the Puritans were in power?" she asked.

"Madame, it was—moribund as the plague!" In her eagerness to make a foreigner understand just how moribund it had been, Druscilla let her words almost trip over each other. "The theaters all closed, and preachers in steeple hats at every street corner so that one could not sleep o' nights for dreaming about hell.

Nothing but hymn singing all Sabbath and the neighbors spying on you if you so much as smiled at a likely lad. And now—and now—since his Majesty came——"

"You are free to huggle with whomsoever you will—any day in the week—because the gentry do!"

Half-laughing and half-sighing Catherine waved her away to finish her duties elsewhere. At least it was good to know that the people were the happier for Charles's return. "Like my beloved countrymen, oppression does not suit them. They must be free, and proud in their freedom," she thought, sitting down on one of the freshly plumped-up cushions to look out admiringly upon her husband's capital.

For Queen Catherine had come home to her apartments in Whitehall—apartments overlooking the busy river. And Charles had brought her there triumphantly, by water, with a lavish pageantry which had reduced even her incensed compatriots to awed silence. But it had not been the money spent so much as the artistry which had impressed her. No Venetian festival could have been more beautiful, she thought, than the escort of a thousand flower-garlanded boats; and she and Charles in the great State barge with a pillared canopy above their heads, and the coats of the royal watermen making scarlet splashes against the blue sky and the drapery of cloth of gold. There had been music from the smaller boats and wild cheering from either bank and, as they drew nearer, the moving welcome of innumerable church bells. All her life long she would like to look back upon the Londoners' welcome. As smooth green meadows gave place to gabled houses people had waved from windows and even clambered precariously onto roof tops. And at the water gate of Whitehall Palace, Queen Henrietta Maria and all the household had been waiting to receive her.

"And not the least of all my pleasure that day," she recalled with candor, "was seeing that Castlemaine woman waiting uncomfortably with the rest of the crowd trying in vain to catch Charles's unwilling eye."

But that had been weeks ago. And gradually, insidiously, the ill bred creature had pushed her way into every Court function, holding him by reproachful tears to his misguided promise to make her a member of the Queen's household, so that now Catherine was obliged to put up with her hateful presence in her private apartments and to hear her boasting to the other women about the progress of her fine new baby.

Both for her own and for her husband's sake Catherine would have given anything to find herself pregnant. "But how can he expect me to bear him sons when I am kept in such agitation and distress of mind?" she raged, all unaware that this was the very burden of both his mother's and his Chancellor's arguments with the half-shamed, harassed King.

Above everything in those days Catherine hated being dressed before the quizzing gaze of her husband's mistress; for Barbara, offshoot of the handsome Villiers family, had been born so fatally faultless of form and feature that she would probably have looked just as beautiful in the bunchy garments of a washerwoman as in the jewels the King bestowed upon her; whereas Catherine's beauty depended much upon time and mood and, most of all, upon happy animation. She was only too painfully aware that in order to make the best of herself—much more to compete with this Court full of beautiful women—she needed to take thought and care. "I marvel that your Majesty can have the patience to spend so long a-dressing," Barbara would say with every outward show of deference when Catherine, preparing to meet Charles, caused her *friseur* to change the style of her curls for a second or even a third time.

Catherine could have risen from her dressing stool like a Tagus fishwife and scratched the mocking eyes out with her comb. But did she not pray particularly every morning of her life for patience? And had she not lifted herself above the level of her tormentor by keeping her promise to milord Chancellor to make no more angry scenes? "I have vast need of patience, milady Castlemaine," she would manage to say with a kind of spirited dignity.

But in spite of her rival's presence life was easier at Whitehall than at Hampton. There was always something going on to inter-

est or distract. The teeming life of London pulsed about her so
that she was intoxicated by its vigor. The City wharves were always full of shipping, foreign delegates sought audiences of the
King, and discoverers of new, undreamed-of countries brought
strange gifts and stranger stories to the palace. So that Catherine
felt herself to be living in the hub of the world. By the conversation of those around her she was introduced to a new appreciation of art and science, of which she was lamentably ignorant.
Sometimes she would drive with her ladies to see the exquisite
workmanship of famous craftsmen in Goldsmiths' Row or through
the noisy, congested chaffering of East Cheap. Or Charles would
show her his amusing rare waterfowl in St. James's park, or take
her to see some great East Indian merchantman come in. And
wherever she went with him on such informal occasions she marveled at the way in which he would recognize some old soldier
who had fought for his father, or stop and watch some gunsmith
or mason at work. "How can you know so much about their
lives?" she would ask, remembering how Alfonso would scarcely
notice them at all.

"It is having once been poor and honest myself," Charles would
say, in that pleasant, indolent way of his.

But however full and pleasant the days, the winter evenings
were still long and empty for Catherine. Because she would not
play for high stakes or join the noisy, modish throng where Barbara queened it among the men, she often found herself sitting
with the most faithful of her ladies and a mere handful of the
dullest courtiers. All the rest seemed to prefer the loud laughter
and lewd jests, and even those who stayed knew that it did them
no good to be seen too often at the Queen's elbow. Barbara would
be sure to see that they were covered with ridicule before the
evening was out; and because she had a caustic kind of wit
Charles, to his shame, would sometimes smile instead of rebuking
her. And ridicule, as poor Catherine knew only too well, is the
hardest thing of all to face.

Yet all the more decent men at Court and half the shamed syco-
phants were tiring of the once amusing contest, and had begun to

admire the little, lonely Queen who had learned to behave with
dignified restraint and who stood alone, with a courage they
secretly envied, for high principles in her personal affairs. And—
had she but known it—the King himself was tiring too. All that
was best in him was beginning to see her not as the amusing
little innocent to be played with, but as a woman of his own to
be respected. Clearly, if Catherine stood out much longer he
must choose between the two of them. Though he might smile at
his mistress's malicious sallies and walk out in silence from her
tempers, the liberties she took sickened him and he had already
had a word with Will Chaffinch—that ingenious jackal of his
amours—about some suitable pension for a lady in retirement.

But the crumpling of Catherine's fine resolution was precipi-
tated, quite unwittingly, by a young boy of fourteen or so.

One evening when Barbara Castlemaine's behavior was more
preposterous than usual Catherine was touched to see the lad de-
tach himself from a group of baccarat players and take the
trouble to talk with some of her neglected ladies. "Who is that
handsome boy?" she asked.

"I do not know, Madame," answered one of her Portuguese
ladies. "But I could find out if you wish."

Catherine watched him idly for a moment or two, attracted by
his grace and carriage, and by something oddly familiar in his
gestures. But her lady was saved the trouble, for presently a man-
servant came across the room and said to him respectfully, "Your
pardon, Mr. Crofts, sir, but Lady Castlemaine would have you
come and hold her little dog while she plays a hand."

The boy nodded, but was too well mannered to leave Lettice
Ormonde abruptly. And Catherine, glancing contemptuously
towards the gaming tables, observed that Barbara was leaning
familiarly on the King's arm with most of the other men in the
room gathered round her. "She cannot leave me so much as one
unbearded boy," she thought furiously, and, acting on the spur of
the moment, beckoned the young fellow to her side. If he were
summoned by the Queen even Lady Castlemaine would have to
get someone else to hold her pampered spaniel.

He came with alacrity and a charming smile; and Catherine observed that in spite of his gallant bearing his warm brown hair and eyes gave him an almost womanly beauty. "What is your name?" she asked kindly.

"Crofts, Madame," he replied.

"Your first name, I mean."

"Jemmie, my friends call me," he replied ingenuously.

"And how is it, Jemmie, that although I have been here fully a month I have never before seen you?"

Catherine had a way with young people. He pulled forward a cushion and knelt easily and respectfully before her. "Because I have but now come in her Majesty the Queen Mother's train."

"Yet you speak English so clearly that I can understand you more easily than any man I have met—except my husband."

"I *am* an Englishman," said Jemmie, gratified that she should so ignore his lack of years.

How pleasant it would be, thought Catherine, to have an up-standing young boy of one's own—so natural and so lively—about the palace. "But I suppose you live with Queen Henrietta Maria now that her Majesty has her own establishment at Grosvenor House," she sighed.

"At first I did, Madame. But now the King, of his grace and favor, has found me rooms at the Cockpit."

"The Cockpit?"

"That part of the palace which lies across the street, where the tennis court and bowling green are and where the cockfighting is held."

"You do not lodge there alone, surely?"

"With Sir William Crofts, Madame."

"Crofts? Was not that the name of one of those loyal friends who helped my husband to escape after the battle of Worcester?"

"Why, yes, your Majesty." The boy's face lit up with pride. "So you have heard all about that marvelous adventure?"

"The King himself told me, Jemmie. So Will Crofts is your father?"

"Oh, no, but he has brought me up ever since I can remember."

"And you like it better, living at the Cockpit?"

"Indeed, yes. King Charles told Sir Will that it was time for me to study under a proper tutor. You see, when we were in Holland and France we could not afford one. You cannot imagine how poor we were, Madame; and often our lodgings were quite horrible."

"You poor child!"

But young Jemmie appeared to be more concerned with his present good fortune. "Do you know that the King is even paying for me to have fencing lessons at Major Faubert's Academy off Swallow Street," he confided. "And almost every day I am able to watch him play tennis with his friends. And almost always he beats them all."

Catherine found the subject of their discourse so completely to her liking that she forgot all about her former vexation. "He should do so, do you not think, with that long reach of his?"

But the young tennis critic laughed knowingly. "I think he would win anyway, Madame, because he plays with his head," he declared. "Both Sir Charles Berkeley and the Duke of Buckingham have more power in their strokes and the score may be all against him and then, when you think all is lost, the King puts over a cunning one—*et voilà!* You should come across one afternoon, Madame, and watch for yourself."

"I will, Jemmie," promised Catherine, sure that it would please Charles and wondering why she had not thought of it before.

But, even while hugging present happiness, the boy was not unmindful of former obligations. "Do not think me ungrateful to the Queen Mother or tell her that I prefer living with men," he begged naively. "Her Majesty has been very kind to me."

"Then you will be going to her party at Grosvenor House tomorrow?" asked Catherine, who was looking forward to it with pleasure.

"Yes, Madame. But I do not yet know many lads of my own age in this country, so I expect I shall feel rather out of things." For a moment or two Jemmie knelt with lowered eyes, plucking un-

certainly at the cushion cord, so that Catherine had the feeling
that he wanted to tell her of something that was troubling him
still more. "Besides," he added, "I think that milord Chancellor
does not much approve of me. I overheard him tell one of your
other English lords that I ought never to have been brought into
the country."

Although Catherine could not imagine how it could concern
them, she knew by experience just how the boy felt. "Then you
must come with me in my carriage," she invited impulsively.

Jemmie's troubled eyes brightened. "I should like that above
everything, Madame," he declared, getting up politely as if afraid
of outstaying her patience. "When shall I wait upon your Majesty?"

However poor his upbringing, he had at least been taught good
manners. And he had an engaging way of quirking one eyebrow
which reminded her of Charles.

On the morrow he proved an amusing escort and Catherine
noticed that Henrietta Maria and even Barbara Castlemaine, who
had as usual pushed her way into the gathering, went out of their
way to be kind to him. But soon after their arrival at the party
Catherine lost sight of her young protégé because, much to her
joy, the Queen Mother called her aside to talk in private. "Here
is an interpreter whom we can both trust," she explained, laying
a friendly hand on the arm of a priest who had come to pay his
respects to her.

Catherine had already noticed him walking calmly through
the streets and had wondered at the sight of a man who, despite
his tonsured head, was unmolested. Charles, she knew, had fought
hard for religious toleration, but Anglican and Nonconformist
hatred of Rome seemed to be growing rather than waning. She
looked now with particular attention at this unruffled priest and
found him to have a smile of rare spiritual beauty.

"I had supposed that you would already have met Father Hud-
dleston at Whitehall," said their hostess, by way of introduction.
"No one of the people would ever molest him, for he saved the
King's life."

"He must be the priest Charles spoke of," remembered Catherine, turning to him with a little cry of delight.

But John Huddleston laughed deprecatingly. "I was but one of many," he said. "And in those dark days his Majesty's life was from hour to hour in the hands of God. As, indeed are the lives of us all."

There was a naturalness, a glint of humor, about this erstwhile parish priest which Catherine's Portuguese clerics lacked. She felt assured that whatever frivolity or intimate thought she might utter, although translated by him, would be neither repeated nor condemned. "I pray you tell her Majesty how much I have wanted to talk to another woman, wiser than I and of the same faith, who knows the ways of this country," she said, with eager candor. "To ask advice in the—the difficult situation in which I find myself."

"This phase of a malicious influence will pass," her mother-in-law assured her. "But should there be other women try not to break your heart over it, Catherine. I assure you it would be thought nothing of in France. And having had no home or security or steadying hand since they were adolescent, both my elder sons have always been lamentably promiscuous."

"James too?" blurted out Catherine, amazed that Henrietta Maria should care so much for their religion and take their morals so calmly.

"James too," sighed their mother. "Only he sees no reason to pension them or give them the crown jewels or acknowledge his bastards. But it is better to try to condone, or at least to ignore. We foreign brides all have difficulties to put up with at the beginning."

"But I had always supposed that you and the late King Charles——"

"Oh, I did not have that kind of difficulty," smiled Henrietta. "My husband—God rest his soul—was too much taken up with his friend, Villiers of Buckingham, to look at women. Not even at me! So you see that I, too, have no cause to love that family! But afterwards Caro and I were entirely happy. Except that, deeply as he loved me, no arguments or prayers of mine could ever win him to the Faith. And when he was beheaded like that—alone and unshriven——" For a moment or two agony twisted his widow's face and choked her voice; but she was a courageous woman and took a hold upon herself. "It is because of that bitter memory that I took this opportunity to speak alone with you through someone we can trust. As time goes on, Catherine, you may be able to influence my son. . . ."

"I, dear Madame? But I have no influence at all." Although Catherine was relieved to make that humiliating confession, she knew that she could not have brought herself to do so through any official interpreter.

"More than you think, perhaps," shrugged Henrietta. "There may be many mistresses, but there will be only one of you. They may come and go, but you will be there all the time." She came and took her daughter-in-law by the shoulders, looking into her face with dark, compelling eyes. "It is your Christian duty, Catherine," she said solemnly. "I, who was separated from your Charles while he was yet malleable, have tried and failed. Sometimes I think it is out of sheer obstinacy more than from any love of this new Anglican church. Yet he was more angry with me than I have ever known him about Henry."

"What about Henry?" asked Catherine with breathless interest.

But Henrietta had shut her thin lips into a determined line. "No matter," she said. "Save that the boy died, like his father, unshriven."

"It was one of those times when she meddled," thought Catherine.

But Henrietta Maria had already shied away from a subject which shamed her. "I am too old now to pit myself against Charles's obstinacy," she was saying plaintively. "But you, Catherine, you have all your life before you and surely before my eldest son comes to die——"

Before the words were even translated Catherine shrank from them visibly as from a blow.

"You love him very much, do you not?" asked Henrietta, watching her.

Catherine nodded, feeling like a snared bird.

"As I did his father," affirmed Henrietta complacently.

"So much more, so help me God, that I am prepared to take him as he is," interpolated Catherine's frenzied thoughts.

"So that you will never cease trying?"

"Madame, there is nothing—nothing—that I desire or will pray for every day of my life more devoutly than the conversion of my husband," vowed Catherine, knowing, as sensitive John Huddleston did, that the vow was a half evasion.

But, thinking that she had gained her point, Henrietta was satisfied. She became suddenly bright and gay. "Come, *ma fille,* I have something to show you," she cried and, taking Catherine's hand, led the way, blithely as a young woman, to a small inner room where it would seem she wrote her interminable letters to the various members of her important family—to the Medicis, to her beloved daughter, now Duchess of Orleans, and to her august nephew, Louis the Fourteenth of France. It was a bare little room, vaguely reminiscent of a conventual cell, made splendid only by a life-size portrait hanging on the wall. "I take this masterpiece of Sir Anthony Van Dyck's everywhere with me," she said, standing before it. "And I would have you carry the impression of it in your heart. *Le voilà!* Charles, as God made him—before those vile Cromwellian monsters marred him!"

Catherine knew instinctively then that, although their mother might get on infinitely better with James, the belief that she loved him best was a myth. She gazed at the picture of a solemn-eyed small boy dressed up in his first suit of armor, smugly proud of the pistol he held in his hand. Obviously he was aching to get out of doors and play with it, but at the same time trying to be courteously attentive to the requirements of his father's Court painter. Probably, too, that active mind of his was wondering just how the colors got mixed on the palette. "He was a most lovable child, but Caro and I did not spoil him," Henrietta Maria was saying dispassionately. "It was life that did that."

Catherine had taken grateful leave of her amazing mother-in-law, and the sturdy small boy in the picture was safely ensconced for all time in her heart when she happened to meet the original, grown to cynical manhood, just about to take his departure in the forecourt; and some of her tenderness must still have been hovering in her eyes, making her warmly lovely. "Will you not drive home with me?" invited Charles.

Catherine looked up at him in pleased surprise. "With all my heart!" was the laughing formula welling to her lips until she caught sight of Barbara Castlemaine already seated in the gilded coach. Nothing, nothing would induce her to ride with that woman, and suddenly—as a defense—she remembered young Jemmie. "I am honored," she said, drawing back with a face which had become a polite mask, "but I already have an escort and, by your Majesty's leave, cannot well desert him."

"The Queen has a gallant!" she could hear Barbara Castlemaine tittering.

"Fortunate man! May we know his name?" murmured Charles, accustomed to having his invitations accepted as commands.

Poor Catherine wished the ground would open and cover her. If only she could name Prince Rupert or milord Sandwich, or even one of the gentlemen of her household who usually accompanied her! Someone worthy of the scene, instead of a boy whose unimportance would make her look foolish. Barbara's loud laughter would ring out in mockery, and Charles himself would have reason indeed to be insulted and angry. Glancing round apprehensively at the watching company, Catherine saw that Jemmie Crofts had, with his usual courtesy, waited for the moment of her departure and was standing near. Certainly no blame for the situation should touch him!

"A young Mr. Crofts, Sir," she said very distinctly, stretching out a protective hand to gather him to her side against the approaching gust of ridicule.

But if there was amazement, there was no mockery. Charles saw to that. His own delighted, infectious laughter rang out across the expectant silence; his strong hand was beneath her reluctant arm bundling her firmly but affectionately into the coach. "Odds-fish, Catherine, this is pleasant!" he exclaimed. "I will not hear of you and—Mr. Crofts—returning alone. You must both ride with me. Move over, Barbara, my dear, and make room for my wife." And before the astonished eyes of Chancellor, admirals and foreign ambassadors they drove off. "Quite a family party," chuckled the shameless King.

Crofts, who evidently adored him, had climbed in with alacrity; and the great Castlemaine, without so much as a *moue*, was sharing his seat back to the horses. So delighted was she to have got her way at last and to be seen riding with the Queen that she forgot to be feline. And a family party it seemed, with the royal coach full of laughter. Without understanding in the least what was happening, Catherine laughed as happily as any, with Jemmie sitting as mediator in their midst. While passing along the Strand, Charles rendered the lad almost speechless with excitement by promising to take him along next time he went to the Nore to see his ships, and Catherine, watching them, could only think, "What a wonderful father he will make!" For, as everyone knew, Charles adored children. "I vow you are tormenting me, Kate, when you might be making me the happiest man alive by telling me that we are soon going to have a son like this of our own," he declared presently, taking her hand and not troubling to lower his voice in the least.

Catherine blushed as rosily as he had intended her to. "Oh, *no*, Charles, you *lie*," she protested, too flustered to pick her English words with care.

Whereat they all pretended to be horrified. "Do you not know, Madame, that it is high treason to say that to the King?" laughed Barbara.

"Not when it is my Queen who says it," defended Charles.

"People who commit high treason get hanged," insisted Jemmie, leaning forward to draw a hand across his throat with a horribly realistic grimace.

"Very well, confess and be hanged," laughed her sovereign lord. "But at the last moment, when the Calvinists are all thirsting for your Catholic blood, I shall sign a reprieve. And send young Jemmie here riding posthaste with it to Tyburn. Because your brothers might begin to make awkward inquiries and also—" the long, heavy-lidded eyes looked down at her in a way which always made her breath catch deliciously in her throat—"because I find you adorable."

The happy ride was all too short. Back in her apartments Catherine did not even notice the affronted looks her own people gave her because she had ridden in the King's coach through London streets, laughing, with his mistress.

"Who *is* that delightful boy?" she asked again, as they took off her grand clothes. "He must have had very delightful parents."

No one answered. There was another of those queer, hushed silences.

"Young Jemmie, I mean," she added, supposing that she had not made herself clear.

When she turned all her English ladies were looking at her aghast. "We s-supposed your Majesty knew," stammered Lettice Ormonde, with the pearled brocade dress still lying stiffly across her outstretched arms.

"Knew?" Catherine's questioning glance passed from one to another of them.

It was left to the duenna of them all, the Countess of Suffolk, to answer her. "He is James, the King's eldest son," she said at last, without looking at her mistress.

The King's eldest son.

Involuntarily, Catherine's shocked mind began to make calculations. "Charles must have been about eighteen—an exile in Holland or somewhere. "The King's eldest *bastard*," she corrected them haughtily, although her heart was hammering and it seemed that the candles on her dressing table were swaying like flowers in the wind. Catherine let them finish undressing her in silence, but she could not stop her thoughts.

"He, too, thinks I knew. . . . No wonder he called it quite a family party! The oddest, most scandalous party imaginable surely! But he is grateful to me for smoothing over an awkward situation. He'd had the boy brought over against Clarendon's advice because he loves him. But he hates scenes. Clarendon said so. Well, this time there shall be no scenes. I will not be such a fool as to let him guess that I did not befriend Jemmie purposely. . . ."

And later, lying in the darkness, Catherine let her thoughts run on. "Who was his mother? Does it matter now? Just one of Charles's women. . . . 'Lamentably promiscuous,' his own mother said—and she a woman accustomed to the morals of *le Roi Soleil*. 'Don't break your heart over it,' she said too. So armor yourself against the years, my heart, and do not break. . . . I should hate this boy, more than the Castlemaine's. This firstborn. This other James Stuart. . . ."

But when he came to her Charles was happy, grateful and very gentle. And it was difficult to hate young Jemmie.

CHAPTER EIGHT

*A*s the weeks wore on Catherine found herself too happy to hate anyone. Barbara Castlemaine had been presented with a fine Surrey mansion called Nonesuch. There was talk of Jemmie's joining his uncle York against the Dutch to learn the art of war. And she herself became the prime consideration in Charles's mind —she and the child she was going to bear him.

He even gave up playing the exciting new game of pall-mall behind the Cockpit so that he might take her out driving in the spring beauty of Hyde Park. And the Londoners, quick to draw conclusions, cheered with joy. How much better to see the King holding his lawful wife's hand in a carriage by daylight than striding back across the gardens from visiting the Castlemaine after dark. And because the Queen herself looked so pretty, they cheered the more.

Catherine was happier than she had been since those first days at Hampton. What mattered it if she felt distressingly ill in the early mornings and had once vomited suddenly in bed? Charles had been there, beside her; and instead of calling anyone to witness her discomfiture he had risen with alacrity and gone padding around in his nightshirt like any kind, middle-class husband looking for a bowl. He had bathed her face with a towel soaked in rose water and comforted her, and had finally lifted her onto his own unsoured side of the bed before unlatching the door and summoning her women.

Catherine never forgot the ordinary humanity of that episode. Somehow, in spite of infidelities past or infidelities to come, it gave her a sense of security. All the same it was miserably disconcerting to go on with this violent morning sickness for so long. She began to worry about it, not only for herself but lest it should jeopardize the birth of her child.

"What is this place—Tunbridge—that people are talking of? Where they have discovered some miraculous wells?" she asked, remembering how so short a time ago in Portugal she would have sought out some shrine.

"A little town in Kent," Charles told her, tinkering with expert fingers at the mechanism of one of the striking clocks he collected. "But there is nothing miraculous about it. Only medicinal. When the newssheets first began making a stir about the place I sent down one of my apothecaries, and Rupert and I spent a whole afternoon testing the bottle of water he brought."

"And is it really true that it is good for women who are pregnant, Charles?"

"It could be good for most people, for there is iron in the soil there from which the cannon we used against the Spanish Armada were made. And iron enriches the blood."

Catherine reached a hand across the table towards him. "Then let us go there so that I may drink the waters," she urged. "For the sake of our son—that he may grow strong."

Before replacing yet another minute wheel Charles gave her upturned palm a reassuring pat. "Assuredly you may go if you have a mind to," he said. "And God knows I would put everything aside and come with you if I could afford it!"

"*Afford* it?"

"It costs a small fortune to move the Court, and I seem to have to pay for the upkeep of a batch of palaces whether we live in them or not."

Catherine's warm brown eyes opened wide, for there had never been such financial dilemmas in Lisbon. "But are you not the *king?*"

"My dear little plutocrat," laughed Charles, "have you been here so many months without finding out that, for all his fine robes, the king in this country is virtually a beggar? He begs from parliament—from all the fat squires who enriched themselves during the Commonwealth. He has only a small pittance from such personal estates as they have thought fit to leave to him. Those are the terms upon which wily old Monck invited me back, so that I can do mighty little without them. And, consider, my sweet —had I not been damnably hard up, should I have sold Dunkirk to the French?"

Catherine was all loving concern. "And parliament will not— how do you say—vote you any more?"

"For a really popular war they might," answered Charles cynically. "But as long as I keep their country at peace they mutter like a swarm of misers and complain that I spend my wages on wine and women."

"And do you?"

"Some of it. But nothing to what I spend on the navy. My father, having come normally into his inheritance, was free to levy ship money; but I must build ships out of my own pocket, or not at all."

"And they cannot see how important that is—being an island," mused Catherine, who came of a seafaring nation. "Well, at least they cannot mutter that they have been called upon to spend much upon your marriage."

"I did my best for you," Charles reminded her deprecatingly. "I saw to it that they voted you forty thousand pounds a year for your household."

"So I understood from milord Chancellor when I first came," said Catherine. "But I have not had it."

Charles laid down both clock and tools and gave her his undivided attention. "But only last week I heard the Lord Treasurer read out the amount when we were passing current expenditure." His eyes had narrowed shrewdly, and she rose and faced him, her small hands beating indignantly upon the table so that all his small cogs and springs went spinning. "You mean that those— those cheating humbugs pretend in public that I have had the spending of it? That I have not managed with far less in order to—to atone—for my delayed dowry?" Outraged, she seized a bell and rang imperiously for her women. "Bring me my household books!" she ordered. And there and then she insisted upon going through them. She was not Luiza of Braganza's daughter for nothing!

To her husband's shamed amusement, she really understood them. She had, he found, been personally supervising almost every item of expenditure all the time he was twitting her about that wretched dowry. He knew, of course, that in spite of all his gifts, her own private rooms were bare to the point of austerity. Probably she preferred them so, on principle, as his mother did. But, remembering the luxury of his mistress's apartments, it almost unmanned him to find how frugally his wife and her Portuguese people had lived. Catherine was a woman of integrity, and he admired her all the more because it was not the frugality but the cheating that she minded. But figures always had bored him, so he got up presently and took her in his arms, pen, books and all. "We will go to Tunbridge if I have to pawn my crown," he promised, kissing the tip of her indignant upturned nose.

"Oh, Charles, that will be lovely," she cried, standing on tiptoe to return his caress. "But there will be no need to do anything so unseemly as that. I shall fight this thing out with your horrid parliament myself. See, it is all down here in black and white, what I received from them and how much I spent. And they must know very well that I should never have saved and scrimped unless I had supposed that you would have benefited."

Charles knew that she would really be fighting for him, ranging herself on his side against their parsimony, she so childlike and so small!

And fight them she did; coolly, reasonably claiming what they had promised her. It was so mean of them, she pointed out, to ignore the wealth of trade she had brought. They had just thought of her as a nonentity, a gullible foreigner, and had trusted that the King was not interested enough ever to find out. Shrewd London merchants and wealthy squires who called the tune in parliament paid over the arrears of her income and thought the better of her for it.

So by the time the first wild roses were out in the hedgerows and the curly lambs almost outbleating their mothers, Catherine and her solicitous husband went to Tunbridge, thereby lending a luster to that sleepy little country town. Catherine was enchanted with the place and Charles had a right busy time with all the pretty wenches who held up their faces, in confiding rustic fashion, to be kissed. There were picnics in the meadows and dancing on the green; and every morning Charles would accompany his Queen and her new lady in waiting to the wells, where all the fashionable world sat gossiping about the Pump Room and pretending to enjoy the bitter, brownish chalybeate water. Catherine, to her great content, now had a young and innocent girl brought over by the Queen Mother to supplant the hated Castlemaine—a lovely girl called Frances Stuart to whom, because she was a poor relation of her husband, she delighted in showing every imaginable kindness. And although the happy pastoral idyll of their lives was frequently disturbed by the King's being obliged to return to London to pass bills or prorogue parliament, or to attend unwillingly to the quelling of rebellious Irish Catholics, it was observed that he always rode back posthaste to Tunbridge and that Catherine, full of vivacity and charm, would set forth with her ladies, dashingly arrayed in redingotes and plumed hats, to meet and embrace him on the way. Pride and early inhibitions were forgotten; and she was learning that even the lustiest of lovers wearies at times of taking the initiative and can be inordinately pleased by a woman's shameless show of spontaneous affection.

Charles—or Charles's conscience—was glad to see his oft wronged wife so happy; but towards the end of their stay a heavy shadow, occasioned by letters she received from Portugal, began to lie across her new, gay world: foolish, chiding letters from Alfonso, who had heard that she was conforming to a Protestant country's way and had ceased to wear her farthingales; and worried letters from her mother because a Spanish army was again on Portuguese soil and advancing close to Lisbon.

Anxiety tore at Catherine's heart so that Charles, returning from a gallop across Ashdown Forest, found her in tears. "If only you could send your ships again to help us," she entreated, showing him the letters.

"I heard of this when I was last in London, but would not worry you," he said wearily, disliking her elder brother rather more than usual. "Or I would have told you that our Colonel Hunt has already left Portsmouth with a small expeditionary force."

"Oh, Charles! How g-generous!"

"As Hyde will tell you it has less to do with generosity than with our political alliance. Were we at war with Spain I should expect your brother to do the same," shrugged Charles. "And, for the love of God, why must you women always weep?"

Catherine checked herself instantly, realizing that on that last visit to London he had probably been flooded, for her sake, with Barbara's reproachful tears. "It is perhaps a weapon given to us because we wear no swords," she suggested, with a watery smile.

He held out a forgiving hand and drew her to his knee. "Then there is small need for you to use it, since I find myself much more vulnerable to the undimmed brightness of your eyes," he told her.

Catherine lay blissfully in his arms. Through the open casement poured the silver beauty of a nightingale's song, making magic of the still summer evening. "If only I can bear him a son there will be nothing left to ask of God," she thought. But soon the agony of her driven, valiant little country was tearing at her heart again. "Beloved," she ventured, "I have been wondering for days past if you would allow me to write to his Holiness, the Pope."

"And what can the Pope do that my soldiers cannot?" demanded Charles, kissing her white shoulder and marveling afresh at the firm smallness of the breast beneath his hand.

"He could acknowledge my brother's sovereignty and so protect our country from such ruthless rapacity. Spain is a Catholic country and even King Philip would not dare to oppose the authority of Rome."

Charles stopped kissing her and sat up. "My dear child, it

would be most unwise," he told her gravely. "You cannot know
the temper of my people, how fanatically, since the reign of Mary
Tudor, they hate and fear all traffic with Rome. It is like a running fever with them."

"But they need not know. I could send the letter secretly by
one of my gentlemen."

Charles almost brushed her from his knee. "If he were caught
it might cost me my throne," he said brusquely.

But, having seen the way his people loved him, Catherine
found that incredible; and she cared for Portugal more passionately than he, with so many foreign influences and so much to
forgive, could as yet care for England. "There is Richard Bellings,
whom you yourself appointed to be always about me. We both
know that even if he were caught, no Inquisition would ever
make him speak."

Charles, too, got to his feet. Although they stood apart, their
glances held. "And what weight do you suppose a message from
Protestant England could possibly have in Rome?" he demanded.

But over and over again she had thought it all out while he lay
asleep. "I would ask it in return for the good offices I hope to perform for Catholics in this country. I would tell his Holiness that
no desire for a crown—nothing but my ardent desire to serve the
Faith—could have induced me to become Queen of England."

"Then I have only been flattering myself that I had something
to do with it," remarked Charles, bowing ironically. "And may I
ask what good offices you had the temerity to hope you might
perform for us? Or was it," he added, with that shrewd narrow-
ing of the eyes, "to have been for me personally? A zealous wifely
mission recently inflamed by my mother, perhaps?"

Instead of wincing from his sarcasm, Catherine faced him
squarely. "In this matter I was thinking only of my own beloved
country," she told him candidly. "But you must know that, since I
love you, I wish more than anything in the world that you would
become a Catholic."

"And so—sometimes—do I," answered Charles slowly. It was
the first time they had ever spoken together of fundamental

things and he, who seldom talked to women save for amusement, found himself speaking to her as though she were his other self, saying things which he had never admitted even to his own brothers. "It would be a cessation of struggle, a kind of coming home. . . ."

In her utter amazement, Catherine could find no words with which to voice her joy. She went to him and laid her two hands, as if in prayer, against his heart. "I would give *anything—*" she whispered.

"That is just the difference, my dear," he sighed. "I may wish sometimes, but I would not give anything. For in my case it would mean giving up so much."

He saw that she was more deeply shocked than when she had supposed him to be a confirmed Anglican. "What, then, is your religion?" she asked.

He lifted her hands and kissed them lightly. The moment of deep reality was gone. "Never to go on my travels again," he said. "I assure you I am not worth saving. A man with mighty few principles."

"But limitless kindness," said Catherine, seeking to bind up some of the hurts that had been done to the trusting small boy in Van Dyck's picture.

He leaned back against the arm of his chair and, quirking a puzzled eyebrow, pulled her almost roughly towards him. "I have never been loved like this before," he said, half angry because her very simplicity baffled him.

"But everybody loves you!"

"Oh, because I am a king—or for my *beaux yeux*—or because they want something," he jibed. "But you, Kate—" He broke off in mid-tirade, trying to accuse her because he knew so well the tortuousness of men's minds. "But of course it is true, is it not, that my mother urged you to use all wifely wiles to convert me?"

Catherine nodded assent. Her clear, sherry-brown eyes were wells of truthfulness, and he knew it.

"Yet you have never once tried to."

Her gaze dropped before his at last, and the enchanting color rose to her cheeks. "It is because—may the Holy saints intercede for me—I have been wicked enough to——"

"Lie with a heretic and like it?"

She looked up then and saw the grin on his ugly mouth. "I pray you, do not jest about such things!" she begged.

He was all contrition at once. "There at least, my sweet, you wrong me. Never was I further from jesting." Though in part it must hurt her, for once he met her serious sincerity with his own, permitting her a glimpse of the real Charles Stuart whom so few men knew. "Because there is so little else I can give you, I would give you the satisfaction of knowing that none of my mother's subtle plans or impassioned exhortations have ever moved me as you have done, by quietly living your religion and loving me." He got up and strolled to the window, suddenly more king than husband. "For this once I will let you send Richard Bellings to Rome," he said, in that grave, resonant voice she had heard him use to councilors. "But you must understand that having once freed myself, I cannot endure another woman's trying to prose-lytize or meddle politically."

"Are you not—rather hard on her Majesty?"

"Why do you say that?"

"I had supposed that you love her, since you have twice in-vited her to make her home here."

"But naturally I love her, and by God's grace I will never fail in my duty to her. Did she not risk her life for us and do all she could for me in my exile? We Stuarts hold together. But after Cromwell freed my youngest brother from Carisbrook she had him in France and used every device to turn him from the Angli-can faith he had sworn at my father's knee to keep. Henry was but a lad, yet he kept faith, though she had the sheets torn from his bed and turned him out in anger. I sent for him then to Hol-land. Do you not see, Catherine, that had James and I been killed Henry would have been the last hope of our house for the mon-archy? And had he become a Catholic, the English and the Scots would have had none of him. My father knew it."

"I would rather die than endanger you—and your monarchy,"

vowed Catherine, watching his tall, dignified silhouette against the fading sunset.

"So Mam said, no doubt, to the King, my father. Yet it may well be that her meddling cost him his life."

"But she adored him!"

"All the same, being a woman, she talked—at the wrong moment." Charles turned, and although Catherine could scarcely see his shadowed face she knew that it was sad and stern. "Zounds, she had no thought to harm him!" he declared, in the old warm, informal way. "No one had worked more heroically for the cause than she; and when she realized what she had done she was heartbroken."

"Then what made her——"

"It was just Mam's sense of the dramatic. She always had to play a part. And the dangerous way my father doted on her, having to tell her everything. He had gone down to parliament intending to call for his five worst enemies and impeach them. The moment was ripe. He had them in the hollow of his hand that day; and it was their lives or his. He had planned to take them completely by surprise; it was one of the few really clever moves he made against the growing strength of parliament. But Mam had to talk. 'Rejoice with me,' she cried to a lady of doubtful loyalty, 'for even at this hour the King is master of his realm again, for Pym and his confederates must be arrested by now.' But even though she had sat watch in hand, he had in reality been delayed. You know how people with petitions always pester me as I go down to the House. You know what it is—a smile here and a promise there. And he was too courteous and conscientious to brush them aside. And by the time he arrived some cursed Roundhead had warned the five Members and they had escaped through a window, all except one who was enormously fat and got stuck, they say. Just as my father himself, who was not fat at all, got stuck between prison bars trying to escape from Carisbrook Castle before they had done with him. On the Isle of Wight, it was, and I had a French brig waiting for him down in Brook

Bay; but, Heaven bless him for a guileless gentleman, he had to bungle even that!"

There was a long silence while the shadows deepened in the corners of the low-beamed Kentish room. "I am not brilliant like your mother, nor have I any sense of the dramatic. Moreover, you do not dote on me at all dangerously," said Catherine, slowly, borrowing some of his bitterness. "Therefore I think you will always find it safe to trust me."

CHAPTER NINE

*L*isten to what my brother Pedro says, Charles!" cried Catherine, referring to the hastily scrawled letter in her hand. "After the victory, when your British charged up the hill of Amexial and helped us to drive the invading Spaniards back, our general, the Conde de Villa Flor, cried out 'These heretics are better to us than all our saints!' "

"And Alfonso, I understand, rewarded them for their pains with a pinch of snuff apiece," smiled Charles.

Catherine's triumphant gaiety clouded over. "How humiliating! For Pedro and Villa Flor and all the rest of us. Charles, have you thought lately that Alfonso is going a little mad?"

"Judging by the letters he writes you, I should not be surprised. But do not let the snuff incident embarrass you, my dear, for I offset it by ordering forty thousand crowns to be distributed among our men; and, as I told you, it is relatively easy to get money out of parliament for purposes of war."

Catherine, in her unlaced cherry colored waistcoat, regarded him adoringly. "Small wonder the Portuguese think you are some kind of god," she murmured.

Tunbridge Wells had done wonders for her; and after a leisurely progress through the west country where Charles had once been a fugitive, they were back again at Whitehall, a Whitehall stirring with progress and spaciousness of thought, and full of the comings and goings of scientists and sea captains. Such men were forever gathering round a great painted globe of the world that stood before the long window in the King's chamber. James and Cousin Rupert, Admiral Sir William Penn, the Earl of Sandwich,

and frequently, of late, a fearless swashbuckling adventurer called
Robert Holmes. There was gold to be got in New Guinea, Sir
Robert said, knowing well that no man had more need of gold
than a reinstated Stuart.

"But we are not as yet officially at war there," warned Clarendon, who, what with the gout and a long habit of domineering,
grew daily more difficult.

"Take no heed of his croaking, Holmes," grinned Charles.
"What it amounts to is that I can give you no official backing nor
protect you from the claws of parliament should you fail."

"I am well content to take a risk on that, Sir," answered Holmes,
whose daring seamanship had already endeared him to the King.

All that Rupert and James could talk about these days, whether
at meals or down at the dockyards, was the galaxy of fine new
countries to be explored and colonized beyond the mighty Atlan-
tic Ocean, and of Great Britain's rivalry there with the Dutch.
Although they had received the hospitality of Holland, it was
natural enough for the Stuarts to hate the new Lowland republic
which had repudiated their dead sister and young William of
Orange, her son. So when the intrepid Dutch seized the ships of
the African and East Indian Company, the British retaliated by
wresting from them the thriving trade post, New Amsterdam,
which they had built along the banks of the Hudson River.

"What shall we call it?" clamored the explorers and politicians
at Whitehall, when the tremendous excitement of the news had
died down a little.

Charles, after considering awhile, waved aside all suggestions
incorporating his own name and gave honor where honor was
due. "Now that, under the grace of God, this thriving city is ours,
let us call it New York," he said.

And marking the far-off spot on his globe, he hurried off to the
Queen's apartments. For ever since he had found her pouring
over *The Lusiads,* in which Portugal's national poet had immortal-
ized the exploits of her seamen, Charles had begun to talk with
her about such things, recognizing the fact that almost everywhere
his own ships went the courageous Portuguese explorers had been

before them: men like Bartholomew Diaz, who first rounded the Cape of Good Hope, establishing maritime routes to the Indies and actually landing on the unknown continent of America; and the great Vasco de Gama, whose tiny fleet had years ago reached Calcutta and torn the valuable spice trade from the rich hands of Venice. It was a bond between Charles and Catherine at which few people ever guessed.

But although only the passage to the privy landing stairs and Chaffinch's room separated their apartments, Catherine saw comparatively little of her husband. He was a man who must always live his own life, and interests within her own household often had to suffice her. There was, for instance, the training of flighty, foolish Frances Stuart. The girl was so pretty and so much a tomboy that her goings-on began to weigh on Catherine's conscientious mind. Instead of attending to her duties she would sit on the floor building card castles like a child, or escape with other wild youngsters, dressed up and masked, to mingle with the crowds and to cry sweet lavender or oranges in the streets, or run with flying curls through the galleries playing hide-and-seek with all the susceptible young men who shadowed her.

"She is only a child," Henrietta Maria would say indulgently when Catherine tried to hold a family consultation.

"But a cousin of sorts, and so our dear Catherine holds herself responsible," pointed out James, mindful of her kindness to his wife.

"I take no exception to her romping with these young gallants. There is safety, I suppose, in their numbers," Catherine excused herself, with that engaging air of innocence which so intrigued the Stuarts. "But when it comes to hiding in the linen room with the Duke of Buckingham—for you know, Charles, although George Villiers *is* your friend, he has a horrible reputation among my women!"

Whereat her unregenerate husband burst out laughing. "No worse than mine, little Puritan!" he confessed.

But to the Queen Mother, who hated all the Villiers, the linen cupboard episode gave the affair a more serious aspect.

"In this instance, even Buckingham would not dare—" blundered James tactlessly.

"And for all her innocent looks," Charles assured them, hastening to silence him, "the girl is quite capable of looking after herself."

"She needs occupation," snapped Catherine, wondering how he had discovered whether she were or not.

"Then I will tell you of a notion I have in mind," he offered obligingly. "Sir Peter Lely needs a model for a painting to be engraved upon the new pieces I intend to have struck from this Guinea gold, if and when our invaluable brigand Holmes brings it. Some allegorical female figure representing the might of Britain, I thought; for which our Frances, with her little Roman nose, has just the right slenderness and curves."

"A happy thought! And you could call the figure Britannia," agreed James, with unwonted imagination.

But that was scarcely the kind of occupation Catherine had been looking for. And after the family were gone Donna Penelva, who alone had been permitted to remain in England, complained with reason that it would only make the little nitwit more vain than ever.

All the same it passed away the dull autumnal evenings to watch Frances dress up in a white classic robe clasped about her youthful breasts with gold, hide her curls in a great martial helmet, and then, armed with shield and trident, pose in an attitude of graceful defiance—actually towards Catherine's largest mirror, but supposedly towards all the real and imaginary enemies of Britain. All the gentlemen of the Court would gather round—to watch the famous painter at work, they said—and Charles himself was delighted when the first newly embossed coin was brought him from the royal mint.

"How apt to have a Stuart face on either side," observed florid, modish Buckingham, turning the coin on his lace-frilled hand so that the candlelight gleamed first on the fair Britannia and then on the bewigged profile of the king.

"La Belle et La Bête," laughed Charles, flicking the gleaming thing from his friend's hand into his pretty cousin's lap.

But that evening, while her devotional books were being laid out, Catherine was still wondering uncomfortably about the sly, malevolent way in which Buckingham had looked at her whilst he spoke.

"It is a pity that Frances's father, Lord Blantyre, allows her to spend so much time with the fast set in Lady Castlemaine's house," sighed Maria Penelva, settling on her nose the strong spectacles which Charles had had specially made for her.

"Yet, in spite of her flightiness, I am sure that she is chaste," insisted Catherine.

But a few weeks later all thought of *la belle* Stuart was put out of her head by news that Jane Lane was coming to Court; Jane Lane, whose name was so easy to remember, and whose intimate role of gallantry so difficult to forget; the girl for whom a penniless Charles had once borrowed the French King's best horses, for whom he provided a generous pension, and to whom he still occasionally wrote; the woman, it seemed to Catherine, of all others to be envied.

"Jane's husband is bringing her at last," Charles told her, "and I shall be obliged if you and your ladies will be present to greet her."

"Will they be staying with us awhile?" asked Catherine, although her heart sank fearfully at the thought.

But Charles said it would be only a short visit although, for his part, he would willingly find them permanent lodgings in the palace. It seemed that the husband, quite understandably, Catherine thought, had needed practically a royal command to bring Jane at all.

Jane's dress, when she was presented, was that of a country squire's wife and she wore but one of the jewels which the King had sent her; but there was a nobility about her sweet, clear-cut face which needed none at all. Catherine, Queen of England, found herself the more nervous of the two. "For days she held his life steadfastly in the hollow of her hands," she thought, glad that

—with no will to outshine—she had chosen to wear her quietest gray satin.

Withdrawing herself a little from Charles's side, she watched him raise Jane from her profound curtsy and kiss her, calling her his deliverer and his "sweet life," before them all. He spoke with that deep inflection which betokened affectionate gratitude; but, seeing the color flood into Jane's pale cheeks, Catherine knew that however good a wife and mother she might now be in North-amptonshire, she would love Charles Stuart until she died.

"You must find his Majesty very different from the cropped and leather-jacketed William Jackson you served so well," Catherine said kindly.

"It was I who served Jane," teased Charles.

And then for the first time country-bred Jane dared to look at him properly. At the tall, dignified figure with the glitter of Orders across a black velvet coat, the curled and perfumed wig, at the grave lined face and full, licentious, smiling lips and—last of all—at the fine ringed hands that once had watered and stabled her horse. "His eyes are just the same," she said, her own full of tears for the fresh youth of him that was gone.

Charles led her to a chair and began telling her quietly any small anecdotes he could remember of her father, Sir Richard Lane, who had died in exile with him in Jersey; and Catherine noticed how even in that lovely moment Barbara Castlemaine must needs push her proprietory way towards him. Judging by the splendor of her toilette, it would appear that she, too, had feared a rival from the past. "Though, wife or mistress, neither of us need fear; for women made in Jane's mould keep their vows," thought Catherine, gladly watching Charles's happiness as he gathered about him Jane's brother, Father Huddleston, and old Cavalier campaigners like stout Lord Wilmot, Carless and the rest; and then the gradual thawing of Jane Lane's shyness and the breathless outpouring of reminiscences whose every other sentence began with "Do you remember?" Within that charmed circle, warmed with comradery, bursts of laughter and the King's own racy yarns, Jane and the men who had escaped from the carnage of Worcester were living over again what each must have counted his highest hours. Young unfledged fighters of the future hung on the fringe of their fascinating adventure, and while the notorious Castlemaine sulked unnoticed, the Queen graciously drew Jane's forgotten husband to her side, entertaining him as best she could in her still broken English so as to leave the spell of reunion unbroken.

It was not until the King and James had left and the rest of the men were raising their glasses again in boisterous sport to the old, dangerous toast "The Black Boy over the water!" that Catherine, lingering purposely, bade Jane Lane good-by. "I want you to wear this, too, in token of my gratitude," she said, unfastening from her breast a brooch of exquisite Bahia workmanship.

"Oh, Madame!" exclaimed Jane. "From you, whom I have so envied!"

"I had thought rather that people pitied me," said Catherine in a low voice, speaking spontaneously as she was wont to do with those whom she instinctively trusted. "But you are not of the kind who would want to be a queen?"

"No, Madame. And it is not for that I envy you."

"Then our envy is mutual," sighed Catherine. "You see, there is so little that I can ever do for him."

"Yet always, whenever he is disheartened, sick—or dying—you will have the right to be there, in his room." For a brief moment the two women whose lives had been so different clasped hands, and Catherine, crossing herself at the thought of Charles's death, knew that Jane was right. Even now, it was she alone who could bear him a legitimate son, and there was nothing in the world, she knew, that he wanted more. So she bade her guests good night and went early to her room to rest. To rest and to thank God that, after all, one good woman whom she had feared was no menace to her happiness.

To her annoyance she found it was the turn of careless, chattering Frances to attend upon her. "The King and the Duke have gone on to the playhouse," she said brightly, collecting the Queen's jewels one by one on a small velvet cushion, adding, with the licence of a relative, "It seems odd, does it not, that they should go there when that nice woman who helped to save Charles comes at last to Court?"

"Perhaps there is a particularly good play tonight," yawned Catherine.

"It is not a real play by Mr. Wycherley or anybody. But Moll Davis is to dance a jig, dressed as a boy, at the Duke's playhouse," obliged the little chatterbox, who always had all the tattle of the town at her tongue's tip. "And Lady Castlemaine says there is a new, red-haired actress called Nell Gwyn or some such name, whose impudent songs amuse the King."

"And milady Castlemaine hoped that you would repeat her choice morsel of gossip to me."

"Oh, Madame," pouted Frances. "I do but try to liven what must have been a very dull evening for you."

Catherine rose wearily from her dressing stool. "You have yet to learn, my dear Frances, that there are some women to whom an evening is not necessarily dull just because they themselves are not the center of it," she said.

But afterwards, lying quiet within the drawn curtains of her bed, Catherine was so unfortunate as to overhear kind Lettice Ormonde say reprovingly, "You should not have told her Majesty about that Gwyn woman, Frances. After all, she is but a jumped-up orange wench with a drunken prostitute of a mother. The King might have laughed—he laughs at all sorts of things—but it is incredible that he would ever *look* at her."

And then the young Stuart girl's pert retort. "Well, he looks at her often enough at the playhouse. They say he often goes when she is billed to play. And Lady Castlemaine told me that several times the sentries have seen him before it is properly light hurrying across the gardens in that quick, quiet way of his, and along this gallery to his room——"

Catherine did not sleep much that night, and she was still wide awake when the palace servants began raking out the fires and when the river beneath her windows came to life again with the raucous shouts of ferrymen. Of course, there was no truth in the squalid story. It was just something unkind which Barbara had invented out of spite because she and Charles had been so content with each other of late. But presently, while her ladies still slept, she heard footsteps coming quickly along the stone cloister on the garden side of the palace, footsteps which she would have known anywhere. She sat up abruptly. So it was true after all, that Charles was faithless—even now while she carried his unborn babe. Was it always to be like this? From whose bed did he come now, hurrying to beat the dawn? Surely, surely he was not sneaking from some tousled, red-headed slut of an actress?

Indignation boiled within her. She had to know, to see for herself—although, seeing him, she would still be in a world of wretched conjecture. In the anteroom where two of her women slept there was a small window overlooking the cloister. Swiftly, in spite of the vertigo that assailed her, Catherine rose from her bed. Without pausing to put on a wrap she slipped past the sleeping women and silently pushed open a casement. And, sure enough, there in the cold light of autumnal early morning, was her husband hurrying along the flagged pavement below. "Then it is true! Somehow I must get used to it," she told herself, with a shaking hand pressed to her heart.

But although Charles hurried, there seemed nothing particularly furtive about him. The sentry at the garden gate looked as stolidly impersonal as usual, and suddenly Catherine espied two other men rounding the bedewed garth close at the King's heels. Amazed, she recognized Sandwich, the admiral, who was discussing something with a shortish little man carrying a great sheaf of documents. Almost beneath her window Charles stopped suddenly, as if he had just remembered something, so that the other two almost bumped into him. Clearly, from their conversation, they had just come from some sort of committee meeting. Catherine had had no idea that these men were in the habit of conducting State business before she had even drunk her foreign brew of tea; and all her heart was abased to Charles in shame.

"How much gunpowder and cordage was I embezzled out of when the *Royal Duke* came in to refit at Chatham?" he was asking crisply of Sandwich. But it was the little man in the large brown wig who answered, promptly and concisely. With his sensible clothes and expert knowledge of figures he brought a breath of outside commerce into the more rarefied atmosphere of the palace. He appeared to have put a stop to whatever leakage there had been, but seemed to have something else on his mind—something which it had not been his place to speak of in council, perhaps; and although his manner was pleasantly respectful he was obviously accustomed to discussing business with the King. "About the drunken master of the *Unicorn*," he said. "If your Majesty will graciously pass the punishment suggested by the board, the matter need not be left outstanding."

Far from having been caught philandering, they were just three hungry men standing in a draughty passage, each wanting his breakfast but with the same unromantic issues conscientiously in mind. "He was four points off his course with the Dogger bank close on his starboard," recalled Charles consideringly.

"That was not the only charge, Sir," the secretary of his Navy Board reminded him. And Sandwich shook his bared head in friendly exasperation. "It is a question of discipline, Sir," he urged. "If your Majesty is as lenient with all officers who insult him in their cups——"

"What exactly did he say of me?" asked Charles. "My life is not so blameless that I could afford to enquire across a boardroom table."

There was an embarrassed pause during which Catherine noticed that the rising sun was beginning to glorify the dew spangled garth with misty shafts of gold. She saw her husband lay a friendly hand on the smaller man's shoulder. "Come, Pepys, out with it," he encouraged. "I'll wager, for all you have a pretty wife, you sometimes stray."

Pepys looked more embarrassed than ever and would probably have been stricken dumb entirely had he known the Queen was leaning out of a window above him. But he was no sycophant. "Sober, the man is a useful navigator, Sir," he said. "But in his cups he kept shouting above the wind that whereas Dick Cromwell let his father's well tilled land lie fallow, your Majesty had sown it with a fine crop of cuckolds."

Even Charles Stuart was silent; and when he spoke again he had put on that sudden kingliness which dismissed discussion. "Give him the maximum penalty for drunkenness. I will not have my ships mishandled by sots," he ordered. "But as I cannot in honesty take exception to what he said of me, I see no reason why other men should."

He was off to get his breakfast immediately, leaving the two to stare after him with a kind of puzzled disapproval. "But the man held the King's commission," Pepys presumed to mutter. He was some kind of connection of his lordship, as Catherine recalled, and had rendered good service to his wife and household while the admiral was at sea.

Sandwich linked an arm in his and walked away towards the Strand. "I can well imagine, Samuel, that a man of the King's ilk relies more upon spontaneous love than upon compulsory respect."

"However that may be, 'tis a vast pity the other members of the Navy Board do not bestir themselves to attend as many meetings as his Majesty," snorted the conscientious secretary.

"And that old Clarendon nags so tediously about his indolence. But the old bore may be right about him in other matters; for 'tis the navy that is mistress of his heart. . . ."

Their voices dwindled away down the long cloister and Catherine, suddenly realizing how cold she was, hurried back to bed. If she were shivering and shamed, at least she was happier than when she had left it. "There may be other women," her mother-in-law had warned. And Charles himself, who, however much he had learned to mislead the world, was consistently truthful with himself, had just admitted their numbers. Yet none of his women, perhaps, would ever mean as much to him as his ships. Catherine hugged that scrap of comfort to herself; though close on it came the thought, "And neither, for that matter, may I. . . . Shall I ever learn to understand this faithless, loyal, merry, melancholy man I have married?"

And almost before she had finished wondering, Charles was in her room, booted for one of those hard canters of his when he managed to enjoy a little privacy by the simple expedient of out-distancing all his followers. For next to a good ship he loved a swift horse.

"Now that New York is taken from the Dutch and your other colonial news is good I suppose you will be going to Newmarket for the racing as usual," said Catherine, salving her conscience with kindness.

Charles stood regarding her as she lay wanly in the big bed. "I had thought to postpone it this year perhaps," he began tentatively, doing much the same thing by his own conscience.

But deep loving had already taught Catherine something, at least, of his complexity. She could guess how he was chafing because James, not being a king, could get away to sea; and noting his sallowness, she knew, too, in her hardly acquired wifely wisdom, that he was beginning to feel the need of long days of sport and unadulterated masculine society after the stuffiness of Court. And there, thank God, in the wilds of Cambridgeshire, there was no accommodation for women.

"Indeed you must go," she insisted. "You look tired."

He came and sat on the end of her bed. "You do not look over well yourself," he said anxiously.

"It is but the shadow of the curtains," she lied valiantly.

"I should be back long before you are brought to bed," he assured her cheerfully. "And we will go to Hampton if it pleases you."

It did not please her and she shook her head. Hampton, as they both knew, had been a heaven which he had broken.

"Windsor, then? Or wherever you will."

"I will stay here," she told him, "for I think you would like your son to be born a Londoner."

Repentantly, gratefully he bent and kissed the palm of her little hand, closing her fingers carefully as though they could be made to hold his caress until he came again. "Then take every care of yourself for my sake," he bade her. "And above everything avoid going abroad in the City. These mild, humid days after a hot summer we are still cursed with the plague. If I had my way I would tear down half those narrow streets and build afresh more spaciously, to let in the sun."

Catherine promised readily, remembering how some such scourge had already robbed him of two dear ones. "Good-by, my love, and may all your horses win!" she called gaily as he left her.

"If they do I will buy you a new dress," he vowed, turning to smile at her as a page threw open the door. "And even if they do not, at least I can ride across the good Cambridgeshire turf again and forget poor old Ned and the everlasting parliament Zounds, how I love the wind on the heath!"

CHAPTER TEN

*C*atherine never heard whether the King's horses won or not; neither had she any immediate need of the new dress. For a few days after Charles and most of his courtiers had left for the races not only the shadows of her bed curtains lay dark upon her, but also the shadow of death. It was the spotted fever, her physicians said. Her aching body burned and shivered between the sheets; her tongue was swollen in a parched throat. The railed alcove in which her bed stood was packed with frightened women, anxious apothecaries, and praying priests. Their faces seemed at times to be bending over her, at others to be floating afar off like white and disembodied disks. Whenever her head turned on the pillow she heard someone moan and call aloud her husband's name, but in her delirium she had no idea that the cracked, desperate voice was her own.

"Will you not let us send for him now, my lady?" entreated the Duchess of Suffolk, trying to smooth back her mistress's masses of damp, tousled hair.

"Not yet. Not yet."

"But the doctors say——"

Then poor, half-blind Maria Penelva was tenderly sponging the sweat from her forehead. "Oh, my dear, do you not want to see him again before you die?"

"Want to see him again?" ran Catherine's distracted thoughts. "More than anything in heaven or earth, God forgive me! When I should be thinking only of my own soul. . . ."

And then, finally, there was old Doctor da Sousa, who had brought her into the world and whom Charles had suffered to stay, telling her pityingly in Portuguese that there could be no baby now—no baby ever, perhaps. And therefore his Majesty must be told.

"But he so loves the wind on the heath," croaked Catherine obstinately in English.

All through the night they were cupping her, physicking her, exhorting her in Latin, suffocating her with incense.

"*In te, Domine, speravi. . . . Kyrie eleison. . . .*"

"Now and in the hour of our death," breathed Catherine, trying to compose her mind.

It behooved her to forgive all her enemies, they said.

Enemies? Who were her enemies, besides those demons of jealousy and quick temper against which she must strive so constantly? In her extremity the very word seemed to have lost all meaning. Barbara Castlemaine. Buckingham, perhaps? Or even Charles himself because he had, after all, supped with Barbara before leaving for Newmarket. But whatever he did, however much he hurt her, Charles could be no enemy. He was her heart's love. And would he not be punished enough, poor man, if in spite of all his high hopes there should be no heir? She, his wife, who loved him so desperately, had nothing to give him. Barbara had at least given him a bastard to fondle. Jane Lane had risked her life for him. Yet she, proud daughter of Portugal as she was, could not so much as suffer birth pangs to bear him a son.

The fevered days ran into each other and on one of them, rallying a little, Catherine sent for a clerk and made her will, regretting that even to those who had served her best she had so little of her own to give. And once—since even physicians and priests must eat—she was left blessedly alone for awhile with some of the most devoted of her ladies. "You heard what they said? That I may never bear a living child?" she said, exhausted but clear-headed again as they propped her up gently against her pillows. "I suppose that in God's mercy it may be better that I go like this. Then the King can marry again, someone young and full of vitality. Of good lineage—like Frances——"

"But think of his grief," protested Donna Penelva.

"Oh, no, dear Maria, he has never really loved me."

"Madame, you may well be wrong. Consider how he threatened to send us all back to Portugal, and how—ever since you begged that I who am old and dear to you might stay—he has done nothing but spoil me! He is like that, Catalina *querida*. You must not slip from us because you have no heart to stay."

"Only make the effort to live through this night," urged the Duchess of Suffolk, "and I wager the King will have forgotten his sport and be home."

In spite of her former protests Catherine, in her weakness, clutched at her ministering hand. "You mean you have really sent for him?"

"Not I, dear lady, the Lord Chancellor—who should have sent long ago, but that those who have no wish for a Catholic Queen minimized the nature of your sickness."

"His courier should have reached Newmarket two days ago," encouraged Lettice Ormonde, "and my husband calculates that with good relays of horses his Majesty's coach could arrive here by tomorrow morning."

Catherine turned her head away sadly. "I doubt if I can last so long," she murmured, swooning away from very weakness. When she regained consciousness her room was crowded again, and hot with candlelight.

If only all these well meaning people would leave her in peace to lie a while with her burning hand in old Maria's cool one, Maria's loving hand, which she could imagine was her mother's. If only they would stop suffocating her with incense. If only someone would bring a glass of ice cold water. Or open a casement. . . .

Once she roused herself to ask weakly for Father Huddleston. His presence would be comforting, she thought, if one must come to die. And perhaps he might even persuade her own priests to stop the dizzy swaying of the censers. But either they were jealous of their English colleagues or they could not make out what she asked for. And she was utterly in their hands, James being at sea, the Queen Mother on a visit in the country and all the Court except Clarendon away with Charles.

To make matters worse, her own beloved doctor began to quarrel with the priests, saying that the crisis was not yet, that if only the Queen could hold her own until dawn there was yet hope; while they, on their side, argued that since her Majesty had kissed the sacred reliquary they had brought and it had not cured her, nothing remained for her but to receive extreme unction.

But although she appeared to be unconscious Catherine had caught da Sousa's words. If only she could hold onto the thin thread of life a little longer she might see Charles. If only she could struggle on until morning. . . .

But there was no need.

Before midnight there was a great stir outside her door. Above the unending sibilant murmuring of prayers came the dull thud of hurrying footsteps and the sharp clang of sentries' saluting. Even in the strange, lonely borderland in which she tarried Catherine was aware of it, and some faint flicker of revival began to stir in her.

Her door was flung wide and it seemed that the dense fog of people was dispersing. She was not really aware of the amazed murmur that went up because the King had come so soon, nor of his flecked spurs and bespattered appearance. But had she been halfway through the gates of eternity she would have recognized his voice. He was striding towards her bed as he had that first day at Portsmouth, but with far more urgency, and she made a pathetic little gesture sketching her desire to be rid of all else.

"I know, my heart. Even a dog is allowed decent privacy when he is sick!" he was saying, in the tender, practical way of his. His strong arms were raising her so that she could breathe more easily; her wavering heart beats were steadied by his warmth. How reassuring the outdoor, masculine smell of him—heather and sweat and saddle leather—close beneath her cheek! Catherine clutched at him with all the strength left in her wasted fingers, and the awesome mystery of eternity receded, leaving her sentient in his arms.

"Take away all those hideous phials, my good da Sousa," he was ordering reasonably. "Lady Suffolk and I will see to her, with Lady Ormonde here and our little Portuguese countess. Where is young Richard Bellings? Tell the servants to throw more logs on the fire, Dick, and open a window." When the pious foreigners still pressed anxiously about her he rose from the bed, shooing them before him. "Take away your reliquary, my lord Abbot. And get out, all of you!" he cried with concentrated fury. "You have well nigh killed her between you with your cuppings and your wailings. Get out, I say!"

"But—if her Majesty should die without ghostly comfort?" ventured her devoted almoner.

"She is not *going* to die!" Charles told him, and since he was King in this mad Protestant country, they must all needs obey him. In the blessed silence that followed, the first breath of fresh air which she had felt for days fanned Catherine's poor, disfigured face. "The wind on the heath," she whispered, with eyes still closed but cracked lips curving into the painful vestige of a smile.

All night long Charles, who had been in the saddle for the best part of two days, kept at bay those who would have pestered her with experimental remedies. No one but her very own must touch her. The most homely, intimate tasks of the sick room were neither beyond nor beneath him. With his own hand he spooned fresh juice from Dutch oranges into her parched mouth and helped the women to keep her body sponged and the sheets cool and changed. In her unattractiveness he cared for her pitifully, as he might have done for a comrade wounded on the field. It was common sense against leechcraft and, although the risk he took upon himself was enormous, common sense won.

As dawn broke over the City wharves beyond the Bridge, Catherine's lashes fluttered open and she looked at him, at his drawn, unshaven face, at the stained lace ruffs of his shirt sleeves and at his disheveled hair. "It is tomorrow. And you have been with me all night," she said, on a long, contented sigh.

"It is today and you are going to live," he told her.

"But they told me that your coach——"

He had to bend down closer to hear her, and as he braced himself to do so she reached out to touch his arm, her hand traveling up and down it in a satisfied caress. Her sunken eyes grew bright as stars. "Charles, you *rode* all the way—alone!"

"None of them could keep up with me," he grinned, almost apologetically. "Old Ned will probably have apoplexy when he hears of it!"

And then, because he had cared so much more than he had supposed, and because both of them were utterly exhausted, the slow, hard tears welled into those indolent, inscrutable eyes of his. For once in his life his emotional guard was down. "That you should always suffer from my selfishness, my bestial habits of self-indulgence—" he muttered, hiding his face against the thinness of her wasted breasts. Forgiving, mothering him, Catherine stroked his bent head, so dark against the whiteness of her night-gown. And alone, in the peace of early morning, they clung together weeping.

"I tried to live until you came," Catherine whispered at last, still not understanding how he had come so soon. "Lettice said that if Clarendon's messenger——"

"If I had waited for *that* laggard old fool," scoffed Charles equally incoherently, blowing his nose and pulling himself together. "But the lad John Huddleston sent chanced to meet me taking my early morning gallop. Most of the others were still abed, and it would have meant endless delays if I'd gone back to my lodgings. I'd a good horse under me and the road to London ahead. So I did not stop to look back any more than I did after Worcester!" He began to laugh softly, picturing for the first time the astonishment that must have stricken the few men who had happened to be with him on Newmarket heath that wet and windy morning.

"So it was Father Huddleston, may God reward him! . . .

And you missed most of the races after all. . . ." Catherine wanted to tell Charles that he must go now and take a bath and eat and sleep his fill because she was deliciously better and outrageously happy. But instead she drifted off to sleep.

All the same, when she saw him again he looked refreshed and suave and well groomed, as his subjects expected him to look.

"Two kings have come to wait upon your Majesty this morning," he teased. "This one kissing your hand is your loving husband, and the cleverer looking man in spectacles on the other side of the bed is Edmund King, his personal physician, very much at your service."

But Catherine's temperature had risen again, and in consequence she addressed herself to the more learned of the two. "How are the children this morning?" she enquired politely. And while poor Doctor King stood tongue-tied and all present exchanged appalled glances, she turned her head drowsily on the pillow again and added proudly, "God has been very good to us, Charles. We have a boy and a girl."

"Then you must be vastly cleverer than either of us!" improvised Charles, quick to humor her.

Doctor King felt her bounding pulse while Charles and Lady Suffolk, counting, compared it with their own. "Perhaps I should not have come upon her so suddenly last night, King," Charles reproached himself.

"By what they tell me, your Majesty came only just in time."

"Yet now she is wandering in her wits again."

"But the crisis is past I do assure you, Sir. A fever of this kind, coupled with her Majesty's condition at the time, may well recur intermittently for days; and learning of her disappointed hopes must have been a great shock to the mind. In my opinion, Sir, her Majesty should not have been told until the fever had abated."

"Early this morning she was overwhelmed and wept," vouchsafed Charles, though he knew well enough that her tears, like his own, had been the outcome of long tension and relief.

"As to that, Sir, the weeping may have eased her," King

assured him, "for it must have carried away some of the rheum from the head."

And certainly when Catherine roused again, although she was still lightheaded, she seemed to be living in a happy world of fantasy where only one thing worried her. "The boy, Charles," she whispered anxiously. "I am sorry for your sake that he is so ugly."

"Ugly!" refuted Charles stoutly. "You do but confuse his looks with what Mam used to say about mine. He is a fine boy, Kate."

"And like you?"

That was almost too much for him. "If only it were so!" was all that he could think, demanding of God why this ultimate joy, like so many lesser ones, must be snatched from him. But with working face he managed to mumble some kind of assent.

"Charles the Third," murmured Catherine, unaware in her weakness of the hollow jest she offered him in speaking the very words which could have altered his whole life and given his reign and restoration strength.

With healing sleep the fever and the rash abated. Slowly she grew stronger. Gradually the bitter realization that there were no children became an accepted fact in her mind and in her life, albeit a fact of which she seldom spoke. Where Charles had feared lamentations, he found himself respecting her reticence. And because he shared her suffering and knew so much of hope defeated he seemed, during those first dark days, to be always in her rooms. Shone the sun never so brightly on the sleighing in Hyde Park, on the grassy rides at Windsor, or on his new pall-mall court between Whitehall and St. James's, the King's prowess and wit were wanting there until all was well with his barren little Portuguese wife. "I must write and tell Minette that you are sufficiently recovered to watch a Court ball with me," he would say, hurrying away to his *cabinet de travail* to catch the Paris mail. Or would take her out driving in Hyde Park or to watch the orphan children at Christ's Hospital in Newgate Street at their lessons and help her pick out some of the brighter boys for his project of providing properly trained officers for his navy.

One day when it was too wet for Catherine to go out he

brought young Jemmie to cheer her, hoping that graver issues might have burned out all but her liking for the lad; and although the first sight of him, radiating Stuart charm, was as gall and wormwood to her, the irrepressible Mr. Crofts himself soon quite unwittingly put the matter right. For when Abbot Aubigny, congratulating the Queen upon her recovery, claimed that it was kissing the holy saint's bones that had cured her, Jemmie—unable to contain himself—contradicted him, red-faced and roundly. "An' it please your Grace, 't was no reliquary, but the King. Seventy miles he rode in ten hours, and most of it on borrowed nags!"

Charles burst out laughing and clapped an arm about his shoulders. And—Catholic though she was—Catherine could not but love the lad for it; all the more so when, under his father's amused eyes, he installed himself beside her chair to entertain her with a vivid description of the splendid thanksgiving service which had been held for her recovery in St. Paul's. "And there was his Majesty beating time to the music with his prayer book and looking so mighty pleased that all men observed it," Jemmie told her eagerly.

CHAPTER ELEVEN

*M*ighty pleased the King was, although his wife's failure to produce a Protestant heir had plunged him deeper into a sea of political troubles from which James's open adherence to the Church of Rome did not help him to emerge.

But for the moment, knowing her to be out of danger, he was pleased, too, to be free from sickrooms and swooning and to enjoy his own life of varied interests and to see his ships again. Every day in all kinds of weather he went down the Thames to the Nore or round through the Straits to Spithead, reviewing his fleet, discussing with James and his other admirals the range of guns whose wicked muzzles would soon be belching fire, talking to Pepys about shot and victualing, insisting that all foreign shipping in the Channel must dip pennants to his own. For war it was to be, war against the hardy Dutch.

"There is such rivalry that it is they or us, and it is my endeavor to make my country the most prosperous in the world," he wrote to his sister in Paris. "This place New York which we have just taken from them is a town of great importance to trade; and now my good Robert Holmes has beaten them out of their very castles in Guinea, which pleases me inordinately; though what I shall say to the Dutch ambassador God knows! 'Tis too late for aught but a salvo of broadsides. So it behooves you, *ma chère* Minette, as a good Exeter-born woman, to keep Louis neutral! Though if I be forced to war I stand ready with as good ships and men as ever were seen, and leave the success to God."

And before the fleet sailed, knowing his wife's passionate interest in seafaring matters, he sent for her and his mother to come aboard, and enjoyed himself hugely showing them over the *Royal Charles* and impressing the French ambassador with the efficiency of the British navy so as to leave him with no doubt as to which side it would be safer for Louis to be on. There were high spirits throughout the flagship, and over wine and laughter in the wardroom one of James's irrepressible young officers read aloud to the Queen his ditty to sweethearts left behind.

> *"To all you ladies now on land*
> *We men at sea indite;*
> *But first would have you understand*
> *How hard it is to write. . . .*
> *Our paper, pen and ink and we*
> *Roll up and down our ships at sea. . . ."*

And then there was hilarious betting as to when and where the Dutch admiral, Opdam, would put out to sea. It was a cloudless day for Catherine even if her indefatigable husband did catch a well deserved chill through leaving off his wig and waistcoat in the May heat; and she was particularly pleased because the pompous little ambassador was seasick and she was not.

But her happiness was always precarious. She saw little of Charles these days, and missed him sadly. Because of the hectic anticipation of war, whenever he was at leisure he seemed to be engaged in some sport or other, or supping with Barbara Castlemaine again although everyone knew she had a new lover, or at the Duke's playhouse or his own. And on the few occasions when Catherine had pestered him to take her thither she was honest enough to show her distaste for William Wycherley's lewd plays, and too unsophisticated not to be shocked at the sight of brazen young women flaunting their comely legs in jigs before all the company. "A prim little convent bred kill-joy," dissolute beauties whispered behind the fluttering fans which she herself had made fashionable. And poor Catherine was utterly wretched, hating the easy way her husband sat there among them all, laughing with the rest at ribald jokes, obviously adored for it by the populace

and allowing women of doubtful reputation to lean across to
speak to him in the royal box.

"They are all so gay and thoughtless; and that is how he likes
women," she thought. "So I must try to be more gay." But how,
when one was often tired and felt so accountable to God?

Back in the palace against a background of careless chatter,
she patted her thinning hair to rights before a Cupid-wreathed
mirror. Horrified by her own pallor, she leaned forward to peer
more deeply. Illness had certainly taken its toll. The eager fresh-
ness of youth had gone from her eyes, and through building up
her strength with rest and nourishment she was putting on weight
which did not suit her *petite* figure. "My hair has been coming out
in handfuls!" she cried out involuntarily.

Softened from displeasure by her distress, Charles came and
stood behind her, his eyes, sleepy and bantering, meeting hers
in the glass which reflected all the rich treasures of his room.
"Your poor lovely hair," he sympathized, lifting a strand to kiss.
But instead of springing instantly round his finger—"making him
love's prisoner" as he used to say—it lay lank and lifeless across
his palm. Reason enough, perhaps, for his beginning to neglect
her again. That, and the difficulty she found in suppressing a
convalescent's irritability.

"I shall have it all cut short and curled up close round my head
like a play actress," she declared, jerking it from him. "Then
perhaps you will come and sleep with me sometimes!"

But it seemed impossible to provoke him. Could it be that, in
spite of his tears so short a while ago, he did not really care?
In his kindness was he just making allowances for her? Or was
it simply that he was so accustomed to women's jealousy?

"You will never look like an actress, my Catalina, however
hard you try," he told her imperturbably. "And look at my own
hair! If it is of any comfort to you, people say that since your
illness I am going gray."

Removing his wig, he bent his head accommodatingly so that
she might see; and instantly she was pressing against him, smoothing it tenderly with both hands. "Oh, beloved, forgive me! How

could I speak to you so, who did so much for me? And be so intent upon getting well that I did not even notice?" With one of her quick, southern movements she stood back the better to behold it. "But it is distinguished and adorable, your hair! And even if there is a sprinkling of gray at either temple, I shall always remember that it grew that way through anxiety for me."

"Not entirely," he confessed dryly, and stood there petting her absently, thinking of a hundred and one worries which beset him and of which she was blessedly ignorant, until James came to remind him that Sir John Evelyn was waiting upon him to make arrangements for the reception of the wounded.

As he moved across the room, Catherine stood looking anxiously after him. "Do you think that he has aged?" she asked her brother-in-law.

"Aged? Charles? Strong as a horse! Always has been," answered James bluntly, his mind full of how he would catch Opdam with the wind against him off the Texel.

"But he caught that chill and has some gray hairs at thirty-five," persisted Catherine, her own more serious ailments forgotten.

"And small wonder, what with squeezing money out of the Commons for equipment, Castlemaine's tantrums and this nasty business Buckingham and Bristol are hatching!"

"What business?" inquired Catherine, taken aback by his tactlessness.

"Oh, there is nothing they can do," he told her with uneasy evasiveness. "But they are all mighty concerned because there is no Protestant heir to put us Catholics out of the running."

Though what could be their disappointment, Catherine wondered, compared with Charles's and her own? But she must try not to meddle as Henrietta Maria had done. So instead of pursuing the subject she bade James be seated and asked perfunctorily after his Duchess.

"She is far from well, Catherine. The doctors are anxious about her."

"I am sorry, James. Has she taken to her bed?"

"No. She has great determination of character, as you know. I am but now come from St. James's and left her and my two small girls and Jemmie sitting on cushions on the floor playing 'I love my love with an A' or some such foolish game." His face softened at recollection of the domestic picture, for, after all, his marriage had turned out well. But there was something of more pressing importance to speak of. "Anne says that nephew Jemmie is getting spoiled," he said grimly.

"It is not good for him to be always at Charles's heels. He goes everywhere with him now," agreed Catherine.

Looking up from beneath knitted brows James saw his brother and Sir John Evelyn approaching, but before rising he leaned forward and laid a long spatulate finger on her knee. "It is not good for us either," he warned. "As Catholics we are both in the same boat."

Catherine had no opportunity of asking him what he meant, but when she remonstrated with Charles in private about his spoiling the boy she began to understand that the Yorks' resentment was not without foundation. "We must get him married, though no doubt you think marriage has done little to improve me!" he laughed indolently.

"But he is barely sixteen," she said, ignoring the jibe.

"And the bride I have chosen for him is less."

"You have already chosen one? And pray who is she?" bridled Catherine, feeling that at least she might have been told.

Charles wandered to the fireplace and picked up one of his spaniels, fondling her long silky ears. "That charming Buccleuch child who outdanced us all at the masked ball."

"You mean the little Countess Anne who is in my household?"

Charles nodded. "I have heard from Lady Wymess, her mother, and am arranging for them to be married in the chapel at Windsor when we are there for St. George's Day," he told her, a thought too casually because he was also arranging that Jemmie be made a Knight of the Garter.

"But they are no more than children!"

"Probably neither of them is such a little innocent as you were," grinned Charles.

"In years, I mean," she replied with dignity, avoiding his mocking eyes. "In the name of the Blessed Mother, surely you will not let them——"

"Oddsfish, what do you take me for, Kate? Of course, she shall go home to her people once we have seen them bedded—with her nightshift sewn round the edges if you like! My lusty young cub can learn to wait—like his betters!" There was an edge to her husband's voice to which Catherine had not the clue. But he went on stroking the goggle-eyed little dog in the crook of his arm, and added negligently enough, " 'T is a good match for a bastard. And I love the boy."

"That is evident to all the world," retorted Catherine, at her tartest. "But is it a good match for the Buccleuchs? They are a rich family, I understand, and proud."

"Not so proud as to object to a dukedom," Charles assured her cynically. "If they provide the cash, all the more reason why I should behave handsomely about a title, and I propose to make Jemmie Duke of Monmouth."

Catherine felt anger, hot and uncontrollable, rising within her. "The equal of your brothers!" she cried.

"By no means," countered Charles calmly. "You are ignorant of our topography. Monmouth is a Welsh title."

"As Castlemaine is Irish? So that is what you give your by-blow families." It was so infuriating that what to her seemed monstrous left him, by reason of the habits of his associates and upbringing, without apparent shame.

"It is all that I can give them," he shrugged. "Clarendon and parliament and all manner of legalities would have to be invoked to give them English titles."

"Then Clarendon is against this match," declared Catherine shrewdly, driven by a foreboding of she knew not what and wondering if she could induce him to interfere.

"Ned becomes more of a doddering old nuisance every day. It is time he gave over the reins."

"Oh, Charles, how can you! When he has served you so long and faithfully."

"No one can say of me that I forget my friends. He would have been thrown out long ago had I not stood by him and borne with his intolerable diatribes." Nettled at last, he set down his dog, preparing to depart. "But there comes a time when every man, if he live long enough, grows past his task. I pray that I shall not live long enough for that to happen to me."

With whatever good cause she might resent the honors heaped upon her consort's bastard, Catherine found it impossible to bear personal animosity towards Jemmie himself. That very evening she was dancing with him as usual. She adored this new liberty of English dancing, and Jemmie was almost as expert as his father, and as good-natured about teaching her the latest steps. And so Charles found them, leading the *coranto,* when he returned to the Long Gallery from a council meeting.

When all the company would have stopped, he called to them to finish the movement, and stood watching with Buckingham, Shaftesbury and other councilors grouped about him. And coming suddenly upon his son leading that galaxy of elegance, so tall and gallant of bearing, so gravely conscious of the honor of partnering the Queen, an overmastering wave of mingled pride and frustration must have risen in him. "Bravo! Bravo!" he cried, the moment the music stopped; and when "young Mr. Crofts" swept his hat across his heart and then almost to the ground in the most modish of French bows, Charles strode across the floor to the attractive couple and, with an approving hand on his wife's shoulder, before all that bareheaded company, took the beplumed hat and playfully yet deliberately placed it on the lad's handsome head.

Catherine heard the gasp of amazement that rose all round them like a rustle of silk. Allowing Jemmie to be covered in their presence was tantamount to acknowledging him one of the family. Thrilled yet discomfited, the boy himself flushed to the brow, while she felt the smile freeze on her lips, the blood drain from her cheeks. Across her young partner's shoulder she could see the smirking, meaningful glances exchanged between the members of Buckingham's party in the doorway, and close to her the warm happiness of Charles. Though she felt as affronted as though he had struck her she managed to control herself and made no scene, even dancing with him civilly when he asked her.

"A year ago I could not have done it," she thought, passing with chin well up between the ranks of her enemies when the dancing was done. And back in her chapel she fell on her knees to thank God for that measure of grace. "I begin to be a person —self-contained and inviolate."

But she congratulated herself too soon; her own particular devil of hastiness was not yet mastered. For after the crazy act of the King's who could stop the whispering campaign that, since the Queen appeared to be barren, he meant to make Jemmie his heir? Or be surprised at the Londoners for seizing on so choice a morsel of gossip? Or blame the boy himself if, inflamed by Shaftesbury's subtle hints, he began to pretend—perhaps even to believe—that his unremembered mother had been married to the King? Strutting from his chambers in the Cockpit like a bantam, he offered to split with his scarcely flashed sword any man who dared to deny it.

Although all sober citizens laughed at him, so furious was Catherine when she heard of it that she went straight to her husband's apartments, spurning all Chaffinch's frenzied attempts to announce her, and invaded the King's private little work room where no one else dared to disturb him.

"You have heard what is being said since you taught your bastard to wear his hat in our presence?" she demanded, closing the door sharply against the sharp ears of the groom of the back stairs and leaning breathlessly against it.

The King had swung round with an angry reprimand but, seeing who it was, laid down his pen. That he appeared to be writing one of his constant letters to Minette somehow enraged her all the more. "I am sorry, my dear. I had not meant to insult you," he apologized, with an obvious effort at patience. "The young fool shall be taught to hold his tongue. But it is largely the work of his elders, building to suit themselves upon an idle gesture. I know who my enemies are."

Catherine came closer, but his half-finished letter in French which lay unintelligibly before her seemed to shut her out still more. "Who was his mother? After what they are saying I have a right to know."

Charles did not question it, but sat staring straight before him as if looking back into the dubious past. "Lucy Walter, a Welsh woman of extraordinary beauty," he said quietly. "Robert Sydney and a Dutch colonel had her first and I know not how many afterwards." He did not add that in exile, torn from the duties of his birthright, there had been little else to do.

"I begin to understand," said Catherine, after a moment or two, "how it is that you find any chaste woman dull."

Charles had the grace to redden angrily. Her contempt, untempered for once by any extenuating tenderness, was hard to bear. Unconscious of what she did, she bent to retrieve his fallen pen and stood before his table tearing at the gray goose feathers. "How would you feel if I openly started an *amour* with that poet, Waller, who wrote verses to the beauty of my eyes?" she blurted out recklessly. "Or with Ralph Montagu, my master of the horse, whom all my ladies tease for being so hopelessly in love with me? Or do I flatter myself, perhaps? Would you not even care?"

It was a new outlook for Charles, who had supposed her to be occupied with good works and prayers except when she made herself gay for him. And Catherine's voice, even in anger, was as beautiful as her eyes, not shrill, like most of the feminine voices which railed at him. "If your master of the horse is in love with you he will have to be removed," he said sullenly.

"But *why* is it different?" cried Catherine, defying all convention in the obstinate flame of her goodness.

He swung round then and rose to face her. He seemed to tower over her. "Because you are my wife," he stormed. "Because. . . ." But suddenly those stern lines of his face broke into a disarming smile and his hands were raised to high heaven in exasperation. "Because you are you," he added lamely, unable to explain either to her or to himself why the thought of her sullied with intrigue was so unbearable.

In any calmer moment Catherine would have recognized that as a triumph, but she was beyond all blandishments. "If you are set on this marriage, if you must honor Jemmie publicly as your firstborn, then I will not come to Windsor and stand by and see it," she cried shrewishly.

"You are free to do as you please," sighed Charles, opening the door for her and then trying unhappily to collect his thoughts again in time to catch the Paris mail.

But Catherine knew that if she did not go to Jemmie's wedding her husband would take Barbara, utterly wearied of her though he might be. Tired, disillusioned old Ned Hyde knew it too. "In this dangerous mood the King is capable of outraging public opinion, of antagonizing the whole nation," he came to tell her. "So I beseech your Majesty to accompany him. Even if he now takes Lady Castlemaine with him, it will still their tongues."

"Why must one give countenance to things which one knows to be wrong, swallow one's indignation, bear this and that indignity for the sake of expediency?"

It was the old argument, and in his heart Edward Hyde appreciated her attitude all too well. For a few moments he forgot to be the Chancellor of England and sat easing his tired body in the chair she had had set for him. "Because we all love him, I suppose," he sighed gustily, with the beginnings of a reminiscent smile creasing the red puffiness of his cheeks.

"You still love him?" Catherine could not forbear to ask.

He looked up then and smiled outright, albeit sadly, so that she knew what a steady comfort he must have been in trouble. "Yes, Madame. Even though Shaftesbury and the rest, who covet my place, persuade him to send me away."

For a long while after he was gone Catherine sat over the fire struggling with her conscience. The part of her that loved so passionately longed to ease and "gloss over" as he advised, but her integrity was too strict to allow her to retract. Finally she sent for Father Huddleston, feeling instinctively that he must know

Charles—and perhaps, God—better than any of them. "I have prayed and prayed, my father," she said. "But how *can* it be right to condone in the King what we know to be wrong?"

John Huddleston's smile was in itself a healing. "We can at least be careful not to cast the first stone," he suggested.

"But if he seeks to make Jemmie Crofts his heir it is a great wrong to me, to the Duke and to the country."

"But does he? Or is it only what envious men say?"

"Then you do not believe——"

"Madame, this dangerous mood—as you say the Lord Chancellor calls it—may be a recklessness of disappointment. A man has not the outlet of tears that women have."

"Yet he would supplant my unborn baby, so soon, lend so ready an ear to those who say there will be no others."

"Perhaps it is not only that. I was with him when his young brother, the Duke of Gloucester, died. Suddenly, like the snapping off of a spring branch. For days the King was dumb with grief. Then at last he turned to me, who am always waiting. 'Why? Why?' he kept saying. 'When at last I could do something for him and all those unspeakable years of exile were over—and all his laughing, gallant life before him?' Nothing has ever filled Henry of Gloucester's place. But you and I know how the King loves young things; and when Jemmie Crofts came, so similar in promise——"

"And bone of his bone. How wise was milord Clarendon to oppose it," sighed Catherine. "But I begin to see something of the tantalizing agony it must have been for Charles—to have him so beautiful, and a bastard."

"For that sin God has indeed given him his punishment in this world!"

"And you believe that he intends no more than to enjoy and honor the boy?"

"I believe that he would not put him before his brother. Whatever their faults the Stuarts are incredibly loyal to each other."

"You should know. Are you aware, Father, that some tatlers

say you are in secret his confessor and that that is why he keeps you about him when all other priests are prohibited?"

"Would that I were!" Huddleston's strong, tender mouth curved to laughter. "God knows I am unworthy of his dear, ridiculous sense of gratitude, which is the real reason!"

"But you wait—with prayer?"

"Until he shall need me."

Huddleston's quiet confidence watered the seed of hope in her heart. With swift, childlike grace she knelt to receive his benediction. "My prayers join daily with your own," she whispered.

Upheld by his words she went to Windsor and took part in the marriage festivities of her husband's son and bore the liberties of his erstwhile mistress with gentle dignity; and on her return to Whitehall she reaped her reward. Late one evening the King sent for her and to her amazement she found several of his councilors present. It was seldom that he discussed business before women, and immediately she was aware of the tense atmosphere in the room.

"M'lord Bristol here and these other of my loyal subjects appear to have found sudden reason to be concerned about the popish form of marriage we went through upon your arrival in this country, Catherine, and I would have them hear your word on it," he explained, leading her to a chair although he himself chose to face them standing.

"Your Majesty did so solely out of consideration for my peace of mind," she answered, defensive as a tiger.

"You hear, gentlemen?" Charles held some papers in his hand to which he referred contemptuously. "In the indictment they are bringing against m'lord Clarendon they have it that among other enormities he brought us together without any settled agreement as to marriage rites, and that out of bigotry you refused to be married by a Protestant priest. Therefore, they maintain, either our marriage is void or I am exposed to a suspicion of being married in my own dominions by a Romish priest."

"But the Bishop of London performed the Anglican ceremony the very next day at Portsmouth, and I have my women to witness that I lay virgin until then," answered Catherine, quick to appreciate the danger of the situation if Charles should be a party to their wiles.

But Charles was white with anger, angrier than she had ever seen him. He rang for a clerk and had a copy of their marriage lines laid upon the table for all to see. If these intriguers had thought to please him by offering him escape from her to pleasanter pastures, or to push him into alliance with a more prolific queen, they had been completely duped by his neglectful dalliance. Even she, who loved him, had known little of the inner man and his few rigid principles until that hour.

"If this is what you have been concocting over Barbara's supper table, I will never see the treacherous jade again!" he swore. "And because I must needs put up with your prating in council do not imagine for one moment that I will suffer any one of you to meddle in my private affairs. Or in those of my wife. I have brought her Majesty here that you may hear the truth from her uncorruptible lips and that you may humbly beg pardon of her as best you may. Arlington. Coventry. Yes, and you too, George Villiers. There are cheap villainies at which even my easy friendship vomits. And as for you, m'lord Bristol, who had my brother's word that he had witnessed my marriage, take yourself out of our sight and away from Whitehall unless you would have better acquaintance with the Tower!"

Catherine's heart was lifted up in gratitude. All that spring she walked serenely through life, asking nothing of her husband, seeing little of him, but knowing a new contentment. And mingling with her own quiet happiness came the delirious news of victory, James's victory over the Dutch, whose navy he had intercepted off the east coast. Twenty ships he and Charles's sailors had sent to the bottom ere ever their guns came within range of England, and after four days' courageous fighting the redoubtable Admiral Opdam had been blown to the night sky in his flagship. If, man for man, the sailors of Dutch merchantmen had no equals, still the team work of England's trained navy, for which the King and humbler men like Samuel Pepys had worked so hard, eventually told. James was the hero of the hour, and Charles, who had provided the ships partly out of his own pocket, was the popular protector of his people.

As Catherine rode beside him to give thanks at St. Paul's, that seemingly indestructible stone heart of London, the tears that stood in her eyes were as much for the people's love for him as for their victory. Everywhere they cheered and pressed about the two tall royal brothers, and it mattered not to them in those days of national emergency whether James went to Mass or not. Furniture was thrown from the windows of wealthy merchants, to blaze their fierce relief in bonfires, and within the City walls bells rocked half a hundred steeples.

Yet even as the triumphal procession passed along Cheapside and through Ludgate, resplendent in silks and jewels and velvets, with gleaming horse trappings and fanfares of trumpets, a greater enemy came creeping—silent, unsuspected and unseen—along narrow alleys and stinking, back-street gutters and from the crowded hovels of the poor crouching in unplanned confusion outside the City's boundaries, an enemy which neither Charles's forethought nor James's courage nor all the power of Britannia's vaunted trident could stay.

It was a hot and airless summer. Samuel Pepys quarreled violently with a neighbor whose refuse overflowed from his cellar into Pepys's own. The Fleet ditch and Wallbrook, stagnant beneath a blazing sun, discharged their filth into a glassy Thames. And before the roses in Temple gardens had begun to bloom—almost before the shouts of victory were still—the plague had struck at London with a scourge more terrible than any war.

CHAPTER TWELVE

*I*f only the King would come," was the burden of Catherine's conversation throughout the beginning of that summer. He had sent her and all the other women away to safety at Hampton; and although she walked out through the gatehouse every evening to scan the London road, or rode into Kingston in the hope of meeting him, she slept alone half-crazy with anxiety. For plague or no plague, he had a world of other things to see to.

First he must take his mother down to the Nore and see her safely embarked for France, and then there was a plethora of public business to transact: negotiations with Louis to keep France out of the war, trouble with Ireland in which Charles strove as usual for tolerance, hurried conferences with John Evelyn about preparations for wounded, and heartening visits to the naval dockyards with the invaluable Pepys at his elbow and the new young Duke of Monmouth clambering over all manner of deck tackle to talk with the crews about their guns.

But Catherine knew that Charles was often sitting at stuffy meetings while the plague raged outside, reaching right up King Street to the palace doors, that every day more infected houses were sealed with a cross upon their doors, that all night the plague carts creaked through deserted streets collecting corpses, and that instead of pealing for victory the bells in London steeples were tolling mournfully for her dead. And that Charles, wherever he went, would be sure to rein in his horse in that pestilential air to shout up to the victims' windows in that human way of his, asking how they did and promising—and probably paying for—whatever help was possible.

She was thankful when she heard that he was at sea again, meeting his favorite admiral, Holmes, and listening enthralled to his tales of how he had harried the Dutch coast; and that from Spithead they were gone together to inspect the defences of the Wight—that small, vulnerable island lying like a footstool at the foot of England, between the Dutch and the roadsteads of Portsmouth and Southampton.

But during the long summer evenings, listless after each stifling anxious day, her ladies would talk in whispers of fresh horrors culled from the outside world, their faces white with fears they were ashamed to voice. For not one of them had a nettle rash or a migraine those days without beginning to imagine she had the plague. All eyed each other with suspicion, even at Hampton. For were there not infected farmsteads a few miles away at Esher with cattle being destroyed and soldiers set on guard? And was not the terrible Thing spreading its talons further and further out from the metropolis to country towns?

Unlike most of the others, Catherine and Donna Penelva had never experienced even the usual cloud of anxiety that hot summers brought, and the very strangeness of the scourge frightened them. Inevitably Catherine kept recalling how two Stuarts had already been taken by some such contagion. "Snapped off like a spring branch," Father Huddleston had said. And the last courier from Whitehall had brought her a hurried letter from Charles, making kind inquiries after her health—*her* health, when he was already back again in London.

With the letter still in her hand, since she intended to reread it in the cool of the privy garden, she paused behind a group of women huddled on the great wide stairs leading down from banqueting hall to courtyard. They had loosened the departing courier's tongue with potent Rhenish and so wrapped in horror were they that they did not even hear her approach; they heard nothing but the man's voice as it played upon their tensed emotions. And if he, for his part, enjoyed seeing carefully dressed girls again and scarifying a country audience, surely any man who endured London merited so small a compensation.

"You are better off here than there, with not a boat to be seen on the river and the grass growing in Whitehall courtyard. More than two thousand dead this week," he bragged, setting his empty tankard down on the step where he was resting while his horse was being rubbed down, and winking at the inquisitive buttery maid who replenished it. "And what do they do with 'em, you ask? Bury 'em? When every city cemetery was full and over-flowing weeks ago! Shrive 'em? That's a good'un, my pretty chuck. With not enough priests to go round! No, mistress," he answered a more serious woman of the Queen's wardrobe, "there's no holy oil or bell brought any more. Even the church bells don't toll now, for the reason that there's no one left with strength to pull the ropes. 'T is no wonder the Puritans hold up their hands and call it God's vengeance for a whoring Court and some of the graybeards turn back to the old religion and start telling their beads! But half the preachers, be they Romish, Anglican or Dissenters, are either dead or fled."

"With neither priests nor graveyards—then what happens to the —poor dead?" quavered a very young girl's voice out of the gloom.

Over their huddled heads, outlined against the evening sky, Catherine could see the King's messenger stretching out his dusty riding boots and taking another thirsty swig. Obviously he needed it, for in spite of all his braggadocio his hand shook. Noting his thinness and his sense of the dramatic, it occurred to her that it would have been like Charles to give the errand to one of the hungry small part actors from his long closed playhouse.

"Ah, where indeed!" he echoed. "In spite of all the carts that go the rounds at night, I warrant there's many a dead family left stinking behind those sealed doors, all taken within the hour, as you might say, and their neighbors none the wiser. Or, worse still, some poor stricken soul who survived the rest of his household by a day or two, doing what he could for each of them, and now sealed up in his own house knowing that when next the dreaded cry 'Bring out your dead' comes down the street there will be no one to push *his* poor stiffened corpse through the cobwebbed

window. Only the bulging rats come up from the Fleet ditch to
do the grave-diggers' work."

"But the dead that are on the carts? What do they do with
them?"

"Better not to know," the man muttered.

But urged by mass curiosity he took up his tale again and Catherine, still with horror on the stairs above them, stayed to hear.
"Well, since you must know, I saw them at it three nights ago, and,
God help me, I've seen 'em ever since!" The glib voice dragged
with reluctance. All effort at dramatization was gone. "Great pits
they've dug. Anyone helps who can hold a spade. Men from the
deserted Customs docks, out-of-work stall keepers, servants from
the nobility's shuttered houses. Digging all day—shoveling in
lime. At Bunhill Fields, Stepney and out at St. John's Wood. I
followed a cart from Paternoster Row and watched. A mist rising
from the river, there was, so that even the horse looked like a half-
shrouded ghost. The cart was piled so high with corpses that two
of them dropped off as they jolted over the cobbles. There were
flares burning all round the great yawning pit, and I saw the man
who was leading the horse back him as far as he durst and tip the
cart; and as the top ones tumbled in, with legs and arms sticking
up stiffly to heaven, the other fellow, with a scarf over his mouth
and a long pitchfork scraped and shoveled the more laggard of
his cargo in. You could hear the thud and settling together of
shroudless bodies. And then the two of them hurried away into
the night to finish their ghastly work. . . . God knows who
pays 'em, or how much it takes to tempt them to it! All I know is
that all the gold of Indies would not make me look upon the like
again. . . ."

The man shivered where he sat, hands between knees, tankard
and audience alike forgotten. The fine braggart voice had dwindled to a toneless monologue, speaking out of some hideous
dream—a dream which mirrored the unbelievable reality. His
mind was no longer in the pleasant precincts of Hampton, but
had already preceded him into the city of horror to which he must
return.

During those fearful days Catherine learned to be grateful for Frances Stuart's frivolous gaiety. Although some rebuked her, there seemed to be a new gallantry about it, as though she indeed represented a defiant and inviolate Britannia. She was a Stuart and unafraid. Her smooth, childish face was taking on a new gentleness, and her scatterbrained youth developing some personality.

By the end of the month the death roll had risen to seventy thousand and London, once so full of chaffering and merriment, was become a city of the dead. It seemed useless to try to carry on the government of a country at war from a place where the very ferrymen refused to carry fares from suspect landing places and where indomitable little Pepys, hurrying from one duty to another, found his hackney coach slowing to a halt and his driver dead or dying upon the box. And so at last Charles came with a great train of baggage to fetch his queen and all her ladies, and moved the entire Court to Oxford.

"My poor people are in so grievous a state that they firmly believe the new comet to be the vision of a mighty sword hanging over London," he told her. "You remember sitting up with me to watch for it, Kate, in the observatory I had built at Greenwich, and how the second night you really saw it?"

Both of them grieved deeply for their afflicted people and when a chastened parliament sat in the great hall of Christ Church it was found that the King had been subscribing a thousand pounds weekly to the relief fund. Yet he was still spending money on Barbara Castlemaine and her children, whom he had established in a house nearby. "How can you give her countenance when everyone knows she is unfaithful to you and consorts daily, and probably nightly, with that lewd playwright, Wycherley?" demanded Catherine, who had hoped at such a time to be relieved of the sight of her. And Charles, explaining to her more than he would ever explain to a justly incensed parliament, said dourly, "Because she threatens to publish my damned calf-love letters if I cast her off." Whereby much of his lenient subserviance to the woman was made plain.

Catherine could only feel that a person who held him by such means was beneath contempt and, having no more wish than he for such letters to be a joke throughout the country, she never questioned him on the subject again; adding to her maturing qualities a determination to tolerate the woman's occasional presence to their lives' end if need be.

There in the peaceful collegiate life of Oxford, with its halls and spires and quadrangles, its wide learning and its narrow river, it was difficult to believe that only sixty miles away hundreds were dying daily, and that the plague was spreading from the capital to towns and hamlets in all the home counties. In order to keep her mind from brooding upon it, and inspired by the academic atmosphere, Catherine set herself to improve her English; Charles —always at his best in a crisis and his worst in boredom—whiled away the time hunting and teasing any pretty girl he chanced to meet upon the dark, austere staircases, or encouraging the wild orgies of the students whose work the coming of such glamorous company had sadly bedeviled. And in the evenings, in those stately halls of learning, he would make Frances sing French love songs at which all the men laughed and which his wife was thankful not to understand.

Yet when that young lady of the bedchamber came seeking a private interview with her mistress, the reason for her tears took Catherine all unawares. "Sit here on the stool," she invited kindly, sending the rest of her women away.

But Frances, so seldom tongue-tied, remained standing before her twisting her fingers as nervously as any village wench. "Your Majesty is so good, and it is so difficult to explain," she stammered, her lovely eyes downcast.

"Come, come, Frances," rallied Catherine. "We have come to know each other intimately these last few months. Surely you can tell me anything?"

"Anything but this, Madame——"

Catherine stared in amazement. "Is it some favor you would ask?"

Suddenly the girl was down on her knees, her golden head

against the Queen's knee. "It is the favor of your protection——"

Catherine touched her hair reassuringly. "My dear child, being of my household you may always count upon that. But you are very beautiful and, I fear, extremely headstrong. Is it some man, Frances?"

Dumbly, the girl nodded.

"If he has been molesting you surely it is to your cousin the King, that you should go?"

"But, Madame—it *is* the King."

After a horrible moment or two of silence Frances's tear drenched eyes looked up into Catherine's appalled ones. "Oh, Madame, I hate to tell you! But every time he comes into a room his dark eyes cajole me. He has been writing verse and slipping it beneath my door at night. It used to be just friendship and flirting; but now he wants me as he wants those other women. And although I keep trying to elude his advances, he still pursues."

Catherine drew herself up rigidly, no longer able to abide the touch of her, so that the girl's hand fell from her knee. "The King is but mortal. It would be surprising if any man could resist the big eyes you make at them," she said stiffly.

"I know that in the past I have been foolish," admitted Frances, dabbing at her tear-stained face. "But now——"

"And now you are in love with your cousin Charles," stated Catherine, ignoring previous denials.

Retaliation for all the slights which she had endured was in her icy voice; but to her indignation her lady of the bedchamber began to giggle hysterically. "Yes, Madame. Indeed I am," she stuttered. "But not with *your* Charles. It is Charles Lennox, my other cousin. The less important one on the distaff side." Pulling herself together, she went on with more respectful restraint. "At Whitehall, when the King made me his Britannia—it was all very flattering—and exciting. I was young and inexperienced, and your Majesty must know how difficult he is to resist——"

Knowing only too well, Catherine said nothing.

"But physically I have never really wanted him."

"Not wanted him?" echoed Catherine incredulously.

"Oh, please, Madame, believe me! For months this other Charles, so much younger and handsomer, has had my heart."

"Younger and handsomer!" scoffed Catherine, recalling the pretty, callow youth. But the awful prospect of a serious successor to the Castlemaine was beginning to recede, leaving her the power to think coherently again.

"Besides which," added Frances, forgetting in her flighty way the enormity of what she said, "when I take a man I have no desire to share him!"

Catherine rose abruptly and walked to the window, wrestling with the latchet and throwing the casement wide. She felt she could not breathe. "Mother of God, give me patience," she entreated below her breath, gazing unseeingly across a square stone-walled quadrangle. "Merciful Christ, teach me to bear humiliation as Thou didst." Heaven knows what effort she made, what personal pride she jettisoned, standing there before the rain-washed courtyard and the arraignment of her own high ideals; but when at last she turned, the object of her husband's desires was crouching by her vacated chair, frightened as no threat of plague had ever frightened her. "I have always maintained that you were chaste—even when every other woman at Court called you wanton," Catherine made herself say. The words came with slow difficulty, a self-imposed penance.

Frances caught at her cold hand and kissed it. "And you are right, Madame. In spite of past frivolity, I am not as Donna Penelva and the others think. I swear I have never given myself to any man. That is why I grew frightened. Charles—the King—is so experienced—so persuasive—— And I want to go to my husband—as you went to him."

"But why, in the name of all the saints, must you come with this sordid tale to me?" asked Catherine, wearily.

Regaining poise, pulling her disordered laces to rights, *la belle* Stuart excused herself. "I went first to the Queen Mother. I have known her longer and it was she who brought me over. But the plague had come and she was packing. Besides, there had been

Jemmie, and it was the kind of tale she was tired of. So her Majesty suggested——"

"That you should try me?"

Frances nodded shamed assent. "She said you were one of the few really good women she knew outside a convent."

"How imaginatively kind of her," commented Catherine, borrowing her husband's irony. So that was her mother-in-law's last gift to her! A challenge and a test. To some women it was given to live easily, she supposed, but never to herself.

"And Charles Lennox—he wishes to marry you?"

Frances's face was suffused with confident happiness, but her sigh was prodigious. "In the circumstances, the King would never consent," she murmured.

"Never is a long time," said Catherine. "And I think you overrate the depth and permanence of the King's attentions. If you doubt me, you have only to consider your friend, Lady Castlemaine." By voicing the brave words, Catherine was beginning to believe in the truth of them. Frances, she considered, had been candid and not too much to blame; and because she herself loved Charles utterly his very faults became in some sort her responsibility. "You put me in a strange position," she said, touching the girl's hand with a rueful and forgiving smile. "But so far as lies in my power I will help you."

"Oh, Madame!"

Catherine hastened to stave off a torrent of effusive gratitude. "It is obvious, is it not, that I act as much for myself as for you?" she added, with uncompromising honesty.

"Then what must I do?"

"Keep near me always, and when next Lennox comes to see you send him to me. In the meantime, lest you be beseiged with more nocturnal verse, I will arrange for you to share Donna Penelva's room. As every one knows, Donna Penelva is almost blind and therefore whatever happens no one can blame her. But her extraordinary sharp intelligence is entirely at my disposal. Therefore hold yourself in readiness to be even more resourceful and courageous than usual, Frances. And whatever we contrive re-

member that the King invariably forgives women and is too civilized—and too clannish, as you Scots say—to behead this relative
who has the hardihood to become your husband. The worst, or
perhaps the best, that can happen to you both is to be banished
from Court."

Shocked and hurt to the soul as she was, Catherine had sufficient sense to meet the situation with grim humor. At least it was
a change to find a woman who did not want to become the King's
mistress; and when Frances, the brightest star of all that gay company, caused a seven day wonder by a midnight elopement and
a runaway marriage, the Queen and her Portuguese lady appeared to be as amazed as the rest. The Protestant enemies of
James who had hoped for a royal divorce and had seen in this
penniless, well-born girl a possible successor, were checkmated
by the Queen herself. As for Charles, the affair had gone deeper
than she had supposed. He was consumed by silent anger and his
grief was such that he could not hide it even from his wife. But
if he suspected her of connivance he never taxed her with it, and
she for her part never once upbraided him or spoke spitefully of
Frances. Both of them were learning marital forbearance.

And a new trouble was soon on his mind, distracting his
thoughts from women. Negotiations with Louis the Fourteenth
had failed, and France, honoring her treaty with Holland, was
preparing for war.

"Next time I will transact my own diplomacy behind closed
doors and not allow ambassadors to bungle it," he vowed, in the
privacy of his wife's bedroom. "Left alone, Louis and I understand
each other."

No one realized better than she the blow this was to him. Not
only did his cousin, *Le Roi Soleil*, stand for undisputed, unfettered
majesty, but with all his statesman's acumen Charles believed
that England needed the wealth and power and cultural grandeur
of France as Portugal had needed England; and he foresaw that
his own escape from financial dependence upon parliament could
come about only through Louis's support.

Catherine said little and never meddled. Only by a new gentle-

ness did she convey to him her understanding of his dual disappointment. Then one evening, after a long hard ride, he returned in high humor, reminding her of a ship that has come out
of the doldrums and is curvetting before a fair wind again.

"The plague in London is so much abated that I hope to return
to Whitehall in a few weeks," he announced, coming straight to
her room with a letter from John Evelyn in his hand.

"And the rest of us?" she urged, although she was still horribly
afraid.

He glanced up at her, sensing this; and realizing with a little
shock of surprise how essential a part of his life she had become.
"Not yet, I think. I would sooner give the place time to air and be
assured that all is clear," he answered, momentarily sobered.
"But once we are back the Commons may listen to my diatribes
about those streets; and those of us whom God has spared will
take on Dutch *and* French with a right good heart, if need be!
Oddsfish Kate, but I shall be glad to be back in London again.
Will not you, my dear?"

"Why, yes," agreed Catherine, turning her *petit point* about
consideringly. "But for me, be there never so many victories, there
will still be one thing lacking."

He did not answer for a minute or two, but threw his long body
into her chair and his hat across the table in the way she loved,
because then he seemed neither a dignified king nor a careless
lover, but like any man come home to be at ease. And quite suddenly he burst out laughing. "There was a hedge my horse would
not take, out Woodstock way," he began, seeing her pleased, in-
quiring look.

"It must have been a very high hedge," she commented, with
a smile.

Because it was a warm day his wig followed the hat. The dark
hair curled damply on his forehead, giving him what she called
his "young William Jackson look." "A man came and opened the
gates for me—just an honest old countryman driving his cows
home. Yet he knew me at once. 'If only your Majesty would beget

a legitimate son,' he said, as if all the crops in Oxfordshire and
all the kingdom depended upon it."

"Perhaps they do," said Catherine softly. "And what did you
say?"

"I' faith, I promised him I would go home and try!"

"For shame, Charles!" The color flooded ingenuously into her
face just as it was wont to do when they were first married.
"Surely you do not discuss such things with any man at a street
corner or a gate?"

"And why not? It concerns them as well as me," he argued.
" 'T is natural enough they should want to see you with a babe in
your arms. They like you, Kate. In spite of being a 'furriner in one
o' them outlandish fardingales' you have begun to stand for stead-
fastness and chastity and all the things these tough yeomen of
mine really admire."

"And yet they like you," she marveled slyly; whereat he pulled
her to his knee and stopped her teasing mouth.

"Treason," he accused. But she had long since learned not to
be afraid of him. Scenes, she knew, he would not tolerate; but the
truth, wittily spiked and pleasantly thrust, he always received
good humoredly, although whether he was in any way moved by
it was another matter.

Charles kept his word to the old countryman to such purpose
that before he left Oxford the women were all agog because the
Queen had hope of a child again. But this time hope was short-
lived. A few weeks later, in her haste and excitement at the
thought of rejoining him, Catherine again miscarried. Some said
that it was because a pet fox of the King's had jumped on her bed
and frightened her, but she herself felt that that had made no
difference. And before ever she reached Whitehall the doctors
had told her that she would never bear Charles a son.

She had hoped that he would ride out to meet her, but he sent
Monmouth instead. And as she came sadly through the purlieus
of the stricken city in the cool autumnal air the militia were
marching followed by weeping women, and leaden-hued, ema-
ciated citizens were opening their shops and striving to set the

wheels of normal life moving again. Except for the red-coated soldiers everybody seemed to be wearing black, and from the doorways of unkempt houses the bereaved muttered some spiteful doggerel blaming their misfortunes upon a barren, Catholic queen.

Catherine was thankful to be inside the palace again, where fires had been lighted and fresh tapestries hung. But even there grief dogged her. A letter lay awaiting her from Portugal, a shakily written letter from old Don Francisco telling her that her mother was dead.

Doubly stricken as she was, her one thought was to find Charles, Charles who, however much he might hurt her by his way of life, could always be counted on to be understanding and kind about all other hurts. With the letter still in her hand and the tears wet on her cheeks, she hurried alone to his apartments. And this time, seeing her distress, even Chaffinch made no effort to stay her.

But the King was not in his work room. Documents and maps and sea charts strewn upon table and fine French carpet seemed to explain his inability to meet her, and in the midst of them lay a half-finished letter with his quill still wet beside it. It would be like him if he had heard the militia's drums and hastened to one of the long windows in the banqueting hall to hearten them with his personal Godspeed.

With a hand on the back of his pushed back chair, Catherine looked miserably round the room, so empty without him. Her glance came to rest upon the letter and suddenly she remembered it was Sunday. It must be his weekly letter to Minette, of course. And there might be no more weekly mails. Perhaps that had been the real explanation. . . . She leaned forward to look at it, seeking only, through her tears, the comforting sight of the beloved, clear writing. She had no thought of spying, for he often wrote in French. But this time, made cautious by the imminence of war, he must have deemed it safer to write in English.

"I am very glad to hear that your indisposition has turned out to be *un petit Orléans*," read Catherine, who had had no idea her sister-in-law was pregnant, "and I wish you as easy a labor as

James's wife had with her second girl, when she dispatched her
business in little more than an hour. But I am afraid, *ma chère
Minette,* your shape is not so advantageously made for that con-
venience as hers is." For a line or two the words ran on in the easy,
affectionate style of his. And then, towards the bottom of the page,
came the true purpose of the letter. "And now, since we can no
longer write, good-by. Believe me, nothing can alter that passion
and tenderness I have for you, which is so rooted in my heart
that it will continue to the last moment of my life. When this
accursed war is over——"

It was some minutes before Catherine took in the full meaning of the words. But as she did so her own immediate sorrow
faded momentarily into the background of her mind.

So this was what war meant to Charles—separation from Minette.

Here, here, was the only cause for jealousy, the only anchorage
for his love—his family; and more than all of them his one remaining sister, the baby born during the Civil War in besieged
Exeter, whom he had never met until his exiled manhood.

"What a fool I have been!" thought Catherine. The grasping
Castlemaine, Jemmie's disreputable mother, pretty Frances, all
those actress women—they were all nothing to him but passing
playthings. Even Barbara, who had seemed to rule and ruin him
for a time. He had but used them as he used his ministers, treat-
ing them with careless generosity and telling them nothing of his
real thoughts, while here, in this quiet room, he gave expression
to his heart.

Before ever he came back to his room and gathered her in comforting arms, Catherine was cured of any real jealousy of his mistresses, but in her own heart was sown an unhappy, hopeless envy
of Minette.

CHAPTER THIRTEEN

Catherine stirred from a troubled sleep. The hot dry summer had been singularly trying, with the sadly depleted population still exhausted from last year's plague and the dull thud of gunfire still to be heard in the Channel. Someone was calling her urgently. Yet when she opened her eyes it was still dark.

"Madame! Can you not smell burning?"

Bemused with sleep, Catherine sat up to find Maria Penelva standing in her nightgown at the foot of the bed with a curtain held back in either thin hand. "Burning?" she repeated vaguely. "Perhaps the servants have forgotten to damp down the kitchen fires again?"

"My husband is already astir and says it is nothing in the Palace," Lettice O——nde, her Comptroller's wife, assured her. And Lettice, Catherine noticed, was already fully dressed.

"It is coming from the City," cried Druscilla, the pretty chambermaid, rushing unbidden into the room. "Look Madame! Please God it be not the Dutch!" And without so much as a curtsy or a "by your leave" she dragged the heavy velvet hangings apart with strong young arms and pushed open one of the long windows overlooking the river. There was no sound of gunfire but, sure enough, an unmistakable smell of burning was borne in upon the freshening September air and a dull glow made a warm, red oblong of the window.

"It must be a bad fire," said Catherine, now thoroughly awake. "You know, Lettice, only the other evening the King and that clever Mr. Evelyn of the Royal Society of Science were saying how dangerous your old beamed houses are, all overhanging and huddled together, so that one catches fire from another. Now in Lisbon——"

"It is not just a few houses ablaze, Madame," interrupted Lettice, returning from the window too shocked by what she had seen to stand on ceremony. "It must be whole streets!" And, as if to confirm her words, there was a clattering of footsteps on the flagged cloister below their room, while from the riverside there arose a cacophony of shouting.

Catherine sprang from her bed to join the others at the open window. Down on the Strand watermen, still struggling into their coats, were hurrying confusedly to shove off their boats, while women's faces appeared at every casement. And all seemed to be shouting questions at a man and woman rowing frenziedly in the direction of Lambeth, their flimsy craft laden to the gunwale with household goods. "'T is the worst fire ever seen!" screamed the woman, nearly upsetting the boat by clutching at her slipping pots and pans.

"Where?" yelled the men on the bank.

"Corner o' Pudding Lane, it started," called back the man in midstream. "The King's baker was getting his ovens hot again after the Sabbath. Got some new fool of a prentice, they say. An' now the whole of Fish Street is ablaze. Fair gutted out, he was——" His voice trailed away in the morning mist as he made for the hospitality of some rustic relative up river. But the fire went on. As if challenging the placid, rising sun, the angry, flickering glow was spreading.

"I wonder if the King knows," murmured Catherine, shivering with apprehension as she slipped into the fur-lined wrap her women held.

She had not long to wonder. There was more running and shouting outside her own door now and at a sign from Lady Ormonde, Druscilla threw it open upon the spectacle of a group of excited servants all making for the back stairs. "What is it, Dobby?" the girl asked, catching at a small, red-headed boot boy.

"London's afire!" he piped. "An' steward's goin' to let us up on the leads to see." He was away after the rest with never so much as a glance towards the Queen's apartments; and almost immediately the faithful Richard Bellings appeared in the doorway.

"I came in case your Majesty should be alarmed," he said, his good-looking face dependable and solicitous.

"Then it is really serious, Richard? Do the King and the Duke know?" asked Catherine.

"Someone has just ridden in with news. Pepys of the Admiralty, I think. Chaffinch had roused his Majesty and sent over to St. James's for the Duke. So he'll be with them now."

"Then let us go too and hear. You sit quietly here, dear Maria, and I will tell you later. And you, Lettice, come with me." Instead of fluttering round like the others, Lettice was calm and full of common sense; so together the three of them crossed the landing where back stairs and water stairs met, and went through the groom of the back stairs' rooms which gave access to one end of the King's private apartment. The rooms were deserted and Chaffinch himself, too absorbed to be aware of their approach, was standing in the open doorway of the King's bedroom. Passing him, as he sprang hastily to attention, Catherine instinctively pulled her skirts aside. She never set eyes on the man without a feeling of hateful humiliation, for she could not prevent herself from imagining the women he must have bundled up those stairs. Caught unawares and unshaven in the unkind light of dawn he looked the pale, crafty creature he was. And all the more so by contrast with the three vigorous men within.

She could see her husband and her brother-in-law—James fully dressed and Charles in hastily donned shirt and breeches—standing by the window. And in the middle of the room, near Charles's great disordered bed, the secretary of the Navy Board. The fire was no particular business of his but, although red in the face and breathless, he appeared capable as ever of giving an adequate report of all that came his way.

"After three weeks of drought the warehouses in Thames Street are crackling like dry tinder, your Majesty," he was saying, "and with this easterly wind getting up, the fire looks as if it might lick its way right up to Cheapside."

Charles turned and saw Catherine. His face was grave and anxious, and beyond motioning to Bellings to set a chair for her he vouchsafed her no greeting. But, having always been so diffident about visiting his rooms, she was warmed to perceive that he took it for granted she should be there. "And what is the Lord Mayor doing about it?" he asked, continuing his conversation with Samuel Pepys.

"Old Tom Bludworth won't be likely to do much!" growled James impatiently, drawing in his head from the open window.

"Your Grace is right," corroborated Pepys. "He is running about the streets like a fainting woman with a silly scarf tied over his head. 'What can I do? What can I do?' he keeps on bleating. And all the while complaining that no one will obey his orders."

"And will they not?" asked Charles.

"He has given them none that I know of, your Majesty. Or none that are likely to meet so great an emergency. This calamitous thing broke out so suddenly that half the people are too stunned to do aught but stand and stare. While the other half, instead of lending a hand with pump and bucket, are set only on saving their own possessions, borrowing a cart if they can, staggering beneath their belongings over the Bridge to the safety of Bankside or offering more than their gear is worth for a boat. Those rascally ferrymen are making a fortune, m'lord Duke; but the fire blazes on."

Catherine saw the two Stuarts exchange glances, and Charles nod assent to some unspoken desire of his brother. "Better go, James, and take some of your troops," he said briefly.

But besides warehouses and the huddled houses of the poor, Pepys had seen the gracious gardened homes of wealthy merchants writhing and twisting like burnt paper. "It will take more than troops to put it out," he told them flatly.

"What, man! Would you have me stand by and do nothing?" snorted James, halfway to the door.

"God forbid, your Grace! But with this wind only one thing can save the city."

"*Save the city!*" there was incredulity and anguish in Charles's

voice as he strode back into the middle of the room, making a
sign for the navy secretary to speak his mind and for James to
stay and hear it.

"It is as grave as that, Sir," said Pepys, holding his ground. "But
gunpowder might do it. In my humble opinion the only hope is to
blow up some of the houses as yet untouched. Make a clear ring
of space around the burning areas and so prevent the sparks from
spreading."

A heavy silence hung in the room, as heavy as the acrid smell
that filled it. Charles began to pace up and down. "It is heart-
rending—deliberately to blow up people's homes," he demurred.
"What say you, James?"

"No worse than things one has to do in war," shrugged James,
who had earned the bread of exile as a mercenary in more than
one foreign army sooner than accept the hospitality of France.
"What are a dozen or so homes to save hundreds?"

"Well, then. I will abide by your judgements," said Charles reluctantly. "If there be no other means send to m'lord Albemarle
for what gunpowder is needed. Your men can dispatch the business, James. Only tell that fool Bludworth to make certain every
living soul is safely out before you begin blasting. And, Pepys, tell
the poor devils they may borrow my palace carts to save their
bits of furniture."

"I doubt if there will be time to save more than lives, Sir," said
Pepys, to whose wig and eyelashes still clung the dust of the conflagration he had ridden from.

Charles walked briskly to a table and scrawled something upon
a piece of paper. "Lest there should be any questioning of your
authority, here is my name to it," he said. "And tell them I am on
my way to see that it is done."

"I will ride with you, Master Secretary," said James, hurrying
with his long strides after the rotund Pepys; and before they were
well out of the door the King was struggling with his cravat.
"Toby! To-bee! My coat and boots," he called.

Through a small inner doorway, as if by magic, appeared Toby
Rustat, the King's old Scots valet, with a coat over his arm and

the riding boots already in his hand. Quietly, without fuss, he laid
aside the fine gold-embroidered coat proffered by a flustered
courtier and helped his master into the plain brown one which
Charles was wont to use for his morning gallops at Newmarket.
For once he did not stop to brush off some almost invisible speck
of dust; and Catherine, watching him, could only suppose that
during long years of service he had come to anticipate the
thoughts in Charles's mind as quickly as his sartorial requirements. He probably guessed that before his master's return the
coat would be too drenched and dusty to be used again.

But as the King turned to speak to her, Richard Bellings made
so bold as to join them. "What is it, Dick?" asked Charles.

"I think, sir, you should know that there is a malicious rumor
abroad that we of my faith started this," he warned, in a low
voice. "Your Majesties know how the least thing inflames the Londoners on that subject. Mobs of them who have lost their homes
are rounding up every professed or suspected Catholic they can
lay their hands on. That is partly why they are so out of hand.
They will listen to your Majesty, but in their present temper
might do His Grace the Duke some injury——"

"Plague or fire—it is always the Papists!" cried Charles, in exasperation. "Have they no sense, since all men's houses burn
alike?" For a moment or two he stood in deep thought. Then,
slowly, reluctantly, he took off the favorite old brown coat and
handed it back to his valet. He sat down and signed to a hovering page to pull off his riding boots. "All the same, we will let
James go first," he said to Catherine. "He is absolutely master of
his profession and will soon have the mob, if not the fire, under
control. This is really a heaven-sent opportunity for him, Dick. If
they see him laboring to save their City it will still their fears and
serve his popularity as well as war, when they care not whether
he be a Catholic or an Anabaptist so long as he wins them victories!"

"And you, Charles?" asked Catherine.

He turned to her with that devastating smile of his, suddenly
as suavely attentive as if no emergency raged. "I will stay and

drink a glass of your abominable newfangled tea with you, my dear, if you and my little Donna Penelva will invite me. And then go along unspectacularly by water."

It was characteristic of Charles that he was completely without vanity. Expediency with him always came first. He minded not at all that his brother should be thought the more capable. Unlike most of the men about him he was content to hide his talents rather than to parade them, so long as he ultimately attained his own ends. Indeed, as his wife was beginning to perceive, he often deliberately hoodwinked them by a show of careless indifference in order to profit the better by his shrewdness.

Shrewdness he needed more than any man, being kept perpetually short of cash. Catherine knew only too well that, although he never reproached either of them, she and James between them —she by her childlessness and James by his openly professed religion—had made the restored monarchy a difficult thing to hold, so that Charles must juggle skillfully each event as it came, seeing no security for the future. Small wonder there were those few gray hairs of his, seeing that he had no Protestant heir and the majority of his subjects were so opposed to a Catholic one.

And in this present decision, in spite of Bellings' fears, he was proved abundantly right. While he himself, remembering the first danger of all, went quietly down to the Tower to have the small dwellings round the moat destroyed lest the gunpowder stored within the fortress should blow up docks, shipping, houses and all, James, the trained soldier, completely impervious as ever to public opinion, kept order in the City, blasting spaces in the path of the fire, organizing chains of men to bring water from the Thames, the Fleet and Wallbrook and putting the aldermen of each ward in charge of the homeless for whom they set up a camp on Moorfield. Pepys, too, got workmen from the dockyards to keep watch round the Navy Office and buried all the King's private Naval papers in a friend's garden.

But throughout that hideous Monday night, in spite of all that willing hands and encouraged hearts could do, the east wind still blew and the great fire still raged. Fenchurch Street, Gracious

Street and Lombard Street lay in smoldering ruins. Baynard Castle and half the City churches were gutted out.

Early Tuesday morning, without fuss or ceremony, the King called out the trainband and set out to join his brother in that inferno.

"Must you, Charles?" asked Catherine, standing in the dawn light beside his horse in Whitehall courtyard.

"*Pour encourager les autres,*" he said lightly, those grim lines on either side of his mouth relaxing for the first time.

And because it was London, which he had learned to love as only a returned exile can, she made no effort to dissuade him. As she watched him ride out into King Street she noticed that his valet followed him, keeping as close to him as the presence of his betters permitted. There was no need for a valet to go, but if so much as a breath of danger blew upon his master Toby Rustat was determined to be there. And with all her heart Catherine envied him.

Each gentleman about the Court was told off to perform some task or put in charge of some street or sector. When evening came none of them had returned, and the night sky was so red that no candles were needed in the deserted palace rooms. "What is that great hoop of flame stretching across the bend of the river beyond the Surrey marshes?" asked Catherine, from the vantage point at Charing whither she had begged Lord Ormonde to take her.

"Madame, it is the Bridge," her groom told her. He had been born and bred within sound of Bow bells and by the way he spoke he might have been referring to the Holy Rood.

"The Bridge? *London Bridge?*" cried Lady Ormonde, moved from her composure at last. "Then we are completely cut off from the South bank, with no way by road nearer than Kingston?"

"It is only some of the houses upon it which are burning," pointed out her husband. "The bridge itself is built of stone."

"Why, only a few days ago the King and I were driving over it," remembered Catherine, with a heavy heart. "And he showed me with so much pride the Lord Mayor's fantastically lovely mansion overhanging the water and a warehouse that once had been a chapel dedicated to your St. Thomas à Becket."

But it was not only the Bridge. Soon the flames were shooting up as high as St. Paul's on top of Ludgate Hill, St. Paul's with its old cruciform fabric and its exquisite new portico. Smoke began to envelop that beloved, familiar landmark. Like a pillar of flame the very heart of London was burning. And the heat was so fierce that there was nothing her citizens could do but stand and watch until, with a crash that could be heard at Westminster, the massive roof fell in. In the following silence a great gasp of horror seemed to go up from thousands of throats, drowning the crackling of the flames and the shrieks of terrified women and children. Foreigner though she was, Catherine—striving to quiet her frightened horse—could feel all about her the people's passionate, incredulous grief. And then, as if to relieve the tension, some Cockney wit—jauntily indomitable as ever—was heard to remark, "Well, at least that's saved Master Christopher Wren the trouble o' repairing the old place, and the Aldermen squabblin' over whether we're to have a dome or another steeple!"

But from that hour the wind began to drop and the fire gradually to die down. Begrimed and bemused, the City dwellers found what shelter they could. And slowly, bleakly people living in the suburbs betook themselves to their beds although even out at Charing their gardens were white with ashes and bits of plaster and torn paper borne on the breeze. Scraps of their conversation reached Catherine's ears as she and her escort returned in sad silence to the palace, remarks shouted above the turmoil by people too excited and too worn out to notice that she was the Queen.

"Over ten thousand houses must have been destroyed," they told each other.

"More like fourteen thousand, the Recorder says."

"And thanks only to the King and the Duke it wasn't more."

"From the moment *they* came, things got done. Did you see them these last two nights?"

"Standing knee deep in water the Duke was. Giving orders here and helping there——"

"And the King in his shirt sleeves pulling aside flaming beams and passing buckets with the best o' them. Jesting, even. Lord, how the people love him!"

"Reckon Parliament won't grudge him an expensive whore or two after this!"

When Charles at last came home he was just as full of praise for his people. "It was the troops and the trainband got it under," he declared. "And even graybeards and prentice boys lent a hand. And those poor, uncomplaining women, James. I am just come from trying to cheer them on Moorfield. Some of the children have not so much as a tent to cover them. We must appeal to the country folk to send them in food, and give shelter to as many as they can." He stood stamping the water from his squelching boots and rubbing his reddened eyes. "I managed to save all our smaller ships in the Pool, Kate, and the docks for those at sea to come home to. But, zounds, what will they make of the desolation which is London! Over eighty churches gone, John Evelyn tells me. And St. Paul's. . . . It is incredible—incredible! But one day we will build it up again—finer and more spacious than before. Before I die I'll hear the bells of London ring again!"

His clothes were torn, his face blackened and his curled wig long since lost in the rubble. He might have been escaping from a lost battlefield or turning a kitchen spit again. But Catherine came and put her arms about him before them all. "You have done marvelously—William Jackson!" she told him, torn between tears and tender laughter. But although there were tears in his own eyes for his ravaged capital, his immediate request was commonplace. All he called for was a bath and fresh linen.

"And not you this time, Toby Rustat! You get to bed!" he ordered, as his worn-out valet would have rushed with the other servants to do his bidding.

With the liberty of long service, the old man began protesting but Charles, seemingly indefatigable, gave him a friendly push. "Ye're nae sae young noo, Toby," he told him, relapsing into the tongue of their common ancestry. "Nor sae teugh a blade as when we twa went gallivanting unkenn'd frae the Hague tae Paris tae see my young sister, wi' nae mair than a poke fu' o' bawbees atween us. Hoots, mon, gang an rest yersel' a wee."

While Charles took himself off to change, Catherine caught up with his disgruntled valet making for the back stairs. "That was just before he came to England, wasn't it? What was she like then, his sister?" she asked softly, with an urgent hand on his grimed sleeve.

The tired old Scot straightened up in surprise. His inflamed eyes blinked at her. "Jist a wee bit lassie, M'am, aboot savanteen. Slender as a willow, an' as sweet," he answered in the same guarded tone. "A' thae years awa' in France he'd been her world, an' she the one body he was de-tair-mined to see again afore he crossed the water to be King o' Scotland."

Even after six years' residence at Whitehall the little man from the Lothians had a way of ignoring the rest of the realm which maddened his fellow servants and was an unending source of enjoyment to the Stuarts.

"Was she so beautiful?" insisted Catherine.

The inimitable Toby pursed up his lips consideringly. "She had but the glimmer o't then, I'd say. Ower thin an' ne'er a bonny goon like he gied her when she cam' for his Coronation. I ken there were times, lang syne, when our guid Queen hadna muckle for the puir bairn to eat. But our Princess Henrietta—Minette as he always ca's her—has that aboot her, the same as his Majesty——"

"Has what, Toby?"

"I canna put a name to it, M'am, unless it be the couthiness—the grace—that begets responding love. An' as to my master hissel'——"

Toby was started on a topic dear to his heart; but he had been wet to the skin off and on for hours and his voice croaked into something between a chuckle and a cough.

"Yes?" urged the Queen.

"He hadna but yun decent shirt tae his back the time we went to Paris. I'd no have these upstart Sassenachs hear o't, M'am, but mony's the time I've wash't it oot for him at the pump o' some

lousy foreign inn an' took the lib-air-ty tae dry it oot ower nichts
on my ain body!"

"The liberty! Oh, Toby, you might have caught your death of a
chill. Small wonder he loves you!"

Weary as they were, the old man's eyes glowed and twinkled.
"He does that," he agreed, with immense complacency. And then,
surprising the look on Catherine's face, he saw her for the first
time not as the Queen, but as Charles Stuart's wife. And before
bowing himself off to bed he grinned raffishly, perfectly certain
that, given the chance, she would have done the same herself.

CHAPTER FOURTEEN

For weeks to come Londoners slept fitfully between night-
mares of fire and woke each morning to the terrible realization
that half their city was no longer in existence. The lovely silhouette of a long, narrow riverside town with over a hundred spires
rising above medieval streets was gone, and so mercifully were
the rat-infested, overcrowded alleys leading down the slope to
Thames Street and the wharves. When the ground was sufficiently
cooled and cleared for Catherine and her ladies to ride out and
see what damage had been done, they found fashionable houses
and pleasant gardens along the Strand and around Lincoln's Inn
fields still there, but once they had passed within the City wall
at Temple Bar they saw only half a dozen buildings standing up
like gaunt, discolored teeth at the beginning of Fleet Street. And
from there, looking eastwards across the Fleet bridge, up Ludgate Hill and past the ruins of St. Paul's, through the still smoldering waste where Cannon Street and Eastcheap had once been,
right to the very moat of the Tower, all was flat desolation. All
along the river front from wall to wall the fire had raged, so that
only a comparatively small area by the northern gates remained
untouched, brooded over by the massive bulk of St. Bartholomew's age-old monastic church.

For months families lived as best they could in army tents lent
by the King and bivouacs set up on Smithfield and other open
places, or they sought shelter in the sooty cellars of what once
had been their houses. Others, searching through all those acres
of devastation, could not even tell the exact spot where once their
houses had stood. Yet the life of crippled London had to go on.

Carts came in from the country with food, and ships—their crews stricken with amazement—unloaded merchandise. And even while people struggled to clear away the debris of their old city, master builders appeared with plans and masons with cartloads of stone. A new city began to rise, a more spacious, sanitary, stone city where large tall windows would one day supplant leaden casements, and lofty porticoes take the place of timbered eaves.

But all this was a dream which would take years to materialize. And in the meantime the Dutch, unimpaired by plague and fire, chose their moment to avenge their defeat in Sole Bay and the filching of New York. While all thinking people were hoping desperately that the talks going on in Breda would result in peace, seventy ships set out from Holland and stormed Sheerness, catching the English all preoccupied and unprepared. Almost as soon as enemy gunfire was heard in London the ominous sound of it was drowned by drums calling out the militia and charges blasting hulks to block the Thames below Barking Creek. Press gangs were busy in all the ports and every soldier in the country was called up, the King promising that whatever venture might befall he himself would be in it with them. But with half her ships uncommissioned England was powerless. Too late did a niggardly parliament push through a levy long withheld. Though troops massed along the Kent and Essex coasts, guarding the Thames' mouth, the great Dutch ships circumvented them and sailed up the Medway, broke through the boom below Chatham and fired Charles's impotent, ill-manned, home-berthed fleet. Five of the British warships the great Dutch admiral, De Ruyter, set ablaze, while their unpaid crews made shift to swim ignominiously ashore. The flaring ships rivaled the scarce extinguished fire of streets. And then—worst humiliation of all—the Dutch admiral's flagship made fast the *Royal Charles* and, beneath the very noses of raging Englishmen, towed her back to Holland.

To Charles it was as if part of his heart were being tugged away.

That day the English bit the dust indeed. That day, following all their disasters, they touched their lowest ebb. Fire, pestilence, rebellion, war—all these things they could encounter; but no man questioned the saying that every time one of her ships is lost the hearts of all true Britons bleed. Returning like whipped dogs to their homes, no man durst look his neighbor in the face. And, having endured more than they could stomach, something soured in them, soured so that with distorted vision—uncorrected by their accustomed humor, blurred by suspicion and intolerance—they sought some scapegoat for their common shame.

Though all their recent misfortunes were more the King's sorrow and less his fault than any man's, they began to whisper that had he been less indolent and pleasure-loving and his Court less licentious such disgrace and misery never would have befallen them. Adversity brought out the sturdy old Puritan spirit, and up and down the country it was remembered that Oliver Cromwell had believed in discipline and been a good living man. When a Quaker ran naked through the palace precincts with coals of fire on his head calling upon the profligates of Whitehall to repent, although Charles enjoyed the spectacle as much as graceless Buckingham, he was not so deluded by laughter as to have no uneasy inkling that the poor fanatic was right. For somewhere hidden beneath his easy cynicism Charles Stuart kept a conscience. And although he could gull the wiliest statesman, himself he never could deceive.

In his uneasiness and regret he found solace in a wife who said little but understood, a wife who had loved his lost ships as his mistresses loved jewels. Irritated by the formality and constant coming and going in his own apartments, where men were always pressing for audience, he fell into the habit on those days of slipping away to "the Queen's side," as the apartments to the east of the water stairs were commonly called. If it were a matter of making a bid for a separate peace with France or finding a politically useful second wife for his recently bereaved brother, he would say to such men as he wished to talk to in peace and privacy, "Let us go over to the Queen's side."

Besides the people he wanted to talk to there were the people he wanted to be rid of, for Charles's kindly impulses often outran his ability to perform.

There was the morning, for example, when he surprised his long-suffering wife by having a great carved wooden crucifix carried into her room. "My dear, I am in a devastating hurry," he announced, "but would have you look at this exquisitely wrought thing. A man with the extraordinary name of Grinling Gibbons carved it. Master Evelyn here found him working in a cottage turning out a mound of such masterpieces and the man only wants a hundred pounds for it."

"The frame alone is worth that, Madame," urged John Evelyn, who knew more about such matters than the King. "And the original design is taken from Tintoret."

Charles was always in a devastating hurry these days with the whole of London to rebuild. "I will leave our good friend Evelyn to tell you about it as I know you care for such things," he said. "For I am on my way to meet Christopher Wren in Fish Street; we hope to find a fitting site for some kind of monument to commemorate the fire. A tall column in the classic style, he thought, surmounted by a great ball of fire."

Examining the crucifix after he was gone and only half-listening to the scholarly Evelyn, Catherine realized that Charles was more anxious to encourage the arts than to own this. She guessed, too, with a little spurt of wifely wisdom, that the reason for his hasty departure was less his appointment than his intolerable penury. For only that morning she had overheard him complaining that he possessed but three decent cravats in the world, less than some impudent puppy of an ensign called John Churchill who was trying to cut him out with the ladies, and discussing with Toby Rustat their hopes of further credit with the linen draper.

"Poor Charles! He probably promised weeks ago to see this protégé of Master Evelyn's, and was then badgered into buying something expensive for Barbara's children or some down-at-heel Royalist who had fought at Worcester," she thought. But in spite of all her economies the state of her own exchequer was little better; and apart from a liking for lively music, she never had professed to know anything about the arts. So, like a good and thrifty wife, she took upon herself the unpleasant duty of sending the cross away, thanking Master Evelyn civilly for his pains and damning her own taste in his eyes for ever by picking imaginary faults in a masterpiece of perfection. Very sensibly she assured him that no clever woodcarver or mason need want for opportunity with so much rebuilding going on, for which parliament would no doubt foot the bill.

Then there was the afternoon when, forgoing his usual walk in the park, Charles sat late discussing business with Lord Arlington, the man who had waited so eagerly to succeed Clarendon in the Chancellorship.

"Without my protection Ned would have been hounded out years ago," Charles said, after Arlington had taken his departure. "And of a truth I cannot any longer endure his domineering pomposity. You should have seen Buckingham last night imitating his entry into the High Court with the fire shovel for a mace and my new French watch for the Great Seal!"

Catherine sent for a bottle of the Portuguese wine her brother Pedro had sent her, and poured some for Charles. Then she got her needlework and went to sit near him by the window. "But what will Clarendon do, poor man?" she asked.

"I had arranged a pension for his honorable retirement. But James says he will probably go abroad, which seems hard after so many bad hours in my service. I am hoping he will console himself by finishing a history of the Cromwellian rebellion which he was always talking about when we were in Holland." Charles sighed prodigiously and laid aside the papers Arlington had been pestering him to sign. "And how have you spent your day, my dear?" he asked.

"Trying to amuse James's two motherless girls. Anne's death was hard on them, and I am sorry, but I am afraid I do not care for them very much."

"Mary is not bad looking," submitted her uncle without enthusiasm.

"But sly. Oh, she is stoutly Anglican, as you have had her brought up to be. But I have a feeling that, good as you have been to her, she is not a very loyal little person."

"Well, she will be a very important little person unless James hurries to a new marriage bed and begets sons. Quite soon, I suppose, I must begin looking for a suitable husband for Mary." He turned in his chair to scrutinize his wife in the somber simplicity of her mourning, reaching out a hand to touch hers as she selected a skein of silk from a small table that stood between them. "You are very good to all my oddly assorted relatives, Kate. And how well black becomes you! You look now as you did when I had Lely paint you in those fabulous pearls of yours as a bride. Do you remember?"

"Do I remember?" thought Catherine, whose heart cherished every moment of that happy month at Hampton. But she managed to laugh lightly enough. "I am afraid it is only the fading light that makes you say so."

She sensed that he was tired, so she quietly laid aside the work she could not longer see and sat in companionable silence without calling for candles, knowing how he loved to watch the lights come out at prow and masthead over the darkening river. "Why do you come here so often now?" she asked at length, out of the gathering shadows.

"Come here?" he repeated, stirring from his dreaming and his scheming.

"You used to come only at night," she explained, carefully eliminating all complaint or emotion from her voice. "And now you come seldom at night but much more frequently by day. And bring all these men."

Charles sat up straight. "Do they incommode you, my dear?" he asked, shocked by his own thoughtlessness.

"Oh, Charles, you must know better than that!" He could scarcely see her face, but her laughter was low and delicious. For the hundredth time, hearing her in the darkness, he thought what a lovely voice she had. "Your coming—and your friends'— could never make me anything but infinitely happy. There have been so many times when I have been alone. It was only that I was wondering why you come."

Not a little embarrassed, he sat there thoughtfully twirling the stem of his empty glass. "For a little peace and quiet, I suppose," he said, with a short answering laugh. "And because—just now— I have matters on hand which I dare not talk of freely save among those whom I can trust."

A warm happiness of achievement flooded Catherine's heart, only to be pricked like a bubble by some sharper, smaller, less mature emotion. "And at supper time do you not speak of these things in Lady Castlemaine's rooms?" she heard herself asking sharply. The words seemed to be torn suddenly out by past hurts, and to be quite beyond her control.

A moment or two of silence showed her that he, too, was jolted by surprise—and disappointment. "Do you really suppose so? When it is common gossip that she lies with Wycherley and my own friend, Killegrew?" he asked, coldly sarcastic. "When only last night, going to ask after one of my children who has been sick, I caught young Churchill scrambling out of her window in his shirt?"

So that was why he had been so peeved about the paucity of his cravats! "What will you do to him—relieve him of his commission?" asked Catherine, momentarily sidetracked.

"God forbid! James says he is a remarkably good ensign. One day he may be of considerable value to his country."

So that, apparently, was all Charles cared for Barbara's constancy. Yet for hers—his wife's—he did care. Had he not told her so? But, since good women must needs covet the cheap benefits of the bad, even that knowledge did not give Catherine the thing she longed for. "Sometimes trust between a man and a woman can be a kind of insult," she said, rising from her chair. "It can imply that she is not attractive enough to engender distrust."

It was a long time since her jealousy had flared openly like that; but in that intimate hour, when all the semblance of possession was hers, she wanted desperately to hold his senses.

There was a moment or two of silence while the shadows deepened. Catherine was grateful for them. Hands pressed to her flaming cheeks, she felt as though she had laid bare her heart before him.

"I know I am a shocking husband, Kate," he admitted harshly, mocking himself as much as her. "But I do assure you my trust goes deeper than such matters of the flesh," he added more gently. "Have I not trusted you, without so much as giving it a thought, not to interfere with my niece's religion, though it is just conceivable that she may one day reign after me? It is implicit, Kate —my trust. Bound up with my respect for you——"

"Respect!" echoed Catherine, almost as if she would cast the cold word from her. Yet more than once he had given her, as he was giving her now, the rare gift of his sincerity. And often his tenderness. And here she was creating discord like a thankless churl! But always it was his passion that she hungered for. "Sometimes—of late—when you have been so charming to me," she began haltingly, "I have wondered, had I been some other woman —not your wife——"

"God preserve us from such a calamity!" he exclaimed, wholeheartedly. "You women are always setting yourselves up to be intuitive but, Lord, how little you understand us poor men!" Fleet as ever to avoid the analysis of feminine emotions, Charles dragged himself from the comfort of his chair to the protection of a fresh appointment. "While I think of it, the French ambassador is back," he told her, preparing to take his leave.

"Colbert de Croissy? Then we are at peace again?"

"Yes. Colbert coming and Ned Hyde going," he added ruminatively.

"That should make it possible to be on better terms with France than ever."

"For more reasons than one, I hope so. He is coming to supper and I should like you to wear that lovely gown you have on. A pity you do not speak French like the other ladies!"

"I will begin to take lessons at once," she promised, both pleased and humbled.

"It means we must sup in public in the banqueting hall,"

he reminded her from the doorway, with an inelegant grimace.

It was while they were standing together waiting to receive their guest that she again became aware of his dislike of his surroundings. "Why do you hate this lovely room?" she asked, looking along the lighted tables laid with gold plate.

"Hate it? What do you mean?" he asked, with that aloofness with which he habitually met advances upon his privacy.

"I have never known you to come here unless forced to by some formal occasion such as this."

"You watch me too closely."

"I love you."

They were talking in quick undertones so that the courtiers grouped about them might not hear, yet holding themselves ready for the State reception. And being so hemmed about by formality, Catherine found that she could quite easily say the words which in private shamed her.

The very simplicity of them melted Charles's resentment. "It was from here that my father was beheaded. Did you not know?" he said tonelessly.

"Every reigning family knew, and wept for him, and was afraid. But do you mean—from this very room?"

"From that window where Dick Bellings is standing. They built out a kind of platform. Going to it, alone—not one of us with him—he must have walked across the spot where we are standing."

His sad horror of the place communicated itself to her, so that she turned her head, as if half-expecting to see that gentle, dignified figure Van Dyck had painted crossing the hall towards them. "And they expect you to eat here?" she whispered, with a shiver.

"They have very little imagination."

"How tolerant you are!"

"Tolerance is a virtue which can soon run to seed and become indifference."

There was a great stir down in the courtyard as the guard sprang to attention and the ambassador's coach rumbled to a standstill.

"Tell me about that gallant Protestant. If it does not hurt you too much," begged Catherine.

Charles's fine, tapering fingers were toying with the St. George badge suspended from his gold collar of the Order of the Garter. He looked poised and debonair as usual. Except for the timbre of his deep, cultured voice he might have been discussing the chances of Woodcock, his new horse, at Epsom races. "He walked out through that window," he was saying. "Cromwell's soldiers were rows deep, lest the people should attempt a rescue at the last moment. The roadway was black with weeping women and Puritans in steeple hats, and the snow white on the ground. He'd asked for an extra shirt, Toby says, in case he might shiver with the cold and Cromwell think he was afraid. *He—my father—afraid!*"

"Did you love him very much?"

"Yes. He was the best of fathers. But I did not understand him. He was too good for me. His single-mindedness sometimes seemed to me like stupidity, even then when I was a lad. He endured imprisonment and walked out there to the block sooner than budge one inch from what he believed to be essential and right. James is like that too." Charles glanced round to make sure that not even a page was within earshot. "I would not have you repeat it, even to Maria Penelva, Catherine, but feeling against James is growing so strong that only yesterday I sent the Bishop of Winchester to beg him to appear beside me, just once, in the Chapel Royal. For his own sake and for England's. But he sent back word that he would sooner die." Charles's eye was on the door at the far end of the hall, his mind and body already braced for official duty. "I would have you know that I admire him for it. Envy him, even. But to me, were our positions reversed, it would always seem better to attend Mass and prevent bloodshed."

The great doors of the banqueting hall were thrown open. There was a vast bowing and scraping. His Excellency the Ambassador of his Most Christian Majesty King Louis the Fourteenth of France was coming.

"So it is as grave as that," murmured Catherine. There was no more time now to consider the matter. Conscious that she looked almost beautiful in the black velvet, she hurried to finish what she had to say. "James will never be beloved as you are, but perhaps in his heart he is happier."

"I make no doubt he is," agreed Charles, going forward to greet his welcome guest.

$\mathcal{M}$aria Penelva was aging and delicate, a more shriveled little woman than ever, and often during the cold English winters she longed to go back to end her days among her own people in Portugal. But she had promised her late friend, Luiza of Braganza, to see her daughter through the difficulties of her foreign marriage; and, half-blind as she was, she saw them and the quiet fight which Catherine put up against them more clearly than most people.

"At first, when one is young, it is one's own happiness and hurt that one clamors about," she had been wont to tell a young indignant bride. "But as the years go by, if one really loves, it is only the happiness and hurts of the beloved that matter."

Now she was able to watch this very miracle happening in Catherine. A patient wisdom was growing in her mind, and her turbulent heart was gradually attaining some kind of peace because, loving one man to the exclusion of all else, even the sharp goads of pride and self were wearing smooth.

Maria knew well enough that when young Jemmie, almost grown to manhood, went swaggering about the town with bad companions and finally brutally murdered a parish beadle, most wives as neglected as the Queen was would have shrilled triumphantly, "It is his mother's base blood coming out!" or "What can your Majesty expect after making so much of him?" But Catherine seemed to have forgotten how Charles had insulted her by raising him to his dukedom, forgotten even her bitterness about the boy's birth. When her name was linked to his in a cruel lampoon merely because she had been kind to him, all she thought of was how to console his shamed and disappointed father.

Maria knew, too, how Catherine comforted Charles when the letter came from France to tell him that his mother had died.

But even shrewd old Maria could not have known about the morning when Catherine, hurrying into Charles's room to tell him the news of crazy Alfonso's deposal in favor of her beloved Pedro, observed a woman's small, rosetted slipper lying by his bed. And how, sooner than provoke a scene, she had brought herself to stop and say some idle thing to Chaffinch in order to give its owner time to escape from behind the bed hangings to the back stairs. "You must learn to shut your eyes," Queen Luiza had said, that last night in Lisbon. And, remembering her words with a rueful smile, Catherine had unobtrusively kicked the frivolous footgear out of sight. Charles had come late from the playhouse the night before and the hussy with him, she suspected, had been that pretty red-headed actress, Nell Gwyn. Well, at least, thought Catherine, she took the King's mind off his cares with her wit and mimicry and was not always plaguing him like the rest for favors he could ill afford. It all hurt less now because she had come to realize that although he might share his moments of amusement with such women, he spoke of his inmost thoughts only to her. In such things, she was sure, no other woman had any part at all. Except, of course, Minette. And Minette was across the sea in France.

But England was at peace again; letters were passing back and forth across the Channel and Colbert de Croissy was busy between those two arch-schemers, Louis and Charles. Almost inevitably there came a day when Charles, after a session with the French ambassador, flung out of his workroom like an eager boy and came striding in search of her. "She is coming to England! Minette is coming!" he announced, finding her in the Matted Gallery.

In four years of married life with him, Catherine had of necessity acquired considerable self-control. And because she had never before seen such unalloyed happiness illuminating his swarthy face she managed somehow to clamp down her own dismay, to clasp her hands and say, "Oh, *Charles!*" as if the most

wonderful thing in the world were going to happen. And he, supposing that she shared his delight, began pacing up and down
with her in uncontrollable excitement. "I had begun to despair
that he would ever let her!"

"Who? The French king?" asked Catherine, stupefied by the
rush of conflicting emotions and already out of breath through
trying to keep up with him.

"No! No! Her husband, Philippe, Duke of Orleans. Louis was
willing enough. Louis is civilized. Moreover, he admires my sister more than any woman in his kingdom. Too much, the malicious say. But for weeks that poisonous little popinjay has been
putting every conceivable difficulty in our way."

"Is he so very unkind to her, Charles?"

"Unkind!" snorted Charles. "Surely you know that he——"

His glance came to rest on her childishly uplifted face and
suddenly recalling how she had looked when she had first come
to him, he decided that perhaps she did not. He and his Court
must have tarnished her lovely innocence with much that was
evil, he told himself bitterly, but at least not with Philippe of
Orleans's particular brand of perversion. "Like many vain little
men, he is spiteful and jealous. I abhor jealous people," he said,
more calmly. "The main thing is that Louis has at last persuaded
him to let her come. He and the Queen will see her part way on
the journey, Colbert tells me, and I am sending Sandwich with
the fleet to fetch her from Dunkirk."

"And then you and James will bring her here? We must do
everything possible to entertain her," said Catherine, remembering her responsibilities as hostess.

Much to her physical relief, Charles pulled up short in his
pacing. "But that is just the trouble. That dog in the manger will
allow her only three days. He is the only person who does not
want her, yet he will not let anyone else have her. So there will
be no time to go anywhere. We shall all have to herd like cattle
in Dover Castle. And I had set my heart on giving her the most
wonderful time imaginable, something she would remember all

her life. All her life," he repeated, falling into a reverie, his stern dark face suffused with tenderness.

"I think perhaps she would prefer to be informal and so see more of you and James," soothed Catherine, hugging to herself the thought that at least he appeared to be expecting her to come too.

"And we must take Frances with us—and her husband, I suppose."

This was an added pin prick. "Frances, Duchess of Richmond! But I thought you would not forgive that runaway marriage."

"Oh, one must not bear animosity at a time like this. After all, she is one of the family, and she and Minette were always friends. It will give my sister pleasure. You will love Minette, Kate."

He said the words as if there were no possible doubt of them, all unaware that his wife was thinking, "Only three days. One can put up with any kind of pain for three days. And how can I grudge them anything? I, who have him for a lifetime—or at least some part of him——"

It was not that she held anything against Henrietta Stuart—"Madame of France" as the second lady in that land was called—only that it was so hard to see that light in her husband's eyes which she, with all her love, could not ignite.

But after that there was no time to think. Everything was bustle and preparation. Charles was so impatient that he tried to set sail from the Nore, but a storm blew up and the wind was unfavorable, and in the end he was forced to go by road to Dover and content himself with meeting the fleet offshore with James. And meanwhile Catherine established herself in the old castle on the cliff while half the Court had to pack themselves, with their best clothes, into the small inns and fishermen's cottages in the little port below.

She never forgot her first sight of Minette. As she saw her standing between her two tall brothers, in the elegance of her sophistication and her Paris clothes, Catherine was almost shocked by her fragility. Worn out as she must have been by her journey, there was yet a radiance about her, a lightness of voice and step, which made the vitality of her spirit shine through the pallor of her small-boned face. A flush of color high on either cheekbone accentuated the brightness of her eyes, and although her beauty was of the spirit rather than of the flesh, her naturalness and spontaneous gaiety bound her warmly to this earth. As she ran forward to greet her sister-in-law, Catherine appreciated the truth of old Toby Rustat's words. "She has that thing about her which his Majesty has."

Sitting at table, dancing in the torch-lit hall or riding with her brothers to Canterbury, Minette was always the center of liveliness and laughter. She had that easy charm which holds all but clods beneath its spell. And passionately Catherine envied her.

"I had desired to see the so terrible damage which has arrived to London," she said in unaccustomed English, as soon as they were seated at table that first evening.

"It would only have distressed you," said her cousin Frances, who had grown more gentle.

"One thing at least which Philippe's niggardliness has spared you," consoled James.

"We are trying to have it rebuilt in time for your next visit," promised Charles. "We have a genius of a scientist turned architect——"

"Every single church he will rebuild," put in a chastened and forgiven Duke of Monmouth, who had known and adored Madame when he was a small nobody in France. "Even St. Paul's, with a great dome that will dominate the City."

"You should see the palace Louis builds at Versailles! A hall lined with mirrors, *our* architect plans."

"I understand some unfortunate courtier was tactless enough to entertain him in a mansion bigger than any of his own, so he feels he must outbuild him," chuckled Charles.

"Hundreds of peasants he has set to drain the surrounding marshes so that he may lay out gardens, and many of them were drowned. His parterres and his fountains will be *magnifique—incroyable*. But I am sorry for the poor peasants."

They were all talking at once, as reunited families will.

"And what sort of journey did you have from Paris?" asked James.

Minette set aside the strawberries with which Charles was plying her. "As to the journey—oh, if you could but have seen us!" she cried on a trill of laughter, although she had well nigh died of it. "Milor' Sandwich here has already heard enough of it from my people. For see, it was pouring with rain and the river Sambre had overflew——"

"Flowed," corrected Charles, enjoying himself hugely. "For an Exeter woman you really speak the most execrable English!"

"Overflowed, then. And the bridge *tout à fait détruit*—quite broken. We had to refuge ourselves in a very ill-smelling cottage."

"*Le Roi Soleil* in a cottage!" It seemed to amuse Charles immensely to hear that his all powerful cousin had at last been brought within smelling distance of ordinary humanity.

"Oh, Louis was quite agreeable. It was the Queen who protested. She would have had us spend the night in our coaches sunk in mud to the axle. It was not *comme il faut,* she said, for him to sleep in the same room with me—although with two of his mistresses and at least a dozen ladies in waiting lying on the floor I do not know what we could have done! Besides, dear Charles, I do assure you I was feeling too ill just then to sin with anybody."

"Perhaps Queen Marie-Thérèse was suffering too—from the mistresses and from wishing she were as lively and slender as you," suggested Catherine, unable to refrain from joining in her menfolk's ribald laughter.

"And Louis?" asked James.

"Louis? Oh, he was furious with her. So he stamp out of the little room to sleep in the coach, but *malheureusement* he trip over Madame de Mountespan and put his muddy spur right through the lace nightcap of the Marquise de Lavallière, who was lying by the fire. The Marquise was furious. And, ill as I felt, I catch his eye and then we laugh and laugh——"

"Poor Louis! He should have known better than to crowd all his mistresses into one cottage," said Charles, when their merri-

ment had subsided. "But let us drink to him. And may he allow
you to stay longer!"

But neither Minette nor anyone else remembered to drink to
the Duke, her husband.

Minette was able to tell them about their mother's last days in
the convent she had founded in Chaillot. "She spoke of you both
very often, the Mother Superior tells me, and with special affection of you, *ma belle soeur.*"

They talked for a time of the memorial to be erected to her
memory, for which Charles was contributing the greater share.
But their time together was pitifully short; and in the middle of
it poor James was obliged to return to London to quell a rising
of the Anabaptists. It was strange of Charles to send him at such
a time, Catherine thought; but perhaps James did not mind so
much because it was Mary of Orange who had always been his
favorite sister. And after he was gone, although all serious motives
were masked by hilarious entertainments, it seemed that Minette
must often be cloistered with the King, Arlington and the French
ambassador hovering near, talking business. That there was some
secret State deal afoot Catherine did not doubt, although others
less watchful of the King seemed unaware of it. And Minette
would try to make up for the hours so lost from pleasure by dancing and talking far into the night.

"You will wear yourself out, Madame," remonstrated Catherine,
recognizing because of her own long illness the signs of exhaus-
tion.

Even Charles would say gently, "You really must rest, *ma mie.*"

But Minette would only laugh and settle herself upon some
cushions on the floor and drop off to sleep in the midst of all the
lights and laughter, with her hand fast in her elder brother's and
her neat dark head against his knees. "You remember how even
as a child I liked to sleep like this," she would apologize; but
everyone knew that it was because neither of them could bear to
spend the precious moments apart. And Charles, who loved to
surround himself with chiming timepieces, had the only clock in

the castle stopped so that he need keep no account of the swiftly passing hours.

Catherine left them to themselves as much as possible, but one morning when their guest slept late Charles returned to her room before the castle was well astir bringing with him five other men. While still in her wrapper sipping her morning brew of tea, she looked up to see Arlington and Arundel, Sir Thomas Clifford and Sir Richard Bellings, together with the French ambassador, bunched together in her doorway as if fearing to intrude. But Charles, after a hasty look round to assure himself that no one but her dresser was there, came swiftly across to her. To her surprise he said nothing but, looking her in the eyes, pressed her fingers urgently with his own and jerked his head backwards with a meaning gesture towards his silent companions.

Remembering how overcrowded Dover castle was and how often, even at Whitehall, he had brought people to her rooms for privacy—albeit at more suitable times of the day—she was quick to understand his need. "Good morning, gentlemen," she said lightly, turning towards them. "I hope you have slept reasonably well in such makeshift accommodation as we have been able to offer you. For myself," she added, as the ambassador came forward courteously to kiss her hand, "I find this old room mighty oppressive and have slept but ill. Indeed, I was about to take a turn upon the battlements to refresh my poor head with some sea air. So if your Majesty will excuse me. . . ."

She saw the quick, warm, approving smile in the beloved brown eyes, and was rewarded. Beckoning to her woman to bring her cloak, she lost no time in passing between the bowing gentlemen. Waving Bellings aside, Charles himself went to the door with her and opened it. As she turned her head to smile at him she noticed that the rest of them were clustered around de Croissy and the paper he was holding, and had already forgotten her existence. And as she began to climb the worn turret stair she was certain that she heard her husband push home the massive medieval bolt.

"It is something extraordinarily secret. Something to do with France," she thought, emerging from the gloomy spiral onto the breezy, sunlit battlements, where the blue Channel, with gray stone quay and gaily dressed ships, was spread like a brilliant tapestry below her. "Something, quite certainly, which his sister knows about and I do not."

The sharp prick of personal jealousy was swiftly followed by a larger racial one. Ahead, a faint smudge on the horizon, lay France. Even now a frigate flying the golden fleurs-de-lis hove to beneath the dazzling whiteness of the cliffs, seeming to emphasize her neighborliness. But somewhere away to the southwest, if only one could see far enough, lay Portugal, the firm ally of England. Catherine's longing gaze was blurred by tears as homesickness surged in her. The Portuguese ambassador was aware, as was all Europe, of the peace treaty Charles had discussed some days ago. Why did he want to come now, quite secretly, to her room to sign something else? Could it in any way be to the disadvantage of her brother? Something that might curtail the trade of her people? Leaning against the battlements, forgetful of the patient woman behind her, Catherine knew herself to be first, foremost, and always Portuguese. Slights and betrayals received in this country crowded to her mind. England had not been so extraordinarily kind to her. And the young, laughing image of Pedro was at that moment very clear and dear. Ought she to warn him? Although she never meddled in State affairs, she had wit enough to do so. Just a word dropped in a personal letter perhaps. How could it be disloyal when Charles wrote so many urgent words—not all of them personal, she now suspected—to his precious Minette?

But suddenly she remembered his telling her how Henrietta Maria had dropped a casual word and so destroyed his father's fortunes. She remembered, too, the urgency in his eyes a few minutes since, and realized how vital this half-entrusted secret must be to him. And Charles was the very heart of her. Charles she never could betray. Whatever he was signing, whoever might profit or suffer by it, she would stifle her own intelligence and keep silent. Surely, surely, she could trust him to do nothing that would harm her own country.

After a while, when she had descended to her deserted bed-

room to be dressed, she found the whole company, French and
English alike, filling the great hall with excitement, and the captain of the newly anchored frigate talking to Charles.

"King Louis has sent Captain Fallière to say that I may stay
another week!" cried Minette, running to embrace her. "Seven
more whole days at home!"

"So after all the splendors of Paris you still think of our barbarous little island as home?" teased Charles.

"Wherever you are, *mon cher,* that is home," she assured him
recklessly, even before King Louis's officer.

"My only regret is that we must stay here in Dover, that time
does not permit the Queen and me to offer all of you the hospitality of Whitehall," he answered. "Your compatriots must think
us barbarous indeed, my dear Fallière. Knowing the limitations
of this village I did warn my sister to bring but a limited retinue,
but she appears to have brought all the pleasantest persons in
France!"

"Louis himself selected the women for their beauty, knowing
you to be somewhat of a connoisseur," she bantered back, in high
spirits. "*Voici, par example,* my little friend Mademoiselle Louise
de Kerouille. Have you any quarrel with Louis's taste?"

All eyes were turned on Madame's favorite attendant, a young
Breton with a lovely oval face framed in red-brown curls, who
laughed in pretty confusion. "Mademoiselle knows that I am the
devoted slave of her charms," Charles said, gallantly kissing her
hand.

"And Monsieur le Capitaine will also remain with us?" invited
Catherine, conscience driving her to join in hospitality to the
French.

"Your Majesty is too gracious—*et moi je suis desolé,*" he replied,
looking round regretfully at the merry company. "But duty com-
pels me to return immediately."

"And take Monsieur de Croissy and that intriguing paper with
you," thought Catherine.

But from that day it seemed to her that some cloud was lifted
from her husband. He might have been an anxious merchant who

after many scrimping, anxious years at last finds resources at the
back of him and can look forward to security ahead. A new sense
of confidence seemed to inform him, so that there and then he
was able to put all further care from him, mingling his wit and
merriment with Minette's so as to pack into one short week, for
each of them, the happiness of a lifetime.

It was perfect May weather and every kind of pastime was invented to celebrate his birthday and the anniversary of his restoration. But such a round of gaiety was a strain upon Minette.
"She has never been strong," confided Charles in a conjugal aside.

"And, now, obviously, she is far from well," insisted Catherine.
"I pray you, Charles, take James and Jemmie to review the forti-
fications or something, while I persuade her to rest."

"But I cannot bear to waste one hour, or to spoil my brother's
pleasure," remonstrated Minette when pressed; and in the end it
was Mademoiselle de Kerouille who persuaded her.

"Your Highness knows how you tossed and coughed half the
night," she said. "If you do not get some sleep you will make yourself ill and then his Majesty will have no pleasure at all."

Catherine bore Minette off but she felt sure that her husband's
immediate pleasure would be well catered to just the same; for,
being sadly experienced in such matters, she doubted very much
whether solicitude for her mistress actuated Louise so much as
her desire to be alone with a king who obviously admired her.

Lying in the quiet of the Queen's bedroom at Dover Castle, the
exhausted Duchess looked little more than a girl; yet in the defenselessness of sleep that small-boned, piquant face took on a
worn aspect which revealed how much she had been through.
And Catherine, sending her women away, sat by the bedside
wondering about the strange life she must have led—as fantastic
with sudden changes as the King's: birth in a besieged city, an
unknown murdered father and a domineering mother, exile and
poverty—real poverty, so that when her eldest brother had wanted
a portrait of her the artist had perforce to paint her in her pina-
fore; and then quite suddenly the change in the family fortunes
with the Restoration, her own brilliant marriage, the friendship

of the most powerful monarch in Europe, extravagant gaiety, painful motherhood, the cruelty of a jealous husband. All these things Henrietta Stuart had known, and in knowing them had acquired much the same attributes as Charles.

Just as this charming woman, who wore herself out in order to savor life to the full, had a facility for falling asleep anywhere at any time, so she could wake instantly, as unrumpled as an infant. As Catherine sat dreaming, hands in her lap, she was startled to find her sister-in-law's bright eyes fixed upon her in kindly, ironic amusement, and to hear her say in her improved but still elusive English, "I am so glad you married Charles!"

"B-but it is scarcely a success," objected Catherine, shaken out of her slowly acquired reticence as perhaps Madame had intended her to be.

"Why do you say that?"

"In the first place," answered Catherine more warily, "we have no children."

"For that I am sorry—deeply sorry. We all are."

"It is not Charles's fault!" said Catherine quickly, defensively, idiotically.

"Obviously," grinned his unregenerate sister, who had met at least three of his children.

"It is not only our disappointment, but the difficulty it makes for him—about the succession," added Catherine hurriedly.

"Of course. But apart from that—come, come, Catherine, what did you expect? Your marriage is more of a success than—let us say—that of Louis, who imagines himself the Sun God, and poor, stolid Marie-Thérèse."

There was much of her brother's sophistry and a wealth of worldly wisdom in the light, tired voice.

"But he is not in love with me," blurted out Catherine, looking down at the hands in her lap.

Madame of France made a gesture of helpless exasperation. "Not *in* love. But that is not to say that he does not love you."

"As he loves his spaniels, or Toby Rustat, perhaps," said Catherine bitterly.

"Say rather as he loves James—or me."

"Not as he loves you, Madame."

"For the love of God, can you not call me Minette?"

"It is his name for you," objected Catherine mulishly.

"Henrietta, then. And you cannot imagine how often he mentions you in his letters."

"But he—he— You must know there are so many other women." Catherine knew that she was behaving like a gauche child. So often these two brilliant Stuarts made her feel like that, although somehow James, with his slower mind, did not.

"He seldom mentions any of them. Pah!" The second lady of France blew out her lips in the contemptuous grimace of the Paris gutters. "It is always 'I have just caught my wife teaching three of her chaplains country dances in her bedroom.' 'I would have you get some images in Paris for my wife's prayer book,' or when he first saw you, 'She has wit enough and a most agreeable voice.' 'My wife mends but slowly from her illness,'" mimicked Minette in her brother's deep voice. "'My wife, thank God, continues to improve.' Or 'My wife is calling me away to dance.' And always that smug husbandly satisfaction of a man who likes to grumble that he is busy and yet likes to be dragged away." Minette watched her sister-in-law's cheeks grow pink, and because she loved to radiate happiness she warmed again to her theme. "And he never writes 'Catherine' or even 'Kate' as I so often hear him call you. It is always *tout simplement* 'my wife.' Oh, most certainly, *chère imbecile*, those other women may take more of his time and money, but there is only one of you!"

Catherine leaned forward, breathless with happiness. "My old Maria says something like that. Minette—*dear* Minette—you really think so?"

And Minette, grown grave, cupped the Queen's radiant face between kind jeweled hands for a moment, her long dark lashes suddenly bedewed with tears. "Mother of God," she murmured, "what would I not give to go home to a husband who found me amusing and liked me to call him away to dance!"

Catherine managed to put aside the joy that Minette had given her, holding it in her mind to be cherished later, and became all grateful compassion. "Is he so very cruel, your Philippe?" she asked.

"Cruel? He is unspeakable. Listen, *mon amie*, when I was first married I had clothes, jewels, admiration for the first time in my life—and men made love to me. It went to my head a little. I was gay, indiscreet. He would have it every man I smiled at was my lover. And then Louis regretted, perhaps, that he had not married me himself. Philippe was jealous. Jealous even because the people love me. And not daring to rage at Louis he did everything possible to punish me. My husband insults me in public, and whenever we are alone at St. Cloud he sulks. There is a marriage for you!"

"And there is nothing you can do to mend it?" asked Catherine, realizing how much effort she had put into her own.

"There is nothing to mend," shrugged Minette.

"You mean—he does not sleep with you any more?"

Minette laughed, suddenly and harshly, so that she was again wracked by coughing. "If that were all! My dear cloistered saint, surely you have heard of that painted fop, the Chevalier de Lorraine, who goes everywhere with him? Whom he fondles even in public?" she tried to explain between paroxysms. "Naturally Lorraine hates me. He would do anything to humiliate me—to get me out of his way. It became such a scandal that Charles wrote and protested and Louis forced my husband to send him away."

An unknown world of violence and evil opened before Catherine. "So that is what Charles was going to tell me."

"And what I *have* told you," said Minette crisply. "When it was first suggested that I should come to England, Philippe threatened to bring that creature back to live in the same house with my innocent little children, if I persisted in the idea. Then he tried to spoil everything by accompanying me, only Charles staved him off somehow. And finally when Louis insisted upon his giving me permission to come, Philippe returned to St. Cloud and slept with me, night after night, out of spite."

"Out of spite?"

"Hoping to make me pregnant so that I could not undertake the journey. So that I should not have even this short respite of happiness. So that I should not see Charles. That is the kind of husband some women have. You should go down on your knees, Catherine of Braganza, and thank God for yours!"

CHAPTER SIXTEEN

From her window Catherine had watched the great, tall ships weigh anchor and all the French company go aboard. She had seen Charles and James, now returned from London, board the royal yacht, taking Minette and Jemmie and Frances Stuart with them so as to have that last half hour *en famille*. A few miles off shore the fleet had anchored again, and Charles's *Grayhound* was bobbing against the flagship's dark hull. Using his Dutch telescope, she had been able to make out people, like black ants, climbing from yacht to warship. It had seemed an age before the ships had disappeared from a hazy horizon and the yacht, with billowing sails, had scudded back to Dover. Charles, a detached foreshortened figure, had disembarked and was striding off the quay, the rest of the party streaming after him in dispirited groups. Later she had heard his footsteps echoing along the stone passage, and then the banging of his door.

Now a baleful silence reigned over the Castle. James and Frances were up on the battlements, talking over old times no doubt. Catherine's women whispered in corners. But she was scarcely aware of any of them, her heart being in that quiet room with Charles. Then suddenly her own door opened behind her and was shut quietly. She swung round with a flurry of skirts, half-hoping that her husband had come to her for comfort. But of course that was absurd. It was his eldest son who stood there, handsome, charming Jemmie, his face alight with facile emotion.

Miming the mournful silence, finger to lip, he tiptoed across to her with exaggerated caution. "This is the castle of the Sleeping Beauty," he remarked in a penetrating whisper, raising a laugh from the younger women. And then, with histrionic gestures towards the open window, "Is it permitted to relieve the gloom by telling your Majesty all about it?"

Catherine had to smile. She held out a hand and drew him to a stool beside her. "How dear of you to come!" she said.

No one else had thought of it, not even James. Certainly not Andrew Marvell, the court poet who had lampooned her so cruelly and who was no doubt already shut in his room immortalizing the scene in verse. And none of them, she was sure, would give her so pungent an account of what had really happened as Jemmie, with his observant young eyes and his racy, unstudied words. Besides, no poet—however pampered—would have been allowed so intimately close.

"Is the King grievously distressed?" was the first thing she asked him. And the ingenuous young face of her visitor had clouded over. Even Jemmie had no words in which to answer that.

Catherine would have preferred to hear his story alone, but had not the heart to send her eager, curious women away. They had been with her through so much; and often, at Whitehall, their lives must have been extraordinarily dull compared with that of the ladies who attended Madame. These last ten days at Dover, she supposed, had been a God-sent oasis of gaiety to some of them. "The yacht seemed to stay a great time alongside," she prompted, drawing Maria Penelva's hand through her arm and making a little gesture of welcome when the others crowded round. It was so difficult to believe that this delightful young man in their midst had, in his high spirits, murdered a defenseless old man—and so fatally easy, because of his Stuart charm, to forget.

"The King loaded her with gifts. A veritable armory of jewels. A pup from White Lady's last litter, and even one of his favorite clocks which he had brought specially from London—and which I wager she will forget to wind! But of course, dear Madame, you saw all that before they left."

"Yes, yes. Tell me what they said, Jemmie."

"Well, at first, when we were all settled in the *Grayhound*, no one could think of anything to say at all. Uncle James does not help much on such occasions, except that he kept fuming about some fault in the rigging of the *Gloucester*. Poor Madame just held tight to the King's hand. If I were a woman, I would not be going back to the Duke of Orleans for anything! If it had not been for my father himself——"

"Yes, Jemmie. What did he do?"

"He was marvelous, your Majesty. Although his voice sounded odd he kept making her laugh right up to the last, so that there was scarce time to think. 'You must be sure to wear those jee-jaws all at once,' he insisted. 'I want you to outshine Louis himself.'

"'Remember what happened when someone outshone him with a house,' she said, laughing and crying both at once.

"'Pooh! Versailles! It will be nothing to our new London!' he bragged. 'I shall bribe that husband of yours to let you come again and get Christopher Wren to clap the dome on St. Paul's all ready for you.' By that time he had got her up the side of the *Henrietta*. He lifted her on deck himself. 'And feed yourself up, woman,' he chided, feeling how thin she was, 'or next time my bo'suns pipe you aboard they will blow you away!'

"Even the sailors were grinning, bless their stout hearts.

"She clung to him then. 'Oh, Charles! Charles! *Je ne peux pas——*'

"'And speak English, will you!' he scolded, shaking her. 'I would have you remember that as long as you are on one of my ships you are on English soil and that every foreign ship in the Narrow dips her flag to us. And in future you must write home in English, too, lest you forget the use of it.'

"'Forget! How can I forget anything. You have been so generous to me. I only wish that I could give you something in return!' And then she turned to that pretty Breton girl she has. 'Louise,' she called. 'Bring me my jewel box and let us see if there is anything in it good enough for my brother to keep as a souvenir.'

"But when Louise de Kerouille brought it and was fumbling

with the lock, the King caught hold of her hand, key and all, and laughed and said, 'Here is the only jewel I want to keep!' "

For the first time the impetuous young man stopped short, realizing what a *gaffe* he had made. But Catherine, stricken by it though she was, asked steadily, "And what did Madame say to that?"

"Faith, she looked grave the way she does sometimes in the middle of her wildest fooling—with what King Louis used to call her 'pious look'—and said 'No.' Mademoiselle de Kerouille was very young, she said. The parents of Mademoiselle had entrusted their daughter to her care and therefore she must return their dear Louise as virtuous as she came. And she hardly supposed that if she were left as a souvenir——"

Catherine breathed again. Dear Minette, who had perfected the art of living in the gay world without being really of it!

Jemmie's audacious brown eyes were quizzing her, half apologetically, but she did not reprove him. "And then they all laughed and went below," he continued. "I do not know what they talked of, crowded in the cabin down there, with Uncle James, Arlington, George Villiers of Buckingham and the rest. All I know is that my lord Sandwich was stamping the quarter-deck, mighty impatient to get away while the wind served. So that at the end, when they came up again, the men were already standing by at the capstan and there seemed no time at all. Perhaps the King meant it to be like that. . . ."

All lighthearted jesting seemed to have slipped from the young Duke. He sat staring abstractedly before him as if at some scene which, even in the midst of the affairs of hot and urgent youth, had impressed him indelibly. Some scene in which, for all his glibness, it was not easy to make others share.

"And then they parted?" prompted Maria Penelva, softly.

"Yes, Madame. The Duke and I bade her farewell and went down to the yacht. And after what seemed a long time the King came down the ladder after us. We in the *Grayhound* were swaying and bumping against the *Henrietta's* side, but for a moment I saw his face. Our bo'sun was braced on a thwart reaching up a hand to him, but he seemed quite unaware of us all gazing up at him. And halfway down he stopped. And then, as if something stronger than all Europe drove him, he clambered up again. Your Majesty knows how agile he is when he mounts a horse or plays some game, suddenly discarding that indolent pose of his. Madame was standing by the gunwale, her face towards England, crying as if her heart would break. As our bows rose I could just see her. And he took her in his arms and they clung to each other —as if——"

Monmouth's voice trailed off and there were tears in his own eyes.

"As if what, Jemmie?"

"As if they could not bear to be parted for so long, I suppose," he ended lamely.

"Perhaps it will not be for so very long this time," sniffed one of the women, unashamedly blowing her nose.

The tale was told and the dusk gathering; but Jemmie was not one to sit in silence for long. "She was always extraordinarily kind to me when I was so poor in France," he recalled.

"Perhaps it was because she had known poverty herself," suggested Lettice Ormonde.

"Or for your father's sake," said wise old Maria.

But Catherine roused herself and flipped his smooth cheek with the bright feathers of her Brazilian fan. "I think all women are much too kind to you," she told him.

In spite of the brittle edge there was to her voice he grinned back at her, unabashed. "Except my wife," he said.

"Have you given her much cause to be?" she asked.

Jemmie had the grace to say nothing, guessing that she must have heard that he already kept a mistress in the town; and was relieved to see Lord Aubigny appear in the doorway to summon the Queen to vespers.

"She is a gentle child, your wife," said Catherine, rising and dismissing him. "Even if it be only her wealth and title you value, try to be kind to her. For I can assure you it is not easy being the wife of a man to whom other women are too kind!"

Once they were back in Whitehall, life went on much as usual. Charles set himself more vigorously than ever to the rebuilding of the City; and once again, in spite of the coarsening Castlemaine's demands for dukedoms for her sons, he tried to retrench on his private expenditure, having paid the whole of his sister's traveling expenditure sooner than leave her beholden to her husband.

"You did like her?" he asked Catherine, pausing one sunny afternoon by the tennis court, whither she had come to watch him play.

And she, proud to have been able to hide from him every poor scrap of her jealousy, had answered spontaneously. "Meeting her was like opening one of those exquisite old illuminated romances you have, so full of warmth and color that, after losing yourself in them awhile, all ordinary printed books seem dull."

And he had looked at her in pleased surprise, knowing her to be a person not given to fantasy. "I' faith, it must be mutual," he said. "For when I told her we hoped to have found her a new sister-in-law by the time she comes again she said that, much as she wishes James joy, we could nowhere find so pleasing a one as she now has."

"She, who is so gifted, said that of *me!*" Catherine was inordinately pleased, and none the less so because Minette, in her generosity, had chosen to say it to Charles.

Although his partner was waiting for him, and the pages standing ready with their gear, he stopped to draw a letter from his pocket. "I find Ralph Montagu better placed as our ambassador in Paris than as your master of the horse," he teased, unfolding it. "For besides being out of range of your *beaux yeux* he keeps me informed most efficiently on all affairs. The French it seems, turned out in their thousands to meet her and Louis himself would have gone but that his surly brother would not, and so malicious tongues might only have wagged the more. Listen to this. 'She looked beautiful as an angel, so amiable, so charming; and everyone was delighted to see her again. The King received her with joy. Not so Monsieur.' Very pithily put, Ralph Montagu! It seems,"

added Charles, refolding the letter, "that Louis wished to celebrate her return by a week of festivity at Versailles, but Philippe
insisted upon her returning to St. Cloud."

"How can she tolerate him!" exclaimed Catherine, beginning
to believe herself by comparison the most fortunate woman alive.
"But no doubt she had great joy in seeing her children. And she
must have been very tired."

"So tired that she went straight to bed, Montagu says. But she
must have been up with the lark next morning for she actually
wrote to Sir Thomas Clifford in English," laughed Charles, divest-
ing himself of his coat in readiness for the game. "Besides which,
Louis, having much to discuss with her touching her visit here,
ordered her husband to bring her, if only for a few hours. But
because their private conversation languished whenever he went
into the room, Philippe seems to have sulked for the rest of the
day and finally dragged my poor Minette away in tears."

Happily for Charles he could forget his anxiety for one member
of his family in a good, hard set or two of tennis; but as soon as
he and Buckingham had laid down their rackets he was being
coerced to a council meeting to decide on a new wife for James.
"Last time you took your own way, and a useful foreign alliance
it cost us," Catherine overheard him telling the reluctant bridegroom as they all left the court. "You cannot make a fool of yourself now at your time of life."

And afterwards, in an anteroom where they passed her unawares, the argument still seemed to be going on. "Seventeen
eligible princesses Arlington here has found for you to choose
from. A far better selection than I ever had."

She could see James being mulish and Charles puffing out his
thick underlip as he always did when he was annoyed, but they
had passed beyond her hearing. Only when James was gone did
she hear her husband complaining coarsely to Clifford and Arlington, "Of course, as long as he gets what women he wants . . .
though he might as well keep them in the cellars of St. James's for
all we ever see of them except pretty Arabella Churchill! But
judging by his usual taste in feminine charms 't is but little loss."

As the days passed lighter spirits, like Killigrew and Bucking-ham, began laying wagers.

"York had more than enough managing from old Hyde's daugh-ter," they said.

"Then 't is likely he'll choose that convent-bred chit, Mary of Modena."

"Italy should prove a useful ally."

"And she being but fifteen, he can mold her."

It was in the midst of all this marriage speculation that the un-believable blow fell.

The candles had been lit and Charles and half the Court were in high spirits, watching an absurd steeplechase of spaniels which Buckingham and Monmouth were trying to organize in the Stone Gallery. "Put your money on White Lady. She will jump anything for a sweetmeat," Charles was urging Catherine when Prodgers, one of the senior servants, touched him on the arm. "From Paris," were the only words distinguishable above the shrill yapping, the betting, and the shrieks of laughter. But the King turned instantly from the hilarious fun, with extended hand. "The letter," he de-manded impatiently, when the man failed to produce one.

"There is no letter, your Majesty," mumbled Prodgers.

Charles put down the dog he was holding. "No letter? But a boat is in?"

"Sir Ralph Montagu has sent Sir Thomas Armstrong."

It was only then that something in the man's demeanor struck him with foreboding. All the happy animation was wiped from his face. Something must have gone wrong with the negotiations. "Send him to me at once," he ordered curtly.

"He is here, Sir."

Sir Thomas came limping along the gallery. Although he was elderly and had been wounded at Naseby, his boots were lath-ered with foam from his sweating horse. He looked unhappily at the company, arrested in their crazy pastime, as if he found them incongruous with his errand, but never once at the King. He was dressed from head to foot in black.

Catherine sprang up with a little cry and ran to Charles, casting a shielding arm about him. She knew that he was completely unaware of it. His lean body was taut as a drawn bowstring, his eyes upon the envoy. "Is it—my cousin, the King?" he asked. Sir Thomas just stood there with lowered eyes. "It is—Madame," he said.

For once Charles said nothing, asked nothing. And Catherine knew that he dared not. "What about Madame?" she asked for him.

The ambassador's envoy appeared to be bankrupt of words. He went down on his knees and as he did so he crossed himself. "God help me to tell your Majesty," he groaned.

But still Charles said nothing.

"In the early hours of Monday morning—she died."

"She. . . ." Charles Stuart brushed aside his wife's arm, freeing his own to run a finger round the inside of his cravat as if he could not breathe. "But this time last week she was laughing—laughing, I tell you! She was alight with happiness. You must be mad!"

"Would to Heaven that I were, if it would bring her back," muttered Sir Thomas.

"How—did it happen?" asked James, striding from the fireplace to join them.

The brief story came in pitiful, broken sentences. "She had gone back to St. Cloud. The weather has been so hot. . . . She bathed in the Seine against her doctor's orders. And that same evening when they brought her some iced chicory water she was taken with violent colic—and died."

"It was poisoned!" The words shot thickly from the King's lips. His hands fumbled blindly before him and he lurched into a chair like a drunken man.

"That reptile, Lorraine!" supplemented Buckingham, loosening the laces about his friend's throat.

"Did she suffer?" asked Charles, after a long silence.

"Hideously, your Majesty."

His face was ashen. The others had crowded close behind him and Catherine stood behind his chair, praying that in his bitterest hour she might be given the strength not to faint.

"Tell us, Armstrong," said James, seeing that his brother could not speak.

"It was on the Sabbath. They called Monsieur, who was on the point of leaving for Paris. Madame's friend—the one she calls Bablon—was with her, and Mademoiselle de Kerouille. As soon as the King of France heard of it, he came. He brought his own physicians and entreated them to save her. He tried to comfort her by telling her that she would get well again, but Madame knew better; and when he left her room he was sobbing. After that—they administered extreme unction."

"Do not tell me that she just went out like that? That she was not—able to say anything, to leave some message?" entreated Charles.

Some faint glow of comfort seemed to come into the old envoy's face. "She did, your Majesty. She lived through the night," he said. "Her beloved Bishop Bossuet was with her at the end. But before that her first thought had been to send for the British ambassador. Our beloved Princess sent her love to his Grace, the Duke of York, and this ring—which she always wore—to your Majesty. She told Montagu that her sole regret in dying was to be leaving your Majesty. 'Tell my brother,' she kept saying, 'that I have always loved him above all things in this world . . . above all things in this world. . . .' "

Charles, who had born so many sudden bereavements, broke from them all before he should break down. The servants who flung open the doors stared at him, afraid. He groped his way to his workroom, went in and bolted the door. Catherine alone dared to follow him, casting herself against the unresponsive panels that shut her out. "Minette! Minette! Minette!" she heard him call over and over again in anguish.

CHAPTER SEVENTEEN

In the dark days which followed the youngest Stuart's death, anger ran riot in London, and no Frenchman's life was safe. Buckingham and Monmouth, in their tempestuous indignation, fed the blaze. And it was characteristic of Charles that, although in the first fury of his grief he had cried "Poison," he now did everything possible to restrain them until proof could be obtained. He would not condemn on suspicion even men whom he had such good reason to hate.

Time proved him to be right. Much to Louis's relief, it seemed that his younger brother was at least not implicated in murder.

Charles sent Catherine's cleverest surgeon to attend the autopsy which the French king had ordered. More than one hundred persons of unbiased integrity were present, and although poor Minette herself had believed her chicory water to be poisoned, she must have been prejudiced by the cruel daily knowledge that Lorraine, and possibly her husband, would like to be rid of her; for no sign of anything but natural disease was found in her body. Moreover, as letters began to pour in from France, it was established that Monsieur, although little moved by his wife's sufferings, had made no objection to having the remainder of the water immediately tested upon a dog. And two of Madame's women, in their detestation of him and their devotion to their dying mistress, had courageously put their lips to the same cup in order to prove whether or not there had been such wicked treachery.

Madame had always been delicate. She had been ailing of late, and she had overtaxed her strength. That was the unanimous verdict, although, just the same, those who loved her would always feel that the misery of her marriage had been the culminating factor. "Had she been happy as she was at Dover, had I been able to keep her here, she would have lived!" Charles was heard to say repeatedly. But no one in his senses, reading Louis's letter of condolence, could have doubted the deep sincerity of his grief. So the pact between France and Great Britain stood, not broken as it might have been, but sealed all the more firmly between the two kings because of Minette's death.

For days Charles shut himself in his room with only White Lady, his bitch, for company, and a silent, soft-footed Toby to wait on him. Then somehow he took up life again. But it seemed to Catherine that for a long time he lived only on the surface, giving to all a superficial geniality but hiding his real self still more deeply from the world. He went to Newmarket as usual, riding harder and more recklessly than ever, and when in town he moved idly from one amusement to another. Although he seemed to have lost much of his interest in the replanning of the City, he was often to be seen at the playhouse, caring little what he saw there so long as it whiled away the hour. Glad of her audacious merriment, he set Nell Gwyn up in grand lodgings in Whitehall, delighting in her generous inability to forget disreputable old friends from Drury Lane. He sent Jemmie soldiering to make a man of him. But he listened with more irritation than ever to the bickering between religious sects which began to make a contentious bear-garden of every meeting house and pulpit in the country. "Can it matter so supremely whether a man holds by total immersion or by a baptismal sprinkling, so long as he practices charity?" he would protest, with that tolerance which so exasperated the zealous.

Practicing charity himself, he rescued Sir Robert Holmes from the displeasure of parliament and made him Governor of the Wight, where the Solent would protect him in some measure from their malicious interference and where the hardy, seafaring islanders would be more likely to appreciate him. In return, by their parsimony, the Commons forced him, their Sovereign—in spite of all his wife's protests—to withdraw the British garrison from Tangier.

Indolently, Charles drifted, discussing the uses of mercury with the Royal Society, going to sea in a gale so that the nation had no idea of his whereabouts for days, waiting always, it seemed, for any new interest to catch at his attention.

Then Fortune sent two topics of interest sensational enough to stir him and the whole country for weeks.

The first was the finding of two small skeletons buried beneath a staircase in the Tower. Masons who had been repairing the old Norman chapel came upon them hidden, coffinless, only a few inches beneath a flagstone. Immediately everybody remembered the two imprisoned little Plantagenet princes who were believed to have been murdered, and whose bodies had never been found. Scientific experts who were called in confirmed that the bones must have lain there, beneath the passing feet of worshippers, for nearly two hundred years, that they showed signs of strangulation and had been the bodies of a boy about fourteen and of one a few years younger. And it was found that the villains who had hidden them there had done so in such fear and haste that a ring of apparent value had been left upon the finger of the elder boy.

The lieutenant of the Tower brought the ring to Charles, and when the dirt of ages had been cleaned from it it was found to be almost an exact replica of the great ruby ring he himself always wore. Charles put off an important meeting, called for his State barge and set off down river as if he were going to meet royalty. Standing in the Tower chapel shut away by massive stone walls from the surge and hum of London, he stood looking down pitifully upon the sad little skeletons. "Like me, he was King of England. But only for three short months!" he said.

Back at Whitehall, he told his compassionate, child-loving Portuguese wife the story of fair young Edward the Fifth, whose father died when he was fourteen, and of his little brother Richard of York: of how they were torn from their weeping mother "for their safe keeping, and because it is the custom for kings to lodge in the Tower before their coronation," as their ambitious uncle, Richard, Duke of Gloucester, had said; of how they must have looked down from their window to watch the stands being put up for their procession, when all the time their uncle meant to smother them in their sleep before ever the great day came, and wear the crown himself.

"Oh, Charles, how horrible! How could a man do that to his own flesh and blood?" cried Catherine.

"It passes my comprehension," sighed Charles. "But it seems to have been so through the centuries where a crown was concerned. I thank God we have never had to suffer such disloyalty and suspicion in our family. I verily believe that James—who may ache to turn the religion of this country upside down for aught I know—would sooner have my company than hurry his inheritance by a single day."

In shops and taverns people talked of nothing but the gruesome discovery. Mothers of living children stood gaping and weeping round the grim Tower walls, and gathered round the fireside o' nights to harrow each other's imagination with old tales of bygone ghosts. The playhouse on Bankside was packed when the enterprising producer revived a play by one William Shakespeare about the hunchback king, Richard the Third, in which the very murder scene was faithfully enacted. And the people loved the humane, athletic king they now had more than ever when he had the remains of the unfortunate little brothers brought to the Abbey at Westminster for proper burial.

"At least they will lie among the rest of us," he said.

Catherine, who had been helping him to compose the lines for their pathetic little memorial, looked up and asked unexpectedly, "Charles, do you know where your father is buried?"

Charles was a long time answering. Indifferent Latin scholar that he was, he fiddled meticulously with the alteration of a phrase; finally, since they were alone, he said, "Yes."

Catherine looked lovingly at his diligent, down bent head, illuminated by the light from a tall, branched candelabrum. "You were all so far away," she murmured.

"Some loyal friends of ours begged his body of Cromwell."

"And he let them have it?"

"Yes. Provided they bury him privately in some humble place."

"And they did?"

Charles laughed shortly. "No. They were better royalists than that! They fooled him—and everyone else—utterly. Unknown even to my people my murdered father, too, lies among kings. Otherwise, do you not suppose I should have searched the graveyards of England?" He put the finished parchment aside and looked across at her. For a moment a flicker of amusement crossed the gravity of his face as if he found it difficult not to share with her some secret which she, particularly, might appreciate. But nearly twenty years ago he had given his word to men who had risked their lives to do this thing, and he was content to leave it as their loyalty had planned it. "Your knowledge of English history is woefully lacking, my sweet," he said, ringing a handbell for his secretary, "but I can assure you he has no worse a tomb than the only other ancestor of mine I have ever heard you mention."

And no sooner was the excitement over the skeletons beginning to die down than London was all agog again over a daring attempt to steal the crown jewels. After carefully ingratiating himself with the warder and then well nigh murdering him, an Irish adventurer who called himself Colonel Blood had got as far as the drawbridge with the crown hidden beneath his cloak, the orb ignominiously stuffed into his breeches pocket and the sceptre sawn in half by a confederate. But for the unexpected return of the warder's son and a regimental friend who both gave chase he would have got away with them altogether. Once again Charles went down river to the Tower, so intrigued by the cunning by which the theft had been contrived that he insisted upon interviewing the desperado himself.

"But whatever moved you to pardon him?" asked Catherine, when she heard that the man was at liberty again.

"His cool audacity mostly, I suspect," said Charles. "It is not the first *coup* of this kind he has almost brought off."

"But your Majesty's crown!" protested Donna Maria, who was sitting with her mistress in the palace garden.

"My dear Donna Maria, even the crown was not the original," explained Charles. "The Roundheads melted everything down the moment they got their hands on them! Most of the insignia Blood took were made specially for my coronation. It was not as if he had tried to take the Stone of Destiny."

"I believe you really like this horrible man in the same way that you like Admiral Holmes," laughed Catherine.

"Heaven forbid that you should compare them! For all his lawlessness, Holmes is a gentleman."

"But you do have an odd variety of friends."

"'T is my poor upbringing, Kate. Is it not, Donna Maria, my staunch supporter?" he said, appealing to the frail old Countess, culling for her one of his most sweetly scented roses and himself fastening it in the voluminous silk of her wraps.

"Take scholarly John Evelyn, for instance—who I am sure disapproves of us—" continued Catherine, "and that little Navy Secretary you often speak of as 'friend Pepys.' Surely no two men could be more different!"

"But both are singularly intelligent, and so one gets a rounded view of life. Evelyn, for all his aesthetic taste, sees things with his head; while Pepys, for all his ready reckoning, sees 'em with his heart."

Privileged by her age and the King's kindness, Donna Maria began dozing a little and Catherine caught at her husband's hand and pulled him to the garden bench beside her. "And you, Charles?" she asked. "How do you see them?"

"I, my dear? Oh, with my heart, I suppose. But my mind is always there—at the back of it—jeering." For a few leisure moments his somber eyes rested on her consideringly. "That is probably why I thank God for you, Kate, who are no fool and yet so blessedly uncomplicated," he added.

Catherine knew that these days he paid her the compliment of answering her questions with sober truth and, thinking of all the people who came and went through the palace to see him, she bethought her of something else she had wanted to ask. "And there is another man I have seen of late, Charles," she began, less lightheartedly.

"What sort of man? This place is like an accursed rabbit warren."

Catherine wrinkled her short nose, trying to give an accurate description. "A strange, tall man in some sort of clerical garb. I heard him haranguing some down-at-heel individual once in an affected, drawling falsetto. His eyes frighten me."

"Frighten you, my child?"

"He lowers them obsequiously enough when I pass and then glares at me as if he intended me some injury. Surely, you must recall him if you have ever seen him. His chin is even longer than James's, like a nut cracker, so that his great fish mouth appears to be almost in the middle of his face."

Charles burst out laughing. "Oh, you mean Titus Oates! Being of extremely dubious origin the fellow considers it effective to imitate m'lord Sunderland's preposterous drawl."

"And who is this Titus Oates?"

"One of the biggest scoundrels unhanged, I should say! But other people appear to believe in him. He is said to have un-earthed yet another popish plot."

"What, some other city fired? Or a plague brought straight from the Pope?"

"Oh, nothing so serious as that this time," smiled Charles, sympathizing with her bitterness. "Just a plot on my life."

Catherine gave a low cry, and was suddenly clinging to him so desperately that he had to laugh.

"Fond little faint-heart!" he chided. "I do not credit a word the fellow says; and neither, I should imagine, will any other sane person. All the conceited hypocrite wants is publicity."

Touched by her concern he bent and kissed her affectionately before joining James and his cousin Rupert for a game of pall-mall, and after he had gone Catherine sat there for a long time without stirring. It was pleasant in the June sunshine and she was thinking back over the years since she had known him, thinking of his infidelities, of her anguishes and her jealousies, and of how these things had somehow come to matter less. She had long ago come to realize that all he knew of real loving was reserved for his family and friends. Slowly, prayerfully, patiently she had put herself within the circle of both. Never, she knew now, would she possess the long yearned for joy of his undivided passion. But at times she was almost resigned to this unspeakable loss. For as the hot urgency of passion dimmed in each of them a sense of fixed security was growing in its place. If she had missed the ecstacy, she had at least won a finely tempered affection which she felt sure would outlast the years.

She came back to the sunlit garden and the present with a half regretful sigh. "You were right, Maria," she admitted, as if concluding some previous argument.

"Right about what, *minha cara?*" quavered Maria, waking abruptly.

"About marriage."

But the old Countess's vivid memory was beginning to fade at last.

"That the ardent beginning is by no means the whole of it," Catherine reminded her.

CHAPTER EIGHTEEN

Catherine's acceptance of the second-best in marriage was still to be sorely tried, and her patience with her husband's short-comings was to be called upon to withstand yet another blow. For during that summer Louise de Kerouaille returned to England. Ostensibly, she came to tell Charles all the more intimate details of his sister's last hours, but in reality, Catherine suspected, to take her place politically; for she came with Louis's blessing and at his expense, and since she was a young unmarried woman it was taken for granted by both kings that she should be received into the Queen of England's household.

Charles himself brought her to Catherine and very charmingly committed Louis's protégée to his wife's care "as a welcome souvenir of our beloved Minette." Undoubtedly during the first few weeks when he and the pretty Breton were to be seen so often walking and riding together, they were talking about Madame; and because Louise was essentially tactful each little detail and each scrap of Minette's conversation she was able to recall was of real solace to him, for which Catherine could be vicariously glad. But behind the girl's guileless baby face moved an astute mind, a mind sharpened by contact with Minette's, no doubt, although unsweetened by her selflessness. Else why should Louis have chosen her to look after his interests, to be the feminine counter-part of Colbert de Croissy, his ambassador, and as such, under the guise of a tender liaison with the lost loved one, to keep France ever in the forefront of his cousin's mind. There at his Court, day and night, she was a pretty persuasive reminder.

Gradually it was born in upon Catherine that that was exactly what Louis did want. Understanding his cousin's tastes only too well, he hoped the jewel Charles had once begged from his sister would be with him, quite literally, by day and by night.

Having the girl in her household, she had ample opportunity to observe the handsome jewels with which the French King had loaded her, and to know that, like many girls brought to Court from comparative poverty, she was as acquisitive as a jackdaw about sparkling things. And as time went on Catherine seemed to recognize some still handsomer pieces which her own husband must have contributed to the collection.

Sore at heart, Catherine watched and waited. For a long time the French girl was clever enough to resist Charles's advances. She played him like a fish. "She is one of those people he was talking about who see things with their minds and not with their hearts," concluded Catherine bitterly. For certainly she herself, if so besieged, could not have kept her chastity so long. Her emotions, proof against all other men, would have betrayed her. Always she had been trapped by her desperate love for him.

And inevitably the day came when Louise de Kerouille succeeded Barbara Castlemaine.

Charles had taken her to Newmarket, where he had always said there was no place for women. But both of them had been the guests of Lord Arlington in his huge mansion at Euston; and back along the country roads to Whitehall sped fantastic accounts of the brilliance and gaiety of that houseparty and of the game of charades which had ended, one hilarious night, in a mock bedding of Madame Carwell, as the English called her, and the enamored King. Few, knowing Charles, were such fools as to believe that there had been much mockery about it.

Catherine hid her grief as best she could. "Even the brief fires that consume a man in later life do not matter so much," her mother had said, that far-off day in Lisbon; and certainly Maria Penelva's conjugal love had survived unfaithfulness. Withdrawn and hurt, she tried to wait with dignity for the day when Louise would return to France. But Louise did not return. And by the time winter came and there were perpetual rough seas in the

Channel, Catherine had to face the fact that here was another woman who was no brief fire, but a habit, in her husband's life. Another Castlemaine.

Catherine never hated Louise as she had hated Barbara. Mainly because she herself had matured. But also because Louise's manners were at all times respectful, and in spite of her extravagance she never plagued Charles with tears and tantrums or took vulgar delight in humiliating his wife. Neither did she allow the least liberty to other men. Indeed, one of the things which Catherine found most hard to bear was the virtuous mien with which the Frenchwoman performed what no doubt she considered to be the patriotic duty for which she had been sent. But the pensioned Lady Castlemaine and all her brood—whether by the King or not—had been given titles, and when Louise became pregnant she naturally expected, following the French fashion, to receive one too.

On the day when Charles created her Duchess of Portsmouth Catherine quietly removed herself and her people to the late Queen Mother's dower house. There would be no scenes, no recriminations, this time, but neither would she permit herself to be humiliated by those long, neglected evenings spent in the new favorite's presence or become involved in any of the ridiculous occasions for rivalry which propinquity might provide.

It was the people who hated Louise so savagely for her Catholicism, her French influence and her fine, superior ways. In leaving her the field Catherine, without intent, had left all reprisals in far more capable hands than her own. Where she would probably have bungled veiled, sarcastic shafts, the Gwyn woman's aim was primitive and sure. Witty and good-humored, with her adoring public behind her, she never lost an opportunity to score off her contemptuous rival. Although Catherine would infinitely have preferred less publicity for her husband's sake, she forgave the actress much in return for the stories of her spirited warfare. If the new Duchess of Portsmouth tried to lead London fashions with the largest plumed hat from Paris, buxom Nellie was sure to appear in one even larger borrowed from the comedy wardrobe at the playhouse. When the Duchess, over-emphasizing her high lineage, went into mourning for some important personage in France, Nell drove weeping disconsolately through the streets of London in even deeper weeds—for the Cham of Tartary, or some such person, she said. It was all manna for the editors of the newssheets, and free entertainment for the prentices. And when a mob of exasperated citizens pelted what they supposed to be the Frenchwoman's fine carriage with stones and yells of "Pope's daughter!" and invective borrowed from the more outspoken prophets, it was Nell's irrepressible red head that was poked fearlessly through the window. "I pray you, save your breath, my good friends. 'T is only the Protestant whore!" she cried, above their sudden delighted laughter.

And what afforded Catherine the most satisfaction was that Louise, less clever than usual, made the fatal mistake of appealing to the King himself about the insult to her faith. For Charles, who could probably have shaken shameless Nellie for drawing attention to his morals, had only laughed like the rest, and calmly told the lady that it was not women's souls he was interested in. Lady Suffolk, who had been in the room, had heard him say it. After that Catherine had not minded nearly so much about his casual faithlessness because she knew that for her soul he did care.

She tried to hold her peace and to occupy herself with quiet, uncontroversial things. Happily she found plenty to do just then with James's family, trying to console the two unwilling, fifteen-year-old brides—Mary, his elder daughter, and Mary from Modena, his new wife.

Realizing the increasing animosity against a Catholic heir, Charles was marrying Anne Hyde's elder daughter to her Dutch cousin, William of Orange, who was so tenaciously defending his gallant little country from the French that even the revolutionaries had invited him back to power as Stadholder. Without much enthusiasm Charles invited the taciturn young man on a betrothal visit, and while he endured the boredom of trying of entertain so serious minded a guest, it behooved Catherine to try to comfort William's weeping bride.

"I felt as you do, child, when I had to leave home," she reminded her.

"But then you were coming *to* England, Madame!" protested the girl between unconsolable sniffs—whereat Catherine had to laugh. "It did not make it any easier, since it was Lisbon I loved," she pointed out patiently. "But perhaps you, too, will come to love your husband."

"I may," admitted Mary, giving her a long, quizzing look and seeming to doubt, with all the censoriousness and incomplete knowledge of youth, how any wife could possibly forgive, much less love, immoral Uncle Charles.

"Oh, well, Mary, in your case—since your husband is a relative —it is quite probable that you may come back again and visit us," sighed Catherine, thinking of her own country and of dear, faithful Maria who was dying without ever having seen it again. And her well meant though rather half-hearted ministrations must have had some effect for, although Mary Stuart was at present the only legitimate hope of a strong Protestant cause, it was to her Catholic stepaunt that she clung until the last minute before she embarked for Holland.

With dainty, sloe-eyed little Mary of Modena Catherine found more in common. Both were convent-bred and made in the emotional, southern mold. But unfortunately when the young Italian princess arrived she hated James at sight. "The King, he is distinguished and dark, like the gentlemen at home," she confided ingenuously. "But your Duke, he does not pay the compliment. He has a wig the color of corn and long fair hairs on his arms— ugh! You do not like him, no?"

"But I do," Catherine assured her. "And so will you, little goose, when you cease casting languishing glances at my husband, who is old enough to be your father."

"Ah, how I envy you!" cried Mary ecstatically.

"You have good reason," said Catherine quietly. "But they make ballads about me and call me the barren queen. You would not like that."

"No. I should like a little son," admitted Mary more docilely.

"He may be fair-haired too," teased Catherine.

"But he will be James the Third of England," said the new Duchess of York, who evidently understood very clearly what she had come for.

Catherine saw little of the King these days and was sure that her new sister-in-law would hear soon enough all the stories of his amours and his neglect. Few people had the faintest idea of the bonds of common interest which made Charles and her pleasantly contented with each other upon the family or formal occasions when they did meet. Even now London was buzzing with the scandal about his clandestine visit to his cousin Frances. She had suffered from a pox and everybody thought it calamitous that her famous beauty should be marred—that this horrible thing should have happened to her, *la belle* Stuart, the familiar Britannia on the coins in their purses. But Charles, in a rush of compassion, had tried to see her; and when her irate husband had made all manner of excuses, sooner than issue royal commands about it, he had gone quietly down to the water stairs as dusk was falling and had rowed himself up the river to the Richmonds' house, and, of course, some delighted busybody must needs see him mooring his skiff and climbing over the garden wall. Catherine heard the tale with serenity, for whether he succeeded in seeing the lady or not—being Charles he almost certainly had—she knew Frances's exemplary motherhood and her husband's clannish affection too well to have been prompted by anything but past tenderness and family affection.

Indeed, he seemed to have little mind for philandering at present. Without fully understanding, Catherine knew that he was extremely anxious, that there was a new tension between him and parliament which made him walk very warily. Fight for toleration as he would, they were forcing through what they called a Test Act which would create an impossible situation with regard to his brother's succession. Under this law no Catholic might hold public office and poor James was obliged to give up all connection with the navy. Once again, although it was against his nature to urge any man in spiritual matters, Charles besought him to make

outward profession of the Anglican faith. But beyond consenting
to go for a short time as Governor to Scotland, where he was anything but a success, James was adamant.

And the main source of trouble, it seemed to Catherine, was
that hatchet-faced man, Titus Oates, whom she had seen about
the palace and whom Charles had called lightly a "plausible
scoundrel."

For once, it seemed, his tolerance had been ill-advised. He had
not taken into sufficient account the almost crazy credulity of the
Londoners where anything popish was concerned. True, the
Anabaptist rising which James had been sent to quell had
amounted to little a year or two ago, and Catherine had even
wondered if Charles had invented the errand for his brother's
future protection, so that no one could ever say he had had anything to do with that mysterious paper Charles had signed at
Dover. But now Oates had a fervent following and, goaded by an
extravagant French mistress in their midst, the people were ripe
for suspicions sown by fanatical preachers. A series of unprec-
edented misfortunes had driven them from their normal cheerful
sanity to a kind of mass hysteria, in which they lost all sense of
proportion and with it, as Charles lamented, their saving grace
of humor. After the horror of the plague pits, the razing of their
city by fire and the sight of their finest ships being filched by
the Dutch, the wildest rumors were not too much for them to
swallow.

At this moment megalomaniac Oates, for his own advancement,
arose like a prophet of old and accused the Papists. Cunningly
taking advantage of a swing-back to Puritanism, he played off
Rome against the monarchy, inventing plots and pinning onto
loyal and inoffensive Catholics plans to kill the King. Encouraged
by the credulity of his dupes, he became more circumstantial and
began to prophesy the actual time and place.

Catherine first heard about a specific attempt from pretty
Dorothy Howard, the lady of the bedchamber who had taken
Frances Stuart's place. "Three hired assassins hiding behind the

bushes in St. James's Park—with pistols—when the King takes his walk," she babbled, running into the Queen's room.

"Three *Catholic* assassins, of course," jeered her mistress, without raising her head from her book.

"Why, yes, Madame, of course," agreed the girl guilelessly. "About two of the clock this afternoon, that good looking assistant in the King's laboratory was telling me. No doubt they will set a double guard."

Suddenly Catherine's scanty attention was fully caught. A man who worked in the King's laboratory could not be stupid. Suppose it were really true this time, and not part of all this wearisome, insulting fantasy? She threw down her book and seized the girl by both arms.

"This afternoon, did you say?" she demanded.

"Druscilla and Master Kirby both swear to it," spluttered poor Dorothy Howard, goggle-eyed.

"Then come with me this instant."

Catherine released her only to seize a wrap. Her eyes went to the clock. Ten minutes to two. It was further to the park from the dower house than it was from the palace, but if she hurried she might just meet the King on the path to the lake where he sauntered most sunny afternoons. Breathlessly she set forth, without any clear idea of what she was going to do. She could see them coming now, a shorter string of courtiers than usual, led by two tall figures whom she recognized as the Stuarts, and followed by one of the pages bearing the usual platter of scraps for the waterfowl. "I shall come upon them suddenly at the end of the old tiltyard wall," she calculated. Louise, Duchess of Portsmouth, was wont to employ the same tactics, she had heard; and frequently of late had shared the King's postprandial stroll as she herself had been wont to do. The absurdity of it stayed Catherine's hurrying footsteps. Were they to arrive at the same moment it would make a rich jest for Buckingham's biting tongue and create the sort of situation which Andrew Marvell could write so scathingly about. But even ridicule was as nothing compared with the possibility of danger to him. She could perhaps warn him, or at the worst throw herself in front of him if anyone really did fire. She had much in common with Toby Rustat, she supposed, remembering with an affectionate smile how, for all his unobtrusiveness, he had ceased to mind his own business when it had been a matter of going with his master to the Great Fire.

But this particular afternoon the Duchess of Portsmouth had not ventured forth. "So much for her affection!" thought Catherine, in a dither of fear herself.

With an ill-feigned start of surprise she fell in with the King's party. He broke off courteously in the middle of some technical discussion to greet her, and when she asked if he would like her to go along with him to see his new pintail ducks he replied in his usual pleasant way, "With all my heart!" But there had been just that momentary hesitation, that quick, alert look round, which had betrayed to her that there was no need to warn him. He, too, had heard the latest rumor but had chosen to disregard it—until there was some question of her coming too. And even then, since he let her come, she supposed he could not have taken it seriously.

"I thought you did not care for waterfowl," she said to James, for the sake of making conversation.

"I am but returning home this way," he answered with a brevity which made her suspect him of accompanying his brother for much the same reason as herself.

Across the park rose the squat, Tudor bulk of the older palace of St. James, pleasant and familiar. But between it and Whitehall lay the long, narrow sheet of water, the winding paths, the elm trees and those innumerable clumps of bushes of which only John Evelyn knew the names, far more bushes than she had remembered, bushes big enough to afford excellent cover for traitors with primed pistols. She viewed them covertly and her legs trembled beneath her as she tried to talk naturally about what James called "Charles's wretched birds."

"See the little gray fellow with the scarlet tuft?" their owner was saying, with calm enjoyment. "Throw him a titbit, and see

how amusingly he catches it. Here, boy, pass the platter to her
Majesty."

The trouble is, Catherine thought, one cannot tell from which
direction the villains are likely to fire. Would one know first by
the sharp explosion? Did a bullet travel faster than sound? She
longed to ask James, who had once explained it to her. But she
had no head for such things. She was not of the stuff that heroines
are made. All she could do was to keep close to Charles—just in
case.

"Here comes Columbus," he was saying, walking to the water's
edge to meet a lame crane that was waddling awkwardly ashore
to feed from his hand. Columbus was Charles's pride and the
favorite of the whole queer collection. Columbus had a wooden
leg neatly spliced by one of his old army pensioners.

Catherine and Dorothy Howard made the usual fuss over the
adventurous old bird, but the sun had gone behind a cloud and
the water, ruffled by a sudden chilly wind, looked gray and steely.
The manner of the handful of attendant gentlemen was as distrait
as her own, and even James, who knew nothing of personal fear,
seemed surly and uneasy. "Of a truth, your Majesty tempts
Providence!" he blurted out at last.

"By feeding a few harmless fowl?" inquired Charles blandly.

"By walking abroad without a guard during all this ridiculous
disturbance," said James, to whom all subterfuge was alien.

Charles gave him a warning glance. It was not a subject which
he cared to discuss in public.

"Today I took it upon myself to double the guard at the gates,"
persisted James obstinately. "But must you ride unattended
through Windsor park or row alone on the river after dark?"

Fastidiously, Charles brushed the last of the crumbs from his
fine long fingers. He might have been brushing the soil of
religious faction from his sorely tried kingdom. "My dear James,"
he countered calmly, "you should know the real temper of the
people better than that. Surely you do not suppose that they
would seriously try to kill me with you as the only alternative?"

They parted then. James strode angrily away towards St.

James's while the King's party strolled back towards Whitehall, Charles idly discussing with Sir Charles Berkeley a performance of "The Country Wife" and the evil times upon which its author, Wycherley, had fallen. After all, no violence had disturbed the autumn afternoon, and most of them felt rather flat and foolish. At the branching of the paths by the tiltyard wall he took his wife's hand and, bowing, kissed it. It was his usual formal gesture of farewell. But when the long curls of his wig hid his face from the others he said gently, "I should go and lie down, my dear. These scares are all poppycock, of course; but it is good to know how you and James love me."

$\mathcal{I}$f the plots against the King's life were all inventions, many an honest man lost his life on suspicion of his being involved in them. Titus Oates began to be a kind of god to the people. Although he was only an unfrocked parson who had sought refuge in a Catholic seminary abroad, and who had been expelled from it for unsavory conduct, he had gleaned there a superficial knowledge of Jesuit affairs which, added to his lying audacity, made him exceedingly dangerous. He had only to point his finger at an enemy and employ enough false witnesses, and over-zealous judges passed sentence of death. But such power could not have come into the hands of so unimportant a man had he not been secretly backed by political enemies of James and unimpeded in his apparently patriotic activities by Scroggs, the Lord Chief Justice of England.

The King did what he could, going down to the law courts, cross-examining witnesses himself and trying to instil some measure of common sense into the morass of hysterical credulity; but life had taught him just how far the steel of authority must bend before the weight of popular opinion. When, inevitably, members of the Queen's household came under suspicion and she appealed to him he found himself powerless to protect them.

"But, Charles, these three servants of mine could not possibly have the least desire to harm you," she pleaded. "It is only that those fiends of inhumanity put Prance, the goldsmith who cleans my altar plate, in irons in Newgate and tortured him until he laid some ridiculous false charge against them. They are being tried for their lives, and they are innocent!"

"I make no doubt of it. So were many far more important people who have been executed these last few weeks," said Charles grimly.

"Yet you go to your cockfighting and your tennis and do nothing!"

"What can I do?" asked Charles, morosely. "This brilliant new man Jeffreys has the case in hand, and justice must take its course."

"Justice! They say that he is the most merciless of all. Say rather malice! At first you went down to the courts and cross-examined this Oates yourself."

"Yes. And caught him out in a couple of barefaced lies. But what was the use? The people wanted to believe him. And to try to establish his own loyalty Godfrey let him bring in the scourings of the back streets as perjured witnesses and a jury I would not have try a dog. As soon as they had got their hangings, what happened? Poor old Godfrey is found stabbed in a ditch, so that everything looks blacker than ever for the friends of the condemned."

"They even tried to pretend that it was done in my house and the body dragged there. You do not believe that my poor servants know anything about that?"

" 'Zounds, no!"

"I sometimes wonder what you *do* believe!" cried Catherine, in exasperation.

"I believe in religious tolerance, a strong monarchy and unity. I am also one of those bigots who believe that malice is a greater sin than a poor frailty of nature."

"Yet you give this common informer lodgings in the palace—and, for all I know, a pension. Paying a man to hound to death others whom you believe to be innocent!" In spite of the melancholy dignity with which he had spoken, Catherine was more angry with him than she had been for years.

"It is the man who holds the purse strings who pipes the tune," he reminded her. "And the Commons——"

"The Commons! The everlasting Commons! Have you no

authority?" In her grief for her servants and her indignation for her faith she might have been the Castlemaine railing at him.

Yet even then Charles did not raise his voice. He was the last man to hold himself blameless. "If I had, should I have let loyal old Lord Stafford die?" he asked sadly.

"But are you not King?" she cried, thumping the desk by which they stood.

"I am *now*," he said dryly, toying absently with a pen.

Catherine stopped short then in her tirade. Looking up into his drawn face, she realized that for the first time he was envisaging the hitherto undreamed of possibility of his restored crown's slipping from him. He was back to the wall, fighting for his inheritance as his father had done before him, fighting, as he so often did, by seeming to do nothing, waiting for some propitious moment in which to seize his opportunity. Instantly, the burden of her own personal grievances dropped from her. "You mean—" she began, with a terrified little gasp.

Only the snapping of the pen between his fingers betrayed his feelings. "I mean that I will not risk going on my travels again to save any man's skin," he said.

Standing motionless beside him, Catherine knew that he was letting her look for once upon his bared soul, without pretense or barrier. "Not even James's?" she asked presently, in a small voice.

"No, not even James's! That is why I am sending him overseas.

"Into exile?"

"For his own protection. And not, I hope, for long."

"Then *he* must go on his travels again?"

"You do not suppose I like doing it! And I cannot even make him see that it is the only thing which will stop this seething unrest here——"

"Poor James! Then there is no chance for my unfortunate servants?"

"Very little, I am afraid. I shall do what I can for their defense, privately. But I confess to you, Catherine, I must move cautiously. It seems this Oates reptile has nosed out your sending Dick Bellings to Rome."

"Oh, Charles! All those years ago! How could he?"

Charles shrugged contemptuously. "In the same way that he ran to earth some of James's blunt letters, I suppose. James has about as much diplomacy as a bull. He should air his feelings only in code, as I do."

Horrified, Catherine sank into a chair. "But that letter I wrote concerned only Portugal. It had nothing whatever to do with this country," she protested, trying to remember exactly what she had written in it. "Pedro may even be able to produce it."

"And even if he could, do you suppose that Shaftesbury and his crowd, who are at the back of all this, would not find some means to suppress all but the outside of it in court? It would probably be used as evidence that you were trying to convert England."

Catherine buried her face in her hands. "Oh, how wrong I was to urge you to let me send it! You gave in out of kindness, I remember, against your better judgement. I did not realize then how much wiser you are than I."

"Well, it is done now," said Charles, laying a kindly hand on her bowed shoulder.

She sat up, and covered it with her own, comforted that they were in this together. "But how can normal, sane people believe such things about their own kind?" she asked.

"They are *not* sane just now. It is difficult for you to appreciate that there are graybeards still living who can remember the Gunpowder Plot in the time of my grandfather, James the First, when the Papists really did try to blow up King, Princes of Wales, parliament and all. That was no rumor. They caught a man called Guy Fawkes red-handed and have burned him in effigy on every fifth of November from that day to this."

"I know. I have seen them. They are like wild beasts then, although next morning they may be feeding their babies or opening their shops with all the kindliness in the world. And after poor Godfrey was murdered they burned an effigy of the Pope too, with live cats shrieking inside, and brought it beneath my window. It was—indescribably horrible!"

"Oh, Kate, my dear, I am sorry!" There were tears of fear and sorrow running down her cheeks and Charles took her very tenderly in his arms. He could have killed the brutes who had done it. "Do not take this too hardly, beloved. My people are essentially good-natured and fair dealing. They will come to their senses soon and, given rope enough, this Titus Oates will hang himself for perjury."

"And in the meantime innocent men must die."

"It has always been so. I, too, could weep sometimes thinking of the fine young men who gave all the laughter and beauty of their lives fighting for my father and me in battle. But kings cannot live and dwell on such things. Believe me, Kate, with any luck I shall best these hypocrites who pretend they are working in my interest. And then, please God, we shall all live in peace." He pulled her to her feet and wiped the tears from her pale cheeks. "Now rest awhile. I doubt if James will have time to come and say good-by to you," he said.

"Is he being very difficult?" she asked, between sniffs.

"He will obey me. At least one knows where one is with him. He is not like this Shaftesbury—or Shiftsbury, as James calls him— who so lusts after power that he blows from side to side like a weather vane!"

But to Catherine's surprise James did come, straight from the King's apartments. He told her he was leaving for Brussels and began with formal phrases of farewell; but the moment she had sent her women away he paced up and down in obvious perturbation.

"I am truly sorry," she told him simply, realizing what exile must mean to the pride of a man who had so often fought his country's battles.

"Charles was forced to it," he allowed instantly. And then, after a turn or two before her hearth, "I detest compromise, but he is cleverer than I. And if it will preserve the monarchy—but I would not go without his written command."

"So that is why you came back here?"

"I will never let it be said that I fled willingly from religious persecution." He unfolded a sheet of paper upon which the ink was scarcely dry, and Catherine laid a sympathetic hand upon the shaking one that offered it. She had never respected him more.

"*Though I must command you to do this, be assured that no absence nor anything else can ever change me from being truly and kindly your C. R.*," she read, in her husband's familiar hand. Then, refolding and returning it, she added with a smile, "If it is of any comfort to you, his love and regret shine through every word."

James nodded, almost absently, she thought, and replaced his brother's letter in an inner pocket. "But it is not that alone which I had to see you about," he said hurriedly. "I came to warn you."

"To warn me?"

He went and leaned against the chimney piece and spoke with his back towards her. "George Villiers is talking about urging you to go into a convent."

"Pah! He has done that before, after—after my second miscarriage."

"Yes. But now he is talking about it, seriously, in parliament."

"In parliament!" gasped Catherine.

"Trying to make other members persuade the King, so that Charles may settle this succession business once and for all by begetting a legitimate Protestant heir."

Catherine's hands grasped the arms of her chair. She must try hard to keep a grip on herself. No good to indulge in fainting fits now. "Does—Charles—know—this?" she faltered.

"I cannot say. Certainly, he was not present."

"And you did not tell him?"

"No. I felt that he had enough on his plate, with me, and that young fool Monmouth."

"Monmouth?"

"He is back, as you know, and lording it in the Upper House. Elderly peers walking bareheaded before him. One would imagine he had found his mother's marriage lines!" James swung round, red and raging. "Oh, forgive me, Catherine! I am a clumsy brute," he apologized. "But it maddens me, Charles's being so fond with him and his being Shaftesbury's tool. Shaftesbury and Buckingham and the rest are trying to turn his head completely so that he will think he stands as a figurehead for the Protestant cause—a kind of logical sequence to this Oates fellow's ranting."

"You mean that you fear they may really try to put him in your place?"

"With me well out of the way in Brussels. What am I to do, Catherine? He has such a way with the common people."

"If it came to such a pass as that," she said reluctantly, "surely your daughter Mary, who is a Protestant, has more right?"

"But after all that fuss she made, she is quite subservient to her husband; and the English will not stomach a foreign king."

They two, so deeply involved, sat in troubled silence, until James remembered that he must be getting on the Dover road to catch the packet.

"It was more than good of you to come," she said, rising to bid him farewell; and it was only then that he betrayed what was, perhaps, the main object of his visit. "Perhaps if you were to have a word with young Jemmie," he suggested diffidently.

With enough trouble of her own, Catherine showed her surprise. "I have no influence at all, politically. You know that," she said.

"But he was always fond of you. And the young fool is vain rather than heartless. Emotionally, he might be moved," pointed out James, with one of his rare spurts of insight.

"I will do what I can," she promised. "And when is that pretty little wife of yours going to give you the son she was wanting?" she forced herself to ask, almost gaily, seeing her women coming back.

"Not yet, it would seem."

"Poor James! That might be the solution of everything."

But in that she was optimistic. "I would not let Charles's tutors get to work on him as they did on my daughters!" he vowed.

Catherine avoided the delicate issue. "You are happier with your bride?" she asked.

"Yes. Without my pressing it, she has chosen to come with me."

"I am glad. Charles thinks this will blow over and you will both be back again soon. But whatever may befall politically, with all my heart I wish you many years of felicity in your family life, James."

He stood for a moment or two twirling his plain traveling hat. He was looking at her appraisingly—at a small, plumpish, middle-aged woman who could in no wise compare with all those ravishing Court beauties Lely was always painting. James Stuart was not an imaginative man, but for the first time he was considering all she must have suffered, and all the trouble she might have made. "I could wish you had had more in yours," he said awkwardly.

Catherine still showed at times that endearing trait of complete naiveté. "I have had my honeymoon—and my illness, when I learned how much he cared," she said, with amazing humility. "And who knows what the future may bring?"

CHAPTER TWENTY

*C*atherine saw Monmouth the next day, and thought that he avoided her. But she invited him to supper and encouraged him to tell her of his travels. "You are grown nearly as tall as your father," she said, when the cloth was drawn and they were alone. "And you are a fine soldier, your uncle the Duke says."

"The Duke—bah!" scoffed Jemmie, looking flushed and handsome.

"I see no cause for—rivalry," remonstrated Catherine, picking her words.

"You mean because I am of the Protestant party?" asked Jemmie, giving her a keen look. But almost immediately he was his charming, outspoken self again. "The King says I should talk about it less and live up to it more," he laughed ruefully. "That was last time he paid my gaming debts."

"Your father dislikes gambling. Just as he dislikes false pretensions," said Catherine quietly. "What do all these lying boasts about your mother make of me, Jemmie?"

"It is not I who insist upon all this hat doffing," he protested, shamefacedly.

"No. It is the clever men who dupe you for their own ends—whose cat's-paw you are fool enough to become!" Jemmie was a grown man now and he pushed back his chair, enraged, but she knew him through and through and was not afraid of him. "Do you not realize what difficulties your presumption makes for the King?" she went on before he could find words in which to answer back. "And how much it behooves you to show him every dutiful loyalty, even to the extent of refusing lesser men's adulation? Nor realize how much happiness it gives him to be able to be proud of you?"

It was difficult to believe that it was the gentle, unconsidered Queen who was so berating him. "But he has always been proud—" he began ingenuously.

"Oh, I know. Proud of your good looks, your bearing, and now your military prowess. But had you been any other man's son you would have swung for murder at Tyburn. And you would not have been here now to jeopardize the country's peace." With a finger across her throat Catherine mimicked the gamin gesture which he had once made in the King's coach, and which had so imprinted itself upon her memory. This time Jemmie did not find it so amusing. "I remind you but for your own good, because I care for you—I, who have least cause to," she added, more gently.

"He forgave me for that affair of the unfortunate beadle," he muttered sullenly.

"Oh, yes, he forgave you, and that must suffice for us all," allowed Catherine with dignity. "And he may forgive you yet again. But let me tell you this, Jemmie Crofts—oh, James Scott, Duke of Monmouth and Buccleuch," she conceded, at his angry gesture. "If you do aught to grieve so kind a father again I, the Queen, will never either forgive you or receive you—ever!"

As the Duke of York had said, Jemmie was by no means heartless, and it shook him not a little that a woman who had been so consistently kind to him and who so seldom interfered should have spoken to him so. He realized—none better—that for all her unobtrusiveness, she was no nonentity; and that for all her husband's frequent neglect, she was prepared to fight like a tigress for his happiness.

"I do not think you will ever hound her into a convent," he told Buckingham at the gaming tables that night.

"All she has and is, is wrapped up in the value of her marriage lines!" scoffed the coarsening Duke.

"Marriage means more to her than to the rest of us," said Monmouth, more kindly.

"All the more reason why she may listen to me—for the King's sake!" prophesied Buckingham, relieving him of stakes he could ill afford.

"If you mean to try to coerce her I should not let the King hear of it," advised his eldest bastard, who had no reason to desire a more fertile royal marriage.

"I should imagine he would thank me for it," said Buckingham. "And I should know, having been brought up with him."

But, for all her devoutness, Catherine was no saint, and when her husband's friend made so bold as to call upon her with that end in view, she would not listen at all. It was George Villiers, Duke of Buckingham, who did most of the listening.

"When you started all this before, it was out of sheer jealousy, because you feared I might obtain some influence over Charles," she said, keeping him standing before her. "I do not pretend to have any influence—any more than you have, or anyone else. But I showed you very clearly at the time that I had not a conventual life in view. I took to dancing and junketing and going abroad masked in the streets with Frances Stuart and other ladies——"

"And were recognized by the people and grew frightened and had to be rescued by some doddering old courtier and brought home weeping in a cart," interrupted Buckingham, brutally.

It was all too true. Catherine had not been brought up to that sort of lighthearted gaiety. "It would not be the first time I have returned to the palace in tears through the cruelty and bad manners of your kind," she told him. "But that was many years ago and I have learned much since then. Also it takes considerably more to intimidate me. I would have you know that if I do not meddle in State affairs it is from the love I bear my husband. And it would prove more love in you if you too ceased to meddle."

"I am his friend," bragged Buckingham. "In persuading you to retire to a convent I am thinking only of his good."

"Loving him and watching him, I have come to understand him a little. Though you have known him all your life, you have—I should imagine—been watching out only for yourself," Catherine hit back. "Are you really so stupid as to suppose that I could not hold my own Court by now if I chose, as Queen Henrietta Maria did?"

Buckingham found that he had met his match. "But, Madame, you are so devout," he began, more persuasively. "I thought—we all thought——"

But Catherine was not interested in what any of them thought. "A woman can be devout without having a vocation to retire from the world," she told him less heatedly. "And my vocation is marriage."

"Childless marriage!"

"May God forgive you such brutality!"

"Madame, I should have thought that for the sake of England——"

"I am not English. I did not ask to be brought here!"

"Then for the sake of a sore beset husband and your vaunted love for him——"

"I doubt if you know anything about love, unless it be self-love. But, listen, milord Buckingham," she went on quietly, rising to dismiss him. "On the day Charles himself asks me to go into a convent I shall know that he no longer needs me, and I shall go immediately without one word of protest, thanking God for what I have had. Does that satisfy you?"

The flamboyant Duke who provided most of the hilarity at Court collapsed like a pricked bubble before her. In the midst of his surprised confusion, he was even capable of the vague stirrings of pity and admiration. "Your marriage cannot have—amounted to much," he stammered, without malice.

"Whatever I may have been called upon to suffer is my own affair," she told him. "But at least I am the only woman who has been Charles Stuart's wife."

And with that Buckingham and his supporters had to be content.

Tired after so tumultuous an encounter, Catherine sent for her physician. She had not been sleeping well and decided to go to bed early and take a sedative. But Sir George Wakeman was nowhere to be found, and to her surprise John Huddleston came in his stead.

"Father Huddleston," she exclaimed. "I am always glad to see you, and how you go about London unmolested in these troublous times amazes me. But it was Sir George Wakeman I sent for to give me something for my poor head."

Huddleston came further into the room and his sympathy seemed to have nothing to do with her headache. "I greatly regret that he cannot come, your Majesty," he said gently.

"Cannot come! When I specially want him? Is he sick?"

"No, Madame. He has been arrested."

Catherine sprang up, pressing desperate fingers to her throbbing temples. "Yet another of my people! This is more than I can bear!" she cried. "What is he supposed to have done?"

"He was arrested only an hour ago on a charge of treason."

"Since milord of Buckingham left me?" she asked grimly.

"I do not know, Madame. It might well be so. They say that Wakeman, being skilled in drugs, was in a plot to poison the King."

"To poison—oh, no, Father, this is monstrous! A loyal old royalist like Sir George—in my own household——"

"Nevertheless, it is true."

"No one is safe!"

"No, Madame, no one at all." He stood there with hands folded in the wide sleeves of his habit, only his eyes alive and Christlike in their compassion. Something in his very immobility set Catherine's heart racing with foreboding. "Did he send you to tell me?" she asked in sudden terror.

"No. The poor gentleman was seized suddenly on his way to a meeting of the Royal Society. He had no opportunity to do anything at all."

"Then how did you——"

"It was the King himself who sent me. He wanted me to tell you with my own lips before your women heard of it."

"Then there is something more?"

"To tell you," repeated Father Huddleston, "and to stay with you."

Catherine's terrified eyes searched his face. Suddenly she put out her arms and clung to him. "It is nothing that has happened— to Charles?" she asked almost inaudibly.

"No, Madame."

"Then I can bear it. Tell me quickly."

With infinite tenderness he supported her. "Remember, dear daughter, how our Blessed Lord was scourged and buffeted. It will help you to bear it. For you, too, are accused—with Wake- man."

It took some moments for the impossible words to sink into her reeling consciousness. Her clutching fingers bit into his arms. Then suddenly she began to laugh wildly. "I—I accused of plan- ning to poison Charles. . . . Minette would have laughed so! It is so f-funny. . . ."

For a man of God John Huddleston was, for once, violent. "The blasphemous liar stood up in court and said in that damnable drawl of his, 'Aye, Taitus Oates, accuse Catherine, Queen of Eng- land, of haigh treason!' My child, you should have seen the amazement on the people's faces! Why, even the judge——"

But Catherine saw and heard no more. She was slipping from the human comfort of his arms and, shouting to her women, he laid her, mercifully unconscious, upon her bed.

CHAPTER TWENTY-ONE

The Queen had not long regained consciousness before her people gave her the sleeping draught she had been asking for. With frightened faces they listened to her uneasy muttering as, half-drugged, she dozed and dreamed. By some confused association of ideas her mind was back at Hampton. "No, no, not the poor headless Howard girl!" she cried out when Dorothy touched her gently, rearranging her pillows. And then, wandering through the strange memories of dreams, she seemed to be sitting on the sunlit grass, trying to remember that it was Henry the Eighth who had divorced and beheaded two wives who could bear him no son, and pushing away the horrible thought that it might happen to her. "Charles! Charles!" she could feel herself crying, although no sound came. She could see him out on the sparkling river in a rocking skiff, looking like Jane Lane's William Jackson in his white shirt sleeves, his dark hair dishevelled. But he only grinned up at her and rocked the little boat more dangerously still. And then somehow it was she who was being drawn away from him by the racing tide. She was drowning, drowning. . . .

"Why cannot the King come to me?" she asked at dawn, pushing back the damp weight of her hair and remembering only how quickly he had come when she had been ill.

"He must have many important things to do," Lettice Ormonde reminded her gently, holding a cup of hot milk to her lips.

"Then where is Maria?" she demanded petulantly, pushing it away.

But as clarity returned she remembered that dear old Maria was dead. How she needed the comfort of her gentle wisdom now! That last precious link with home. But at least Maria had been spared all knowledge of this last blow—this terrible ending to the marriage they had both striven so steadfastly to preserve.

"I will—I *must* think clearly," muttered Catherine, trying to clear her head of the night's troubled fantasies. "Naturally if Charles thinks that I intended to poison him, he will not come near me." And when Father Huddleston would have prayed with her, she entreated him to go to Whitehall instead. "You alone have access to the King at all times," she said. "Only bring me word whether he believes this monstrous thing of me or not."

But as soon as he was gone her own common sense asserted itself. Of *course* Charles could not believe it! However others panicked, he was always reasonable. What man could believe it, who had seen the daily proofs of her love both in the blinding light of public affairs and in the quiet needs of every day? But even so, believing her to be innocent, what could he do? Oppose parliament and public opinion by trying to override this parody of justice with royal authority? Risk his very crown to defend her? Had he not told her that he would not go on his travels again to save any man's skin? Not even for James, his own brother. So what hope could there be for her? Accustomed to regality as she was, crown, luxury, state meant nothing to her compared with the right to live with him. Willingly would she have gone into exile with him had their positions been reversed. But how could she expect him to take the risk of it, who had more than himself to consider? It was his dynasty, the whole monarchy. Charles must put that first. And he was not passionately in love.

"If only I had not been so obstinate, but had listened to Buckingham and gone into a convent somewhere," she thought desperately. "Perhaps, after all, he was right and that was the only safe solution." Perhaps, even now, to safeguard her life and to save Charles all this dangerous embarrassment—but it was too late. That man Oates had accused her of intended murder, and no one he accused escaped. He would bring false witnesses and swear her life away. Feverishly she fumbled for the jeweled watch

Charles had given her. Even now, perhaps, they were trying her, condemning her unheard. "I must go down to the courts," she said, throwing off the bedclothes. "Face these inhuman fiends, and make them see how ridiculous it is——"

"Madame, you cannot, unless you are called. The doors will be closed," they told her.

She tried to behave sensibly, to tell herself that justice would take its course, that since her conscience was clear she had only to wait, and she and Sir George Wakeman would be proved innocent. But what justice was there when every Catholic was treated as an enemy? Her thoughts turned to poor Hill and Green and Berry, her faithful servants. They too had been innocent, and yet they were condemned to death. And as the heavy hours passed, her fears rose. The man with the pale, magnetic eyes whose long face had frightened her in the galleries of Whitehall seemed to be invested with diabolical power.

She could stay in bed no longer. Although shaking in every limb, she insisted upon being dressed. Only when Dorothy would have fastened her necklace about her throat did she turn from the cold touch of it. Once again she recalled that grimace, that horrid protruding tongue, with which the boy Jemmie had once explained what happened to traitors, and how Charles, laughing beside her in his coach, had told her to "Confess and be hanged!" But of course, Queens and people of quality were not hanged, she remembered, going restlessly to the window to look out upon the ever hurrying river. They were beheaded, like poor old Viscount Stafford, a few weeks ago, like that other helpless Queen Catherine. Like Charles's own father. In this country they walked onto a high scaffold, with the hushed people watching all around, and kneeled down before a gruesome wooden block. . . .

In this country. Unseeingly, Catherine waved aside her people's entreaties that she eat. "But I am not of this country," she reminded herself. "I am a freeborn Portuguese. Even the King of England and all his parliament would not dare do this to me. Our great ships would sail out from the Tagus, some of them mounting seventy guns and each manned by sailors every whit as good

as Britain's. Pedro would send them. Pedro, who loves me . . .
Pedro. . . ."

Catherine, who so seldom wrote a letter, called for pen and
paper and with shaking fingers poured out her frightened heart
to him, imploring his protection. He was all that she had left in
the world, she said. But before she had finished the impassioned
screed it was high noon and John Huddleston had returned.
Springing up, she almost threw herself upon him, scattering the
closely written sheets in all directions. "Did you see the King?"
she cried. "For our Blessed Lady's sake, tell me quickly!"

But first the white-haired priest put her gently back in her
chair. "God has been very good to us, Madame," he was swift to
reassure her. "And—under God—so has His servant Charles."

"You gave him my message then?" she asked, relief surging like
a *Te Deum* in her heart.

"There was no need, your Majesty. He had already left Whitehall and gone down to the courts."

"He went himself?"

"And I, his humble servant, followed him."

"Oh, John Huddleston! They might have killed you!"

But Huddleston only shook his head and smiled serenely. He
was far more interested in his master's doings. "All morning he
has been fighting for you," he told her.

Catherine could scarcely believe her ears. "Fighting for me,"
she echoed. "In spite of all he said? In the face of this wave of
persecution and the powerful backing of the Commons?"

"He seemed to care nothing for any of them," said Huddleston,
looking like a human father trying to hide parental pride. "For
no one, indeed, save for you, his wife."

Catherine sat there with ink stains on her fingers and bits of the
frantic letter to her brother scattered all about her. There was a
lovely color in her cheeks and her eyes shone like stars. She might
have been the Queen of Beauty sitting in a rose-garlanded bal-
cony at some medieval tournament with her lover jousting for her
in the lists below. She felt pride and ecstacy and passion—and a
crowning glory for all the slights of all the years. Her delighted

household crowded round her, hanging upon the beloved priest's graphic words.

"It seems that when I entered, the Judge had just ordered Oates to substantiate his charge. 'How could you, an Anglican, know of such a plot?' some learned counsel wanted to know. But the fellow is full of plausible words. For that express purpose, he said, he had attached himself to a party of Jesuits who were to wait upon your Majesty here at Grosvenor House."

"But I invited no such party!" gasped Catherine, amazed at such effrontery.

"Yet there were many listening to him who willingly believed it," said Huddleston, and went on with his tale. "'I put it to you, Master Oates, that you are not a very easy individual to disguise,' suggested a young advocate, less credulous than the rest."

"But Oates was in no wise outfaced. The Jesuits had never seen him, he explained, and his training in one of their seminaries helped him to seem one of them. And as he was waiting with them in an anteroom he chanced to find himself standing by the door leading into your Majesty's private sitting room."

"My private sitting room!"

"Where you were closeted with your physician, Sir George Wakeman. Presently Sir Richard Bellings arrived and as he passed through into the inner room he left the door ajar. 'Sir Richard Bellings,' repeated Oates significantly, looking round at his audience, 'a wily man who is already known to have carried a letter from your Catholic Queen to Rome.'"

"And I suppose that—since I cannot deny the letter—Oates made his point?" questioned Catherine.

"The court was certainly impressed, your Majesty. And that was the first time I heard the King speak. 'I suppose it did not occur to Sir Richard, who is so wily, to close the door?' he asked almost casually, and for the first time during that tense session a titter ran round the crowded benches."

"Ah!" breathed the rest of the Queen's household in relief. But Catherine said nothing; for she knew that often before, in the days when the King had looked upon it all as an amusing farce, he had made remarks like that; and yet, when the Judge had summed up, he had been obliged to let these fanatical bloodhounds have their way.

"Oates pretended not to hear and proceeded pompously with his indictment," went on Huddleston. "He affirmed on oath that he heard the two men's voices urging some matter, and then a woman's voice exclaim, 'I will no longer suffer such indignities to my bed! I am content to join you.' The King's face was white and inscrutable, and you could have heard a pin drop in the court-room, Madame. And then that archfiend went on to pretend that he had heard it arranged that the physician should prepare the poison and you, the Queen, should administer it."

"God in heaven!" cried Lady Ormonde. "Did no one in that assembly strike him down?"

"The learned counsel, with a great show of impartiality, asked him how he knew it was the Queen who was within, and on this point he was able to satisfy them, having bribed some witnesses from your Majesty's household. And then the King rose and asked the Judge's permission to crossexamine Oates; and it seemed that even Shaftesbury and Buckingham were all for it, supposing his Majesty to be concerned for his own safety.

"'You stood by the anteroom door and were able to overhear a part of the conversation taking place within?' he began. And Oates agreed that it was so.

"'Surely, since these regicides were plotting such wickedness in secret, it would have been scarcely possible to hear so much with the door merely ajar,' said his Majesty.

"'Pairhaps it was raither wider, Sir,' agreed Oates, in his insufferable drawl. 'Although aye regret that aye could not see the parties concairned.'

"'Only a part of the room?' suggested his Majesty.

"'Quaite so,' agreed Oates, falling into the trap.

"'Then perhaps you will be good enough to describe to the court what you saw.'

"It was then that Oates began to be ruffled. 'I haive little concairn for such trifles,' he hedged loftily.

" 'But you would have noticed the position of the window. Or some picture hanging on the wall, perhaps? Come, come, man, you have an amazing memory for detail when it suits you. I advise you to exert it now.'

"There was steel in the King's voice and for the first time it appeared to dawn on Oates that he was dealing with an adversary. He became flustered. Almost vindictively he began to describe a room with rich furnishings such as he was familiar with at Whitehall, even mentioning a portrait of some woman by Sir Peter Lely, and some of the gentlemen present, who knew your Majesty's more austere taste in such matters, began to grin.

" 'And the woman's voice you say you heard,' pursued the King, changing the subject to his victim's evident relief. 'How would you describe that?'

" 'Oh, high-pitched and shrill with anger,' answered Oates glibly.

" 'Strange!' marveled his Majesty, 'for my wife's voice is exceptionally low and pleasant.' And as a ripple of laughter went round, he marveled still more that any man could hear a private conversation across two rooms and a passage—unless of course the Almighty had endowed him with ass's ears! 'For, as many present who are really acquainted with Grosvenor House can testify, it is unlike Whitehall in this, that the anteroom is separated from the Queen's private apartments by a large audience chamber.'

"It was as good as a play," chuckled Huddleston. "And by the time the King had finished pulling the evidence to pieces there was no case left against your Majesty. 'From where you say you were standing, Titus Oates, you could have seen naithing—naithing at all—except a large window and a cushioned seat benaith it!' he summed up, mimicking the wretched man's affected way of speaking, until the whole place was in an uproar of delight. And when his Worship had dismissed the case, and this murderous perjurer would have slunk away, his Majesty called sternly for the captain of the guard and sent him under escort to the Tower."

"To the Tower!" echoed the Queen's women, clapping their hands.

"And so strange is human nature," Huddleston told them, "that the people waiting outside, who only yesterday seemed to venerate him as the savior of the nation, booed him thither through the streets."

Catherine sat in a happy daze, murmuring heartfelt thanksgiving. "And Sir Richard?" she asked presently, feeling that she would never forgive herself for writing that ill-advised letter.

"I left him with the King, Madame."

But almost immediately Richard Bellings himself appeared. Too moved for speech, he knelt at the Queen's feet and pressed her hand to his lips while she, with an arm about his shoulder, kissed his forehead. He had been her friend and secretary since the first days of her marriage and it would have been terrible to have lost him.

"Father Huddleston tells me you have just parted from the King," she said, as soon as either of them could speak.

Bellings rose to his feet and the two men smiled at each other with quiet understanding. "His Majesty was charging me with a very happy duty," he said. "He has sent me to fetch you home." When Catherine stared uncomprehendingly, he added, "He entreats your Majesty to come back to your old apartments in the palace, beside his own."

To go back. To be near him and see him every day. Until that moment Catherine had not known how hard her self-imposed exile from him had been. "When?" she asked faintly.

"This very day, Madame. In order that all the world may see you live beneath his protection, that who touches you, touches him, he said. He blames himself in this matter because, seeing your Majesties parted, evilly disposed persons supposed it safe to attack you."

"But it was I. You and Father Huddleston both know that I had good reason——"

"The King only waits to welcome you. For the rest—can you not trust him to put no further humiliation upon you?" urged Father Huddleston gently.

"He is sending men and carts for the transport of your goods,"

Richard Bellings told her. And when her ladies had dispersed joyfully to their preparations, he knelt on a stool beside her. "Madame, it is not easy to speak of these things, but you should know that when these extremists, despairing of a Protestant heir, pretended to have found the marriage lines of Mistress Lucy Walter, the King denied it. 'I have never in my life been married to any woman but the Queen,' he vowed, and because of the persistent rumors to that effect which Monmouth's boasting has stirred up, he intends to repeat it in a kind of public manifesto. When Shaftesbury and some of the bolder spirits urged him, in spite of it, to take advantage of his brother's exile and proclaim the Duke of Monmouth his heir, he was furious. 'Even loving my son James as I do,' he declared, 'I would see him hanged at Tyburn first!'"

"Oh, Richard, perhaps these trials were sent to force his hand," murmured Catherine. "It is wonderful to see him cease to let things slide. But how do you think? Would it not, perhaps, ease things for him if, after all, I were to go into some convent? For his sake, I would do it even now."

"Of what use would it be since he has already refused to divorce you?"

"They wanted that? And he would not do it?"

"They urged him in parliament. They thought that for the sake of a son he would be only too glad."

"And milady of Portsmouth hoped it!"

"If she did, Madame, she must have been grievously disappointed. 'If my conscience would allow me to divorce a virtuous woman, it would also allow me to put her to death,' he told the Commons. 'And if you think I have a mind for a new wife, all I have to tell you is that I will not suffer an innocent woman to be wronged!'"

"Oh, Charles! Charles! How often you have wronged me in the flesh, who will risk so much to keep faith with me in the spirit!" thought Catherine, after they were both gone. Was this, then, the "whole of marriage" of which Maria had spoken? The ending which was worth so much bitterness and striving at the beginning?

In a shining cloud of happiness, while chattering women packed her clothes and menservants moved to and fro with her furniture, Catherine finished the letter to her brother. "The King releases me from all trouble by the care which he takes to defend my innocence," she wrote. "Every day he shows more clearly his good will towards me, and thus baffles the hate of my enemies. I cannot cease telling you, dear Pedro, what I owe to his benevolence, of which each day he gives better proofs either from generosity or from compassion."

Even then Catherine could not bring herself to believe that it was simply from love.

But once she was back at Whitehall, her husband treated her with such tender affection that many a wit laughed and said she might well have been his mistress. He took her everywhere with him, to Newmarket, to Windsor, to Oxford. And while at Oxford, where a new parliament was sitting, he finally outwitted the trouble makers.

"The Commons are trying to follow up the Test Act with an Exclusion Bill which will debar James from the succession," he told her. "But before I see that done I will dissolve them."

"But without parliament to vote supplies what will you live on?" she asked, ever practical.

"We must economize," shrugged Charles, at which she smiled, knowing only too well his efforts at economy, but feeling certain in her own mind that because of that secret agreement made at Dover, he had other resources to draw upon and so preserve his independence.

Going into her bedroom a week later she found the King's valet standing like a sentinel at the foot of her bed, and no one else present but Charles.

"Whatever is Toby doing here?" she asked in amazement.

"Looking after my clothes as usual," said Charles, sounding both amused and elated.

"*Here?*" And noticing that both of them seemed as pleased as schoolboys perpetrating some practical joke, she crossed briskly to the bed and jerked back the closely drawn curtains. There on her pillow was the crown of England with all her husband's State robes spread across the coverlet. "Charles, are you crazy?" she exclaimed. "Or has your friend Colonel Blood been busy again?"

With a hand still on a fold of the tapestry, she turned to him for some explanation, but before answering her he strode to the door and locked it. "My dear," he said, with comical diffidence, "loath as I am to inflict yet more hardships upon you, I could find it in my heart to wish you a very severe headache this afternoon, so severe that no one—not even Lettice Ormonde—will be allowed in here. Everyone knows that you do have such migraines, do they not?"

Catherine nodded. She would do anything for him, within reason. "But why?" she asked.

"Because today I am going to dissolve parliament and, as you know, I cannot do so except in full robes and regalia."

And then, seeing how mystified she still looked, he drew her gently to the window seat beside him. "Listen, sweet, for I have very little time in which to explain," he said. "I have been in consultation with my ministers this morning here in Merton College. They are in full agreement with me that it is the only thing to do in order to save any semblance of power to the Monarchy. Today the Commons are hoping to pass this Exclusion Bill, and if they should succeed, then—good-by James!"

"And so you will go down to them in your robes?"

"Oh, no, my dear. Forewarned is forearmed. That would give them just the advantage which they had over my father when, hard pushed, he tried to do the same thing. I shall walk down to Christ Church in the pleasant sunshine, as usual. Lest there be any tattle, a sedan chair has been ordered to your back stairs to take some of your dresses to the fuller's. After dinner Toby will fold all this sumptuous velvet and ermine into an inconspicuous bundle and take it through the side streets with drawn blinds. It is after all, my dear, our turn to hatch a plot!"

250 `

"And the crown?" asked Catherine, looking at its jewels scintillating in the sunlight.

"I will haud the braw thing richt warily upon my twa knees, Madame," promised Toby, as imperturbably as though he were accustomed to carrying it about in hackney vehicles.

"And when he has dressed me I will take my seat in the House of Lords and send Black Rod to summon the Commons," said Charles. "And they will come crowding eagerly to the bar assured that I have sent for them to say I have given in at last, having so poor an opinion of me that they cannot believe I would ever face poverty sooner than not be master in my own house!"

"And then?" asked Catherine.

"Then I shall make a brisk little speech which will be reported in all the newssheets. About the necessity of unity to restore the vigor of the country, and so forth. About how the eyes of all Europe are upon us and these disputes only gratify our enemies and discourage our friends. I shall finish up by pointing out that I have always done everything possible to keep my people in peace and religious toleration and that, by taking this unexpected action, I hope to leave them so when I die. And, having said my say, I shall send them about their business, wishing with all my heart that you could see their faces!"

"And after that?"

Charles rose from her side and turned to the window, looking out at the lanes and spires of Oxford, but seeing with his mind's eye the whole realm. "After that," he said on a satisfied sigh, "though it will have taken me twenty years and more—I shall be King."

Catherine could not see his face, but after a few moments he roused himself from his long, deep thoughts and turned to her with all the cheerfulness imaginable. "But I must be going, to dine pleasantly in hall, while you mope here with a migraine. I pray you tell your women not to disturb you; and Toby, who will hide behind the hangings, knows just what to do with those geegaws. Like the solicitous husband I am, I will send you some special dish from my table, and because you are an angel of complaisance I shall regret that you cannot be with me this day."

But Catherine had no regrets. Pleasantly, it passed through her mind that even Jane Lane had had no adventure with him that she need now envy, Jane, in whose capable little hands the crown of England had once rested. "And you are stupid and doting enough to tell me all this?" she teased softly.

It was Charles's turn to look puzzled.

"After what happened when your father shared the same secret with *his* wife."

Remembering what he himself had told her, Charles chuckled. He put a finger beneath her chin and tilted up her laughing face towards his. Because of Toby's presence he did not kiss her. Only his dark eyes, between their smoky lashes, grew grave and tender. "God knows I am a sinner," he said, "but at least I have the grace to value aright the gifts he vouchsafes me!"

CHAPTER TWENTY-TWO

With the removal of Titus Oates and the suppression of his supporters, sanity and tolerance had gradually returned. Shaftesbury, knowing his day was done, betook himself abroad; and young Monmouth for once had the sense to keep in the background, enjoying the popularity he always enjoyed in the west of England. The tide of public opinion had turned, and people ran beside the King's coach, cheering him wildly in the streets. Peace and prosperity, with something of the good-humored May-day spirit of the first days of his restoration took possession of the country.

But this time it was a quieter, more settled sense of well being. Having suffered much and lived in fear, men thought more soberly. There were none of the extravagant excesses that had been the natural outcome of Puritanical suppression during the Commonwealth. In this a less scandalous Court set better example than before. Besides which, people were heartily tired of persecution, so that Anglican and Anabaptist, Catholic and Quaker made shift to live amicably side by side—which was what Charles had always hoped that he would live to see. And it was entirely with his blessing that the Nonconformist son of James's friend, Admiral Sir William Penn, set out with a staunch following of Quakers to found a new colony along the shores of the Delaware river, just as the thriving settlement of New York had sprung up beside the Hudson.

A new London—so recently but a dream on paper—had risen phoenixwise from the ashes of the old, to be the wonder of all foreign visitors. Below the Bridge, beneath the shadow of a domed St. Paul's, foreign shipping and the King's fine merchant navy thronged the Pool. When Dutch William would have drawn England into war, Charles would have none of it; and instead of being used for military embarkations, the busy wharves of London were a link with America, Bombay, Guinea, the East Indies and a score of other places, while merchant adventurers sailed out to explore the northern regions and the South Seas.

At long last Charles had leisure in which to indulge the varied interests which had always made his life so full. Often that summer he was àt sea, navigating his own ship as he loved to do, scudding over a choppy Channel or visiting Sir Robert Holmes who, as Governor of the Wight, had built himself a fine house within the walls of Yarmouth castle; and, while there, riding to Carisbrook to see the place in which his father had been imprisoned and where his lonely little sister Elizabeth had afterwards pined to death.

For the Queen it was a happy year, because Charles had suggested firmly to Louise de Kerouille that she might benefit from a holiday at home in France. And on his return to the mainland he took Catherine to the races, to visit the hospital for his wounded soldiers at Greenwich, and to Winchester, journeying leisurely through the hot summer weather to see the fine house Wren was building for him upon the hills. "This County of Hampshire begins to grip my heart," he told her, standing upon the thyme-sweet turf.

"Or is it only because through your telescope you will be able to see your shipping in the Solent?" she laughed.

"You may be right," he admitted, tweaking her ear. "But the place will have other charms. John Evelyn is advising me about the gardens, and though we cannot aspire to anything like Louis's fountains and parterres, here, between a long avenue of English trees, we will look down upon the lovely cathedral city where once our Saxon Kings were crowned."

Once more he was sauntering through life, talking to the people who interested him and passing the day in the country pursuits which he loved. At a year or two short of fifty, he was as lean and athletic as when he had outwitted the Roundheads after Worcester, searching for an unwatched ship.

"You should walk miles a day like me, George," he would say, poking the Duke of Buckingham in his thickening stomach.

"But what would be the use of it if he came in with the wolfish appetite that you acquire?" pointed out Catherine, who often worried lest her husband overdo such strenuous exercise.

And time proved that her anxiety was not without cause; for there came a day at Windsor when he insisted upon playing singles against John Churchill—that same John Churchill whom he had caught in Barbara Castlemaine's bedroom and who had justified his indulgence by a meteoric rise from beardless ensign to full-blooded Colonel. Besides being the acknowledged tennis champion, Churchill was many years his junior. Catherine watched Charles put up a magnificent fight and take a beating with his habitual good grace, but she knew that, much as he had enjoyed the game, it had been a strain, and she wished that he had not got so hot, all the more so as he was obliged to return to London immediately to meet the commissioners of accounts, to enquire into alleged evasions of the Hearth Tax.

After a rubdown and a too hasty meal he went aboard his barge and Catherine, accompanying him to the water's edge through the airless afternoon, called after him, "Be careful not to catch a chill!" Charles waved and nodded, but she knew as well as he did that the moment he was round the bend of the reach he would throw off wig and coat and order all the cabin windows to be opened. And, of course, the next day he was down with a raging fever. However lightly he weathered them, past anxieties must have taken their toll, and by the time his ministers had sent for her he had had some kind of fit so alarming that he had gasped out orders for James to come home from Brussels, and in the general consternation no one had raised the least objection. Mercifully for Catherine, by the time she reached Whitehall Charles was already partially recovered, his life having been saved, the doctors said, by the new remedy of Jesuits' bark which caused high fevers to abate. She found him scarcely able to breathe for the press of anxious surgeons and apothecaries and the surge of curious people about him and, remembering what he had done for her when she had been so ill, she tried her utmost to have most of them turned out and to give him some peace and privacy. But so patient and sweet tempered was he with them all that she began to think it was more the calmness of his disposition than the Jesuits' bark which had restored him to her. And by the time James arrived, hurrying breathless and unannounced into the room, Charles, in spite of all medical warnings, was up and about again.

But his short, sharp illness had been dangerous enough to teach his people how much they loved him, how much they depended upon his wisdom and lack of all vindictiveness for their untroubled way of life.

"Now indeed, *caro mio,* you will have to take life more easily," Catherine insisted; and for several happy weeks he heeded her, convalescing at Windsor, going to bed at sunset and indulging in only the gentler sports. She would sit beside him quietly while he fished, play basset with him after supper or join him in archery contests at the butts, becoming so proficient with a bow herself that, to the equal delight of both of them, the Fraternity of Bowmen of London invited her to become their patroness.

As the pleasant months slipped by Charles, with his amazing constitution, seemed to be as well as ever. Soon he was off to Newmarket with James, where he watched the hawking and the cockfighting, and rode again upon the heath. Catherine was glad to have him there, with a chance to forget all the ugly things which had happened in London, but gladder still to receive his letter telling her that he was coming home again. "James and I think to leave here on the twenty-fourth, lodging the last night of our journey at the Rye House in Hertfordshire, so hope to be with you by the end of the week," he wrote.

The messenger had scarcely gone when she was amazed to hear him at her door, laughing with James at the surprise they would be springing upon her. "Whatever has happened?" she cried, the letter still in her hand.

"Yet another fire," grinned Charles, shaking the rain from his hat and coming to greet her.

"Not here in our newly built London?"

"Oh, no, my dear. Only my poor tumbledown racing place at Newmarket which I have been intending to rebuild these years past. And the weather turned so atrocious 't was not much loss of sport."

"But what caused it?"

"A stable boy lying in the hay with a borrowed pipe smoking some of Admiral Penn's pernicious Virginia tobacco," James told her.

"But we saved all the horses," said Charles.

"And the rest of you? No one was hurt?"

"No, my dear; though we lost some of the coaches that could not be pulled out in time. But I assure you 't was a great deal of panic and pother about nothing. They forgot they had two experts from the fire of London on the spot! James rescued two shrieking chambermaids from a top window and I contented myself with the head groom's fat wife."

They were still laughing and telling her all about it when, from her vantage point by the fireplace, she saw the Earl of Ailesbury's young son, whom her husband had just taken into his personal service, come running into the room through the open door behind them. The young man's face was white with agitation but at sight of them he stopped still in his tracks and stared as if he had seen a couple of ghosts. His behavior was so odd that although they were still talking to her, Catherine could not help watching him. But as soon as the King and his brother became aware of him he seemed to make a great effort to pull himself together.

"You did not expect us for a couple of days?" said Charles kindly, noticing how strained he looked and putting it down, no doubt, to some neglected new duty.

"Why, no, Sir. I—I certainly did not. But I thank God you have come!" And quite inexplicably the agitated young man went down on his knees and began fervently kissing the King's hand.

"Why, Bruce, you are a bundle of nerves, man! Get up!" Charles ordered him testily. "You cannot be fully recovered from that ridiculous duel wound yet. We must feed up my good friend's cub, Kate."

But after the King had taken himself off to change and James had gone to his now adoring Mary, the young man just slumped down onto the nearest window seat. "What is really the matter, Bruce?" asked Catherine, going quietly to him.

Feeling her hand on his shoulder, he managed to spring to his feet. "I beg your Majesty's pardon," he began evasively.

"I think you came to tell me something and would have done so had they not been here," she insisted.

Bruce began to laugh at himself with boyish awkwardness. "The most absurd thing, I suppose, Madame! But I had not heard the King and the Duke arrive. When I was over at my lord Chamberlain's lodgings awhile since, a man rode in from Scotland, a servant of my lord Provost. For days he had been in the saddle. He had been sent to find out if it were true. And when I saw them here I thanked God and could not bring myself to speak of it."

"Speak of what?" asked Catherine, touched by the young man's obvious devotion.

"It seems it is rumored all over Edinburgh that—" he gulped and nodded his head towards the door through which his master had just departed—"that both of them are dead."

"Dead?" Catherine recoiled in horror. Then, since only a moment ago she had both touched and seen them, she began to laugh with relief. "Oh, I see. Just another of these absurd plots," she chided.

"Of course you must be right, Madame," he admitted, reddening. "It was foolish of me to think of alarming you."

"No, no, Bruce. We have all lived through such alarming times of late that 't is but natural. I suppose they said it was a popish plot?"

"Why, no, Madame. Not this time. It was thought to be the work of a remnant of political malcontents. They were supposed to have set an ambush near a place called the Rye House by supporters of his Grace of Monmouth."

Catherine's whole demeanor changed. "The Rye House," she repeated, unfolding the King's letter again.

"Is there such a place, Madame?"

"Yes, although I never heard of it until this day." In silence she offered him the King's brief note to read. "It is strange," she murmured, searching his intelligent young face as he handed it back to her.

"So strange," agreed the young man gravely, "that it almost looks as if some impatient person with foreknowledge of what was going to happen sent to rouse Scotland—some hours too soon."

It was decided that the King must be told of it but in his comfortable frame of mind and lulled by the love his subjects showed him, he dismissed the matter lightly. It was like the old fable of the shepherd boy's calling "Wolf! Wolf!" so often that when the wolf really descended upon his flock nobody heeded. When a wild eyed Anabaptist named Keeling came to the palace to pour out the same ambush story to one of the upper servants, he was laughed at for his pains. But fortunately the man had the pertinacity to return. And this time he brought with him solid witnesses, one of whom openly acknowledged his own intended guilt, so that the corroboration of the affair reached higher levels. Charles himself interrogated the men and was convinced that but for the last minute alteration of their plans he and his brother would both have been dead by now. This time the intended plot had been all too real.

A haycart was to have been pulled across the road just outside Ware, and a dozen or so conspirators were to have been lying in a wayside ditch with loaded muskets waiting for the holdup of the royal coach which so invariably outdistanced the rest of the cavalcade. There was no doubt at all that Russell, Howard and Essex, together with Algernon Sydney and a handful of others, had intended to murder the Stuarts and had made grandiose plans for seizing Whitehall, rousing Scotland and the west of

England and setting up Monmouth as a puppet king, with the real power in their own hands.

The whole kingdom was profoundly shocked. The regicides were to be rounded up for trial. " 'Forgiving, humble, bounteous, just and kind,' John Dryden wrote of me in his sweet partiality," said Charles. "But this time he and all men else will find me more just than kind. Send me," he ordered his secretary, "a list of the conspirators. Of them all, I will spare only Essex because I owe him a life. His father died for mine."

But Essex, in an agony of remorse, had already cut his own throat.

The plot—abortive as the Gunpowder Plot—was over and done with and so, very soon, would be the traitors who had planned it. So small a remnant of dissatisfaction had fermented it that, unlike that popish effort, it would soon sink into oblivion. But though thanks were offered in every church in the country for the sparing of King Charles's life, Charles the man was not to be spared a stab almost as sharp as death itself.

The first Catherine knew of it was when he came to her room one evening, and even then, because it was growing dusk, she was not at first aware of anything amiss. Putting down her book of evening devotions, she would have risen from the small circle of candlelight in which she sat, but that he made some vague gesture which forestalled her. She saw then that he had a roll of thick parchment in his hand. He came straight to her and unrolled it for her to read. Instead of his usual indolent grace there was a brusqueness in his movements. In the stillness of the room she heard the parchment crackle sharply between his hands. It was the list of the men who had plotted to take his life. And in the steady light of her tall candles she saw that the first name upon the list was James Scott, Duke of Monmouth and Buccleuch—his own firstborn.

"Jemmie," she cried, scarcely above a whisper.

Charles let the accursed list roll back on itself and threw it aside. "He was away in the west," he said in a voice thick with suffering. "I thought he was just a handle for their vile treachery.

No more than a headstrong, affectionate young fool. . . . I
would have sworn on God's Body—that he loved me. . . . But it
is I who am the fool, Kate. . . ."

He was down on his knees with his head in her lap—he, the cool,
cynical King of England. Tomorrow no one would guess at it. His
eyes would be amused or mocking, his voice as crisp as ever. This
was just a moment between man and wife—one of those moments
which show them to be one in something more than flesh. It mattered nothing to Catherine that it was the fruit of his sin with
which she condoled. Her pride was nothing. Her arms were about
him, holding him, her pitying hands stroking his bent head. All
her frustrated motherhood leapt to join forces with her wifehood,
pouring out in one stream to comfort him.

He had come to her for consolation.

And after awhile as his loved body relaxed a little the thought
came to her, like a warming flame through the gathering darkness: "Even Minette, whom he adored, had only his glad moments. It was always he who comforted and protected her. His
heart, when it is wounded, is brought to *me*."

CHAPTER TWENTY-THREE

As the evidence was sorted out it seemed possible that Monmouth had not known of his associates' intent to kill, and that he had been led to believe that the King and Duke would only be held as hostages. Certainly, he had not been present.

"But it is horrible to imagine," protested all thinking people, "that with even the least suspicion of this foul plot he should not have quit whatever dubious company he was in and run himself out of breath, without food or sleep, to lay his fears before the King!"

James, for his part, would have had him executed out of hand.

But Catherine understood how Charles must temporize, how he could not bring himself to destroy one so dear. She knew how the thought of his son's beautiful head's being severed tortured him through the sleepless nights, and what a cruel temptation it was for him that he had the final power to save. She was with him by the sundial in the rose garden when, seemingly occupied with the setting of his watch, he had said almost savagely to Bruce, who was young and whose life stretched uncondemned before him, "You are a Bedfordshire man and should know all the back ways where a traitor can hide. You had better go and arrest my son who, I hear, is skulking there."

Catherine had not dared to speak but her eyes had met Bruce's entreatingly, and to her surprise the young gentleman of the bedchamber, out of the extraordinary love he bore the King, had dared to hedge, excusing himself on the grounds that he was not well over his sickness and would attend to it later. Catherine held her breath, wondering if he would be put under arrest. She had never before heard a man disobey the King like that. But after Bruce had mumbled on for a moment or two and then fallen silent, she saw Charles slip the watch back in his pocket, straighten himself with a sigh of relief and give the embarrassed lad such a look of affectionate gratitude as she had seldom beheld. And then he left them without another word and went indoors, hoping for strength, she supposed, to bring himself to say those terrible words again some other day.

"I do not know how, if Jemmie were found guilty, I should ever bring myself to sign his death warrant," he told her afterwards, with affecting simplicity.

"My poor Charles! You have but to love a thing for it to be taken from you," she answered, thinking of all he had lost and of how only she with whom he had never been in love, and James who so often exasperated him, were left.

"It is hard for you too, Catherine, who were fond of him," he said gently. "Though God knows why you should have loved my bastard."

But she had turned on him almost angrily then. "Surely you know, Charles, that since he returned your unfailing kindness with treachery I cannot love him any more! Any love I had for him is swallowed up in my love for you!"

And in the end there was no need for him to bring his son to trial; for Monmouth plowed his father's pride into the dust by turning King's evidence to save his own skin, betraying his supporters and begging for a private interview—an interview at which Charles insisted that James, whom he had also wronged, should be present.

"What did the ungrateful wretch say?" Catherine asked of her brother-in-law, feeling that she could not make Charles go over it all again.

"He admitted his knowledge of the whole conspiracy," said James, "except the part concerning our assassination which, he swears, the others withheld from him because they knew he would never be brought to consent. He begged our pardons in the humblest manner and promised us his dutiful behavior for the future. What he says may or may not be true, but how Charles can forgive him I do not know!"

"Jemmie still talks like a spoiled child, always putting the responsibility for his acts upon those who persuade him."

"And changes like a weather vane! But at least Charles, for all his indulgence, had the sense to pin him down to his confession by making him write it down and sign it."

"Oh, James," sighed Catherine. "Were he a son of mine, I would rather see him dead!"

"No son of yours—or Charles's, for that matter—would ever play the coward!" James told her, his face all harsh with bitterness.

Catherine looked at him uncomprehendingly. "But he is—Charles's."

James gathered up his hat and gloves to leave her. "I was in Holland. I often saw this Walters woman," he said contemptuously. "And God knows there were plenty of other men who might have begotten the whelp!"

Catherine would have liked to believe him; but whatever Welsh Lucy's wantonness, she recognized too well that quirk of the eyebrow and all those small mannerisms which mirrored Charles and had always caught at her heart whenever she talked with his eldest son. She knew that the belief growing in James's heart was watered by growing hatred and was certain that if ever he came into power Jemmie could expect short shrift.

But James's power was not yet, and although the chief conspirators, Lord Russell and Algernon Sydney, were executed Monmouth was pardoned.

"Although you have his written confession to everything except murdering you," commented Catherine, alone with Charles.

"I was obliged to make him write it lest it be argued that there was no plot and that I sent men to their death for imaginings as fantastic as those of Titus Oates," he explained.

"And must we have him again at Court?"

"'Zounds, no! He had the impertinence to come back and ask his written confession of me again—persuaded to it, no doubt, by some of his satellites who imagined it might endanger their miser-

able lives. Even after my repeated assurances that the incident
was closed and that no one else would die for it."

"Might he not have been prompted more by fear lest it should
at some future time fall into your brother's hands?" suggested
Catherine.

"He could have trusted me to destroy it."

"Did you give it back to him, Charles?"

"Give it back?" snarled Charles, puffing out his lower lip.
"God's teeth, there is a limit even to my endurance. I told him to
go to hell!"

And that was the last time Catherine ever heard him speak of
charming, faithless Jemmie. How often he thought of him she
never knew. But she was profoundly grateful that at this time of
such personal loss and shame, his people poured out their love to
comfort him.

Ship after ship sailed in bearing indignant letters about the Rye
House Plot from his loyal subjects in Virginia, New Plymouth and
Connecticut and from true Quaker hearts in the newly founded
colony of Pennsylvania. A general thanksgiving service for the
sparing of his life was held in the new splendor of St. Paul's. The
London merchants entreated him to sit to Grinling Gibbons for a
statue, which they set up in their fine new Exchange. It seemed
that with the few rank weeds of treachery uprooted, a stronger
crop of loyalty than ever grew up on all sides to protect him all
his days from aught but pleasantness.

And although, for him, amours and adventures were over, Catherine suspected that these were in some ways the happiest days of
his life. In mellow mood, accessible to all, he reaped the harvest
of kindliness which he had sown. In November he saw to it that
the fierce, controversial bonfires of Guy Fawkes Day were forgotten in the wonder of fireworks celebrating her birthday. It was
as if he wished to mark the day with some special fanfare of appreciation. And from the palace windows that hard winter he
took pleasure in watching his people making merry with their
booths and fairs and skating by torchlight on the frozen Thames.
He spent more time trying out all kinds of experiments in his

laboratory and attending meetings of the Royal Society, where
he listened with absorption to Sir Isaac Newton discoursing on
the various orbits of the planets and to Harvey elucidating his
amazing discovery of how the blood circulates through the human body.

"I am putting on weight at last," he announced ruefully, as old
Claude Sourceau, his Paris tailor, fitted him for one of those dignified, knee-length coats which so became him. Because of a sore
place on his heel, which Catherine was too tactful to suggest
might be the beginnings of gout, he now rode about London in a
coach instead of taking his afternoon walk—a habit which pleased
the citizens as well as his wife since it gave them more opportunity to see him and her more opportunity to accompany him.

True, Louise de Kerouille, was back in England, together with
another old flame of his from France, the Princess Mazarin; but
neither of them was young any more and Louise had grown even
plumper than Catherine. As always, Charles played the complaisant father to the Castlemaine's tall sons. But Catherine had
long ago schooled herself to tolerate and to forgive. Her love for
him had been so screened of all elements of self that she was able
to take a vicarious pleasure in all his enjoyments, and if his more
sedentary mode of life suggested that he was growing old, at
least it gave her more of his company. Although she was nearly
ten years his junior, the possibility that she might outlive him was
something against which she deliberately kept a shutter closed in
her mind. And because she had been delicate and he so strong,
because life was moving along so delectably at last, living without him was something impossible to contemplate.

But at the beginning of February there came a Sunday evening
which she was never to forget. In reality it was no different from
any other Sunday evening. Only by contrast with what came after
did it seem to hold static the whole glow and security of home, to
remain with her as the epitome of all lost happiness.

Charles had come back from evensong in the royal chapel in a
particularly delightful mood, and she had been teasing him about
his hearty enjoyment of a goose egg, a dish he doted on for sup-

per. Afterwards they had all gathered in the Matted Gallery, lovely with its paneled walls and elegant portraits and painted ceiling. He had sat by the fire in his highbacked chair, resting his sore heel upon a stool. The two Frenchwomen were seated near him, the leaping firelight winking on the Princess's exotic jewels and making an auburn aureole of Louise's short, curled hair. Some of his more intimate friends, such as Lord Ailesbury and Harry Killigrew, were grouped informally about him with Ailesbury's son Bruce squatting on the hearth fondling a litter of pups. And in the background a group of courtiers were playing basset at a long table, absorbed and silent save for the occasional clink of stakes and an intermittent burst of conversation as they took up fresh cards.

Catherine sat a little apart with Lady Ormonde listening to the conversation round the fire but saying little, thinking idly what a charming group they made with the rich colors of the ladies' dresses emphasizing the more somber outline of Charles's relaxed figure. She saw him only in silhouette, the darkness of his wig and clothes relieved only by the whiteness of his cravat and a fall of lace at his wrist as he stroked White Lady, stretched in canine comfort across his knees. He had been telling Hortense de Mazarin about his escape from Worcester, a story which he told with so much humor that no one ever tired of it. The faces of his listeners were alight with expectation, sympathy and laughter. "You should have seen me as a cropped-headed groom," he told her.

"And now your people have you pose for a statue as a laurel-wreathed Caesar," smiled the still beautiful Hortense.

"Besides finding it cold to the knees, I am sure that nature never intended me for so formidable a role," said Charles, with a deprecating shrug.

"The people of Paris were putting up a statue to Louis," Louise told them, not to be outdone. "Some marvelous Italian sculptor had made it and was bringing it over to France to finish the face from life, but it seems that he and the statue were shipwrecked."

"Oh, *quel malheur*," murmured Hortense. But Charles burst out laughing.

"Why do you laugh?" asked Louise, offended.

"Because I could tell Louis where his lost statue is," grinned Charles.

"Then why not tell us, Sir," urged Harry Killigrew. Catherine, watching the little group of men, saw their firelit faces warm with affectionate anticipation.

"Shipwrecked, i' faith!" scoffed Charles, folding White Lady's silky ears across her sleepy head. "When I was last on the Isle of Wight I saw it. My governor there must have been doing a little privateering again!"

"Oh, Charles," cried Louise. "You mean that the wretch stole it?"

"Better not ask me how he came by it," chuckled Charles. "But that is not the best of it. 'Zounds, if Louis could see it now! Robby Holmes has had his own face sculptured onto it—and marvelously ill done it is! He intends it for his tomb, he says. You can have no idea how droll it looks, Killigrew, with my cousin's elegant body and Holmes's head on the top of it. For, like me, Holmes is no beauty."

Even my lady of Portsmouth's patriotic indignation melted in such infectious laughter, and the fireside company went on talking idly of this and that. Catherine had had a letter from Mary, who was beginning to like life in Holland, and Charles was full of plans for spending the summer at Winchester where all was finished save the roof. "By this time next week the lead will be on my new house," he told them. And presently he sent for one of his singing boys to entertain them with some airs by Purcell and a new love song which Louise had brought from France. Listening to the music, Charles looked rested and content, half-drowsing at times, and at others beating time with the hand which was not caressing his little dog. Not wishing either to sit up late or to disturb him, Catherine made a sign to Lettice Ormonde and would have slipped quietly away. But as if feeling her departure Charles turned his head and smiled at her sleepily across the room—as though, for all the music and the people, they two were there alone. A year or two ago he would have risen and escorted her formally to the door; but to Catherine that look of friendly understanding meant infinitely more.

Sweeping him a quiet curtsy, she took her leave. But at the door something made her turn and look back at the warmly colored, intimate scene. With a little catch at her heart she thought again how contented he looked, with his trusted friends about him and the last cadence of the music still sweet upon the air. Like a good ship that had seen many adventures and weathered many storms and was safe home in port at last.

Still smiling at the absurdity of the simile which had slipped so involuntarily into her mind, Catherine observed John Evelyn, the President of the Royal Society, being ushered in at the other end of the gallery. Charles was invariably kind to him and they enjoyed talking about gardens together, but somehow she wished that the old gentleman had not come tonight. He was of a more austere generation and by some strangely quickened perception she knew how differently that Sunday evening would appear to his critical mind. The gaming table, the French love songs, the pensioned mistresses—and in the midst of them, Charles. And because Evelyn was a man of integrity whose lightest word could formulate public opinion she was vexed with herself for not sitting up longer and giving countenance to the scene.

CHAPTER TWENTY-FOUR

*I*n the early hours of Monday morning Catherine's women shook her awake. "The King is asking for you," they kept repeating.

"You mean he is taken ill again?" she asked, springing immediately from her bed.

"He has had another seizure."

"They say he rose in the night and came over giddy in his privy closet and my lord Ailesbury and Killigrew, who slept near him, became alarmed and sent for Chaffinch——"

"And first thing this morning, Madame, when Lord Craven went for the day's password the King could not speak but just pointed to the book in which it is always written——"

"And when his Majesty got out of bed he seemed to stagger. But Bruce says he sat down to be shaved as usual with his knees propped against the mirror, and as the barber was tucking the towel under his chin he fell back into Lord Ailesbury's arms. His Majesty's eyes were rolled right up into his head, Bruce said!"

The terrible words buffeted Catherine from all sides as she hurried into her clothes. "They say he is dying," someone sobbed. But she herself was dry-eyed as she ran across the landing. More insistent in her brain even than the suggestion that he might be dying stormed the fact that he wanted her.

Chaffinch's room was already black with people. Frightened servants crowded the back stairs. Catherine saw Druscilla, the chambermaid, standing there, her pretty face all puckered with crying. Although she had probably never so much as spoken to the King, such was the affection in which he was held that by the looks of her she might have lost father, brother, sweetheart and all.

"Make way for the Queen!" some upper servant cried out, and the press of people parted respectfully on either side. Lord Ailesbury, looking gaunt and aged, met her at the doorway and, shedding ceremony, took her cold hands in his own trembling ones.

It was still dark in the King's room. No one had thought to draw the curtains at the tall windows. Only a few hastily lit candles relieved the heaviness of the paneling with their yellow pools of light. Men, half-dressed and tallow-faced, were making up the dying fire and shooing from the hearth a whimpering huddle of their master's dogs. A white-aproned barber stood as if struck dumb by the empty shaving chair, an open razor still in his hand. High upon its stand on the dressing table stood Charles's long dark wig—a thing poignantly ordinary and familiar.

But Catherine's eyes, her mind, her heart went straight to the long, covered figure in the big, disheveled bed. She could see her husband's closely shaven head capless against the pillows, and his gray and twisted face. His eyes, beneath half-closed lids, were watching the door, patient and imploring as the brown eyes of his spaniels. The fingers of one inert, outflung hand managed to make a small convulsive gesture at sight of her.

Unaware of anyone else in the room or in the whole world, she sank to her knees upon the hard bedsteps, so that her face was on a level with his tortured one. She clasped that piteous hand firmly, trying to pierce his dim consciousness with the assurance that she would never let him go. At first he could not speak at all. He lay with closed eyes and labored breathing; but she knew by the clinging of those loved fingers that he wanted her and drew solace from their warm contact. And gradually the terrible twisting of his features smoothed itself out, leaving the stern, lined face she knew so well. "It will pass, perhaps," he muttered thickly. "I am glad—you came."

"I am part of you, beloved," she whispered back.

He had spoken and her first terror passed. Someone had drawn back the curtains, a bright coal fire burned upon the hearth and there was gray February light over the Thames. Catherine was conscious of James's hurried arrival and thankful that Dr. Edmund King was there. "Mercifully, he was here when it happened," James told her, standing tense and tall across the bed. "He had come to dress the King's heel, and took the risk of opening a vein." James kept repeating the information as if it were some kind of talisman, for although he had stood immovable on many a battle deck, before this unexpected calamity he was all bewildered and distraught.

"It is treason to treat his Majesty's body without consultation, but in a matter of seconds he would have been passed beyond human aid," confirmed the little doctor apologetically.

"You seem to be our ever present help in trouble," murmured Catherine, putting her hand on his arm and remembering how kind he had been when Charles had sent him to her in her own illness.

Then the other physicians with whom he should have conferred were arriving, making a great stir, each anxious to hear exactly what had happened and to try all kinds of drastic remedies. To make way for them Catherine moved to the foot of the bed. Bruce was putting hot pans of coal between the sheets and with her own hands she began to chafe her husband's icy feet. For hours she knelt there while he was being cupped and bled and purged. Now and again she heard his voice murmuring some reply to the doctors and once she heard him cry out in agony. It was becoming more than she could bear. The room was now hot to the point of suffocation and crowded with bishops and high functionaries and hurrying servants. How Charles must hate all these people staring at his suffering and having the distressed little Duchess of York and some of her own women in the room while he submitted to the intimate indignities of human illness! "Even a sick dog is allowed more privacy!" he had said when he had ridden hell for leather from Newmarket and cleared her rooms and given her a chance of life. Longing to do the same for him, she looked wildly round. But she had no such authority. "If only they would stop all these exhausting remedies and let him sleep a little!" she entreated, tugging at James's sleeve as he passed. But James did not understand. He thought that the more remedies they tried the more chance of recovery there would be. Unlike his brother, he was no good at all in sickness.

Towards noon her strength began to give out and when Charles slipped into a sound sleep in spite of them, and Doctor King confirmed her assertion that that would prove the best remedy of all, she allowed her women to lead her away.

The next day he rallied. He even sat up in bed and discussed his symptoms, teasing his friends affectionately for their concern. That remarkable constitution of his was putting up a wonderful fight. A hopeful bulletin was given to the people gathered about the palace gates. "Trust old Rowley to cheat death every time," they told each other, calling him by the coarse nickname that referred to a famous stallion, yet loving him and relying on him as they always had.

But the convulsions returned and although Charles bore it all with fortitude, by the middle of the week he lay huddled and exhausted. Knowing that there was no hope, the bishops besought him to consider his soul. For a long time he either did not hear or would not heed them, but lay in delirium sometimes talking disconnectedly in French, so that it seemed that the loving spirit of Minette was very near him. But as the hours crept by and a more lucid moment came, Bishop Kenn, that courageous prelate who had often reproved his Sovereign for his sins and been but the better loved for it, managed to make him understand that he must prepare to meet his God. Charles heard the words unflinchingly and, expressing contrition for all his sins, listened reverently to the absolution. But when the elements were laid upon a table that he might take the Eucharist according to the Church of England he muttered that there was yet time, and that he would think upon it. Catherine, watching him, knew what was in his mind.

"I am sorry," he said, looking round upon the weary company, "to be such an unconscionable time dying!"

And hearing the gallant words and seeing for the last time a faint suspicion of his old ironical smile, Lord Ailesbury was quite unmanned. "Only last Sunday his Majesty was saying the lead would be on his new house before the week was out," he reminded Catherine, with the tears running down his honest face, "and now——"

And now all those happy hopes and plans were finished. Charles would never look down that avenue of English trees to Winchester, nor walk the springy, thyme-scented Hampshire hills—nor ever again see his gallant ships! Of all his houses the only one left him would be that house to which beggar and king alike must come—so narrow, so plain, and so cold! One which even a merciful God would not let her inhabit instead of him—nor even share. . . . A long, leaden coffin. . . .

For the first time acceptance of the truth came to Catherine and she fainted right away.

"Even now, after all these years, I am useless—ignominious beside his immense courage," she thought bitterly, as in the comparative coolness of her own room a blurred sense of her surroundings came back to her. And through her weakness strove a strong sense of something she must accomplish before this accursed swooning engulfed her utterly. If she could not do it herself, she must get someone else to do it. But who, of all these kind Protestant women fussing over her? Or of what use to speak of it to Doctor King who had come to order her to bed? Desperately, Catherine's eyes searched for means. And there, beyond them, alone by the door—neglected for once, and full of apprehension for her precarious future—stood Louise de Kerouille, Duchess of Portsmouth. Louise, who was a woman accustomed to getting her own way—and a Catholic. Louise, who had been her husband's mistress and to whom she could not bear to be beholden.

But nothing mattered now except Charles.

Summoning all her remaining strength, Catherine waved her other ladies of the bedchamber aside and, in full view of them, went to her. "The King has refused the final consolation of his

Church. He is like to die without any consolation at all unless we can contrive to get him a priest," she said urgently, without preamble.

"I have been thinking of this same thing, Madame," said Louise. "And of how the King of France would wish it."

"Long ago Charles said that it would be—a coming home."

"Yet there is nothing I can do. It is not seemly for me to go into his bedroom—*now*," said Louise, with envious bitterness.

"No, it is not," agreed Catherine, holding to a chair back for support because the very walls seemed to be swaying round her. "But you have much influence with the French ambassador. I pray you, ask him to speak to my brother-in-law, the Duke. They have only to turn all those people out and arrange for the Host to be carried from my chapel."

For the first time the Frenchwoman seemed to draw herself from her own personal calculations and to regard the fainting Queen with amazement. "*You* are asking *me* to do this?" she said, with much of her old arrogance.

"I am entreating you," said Catherine humbly.

There was nothing more she could do for Charles this side of heaven. The beautiful babyface of Louise de Kerouille became a blur and faded out of her sight for ever. The chair to which she clung seemed to crumple like paper and she felt herself falling to the floor at her proud rival's feet.

Long afterwards, when Catherine came to her senses, she was lying on her bed. As the terrible realization of her grief came back to her she cried out; but her women had withdrawn themselves and someone was laying cool, steadying fingers upon her wrist. For one crazed moment, in her bewilderment, she imagined it to be Charles. Then, as normal clarity came back to her, she saw the brown habit of a priest. "Take heart, dear child; for God, who has been so good to us, will give you strength," said a voice of rare beauty, and she found herself looking into the face of Father Huddleston, a face so illuminated by spiritual happiness that there was no need to ask from what long desired duty he had come.

Catherine raised herself to meet his look, and peace flooded into her. "It is the perfect ending, that it should be you who have shriven him," she said softly.

"It must have been meant," answered Huddleston, his fine hands now hidden in the rough sleeves of his habit as he stood beside her. "It is over thirty years since I first set eyes on him—a likeable, lanky young man in a torn, bloodstained shirt—and fetched him food and clothing and hid him in my room at Moseley. He passed the time reading my books and questioning me and, being in grave jeopardy, stood long before the altar there. Now, by God's grace, the seed has come to flower." And bending his tonsured head, he murmured, *"Finis coronat opus."*

Catherine covered her face with both hands and gave thanks, and for a long time there was silence in the room. "How did Charles take it—when the Duke asked him if he should bring a priest?" she asked at last.

"With the very words you love and mimic, Madame," smiled John Huddleston. "He said, 'With all my heart.'"

"Oh, Father, what happier words could he have used? And then?"

"Then his Grace ordered everyone to withdraw, save only those two good Protestant lords, Bath and Faversham. He bolted the door himself. 'Here is he who once saved your body and is now come to save your soul,' he said, as I stepped through the low door behind the bed."

"And Charles?"

"He caught at my hand and bade me welcome. And then, when he saw one of your priests bringing him the Body of our Lord, his whole face lit up with radiance and, weak as he was, he tried to kneel."

It was midnight before the doctors let Catherine go to see her husband for the last time. "I have made my peace with God," he was telling the anxious bishops with shining eyes. Although he was sinking fast, the paroxysms of pain had passed, and as she knelt beside him he talked to her very tenderly. It was Catherine herself who could say nothing. She was too dazed by grief and gratitude to do more than gaze on him and hold his hand. And after a short while he fell into a peaceful sleep.

By the time James came to her next day Charles Stuart had passed from sleep to death, and the upholsterers and servants were already draping her rooms with black, making a tomb of memories of her high curtained bed. Recalling that she was now only the Queen Dowager, Catherine rose from a couch in her sitting room and curtsied very low. "How good of—your Majesty —to come!" she forced herself to say.

"I wanted you to be assured, dear sister, that neither Mary nor I will ever drive you from your apartments if you wish to stay," he said.

"That is generous, James!" exclaimed Catherine, who no longer cared where she lived. "I had hoped you had come to tell me— about the end."

"There is but little to tell."

"Did he—speak again?"

"He roused for a moment or two after you had gone and re-minded Bruce to wind that eight day clock. And this morning he seemed to know as soon as there was light breaking over the river. The water was just how he loved it, Catherine."

"At the flood. With the ships straining at their moorings and small waves, still salt from the sea, slapping the water steps!"

"Yes, like that. 'Pull back the curtains,' he said, 'that I may see the sun shine once again.' And after a little he sighed contentedly and was gone—on the turn of the tide."

James moved from her and went to look down upon the river himself, as of some essence of his brother's spirit would always stay there. But there was something else that she must ask him— something that she must be quite sure about for the rest of her life. She followed him to the window. "Did he ask for anyone else, James?"

"Anyone else?"

"Anyone but me?"

Any ambition James Stuart might have had was eaten up by sorrow. When he spoke it was dazedly, as though still missing the master mind which had so quietly directed and controlled them all. "For me, of course, his ministers sent," he told her, without at all understanding why she had asked.

"And you came all the way from St. James's with a shoe on one foot and a slipper on the other," she recalled, loving him for it and smiling for the first time in days.

"I was so afraid he would be already gone—suddenly, in one of those seizures—and not speak to me again. But I was in his room almost constantly for three days or more after that. He gave me his keys from under his pillow and called me 'the best of friends and brothers.'"

James was fresh from his oratory where he had been praying for his brother's soul and his eyes were red with weeping. Catherine hated to add to his burdens, but if she did not make him remember now she might never know for certain. "And who else came? Try, try to remember, James!"

"The young Duke of Grafton came for his blessing. It may well be that Barbara Castlemaine sent him, but Charles was glad to see him. The lad is more credit to him than his other sons."

"And Monmouth?"

"Charles never once mentioned his name."

"And yet the memory of him lay in his heart! And—the fair Louise?"

"She came by the back way secretly while the curtains were drawn, and sat familiarly on his bed."

"And was he—glad to see her too?" stammered Catherine, who had only knelt dutifully beside him.

"He was quite unconscious at the time. I am sure of it because she leaned over and would have drawn off his two rings had she not chanced to see me standing in the shadow of the curtains watching her."

"James! Surely—not even she——"

But he only laughed with something of his brother's cynicism. "She is probably packing up her fine pickings by now and arranging with the French ambassador for a passage to France.

After all, if her status depends now on the good will of the people, there is indeed little for her to stay for!"

"But she did put it into your minds to admit Father Huddleston," said Catherine, forgiving her in her heart.

James turned to her with a radiant smile. "And heavenly glad Charles was to see him!" Then, searching that conscientious mind of his, he brought himself back to the careful answering of her question. "No, Catherine; though many came and went during those three grievous days I am certain that he asked for no one but you. It was only 'my wife.'"

Long after James had gone to take up the new burden of his kingship Catherine sat alone upon the window seat. No traffic passed upon the silent river and the pennants of the tall ships below the Bridge hung at half-mast; but in spite of the grayness of the day and the blinding ache of tears a living spark of happiness warmed her desolate heart. "And at the end—it was only 'my wife,'" she repeated. "If only I could have told Maria!"

CHAPTER TWENTY-FIVE

Catherine, Dowager Queen of Great Britain and Queen Regent of Portugal, sat in the throne room at Lisbon, receiving an envoy from the King of Spain. She was a little old lady with white hair and beautiful dark eyes, widowed these twenty years, and her brother Pedro's throne was considerably too big for her. But since Pedro was a very sick man, it was she who must receive the envoy, with Pedro's eldest son, the little Prince of Brazil, beside her.

The envoy had been sent from Madrid to make peace terms and, although he had been shown every possible courtesy, his chair had been set a little lower than the throne—to show that Spain was at their feet, as the boy Prince put it. And Catherine, too, felt she owed that small satisfaction to the house of Braganza.

King Pedro had been increasingly ill for a long while and this settlement with Philip of Spain had cost her much in anxiety and effort. After the rapturous welcome she had received at her homecoming, there had been hard years during which more and more State burdens had been laid upon her and—under the guidance of the experienced Duke de Cadaval—she had learned to rule her country. But on the whole she had enjoyed it. She had enjoyed the trust her brother placed in her, the devotion of her people and the development of talents which, during her life in England, had lain dormant. Hard work had helped her to bear her grief, and it had heartened her to find that she had inherited her mother's capability, widened and made more flexible by the example of her husband's wisdom. Hard won humility and years of observation had enabled her to learn.

There had been the lean months of war when the Portuguese had fought brilliantly at Valencia de Alcántara, Albuquerque, Salvatierra and Carca, from which victories—thanks to the dogged courage of a united people—Portugal had emerged at last as a free, unharassed nation. And now, representing the worthy ally of the country to which she had gone as an extraordinarily innocent young bride, she was signing the Peace Treaty which the Duke de Cadaval had handed to her on bended knee.

"Is it true that the King of Spain's daughter has a special kind of nut tree?" her nephew asked, as soon as the assembled company moved again and the tension of the solemn moment was over.

"I think that is just a song which I used to hear the children sing in England," answered Catherine, smiling at the envoy.

But Prince John's boyish enquiry had evidently given rise to more serious speculation. "Our Princesses have many nut trees in their gardens," the grandee from Madrid replied gravely. "And when your Royal Highness is a year or two older perhaps you will come to see for yourself. When, with your Majesty's permission," he added meaningly to Catherine, "his Royal Highness would be able to meet the King of Spain's daughter."

"We will think on it," said Catherine cautiously. And, kissing the boy who had done so much to fill her hungry heart, she sent him back to his tutor.

But it had served to show her how high the power of Portugal stood.

"How I wish that Charles could see me now," she thought, looking round the splendid throne room. And she would have been scarcely human had she not wished that his friend, George Villiers, and his poet, Andrew Marvell, could have seen her too. "With their convents and their cruel lampoons," she thought.

Sitting alone in the deserted throne room, she let her thoughts stray back to London, and to those few unhappy years when she had stayed on there as a widow.

Mary of Modena and James had been kindness itself to her, but the time had come when the English would no longer tolerate their religion and their lack of understanding. Then his elder

daughter Mary had betrayed him and with her husband, Dutch
William, clutched at his throne. And the new Queen Mary had
never once lost an opportunity to be unkind. Catherine would have
left England before James's flight to France, but she had stood out
for the considerable sum of money the government owed her.
She was a hard woman to deal with, William and Mary had found.

But now, looking back, she thought only of the two things
she had done for Charles's sake. In neither of them had she been
successful, but at least she had acted as he would have wished.

The first had been to intercede for Jemmie's life, fascinating,
unstable Jemmie who had roused the west counties into believing in his legitimacy, who perhaps had even come to believe
in it himself. Jemmie, who had far better have found death on the
field of Sedgemoor—for, after his defeat, he had not been able to
escape as his father had from Worcester. He had been taken and
tried, and condemned to death by Judge Jeffries. On his way to
London, a prisoner, he had written to Catherine to save him.
She was all he had left in the world, he said. He had always been
terrified of death, had Jemmie!

Catherine remembered her feelings yet, as she had held the hurriedly written, misspelt letter in her hand: the mixture of horror
and indignation with the faint stirrings of past love. For Charles's
sake she, who never interfered, had gone straight to James and
implored him at least to see his nephew. She had hoped that
Jemmie's charm might work. But James was immune to it. For
had he not, all his life, known the same charm united with
personal courage in another? To please her he had granted the
interview; but Jemmie had groveled on his knees and James,
sickened, had been adamant—punishing him more for past
treachery against his father than for treachery against himself,
perhaps. And Catherine had spent the day of Monmouth's execution on her knees, thanking God that this at least her husband
had been spared.

Finally her thoughts, probing through the long years, had come
to the time when James—at the height of his unpopularity and
with what Charles had been wont to call his genius for choosing

the wrong moment—had at last begotten a legitimate son, a son who set the seal upon his father's failure. James, for a few more years, the people might have endured—but not a continuance of his line and faith. And, denying what they would not face, they had invented all manner of perjuries and plots—rivaling even the fertile inventions of Oates—and had produced witnesses who swore that the baby either had been born dead or was a change-ling, and even going so far as to affirm that he had been intro-duced into the Queen's bed in a warming pan.

Catherine had been living quietly at Hammersmith at the time; but she had left her little community of friends and gone to Whitehall at James's request to testify before all the peers and prelates and eldermen who, in desperation, he had gathered together as a tribunal on the ridiculous charges. She was a person of integrity who had nothing to gain either way and her words would have weight, he urged. So she had stood up before them all, because she knew that Charles would have wanted that dark-eyed, luckless babe to become James the Third, and told them the truth. "I went to the Queen's lying-in chamber as soon as his Majesty sent for me, and never left her until the baby was born," she had testified. "If he were not a true Prince of Wales, should I have stood as godmother at his baptism?" But even that had not convinced their contrived doubting, and poor aging James had been forced to go on his travels again.

Clearly as if it had been yesterday Catherine remembered how strange it had felt to be walking those familiar galleries again, seeing at every turn how Charles had walked here or stood laughing there. She had peeped in passing into the banqueting hall and remembered how, while waiting for the French ambas-sador, he had told her about his father's execution. And, although she could scarcely bear to do so, she had passed through that lovely gallery where they had all been gathered on the last Sunday of his earthly life. Her own apartments were occupied by others, but she had glanced down at the courtyard beneath them and remembered how she had watched Charles coming from a meeting of the Navy Board while the dew was yet on the grass, and how he had stopped to talk business with Lord Sandwich and Secretary Pepys. How shocked they had been because he would not punish some officer for shouting the bawdy truth in his cups—how pleasant Charles's voice had sounded, and how long his shadow had looked in the slanting sunlight—how long, and how inestimably dear!

Catherine started when Lady Tuke, who had come with her from England, roused her from her reverie. Because in growing old one lives so deeply with lost loved ones in the past, she was quite surprised to look up and see the terraced vineyards, gray green in the hot southern sunshine, and to see the ships below them riding the Tagus and not the Thames, and flying the Portuguese flag. But proud ships they were, and to her something more than the foreground to a pleasant picture. For her, every bulkhead and ratline had use and meaning; and moored among them, as there so often was these days, lay a British merchantman.

"I see there is one of our ships in, my dear," she remarked pleasantly, taking Lady Tuke's arm because she limped a little of late with the rheumatics.

"Why, so there is," agreed Frances Tuke, following the direction of her gaze. "But how does your Majesty always recognize a British ship so quickly?"

"By the rake of her bows—or by the quickening of my heart, perhaps," smiled Catherine, suffering herself to be led away and made yet more resplendent for supper.

Afterwards, while the musicians were entertaining her Spanish guests and she was sitting back, a little tired, Frances Tuke appeared at her elbow with a letter in her hand. "There is a young Englishman come ashore who begs to present his credentials to your Majesty," she whispered.

"From that ship we saw," said Catherine. "Do I know him?"

"Oh, no, Madame. He would be too young. Besides, he is but a modest sort of youth. I sent word that he must wait. But he bears a message from his uncle, Master Samuel Pepys."

Catherine turned in her chair, all attention. "But how strange,

Frances! Only a few hours ago I was thinking of Samuel Pepys! Let me see the letter."

It was the letter of a blind man, dictated to a clerk, so that nothing of the writer's personality showed in the hand. But all the warmth of his spirit was in the words. *"If this should find you in Lisbon, dear nephew,"* read Catherine, *"I give you in charge to wait upon my Lady Tuke, one of the ladies attending my once royal mistress, our Queen Dowager, for whom I bear great honor; nor if she should offer you the honor of kissing the Queen's hand would I have you omit, if Lady Tuke thinks it proper, the presenting her Majesty with my profoundest duty, as becomes a most faithful subject."*

"Will your Majesty permit the young man to kiss your hand?" asked Lady Tuke.

"But, of course. For his uncle's sake. I pray you tell them to prepare a lodging for him and to have him sent to me immediately."

"But your Majesty's guests," objected the wife of one of the fine Portuguese *fidalgos*, who had no means of knowing that Catherine's world was divided quite simply into those who had known and loved Charles, and those who had not. "The reception is being such a success!"

"Yes, God has granted me success," agreed Catherine, looking round at the glittering assembly. "But it is pleasant to be remembered in England."